Praise for *New York Times* bestselling author

BRENDA JOYCE

and the

MASTERS OF TIME® SERIES

Dark Embrace

"A Perfect 10. Brenda Joyce has created a tale that is full to overflowing with emotion. Passionate, heartbreaking, hopeful, and entertaining, *Dark Embrace* is a novel you do not want to miss. I recommend it highly."
—*Romance Reviews Today*

"Known for her intensity of emotion and superlative storytelling, Joyce draws you into a new Masters of Time® novel that will blow you away with its unforgettable alpha hero and a willful heroine who feels his pain across the centuries."
—*Romantic Times BOOKreviews* (Top Pick)

Dark Rival

"The supporting characters are excellent, the sex scenes are plentiful...and the plot thick, making this sophomore series entry a fine entertainment, sure to gratify fans of the bestselling kickoff."
—*Publishers Weekly*

Dark Seduction

"Bestselling author Joyce kicks off her Masters of Time® series with a master's skill, instantly elevating her to the top ranks of the ever-growing list of paranormal romance authors.... Steeped in action and sensuality, populated by sexy warriors and strong women, graced with lush details and a captivating story...superlative."
—*Publishers Weekly*, starred review

"Sexual tension crackles between Claire and Malcolm as he struggles with his desire for Claire and his protective duty in this sizzling, action-packed adventure."
—*Library Journal*

BRENDA JOYCE

DARK VICTORY

HQN™

Recycling programs
for this product may
not exist in your area.

ISBN-13: 978-0-373-77346-6
ISBN-10:   0-373-77346-3

DARK VICTORY

Copyright © 2009 by Brenda Joyce Dreams Unlimited, Inc.

Masters of Time® is a registered trademark of Brenda Joyce Dreams
Unlimited, Inc. Used with permission.

www.HQNBooks.com

Printed in U.S.A.

To Sydney Chrismon and Michelle Dykes—
for twenty-five years of support, love and friendship;
love you guys!

DARK VICTORY

PROLOGUE

The Future
June 19, 1550
Near Melvaig, Scotland

HE DID NOT KNOW what caused him to awaken.

Guy Macleod sat bolt upright in his bed, his wife's fury engulfing him. Horror began. Tabitha was rarely angry, but now her rage knew no bounds. He went completely still so that his extraordinary senses could locate her. She was supposed to be in Edinburgh, her sister's guest. Immediately he knew she was not there—and that she was in great danger.

He would die for her without blinking. He never panicked, but now he fought to stay calm, searching for her.

And that was when he felt the familiar evil.

Black and vast, filled with hatred and malevolence, they'd lived with this evil for two-hundred-and-fifty years. Criosaidh had powerful black magic. Tabitha had equally powerful white power. But Criosaidh had been stalking his wife with growing determination, as if impatient, and with a new boldness recently. Tabitha had scoffed at Guy's concerns. Now, maybe too late, he knew he'd been right.

He leaped from the bed, his gaze veering to the southern chamber window as he shrugged a leine over his muscular and battle-scarred body. The night sky was still and blue-black, glittering with a billion stars. His stare intensified. His senses sharpened. For one moment, even though Criosaidh's stronghold at Melvaig was almost a day's journey away by horse, he thought the night sky there was on fire. It was so oddly bright in the south. But that was impossible.

Or was it?

Tabitha's power over fire continually amazed him. He had no more doubt now; Tabitha was at Melvaig—and so was Criosaidh.

His alarm vanished, his fear died. He stepped into his boots, leaping as he did so.

He had mastered the art of the leap through time and space centuries ago and he landed upright, dazed but battle ready, in Melvaig's large central courtyard. The sky above was on fire.

Incredulous, he saw huge balls of fire falling into the bailey. Men, women and children were running for the castle's front gates, screaming in terror and trying to escape the inferno. For one moment, he wondered if the sun was breaking apart and falling in blazing pieces to the ground, even though he knew better. His gaze shifted. Above the entire stronghold was Melvaig's tall central tower—and it was an inferno.

Even though stone could not burn, chunks of the gray slabs were falling from the tower, the rocks ablaze, sizzling as they slammed down, only to burn holes into the bailey ground.

Tabitha screamed.

Criosaidh roared in answering rage.

The tower swayed in the fiery night and more blazing stone blocks sheered from it, crashing to the earth below.

They were at war.

He did not have the Sight, but suddenly he experienced the strange feeling his wife so often referred to—déjà vu. He felt as if he were reliving this terrible moment, although he knew he was not.

Only one witch would survive this night.

"Tabitha!" he roared, and bounded to the tower door, leaping to the uppermost floor. As he reached the landing, the heat from the fire inside the tower chamber blasted him, burning his face, chest and hands. He saw the fire scorching a solid wall across half of the tower room. His wife was trapped against the far wall by the flames, which were dangerously close to her velvet skirts.

Horror briefly paralyzed him.

Criosaidh stood on the fire wall's other side, where the rest of the chamber was untouched by the flames. "You are too late, Macleod. Tonight she dies…at last."

He had never come undone in battle, not once in almost four centuries. The heat had caused him to crouch; he straightened and flung all of his power at her, enraged as never before. "Ye die," he roared, but she had wrapped herself in a protective spell, and his power fell harmlessly away from her. As it hit the floor and was diverted to the walls behind her, rock and stone cracked apart.

Macleod looked at his beautiful wife, who was never afraid in a crisis. As their gazes met, he heard her as clearly as ever.

I have known this day would come… You've known it, too.

She thought she would be defeated? "No!" he roared at her, blasting Criosaidh again. His life had been an endless cycle of blood and death, his heart had been stone, until she had come to him two-and-a-half centuries ago, bringing joy and happiness with her. Tabitha had saved his life.

Criosaidh smiled as his power was diverted by her spell, again.

"Command the fire," Macleod shouted at Tabitha.

"I am trying," she cried. "She has new powers!" Tabitha closed her eyes, visibly straining. And suddenly the fire wall shifted and moved back toward Criosaidh.

Criosaidh hissed in displeasure. Macleod stood very still.

His power could not move fire, but long ago he had learned how to use his mind to help Tabitha cast her magic. Now he slipped inside her with his mind. The union always made them stronger—evil had never defeated them when they became one in their thoughts. It could not, must not, defeat them now.

"Fire be hungry, fire be quick. Get the Macleod bitch," Criosaidh said harshly.

And even as Criosaidh spoke, he saw the tears slipping down Tabitha's face. She was lost in this battle—and he was afraid it was a terrible portent of the outcome. "No!" he roared, blasting the black witch again. This time, taken unawares, she gasped in pain and was driven back into the untouched wall, but it didn't matter.

Tabitha went still, eyes wide, as the flames circled her.

He seized Criosaidh, shaking her, wanting to break her. "Stop the fire or die!"

She sneered at him and vanished.

Tabitha screamed.

In horror, he turned—and saw her lavender velvet gown on fire. And then his wife was engulfed in the flames, only a portion of her frightened face visible to him.

I love you...

He knew her so well. It had been two-hundred-and-fifty-two years since he had seduced her in her small loft in New York City and then taken her to Blayde—against her very stubborn will. She was his wife, his lover, his best friend and his greatest ally in the war on evil. She was his partner in every task, both great and small, and she was the mother of his children, the grandmother of his grandchildren. She had taught him love, compassion, humanity. He had never believed in love until she'd come into his life. He'd been ruthless and merciless until Tabitha.

He knew she meant to say more.

Just as he knew these were her last, dying words.

But she did not finish speaking. Instead, the fire erupted, reaching the tower roof, consuming her completely.

"Tabitha!" he screamed.

Then the fire was gone, and there was only the charred ruin of the tower room.

He could not breathe. He could not move. In shock, he stared.

Across the room, upon the floor, he saw the gold necklace she had worn for two-and-a-half centuries, the amulet he had given her. The talisman was an open palm, a pale moonstone glittering in its center.

It had survived the fire, untouched and unscarred; his wife, who had powerful magic, had not.

"No!" He leaped into time.

CHAPTER ONE

The Present
New York City
December 7, 2008

IT HAD BEEN a really quiet weekend. Tabby wasn't sure what to make of that as she and her sister and a friend stood in line to pass through a security checkpoint at the Metropolitan Museum of Art. Her sister, Sam, had even gotten off early enough last night to go out to dinner. Tabby couldn't recall the last time the two of them had been able to go out and have a few drinks and a great meal. It made her uneasy. She was waiting for the ax to fall.

Something huge was going to happen.

She was a Rose, and while she didn't have the Sight like her cousin, Brie, she could feel the premonition in her bones.

"It is weird," Sam said, as they filed toward the security inspector. "There were only four friggin' pleasure crimes yesterday. Not that I'm complaining. But it was Saturday night."

Although they were sisters, they were as different as night and day. Sam was hard and edgy, while Tabby was soft and classic. Two years younger than Tabby, Sam wore short, spiky platinum hair, had an Angelina Jolie body and the face to go with it. Tabby was used to the attention her sister always received. Every male they passed, young or old, gave her a

second glance—male radar gone haywire. Tabby didn't mind.
She knew she was conservative and old-fashioned. Although
it was Sunday, she wore a wool skirt, a cashmere V-neck and
pearls. She didn't even own a pair of jeans.

Sam was being gawked at now. The tall, young male turned
his gaze to Tabby next, giving her the once-over. Tabby was
used to that, too. She was an attractive woman; her sister simply
overshadowed her.

"There was not one Rampage, not in any of the five
boroughs," Sam said. "I mean, it's noon and I haven't even been
called in on a case."

Tabby knew that her warrior sister, who was an agent at
HCU, was bored. Sam was at her best when she was hunting
on the city streets. But the Rampages were terrible crimes.
Innocent victims were burned, medieval style, at the stake. As
eerie as the sudden decline in violence was, she should not be
complaining.

"Why are you so uptight? I saw who you met up with at
Trenza," Kit said to Sam, smiling. "She was with Young, Dark
and Hot."

"Very young, very hot and very, very good." Sam smiled.

"I don't know why they never have friends," Kit complained,
but she winked at Tabby. She was slim, fair and dark-haired.
Tabby had never seen her wear a stitch of makeup—she didn't
have to. Her siren's face and sensuously buff body hid a brilliant intensity and resolve. Like Sam, her first love was the war
on evil. She was one of the most serious and determined women
Tabby had ever met, but Tabby didn't blame her. Her twin sister
had died in Jerusalem in Kit's arms, the victim of demonic
violence. Sometimes Tabby thought she might still be mourning
Kelly. Kit worked at HCU, too—it was how she'd met Sam.

But Sam said, "He *had* a friend. You cut out before you could
meet him."

Kit shrugged negligently. "Had to hit the gym and take care of the bod."

Sam snorted.

Tabby wasn't sure if Kit was as old-fashioned as she was, or if she was simply too obsessed with work to get involved, but she had known Kit for about a year, and she was pretty certain Kit was as celibate as she was. The joke was a front and they all knew it. It was okay—they both lived vicariously through Sam. A stranger might be appalled by the way Sam used men, but Tabby was proud of her. She was a powerful and gorgeous woman; she was the one to say yes or no; she was the one who did the dumping. Sam would never have her heart broken. She would be spared that.

Tabby was relieved when the slight aching in her breast did not suddenly pierce through her heart and soul. The divorce no longer hurt. The betrayals no longer hurt. It was almost two years since she'd learned the extent of her ex-husband's lies and adultery. She'd given him all of her love, and she'd meant every word of their marriage vows. It was the kind of woman she was. He hadn't meant one damned word.

She intended to learn from her mistakes. Randall hadn't been the love of her life after all. He had been a Wall Street investor—a high roller and a player. He'd cheated on her from start to finish, and to make the cliché just perfect, she'd been the last to find out. She was never going near that charismatic macho type again.

But sometimes, especially recently, she wished she was a bit more like her sister when it came to men. She did not want to even think that she might be lonely or that she needed the kind of intimacy she wasn't sure she'd ever have again, but the evenings were getting harder and harder to deal with. She'd started dating again, being really careful to go out with intellectuals and artists, but it felt as if she was simply going through the motions. And maybe she was. When it came to dating and sex, she was the exact opposite of her sister. If she wasn't in love, it wasn't happening. She didn't turn on easily, either. Maybe love and passion weren't in the cards for her. She was twenty-nine already, and beginning to think she'd better focus on her Destiny as a Rose woman.

"You know, I wish you'd let me set you up with the new guy at CDA," Sam said.

Tabby smiled a bit grimly at her. She'd met MacGregor once, when he and Sam had been leaving the Center for Demonic Activity Agency together. "Definitely not," she said, meaning it. The agent had had *macho* written all over him.

"Let her explore the Beta side of life," Kit said, her eyes wide with innocence. "Who knows? Maybe she'll find a match made in some kind of odd, metro heaven."

Tabby felt a pang, but she smiled brightly and said, "That's the plan."

Kit sobered and touched her arm. "I'm sorry. I never met Randall and I shouldn't tease you for going out with his polar opposite."

"It's okay," Tabby said. She smiled firmly. "What's meant to be is meant to be. Maybe the love of my life is a poet with a Ph.D."

Sam choked. "Over my dead body." Then she looked closely at Tabby. "Are you okay?"

Sam always knew when something was really wrong. "It's still hard."

"Yeah, it is," Sam said, and they both knew they were referring to their cousin, Brie. Kit probably knew it, too, but she pretended not to hear them, moving as the line progressed.

The Rose women were special. Each had her own Destiny, tied into the war on evil. For generations, the Rose women had been using their unusual powers to aid and abet good. It had only been three months since Brie had left them to redeem the Wolf of Awe. The year before, their best friend Allie had also vanished. Although Allie wasn't related to them, they had become friends with her as children. That had been Fate, too— it turned out that she was a powerful Healer. Each woman had gone to embrace her Destiny in the past, because it had been time to do so. That was how the universe worked. It was a fundamental Wisdom in the Book of Roses, which had been passed down through the generations of Rose women.

Tabby missed them both, sometimes terribly, but she was also happy for them because Allie and Brie were hardly alone in the Middle Ages. Their Destinies had included powerful, nearly immortal partners—Highlanders who battled at their sides, as driven and committed as they were to the war on evil. But their absence had left a gaping hole in their lives. Sam had helped fill the void by going to work at HCU, the Historic Crimes Unit of CDA, a clandestine government agency dedicated to fighting the evil preying on society. Sam's boss, Nick Forrester, ran HCU with an iron fist but he could be counted on to back them up. And so could Kit. But it wasn't the same without Allie and Brie.

There was no defying Destiny. Tabby's Destiny was magic. Every generation of Rose women had a Slayer, a Healer and a Witch. She had been practicing her craft since she was fourteen—the year her mother had died, the victim of a demonic pleasure crime. There was one big fat problem, though. Rose women usually came into their powers very, very swiftly once their Destiny was made known. Apparently, Tabby was the exception to that rule. Although she'd been practicing magic since adolescence, her powers were still erratic and, once in a while, too weak to do any good. It simply didn't make any sense.

But as the Book of Roses said, there was a reason for everything.

Kit said, "After the gym, I went back to HCU. I was digging around in some older case files. That last Rampage has been bothering me. There were only three in the gang."

"They were doped up on a drug we've never seen before," Sam said quietly.

HCU's jurisdiction was the past—all past demonic activity, even if centuries old. Because so many of today's demons came from previous centuries, HCU's agents worked closely with CDA. Rarely could a present-day crime be solved without HCU's expertise. Tabby had already heard about last week's Rampage. A couple had been burned at the stake in one of Manhattan's most posh neighborhoods. These terrible murders were usually committed between midnight and dawn, with an entire gang present. But it had only been 8:00 p.m. and only three gang members had been there, two males and a female. Were they becoming bolder? Had it even been a genuine Rampage?

The press had dubbed the crimes "witch burnings," a label Tabby particularly disliked, because the victims were average men, women and children of all ages, races, sizes and shapes. But then, evil rarely discriminated—except, of course, when it came to pleasure crimes. Then the most innocent and beautiful were chosen. The witch burnings had instilled so much fear into the general public that no one seemed to care that seventy percent of all murders were still pleasure crimes. What was really scary was how vicious the gangs of possessed kids had become.

They'd once been ghetto gang members or normal kids gone missing. Evil preyed on them, seducing these gang members, offering them power in return for their souls, and then directing them to commit violence, brutality, bestiality and anarchy. The possessed gangs were out of control, ruling the city streets through fear and might. Gang warfare was no longer "in." Now the gangs often worked together to hunt down civilians, cruelly and sadistically. Very few "normal" gangs remained in the country now.

"Something's been bothering me about the Rampages, across the board," Kit said. "I feel like I've missed a really glaring clue."

"I'll go back to HCU with you," Sam decided, "and we can check it out."

They had reached the security checkpoint. Tabby smiled at the guard as Sam flipped her government ID. Sam's messenger bag was loaded with weapons, and she carried a stiletto up her sleeve and a Beretta in a shoulder holster. She would never make it through the checkpoint. Kit flipped a similar ID. Although they were government issued, neither Kit nor Sam were Feds, as the IDs claimed. But CDA was so clandestine that only the top levels of the CIA, the FBI and the Secret Service worked with its agents.

As they passed through the checkpoint, Sam and Kit were both so thoughtful that Tabby had the feeling they were ready to cut out on their plans for the afternoon. She would have to wander around the exhibit by herself, and return alone to the loft she shared with Sam. She'd float around it in the same solitude she did every night—except when she was out with some sweet guy she had no real interest in. It was lonely—Sam was almost never there—but she'd deal the same way she always did. She'd outline tomorrow's curriculum, and then work on her spells.

"So which way to the Wisdom of the Celts?" Sam asked.

Tabby smiled back, relieved. Sam knew she needed company. "Up those stairs," she said, nodding.

The huge front hall was terribly crowded. Every New Yorker knew that visiting the Met on the weekend was a really dumb idea. They started across the granite floored hall, dwarfed by the columns and arches, before going up the broad staircase to the first level of exhibits.

There was no line.

They exchanged looks as they approached the glass displays. Tabby said, "This is too weird. There should have been a half-hour wait, at least."

Kit murmured, "It's an exhibit on medieval Ireland. If you ask me, medieval Scotland and Ireland are peas in the same pod."

Allie and Brie were in medieval Scotland, with Highlanders who belonged to a secret society dedicated to the protection of Innocence. "Are you saying that you think we're *meant* to go in here? That the exhibit is related to the Brotherhood?"

"The earliest Scots came from Dalriada—which is Ireland."

Tabby barely heard them. She realized her heart was thundering as she left them debating the odd lack of a line and walked over to a large glass display case. Inside, there were numerous artifacts and objects. She vaguely saw a large sword with an intricately designed hilt, and a pair of daggers, a brooch and a cup. But her gaze was drawn to the necklace there, instead.

A terrible tension filled her as she stared at the gold chain and the pendant hanging from it. It was a talisman in the shape of an open palm, a pale stone glittering from the palm's center.

Tabby's pulse skittered wildly in her throat. When she touched the hollow of her collarbone, where she wore pearls and a small key on a chain, her skin there felt far too warm. She felt a bit dizzy, faint.

"Are you all right?" Sam asked.

"I feel odd," Tabby said, realizing she was perspiring. She leaned forward to read about the amulet.

It was dated to the early thirteenth century, but had been found in 1932 among the ruins of Melvaig Castle in the northeastern Highlands of Scotland. It had somehow survived the legendary battle of An Tùir-Tara, which meant the Burning

Tower. On June 19, 1550, a terrible fire had destroyed the central tower of Melvaig Castle. Most historians could not decide on the cause of the inferno, because no weapons or other signs of a battle had been found. A blaze that extensive should have been caused by medieval warfare. The most common hypothesis was that the fire was the result of treachery, the kind so often seen in the ongoing clan war between the MacDougalls of Skye and their blood enemies, the Macleods of Loch Gairloch. That bloody and bitter clan feud seemed to have originated in 1201, when a fire set by the MacDougalls razed the Macleod stronghold at Blayde to the ground, destroying the Macleod chief, William the Lion. Very few survivors were left, but amongst them was Macleod's fourteen-year-old son.

Tabby reeled. The words blurred before her eyes. She could not breathe; she started to choke on the lack of air.

The Macleods of Loch Gairloch....

His fourteen-year-old son....

She finally breathed, gulping in air. Were the Macleods important somehow? Did she know the clan? Had they been a part of Rose history? Why did that boy seem important to her? She almost felt as if the clan name rang a bell, as if she needed to reach out to that boy. Yet she did not know anyone named Macleod. Her family came from Narne, in the western Highlands.

But she remained shaken. She could almost see a fourteen-year-old boy, covered in blood and choking on grief and guilt. And suddenly so much conflicting emotion consumed her that she could not breathe at all.

Tabby went still.

She could see the inferno.

The sky was pitch-black, and an entire castle was ablaze. There was dread, fury.

The images shifted. The sky was a brilliant robin's-egg blue. Only a soaring tower burned....

The terrible emotions intensified. Tabby cried out, rocked by the rage and anguish, the fear, the horror, and even the love.

And there was evil, too.

"What's wrong?" Sam asked urgently. "You need to sit down!"

Tabby barely heard her sister. Tabby did not have the power to sense evil, but evil was beckoning her now. It wanted her. Tabby strained to see, horrified and mesmerized at once. And from the raging inferno on that sunny summer day, a dark fog came, slithering over the blazing tower, consuming it. Slowly the dark mists began shape-shifting into a woman—a faceless woman cloaked in swirling black.

"Tabby, damn it!"

The evil woman beckoned. Tabby couldn't see her face but she knew she was smiling the cold, lustful smile of pure evil. Then she realized that *she* was afraid.

Tabby blinked. The darkly cloaked woman became clearer. Night-black hair spilled over her cloak, framing her pale beautiful face. She somehow knew this woman—a black witch or a demon. It was déjà vu. Yet they'd never met.

The woman started to drift away. She opened her eyes—or her eyes were already open and only now could she see what was in front of her. She clung to Sam's strong arms. Her sister was pale and staring at her with alarm. "Evil," she whispered dryly.

She felt Sam's disbelief. "But you can't sense evil. I can, and there's no evil here, Tabby."

There was so much evil. "It's here. I'm sensing it now. It's a woman."

"She's as white as a sheet. She's going to faint—she needs to lie down and get her feet elevated," Kit said quickly.

Tabby then saw Kit beside Sam, the display and the amulet behind them. She stared at the bright gold palm. "I'm okay," she said harshly.

"I didn't feel any evil," Sam said quietly. "Is it coming from the talisman?"

Tabby wet her lips, no longer dizzy but still a bit weak. What had just happened? She'd just felt a huge and threatening black force. And it had wanted her?

Her gaze moved to the glowing white stone in the palm's center. It winked at her and she was stunned to feel its holy power. "It has white light. The amulet is for good, not evil. It has powerful magic."

"It has to, to survive a fire. Gold melts," Kit said flatly.

Tabby trembled. "I think I had a vision." And what about her reaction to the fourteen-year-old boy who had survived Blayde's destruction in the thirteenth century?

Tabby tensed. She felt as if she could almost see that boy. When she'd read those words, she'd felt his grief and guilt.

Sam's dark blue eyes widened. "You don't have the Sight, either!"

"It felt like déjà vu." She wet her dry lips again. "There was a witch—or a female demon. I know her." She corrected herself. "I knew her. And the survivor of the first fire, I might know him, too."

"What first fire?" Sam demanded.

Tabby realized she needed to sit down. "The clans started warring after 1201—it says so right on the plaque, Sam." She glanced around for a bench. There was one across the hall, but she didn't want to leave the display.

A brief silence fell, in which they all considered what had just happened. Kit said, "I get good vibes from the pendant. Maybe I can dig up something at HCU on it, and on these two clans."

"My gut is telling me that we should see what we can find out about An Tùir-Tara." Sam stared closely at Tabby. "Ring any more bells?"

Tabby stared at her sister. Whatever had happened at An Tùir-Tara had been frightening and horrible. What was Sam thinking? She looked far too grim—as if she knew more than she'd let on.

"Want me to dig into the destruction of Blayde, too?" Sam asked quietly.

Tabby became chilled—and even more sick. The boy's grief felt as if it was a part of her. Had she been there?

She thought about reincarnation. The Book of Roses had one mention of past lives, in a Wisdom that had clearly been read over and over again. Tabby didn't disbelieve in past lives, but she didn't believe, exactly, either. "Are you thinking I was there? Either at Blayde, or at An Tùir-Tara in 1550?"

"I don't know," Sam said matter-of-factly. She was oddly poker-faced. What was going on with her?

"Maybe Mom was there, or Grandma Sara, or another ancestor," Sam said. "Maybe it *was* you, in a different life, although I'm not really into reincarnation. Or maybe you are coming into the power to sense evil—to feel across time the way Brie did." Sam shrugged. "It can't hurt to check it out. You're obviously involved with this amulet, in one way or another."

Tabby was silent now. The Book of Roses was very clear about Fate and the fact that there was no such thing as coincidence.

"I hate to jinx ourselves, but I've been waiting for something bad to happen all day. I just thought it would be *really* bad— you know, like vampires from a *Buffy* episode stepping out of the TV and coming to life in our living rooms," Kit said, eyes wide.

Tabby couldn't smile.

"We need vampires like we need a hole in the head. Don't give the demons any ideas," Sam said, amused. Then she and Kit exchanged conspiratorial looks.

Kit was more of a Hunter than a Slayer, and not half as impatient as Sam. She didn't mind spending days poring through HCU's amazing database, while Sam couldn't sit still for very long—or stay off the street for very long. "What are you two planning?" Tabby asked with some trepidation.

Sam put her arm around her. "You're still really pale. I think we should take you home and start checking this out. Tomorrow would be a better time to visit here, anyway."

Tabby knew Sam was worried about her. She stared past her sister at the pendant. The little white stone was glowing now. "I'm fine."

"What does that mean? We can't leave you here, not when you almost fainted," Sam said. "You seemed to go back in time while standing right here with us. I don't like it, not one bit."

Sam was never *this* protective of her. They were a team of equals, backing each other up in crisis after crisis. They fought demons together almost nightly. Tabby straightened and took a deep breath, deciding not to worry about her sister's odd behavior now. She needed to think about that boy and that demon-witch. "I'm staying. I have to stay." When Sam's eyes widened, she said firmly, as if to one of her first-graders, "I am fine. I'm not going to break like fine china. I am going to get some water and then I am going to sit down by this amulet and think—and feel."

Sam finally said, "I am not liking this very much."

Tabby stared closely. "What aren't you telling me?"

Sam's expression became bland. "We don't keep secrets, Tab."

Kit said, "She should stay here, Sam. We were meant to be here today. This is the first time she's ever felt evil—and by God, she felt it across time. This is a medieval Celtic exhibit. Melvaig is in the Highlands."

Kit thought the exhibit related to the Highlanders who were

fighting this war with them—but from medieval times, Tabby thought, surprised. She didn't buy that. This was about a suffering boy and a woman with lots of black power. And it was about that amulet.

But why did everything feel so familiar?

Sam was grim. "That was spoken like a Rose," she said to Kit.

"Hanging around you two, I *feel* like a Rose sometimes," she quipped, her eyes sparkling.

"You know I can hold my own when it counts," Tabby said, which was true.

"Okay," Sam said, shrugging. "You're a big girl and this is obviously in the Big Game Plan. Don't know what got into me."

Tabby walked back with them as far as the closest water fountain. She preferred Giuliani Water to the bottled stuff, anyway. When Sam and Kit were gone and she'd had a drink, she hurried back to the exhibit.

The closer she got to the glass case with the amulet, the stranger she began to feel. Dizzy, expectant, nervous, afraid…and angered.

She paused before the bright gold palm, light-headed and tense, uneasy. She'd been waiting for the sky to fall and it was falling now—this was it, she thought anxiously. The white moonstone blinked merrily at her. She remained aware of the boy and the woman with black power, of all the emotions that were somehow associated with the amulet, or An Tùir-Tara, or Blayde and the warring clans. Just as she had the odd notion that the amulet was protecting her from getting too close to emotions that might be dangerous for her—or a life that might be dangerous for her—so much grief consumed Tabby that she cried out.

It sent her right down to her knees.

It was the kind of grief she'd never felt in her life. It resonated with so much male warrior power and so much rage. On her hands and knees, Tabby somehow looked up.

A Highlander towered over her. He was a huge and muscular man, dark of complexion and hair, his face a mask of fury. His face was blistered, burned and bleeding. She recoiled in fear. He was holding a long sword, his knuckles blistered and bloody, too, and a red-and-black plaid was pinned to one shoulder. Otherwise he was clad in a short-sleeved tunic that hit mid-thigh, and it was charred and sooty. She inhaled—his arms and thighs were also burned and bloody!

His enraged and anguished blue eyes locked with hers.

In his grief, the Highlander looked ready to commit murder.

Uncertain if he was real or not, she somehow got up and reached for his hand. Her fingers grazed his.

Her heart leaped as they made contact for one split second. And then he vanished.

Tabby reeled backward, her fingers burning from the heat of his hands, until she leaned against the case. Her heart was pounding with explosive force. She somehow saw a Met security officer begin to hurry toward her, but she couldn't move off the display. She was shaken to the very core of her soul, his blue eyes engraved in her mind. Finally, she whispered, "Come back. Let me help you."

The security officer grabbed her arm. "You can't lean on the case, miss. Are you all right?"

Tabby barely heard him. She pulled away, rushing to the nearest bench, where she collapsed. She inhaled, her mind racing. She had to cast a spell to bring him back to her while he was still close, before he vanished into time. She had to help him.

Tabby closed her eyes. Beginning to perspire, focused as never before, she murmured, *"Come to me, Highlander, come to me now. Come to my healing power. Come to me, Highlander."*

She knew she had to help him. Somehow, it was the most important moment of her life.

Tabby waited.

CHAPTER TWO

The Past
Blayde, Scotland
1298

"YE HAVE NO HEART!"

"Aye." The Black Macleod stared coldly down at his mortal enemy. The man crouched on his hands and knees, shaking like a leaf, as pale as any ghost, clearly terrified. Panic showed in his eyes. Macleod felt nothing in return.

Alasdair would die that day. It was that simple. He could beg for mercy, but there would be none. He had been hunting down the MacDougall kinsmen since he was fourteen years old. He had lost tally of all the MacDougall men he had wounded, maimed and killed. He did not even care what that count was. Maybe, as his enemies said, his heart was truly made of stone.

"A Uilleam," he said softly.

Images from the past flashed. He fought them, unwilling to ever see them again. His father being stabbed, repeatedly, while he helplessly watched…his father, a still and lifeless corpse, being sent to his burial at sea…Blayde in ruins, a pile of scorched black stone, the sun bloodred as it was rising in the smoke-filled dawn…and a jumbled, unfocused image of the desperate, grief-stricken boy he'd once been.

"My wife is with child, Macleod, I beg ye!" The MacDougall of Melvaig screamed. "What happened at Blayde was long ago. I wasna even born yet! Yer father tried to make peace, Macleod. Let us do what our fathers failed to do!"

His father, William, had tried to make peace—and instead, the entire clan had been murdered in a bloody midnight massacre. His life had become revenge that day. It remained revenge now.

"*A Elasaid,*" he said harshly. Deep within himself, he felt the anger roiling. In war, he never allowed it free rein. "*A Blayde.*"

He knew better than to try to use his god-given powers to murder the other man. A master swordsman, Alasdair's scream sounded and was cut off as Macleod's sword sliced through skin and flesh, tendon and bone, severing his head from his body.

For one moment, Macleod stood there coldly, watching the headless man topple over and finally begin to tumble down the slope. The boy felt a bit closer now. His choked sobs became mere hiccups. Macleod looked at the wide-eyed, severed head, aware that the boy was the only one present who cared. Sightlessly, Alasdair stared back at him.

Sometimes he wished that the boy had died that day, too.

His heart was beating, though, slow and steady, telling him that he did have a heart—contrary to what popular opinion held. His expression never changing, his mouth remaining hard and tight, Macleod reached down, seized Alasdair's head by his golden hair and flung it away, into the ravine and river below. "Join yer ancestors in hell."

The ground rolled ominously beneath his feet. The sky overhead was the color of wildflowers, but thunder boomed directly above him and lightning split the sky. The gods were furious with him.

Again.

He did not care. He looked up and laughed at them—scorning their wishes, their commands.

They could curse him and threaten him, and even spoil his powers, but he was their grandson and he feared no one...not even an angry god. "Do as ye will," he said, and for the first time that day, his interest was actually piqued.

Their response was immediate. Lightning split a nearby tree, and it crashed over at his feet.

He smiled with amusement. Did they think *that* would scare him?

Then he turned his attention to the fear and fury roiling below him.

His smile gone, Macleod turned to stare at the river below, where Alasdair's sixteen-year-old son had fled to hide. Macleod had lurked not far from Melvaig in the hopes of preying upon Alasdair, or one of his brothers or cousins, but Alasdair had ridden out with his eldest son. Macleod had followed and eventually ambushed them.

He was a very tall man, often standing a head over everyone else, with a muscular body hewn from years of riding difficult chargers, running ridges and hills, and engaging in the kind of warfare he liked best—hand-to-hand and sword-to-sword combat. He might have extraordinary powers, but he could not depend upon them—they were often erratic. It hardly mattered. He was stronger than all the men he knew, faster, and more intelligent. He had never lost a battle, not in any kind of combat; nor did he intend to.

It was a pleasant June day, warmer than was usual this far north, and he wore a simple short-sleeved leine that came to mid-thigh. It was belted at the waist, and the bold red-and-black brat of the Macleod clan was pinned to his left shoulder with a gold-and-citrine brooch, where a lion was engraved upon the golden stone. The brooch had belonged to his father, the great

William the Lion. He wore both long and short swords. His boots were knee-high and spurred. Unlike other Highlanders, his skin was surprisingly dark and his hair was almost as black as midnight, but his eyes were stunningly blue. His mother had told him that his grandfather had been the son of a Persian goddess—the explanation for his unusual coloring.

Macleod saw movement below, along the river's banks.

As he did, Alasdair's son's desperation washed over him, and instantly the other boy, the fourteen-year-old who should have died, came back. He almost recalled a very similar moment of desperation, ninety-seven years ago. He decided not to think about it.

He began to move down the ridge, intent, unrushed and very aware of his prey's fear—and his courage. Blue flashed; he heard a branch snap. He slid and slipped down the wet dirt, pausing, listening acutely to Coinneach MacDougall's every thought.

He'll kill me without a second thought, as he did my da'…. He's too fast, too strong, to fight openly…. I ha' to hide…so I can return to kill him another day!

Macleod took a few more steps and reached the rocky bank of the river. A pair of doe took flight as he paused, listening to his victim's thoughts carefully.

He canna be immortal, as is claimed…. Someone will kill him one day—an' 'twill be me!

As if anticipating the kill, a huge black crow settled on the upper bough of a fir, its black eyes bright with interest. Macleod knew that Coinneach hid behind that tree.

He slid his sword from its sheath. Well oiled and bloody, it hissed loudly in the quiet Highland morning.

A nearby saber sang.

The boy had drawn his sword. His thoughts were silent now. Coinneach would die fighting—a true Highlander's death.

His kin would be proud of him—and then they would seek revenge for both father and son.

He did not care. It was the way of this Highland world. Death brought revenge and more death. The cycle was an endless one and to question it would be as purposeless as questioning why the sun rose and set each and every day. He started toward the stand of firs.

Lightning sizzled in the blue sky.

Macleod ignored the warning. As he was about to step into the thigh-deep water, he felt a huge power emerging behind him, almost as holy as that of the gods. The power was so immense that it enveloped him. He instantly recognized its source. Macleod tensed.

Thunder boomed.

"Let him live. He's Innocent."

And finally, he was angered. He turned to face MacNeil, the Abbot of Iona—the man who had become his protector and guardian the day after the massacre, the man he had come to consider both family and friend. But MacNeil was not in the habit of calling at Blayde—except when he meant to harass him. "Dinna interfere," Macleod warned, meaning it.

MacNeil was a tall, golden Highlander with more power and wisdom than any other man, mortal or not. "Of course I will interfere. If I dinna protect ye from yerself, who will?"

"I dinna need protection, not from ye or anyone," Macleod said, his temper lost at last. He would never allow himself any passion during a hunt or a battle, but he was aware of Coinneach running through the forest, toward Melvaig, the hunt now ended. So he would live…only to die another day.

MacNeil's smile faded. "Have I ever failed ye on this day, lad?" he asked softly.

Macleod's tension increased. It was the anniversary of the murders—and the burials. "Ye need not come every single year.

I never think about the past. I ceased thinking about the past an' that day years ago." It wasn't really a lie, he thought. "It serves no purpose. I leave broodin' to the women," he snarled.

"I will always come on the anniversary of their deaths," MacNeil said gently. "Besides, the gods are impatient. I'm impatient."

And finally Macleod felt as if he was on firm ground again. He smiled, but without humor. "So ye say, year after year. Ye bore me, MacNeil, the way a woman does when she's not in my bed."

"Ye're as stubborn as that boy was," Macleod said, unperturbed. "But Coinneach is cunning. Ye're a fool. Ye survived the massacre fer great reasons! And ye heard the gods just now—in a rage over yer pursuit of an Innocent."

"No one commands me, MacNeil. Not even yer gods."

"Now ye deny yer mother's faith?"

He was furious, enough so that the branches on the nearby firs started waving wildly about their heads. "Dinna dare speak to me o' Elasaid!"

"Ye survived that terrible day so ye could become a great Master—so ye could take yer vows to protect Innocence an' keep Faith. Most Masters take their vows at an early age, but yer over a hundred years old now. Ye can hardly delay fer much longer. An' I'll discuss yer mother if I wish. She must be very disappointed, lad."

Macleod was enraged. "Mention her again an' suffer the consequences!"

"I hardly fear ye…an' I willna fight ye, not now, not ever."

His duty was to his father, the great William, first and always. Elasaid would understand. He had no intention of taking his vows and joining the brethren—ever. He did not mind fighting evil—he fought evil as naturally as he took women to his bed. He did both every single day. His heart might be made of stone, but his word was written in stone, as well. If he took the vows MacNeil was speaking of, those vows would rule his life. The gods would rule his life. Protecting the Innocent would rule his life. And then he would have to forgo— or even forget—his duty to his dead kin and to Blayde. And that he would not do.

"'Tis time. Come to Iona and make yer vows." MacNeil laid his hand upon his shoulder again. "Before yer Destiny is taken from ye."

"Let them take my damned Destiny," Macleod snapped. "It would please me greatly!"

"Ye act fourteen years old!" MacNeil exclaimed. "We both ken ye can control that rage o' yours. Ye do so when ye hunt an' war—ye can do so now."

"Ye push me more than I'd ever let any other man push me, MacNeil. I let ye do so because I owe ye still. Ye arrived at Blayde that day with yer soldiers to help me turn the enemy away. Blayde would have been lost if ye hadn't come. Ye helped me bury the dead—ye helped me rebuild. But I watched two Frenchmen stab my father in the back. I was held captive an' I could not go to aid him, to defend him! My mother died in the fires that day, carryin' my brother or sister in her womb. My two older brothers died that day, fighting against all odds." Now, the placid river was raging, racing past them. "When every MacDougall is dead, I will come to yer island and swear on yer holy books to serve the Ancients and protect Innocence. But as long as a single MacDougall lives, my duty is to Blayde."

"Are ye nay tired of yer endless wars? Have ye never thought of havin' a different life—a pleasin' one?"

"Ye're the fool now." He turned and whistled for his horse, aware that it was but a short distance away, grazing in a nearby glen. He'd leaped from it to pursue Alasdair on foot.

MacNeil sighed. "Ye've had yer revenge—ye've had yer

revenge for over ninety years. No man would ever fault ye, Guy. Ye have done yer duty to yer father an' mother."

"My duty will never be done." As he spoke, he glimpsed that young boy again, and his presence infuriated him. That boy was weak and he'd failed everyone. "If ye cease yer harangue, ye're welcome at Blayde an' I will be pleased to offer ye wine, a woman and a bed."

Hooves sounded. The huge black charger came galloping up the riverbank, its eyes bright with interest. Macleod seized the bridle, then gave the animal a single stroke upon its neck.

"Ye've enchanted yer horse. Yer powers are meant to be used against deamhanain an' their lackeys, not on mortals an' not on the gods' earthly creatures."

Macleod shrugged. Shortly before the massacre—as if the gods had known he would lose his family and become laird— he had learned that he could hear the thoughts of others and bend the will of either man or beast with a simple direct thought. It was a useful power. And just after the massacre, he had found his other, god-given powers, powers that could destroy a man or a deamhan with a single blast.

But MacNeil showed no sign of being ready to return to Blayde. "Do ye ever wonder why yer powers sometimes defy yer very will?"

It was common knowledge that he often could not control his own powers, especially when he was angry. Even those closest to him were afraid of his errant powers and his terrible temper. "I dinna care if the occasional stone wall falls when I take an extra breath." But he was curious now.

"When ye take yer vows, ye'll be master of yer powers, Macleod, but until then, they'll escape ye when ye need them most. The gods toy with ye—a punishment fer yer refusal to obey them."

He had seen MacNeil use his powers, and they never failed

him. Suddenly the explanation made so much more sense than his assumption that he was simply less skillful or powerful. "I have enough power, more than any mortal man," he said slowly. "Ye should remind the gods that I never use their powers to dispatch my enemies. I always use my dagger, my sword or my bare hands."

"We ken," MacNeil said. "'Tis hardly enough, lad."

He hated it when MacNeil looked at him as if he was looking into his very heart and soul, seeing secrets even Macleod did not know. MacNeil had great Sight. He could see the future and the past. If anyone could look into a man's most private and unspoken thoughts, it was MacNeil. "I am ready fer wine," he said, leaping onto his horse. "Ye have no mount, but then, ye undoubtedly leaped to Melvaig." MacNeil could leap to Blayde to meet him there.

MacNeil seized the bridle.

"Ye were spared that day because the gods wrote yer Fate. 'Tis time to take the vows an' serve them—or suffer their displeasure."

That sounded like a threat! "Aye, the damned gods wrote my Fate—ye've told me a hundred times. But the massacre was Highland madness. The gods dinna care to save my family and I'm a mad Highlander now!"

"No god can save every man, woman or child," MacNeil fired back. "'Tis impossible!"

"Let go of my horse."

"I fear for ye now."

"Dinna bother to fear fer me. An', MacNeil? The boy will die another day." He reached down and jerked his reins free.

"Ye had better think on yer ways," MacNeil warned, his eyes dark and fierce now. "Because if ye dinna take yer vows soon, the gods will turn against ye."

Macleod froze. The gods could not turn against him. His

mother had been a holy woman. While no one could worship
the old gods openly—it was heresy—she had been their priestess and he had been raised in those ancient beliefs. He still worshipped the Ancients secretly, while outwardly conforming to
the Catholic Church. For ninety-seven years, he had been told
that the gods had spared his life so that he could serve them as
a holy warrior.

How could the gods turn against him? He was one of them.

"I came here today to warn ye, Guy. Continue to displease
the gods, an' they will disown ye. Ye will live a long an' bleak
life, without friends, family, without a wife or sons an' daughters, huntin' yer mortal enemies, each day the same. A man of
stone, without a heart, without a reason to live." MacNeil's eyes
flashed and he vanished.

Macleod stared at the boulder-strewn river, the water
frothing white now. Without a reason to live? He had a reason
to live. He was living each and every day because of that
reason—revenge. His life was the blood feud. It was his duty.
He did not need friends, family, a wife or children. MacNeil's
threats meant nothing, not to a man like him.

His horse knew the lay of the land as well as he did, and it
was eager to reach the stables at Blayde. It was easier to ride
along the coastline than follow deer and game trails in the
interior, even if the going was rocky at times. But when Blayde
appeared high upon the cliffs ahead, Macleod abruptly halted
the animal. It was dusk, the moon beginning to rise. He was
breathing hard and as lathered as his horse.

He hadn't meant to cross this beach, the very same beach
where he'd sent his family and kin to their graves at sea. He
hadn't been back to this small cove since the sea burials, not
once. But suddenly he was at that precise cove. He could smell
the smoke…he could smell the blood, the death.

He slid from his horse and silently told it to go home. The stallion snorted, sending him an almost human glance before trotting away.

Slowly, Macleod turned.

Roiling white waves broke upon the shore and the rocks there. The surf was always rougher at night, boiling and dangerous. But as he stared, the waves gentled, softly lapping at the beach. The dark sand shimmered, becoming the color of pearls—except where it was stained with blood. The sky became lighter as dawn came and the red sun tried to rise in the gray, smoke-filled skies. A boy stood there on the beach, vowing revenge, filled with guilt and desperation and trying not to cry.

He did not want to remember. Another man might hope to go back in time—especially considering that such a power might be attainable—but not he. He'd been told that the past could not be changed, and he believed it.

He started walking toward the churning ocean. The boy knelt in the sand, watching the funeral pyres as they drifted out to sea.

Although he was observing the boy with complete detachment, he was aware of a deep, dark tension. He paused, staring out across the ocean, but not at the rising moon. He still saw the bleak dawn horizon. The galleys were rocking upon the waves, their sails limp and flaccid, eighteen in all.

He had lost everyone that day.

But he'd found his mother's amulet in the hand of a dead enemy soldier. Elasaid had worn a small talisman, never taking it off—a small gold palm with a bright white stone in its center, a pendant with great magical powers. He hadn't been able to send it to sea. He kept it locked in his bedchamber in a chest.

He had not been able to defend his father, his brothers or his mother, or anyone else. He had failed them all. Yet he had survived....

He watched the boy, now on his knees. He began to vomit. Macleod almost felt sorry for him.

It was worse this year, he somehow thought. The boy was closer than ever, when he hoped to forget his very existence. He closed his eyes. Why was the boy so close, after ninety-seven long years?

He was never going to be able to make up for his failures, he thought grimly. He could murder a hundred MacDougalls, but William would remain in his sea grave, and Elasaid's bones would still be dust.

Suddenly Macleod tensed.

He was not alone.

Let me help you.

Surprise stiffened him. *She had returned.*

He began to breathe harder, afraid to move, remembering. The boy had been kneeling on the beach, watching the funeral ships as they drifted away, when he'd felt the woman's soft, warm presence. He'd heard her, behind him. She had said, "Let me help you." When he had turned, he'd thought he'd glimpsed a golden woman, but no one had been standing there.

In that first decade after the massacre, she'd come to him in his dreams, offering comfort, whispering, "Let me help you." In his dreams, she had been beautiful, strangely dressed, with long golden hair, a dozen years older than he was. She had been so vivid and so real that when he had reached out in his dreams he could touch her. Even though her audacity had angered him, he had wanted her immediately, the urgency stunning. But every time he had tried to bring her into his embrace, to take her to his bed, she had vanished.

He had stopped dreaming of the massacre and the dawn burials years ago. But when he was very tired after a terrible and vicious battle, she would suddenly appear. He would feel her strong, comforting presence first. Then he would hear her.

Let me help you. And when he turned he would see her shimmering apparition. It hadn't taken him long to realize she was a ghost—or a goddess.

She had been haunting him now for almost a century.

Macleod was certain she was present now.

Let me help you.

Slowly, Macleod stood and turned.

For one instant, he saw a flushed face, wide, concerned eyes and golden hair—and then he saw nothing but the beach and the cliffs above.

It was dusk again. There was no smoke, and two stars had emerged in the growing darkness, along with the rising moon.

He glanced warily around, straining to see in the twilight, but he no longer felt her presence. He knew she would come back. What he did not know was why. He did not care for her haunting. He preferred a flesh-and-blood woman to an elusive ghost or goddess. But one day he would detain her. One day he would find out what she wanted from him.

He started toward the cliffs, where a path led up to Blayde. At least the boy was gone, too.

HE COULDN'T SLEEP.

The massacre was on his mind now. If he tried, he could relive that day. If he slept, he might dream about it. Instead, he slipped from his bed, clad only in his leine, leaving the woman sleeping there alone. Without thinking, he stepped into his boots, as the floors were icy cold, and picked up his belt and brat. As he stalked to the hearth he belted the tunic and pinned the plaid over one shoulder to ward off the chill. Outside the chamber window, an ebony sky was filled with stars and a waning moon. A wolf was howling.

The woman he'd taken to his bed suddenly awoke. He knew it without looking at her—he felt her fear and nervousness.

They all feared him, although he didn't really know why. He never beat his dogs, much less a woman. He didn't know her name—she was new in the household. Not looking at her, he said, "Bring wine and tend the fire."

She leaped naked from his bed, seized her clothes and fled.

His head seemed to throb, almost hurting him. He stared grimly at the fire, wishing he hadn't decided to hunt his enemies that day.

Let me help you.

She had returned. He was incredulous. His eyes wide, he glanced about quickly, expecting to see her in his bedchamber. She was close by, he was certain, and she was coming closer by the moment. He wanted to end this haunting—he was determined to end it, now, and learn what she wanted from him.

But she did not manifest.

He stared into the shadows of the chamber, waiting for her to show herself. She did not.

"What do ye want?" he demanded of the empty room.

There was no answer.

He smiled without mirth. She'd never amused him, not even that first time.

For one moment, he thought she was about to appear. But as he waited for the sensation to intensify, it vanished instead.

She was toying with him. He did not like that. But suddenly he looked at the chest that was locked at the foot of his bed.

He thought about Elasaid's amulet. Uncertain why he wanted to suddenly look at it, he took a key from his belt and unlocked the chest at the foot of the bed. He took out the gold talisman and stared thoughtfully at it. The pendant had always had great magic for his mother. He almost felt expectant or uncertain—and he was never uncertain.

The moonstone in the gold palm's center winked brightly at him.

The room seemed to shift.

He knew he had not imagined the slight movement of the floor and bed. The sense of expectation intensified. It was as if a gale was about to blow in, but no storm was coming. The necklace burned in his palm.

The maid skittered into the chamber, carefully avoiding looking at him as she set the tray with wine down on the chamber's only table. Macleod waited while she lit the rushes in the room before hurrying out.

He put the pendant back in the chest and was locking it when he felt her presence filling the bedchamber.

This time, he was not mistaken.

This time, he felt the holy power with her.

Startled and wary, almost certain now that she was a goddess and not a ghost, he scanned every shadowy corner. He could feel her power, strong and white and so terribly bright, but he could not see her yet. "Show yourself," he ordered. "I am tired of this haunting. What do ye want?"

In answer, he felt the entire room shift.

Come to me.

Her soft words washed over him, through him. He was incredulous now and even more wary. Her message had changed.

She was summoning him.

"Show yourself," he said again. Could he enchant a goddess with his powers of persuasion? "Tell me what ye want. Why are ye botherin' me so much today?"

Come to me.

His blood surged. Not only had he heard her speaking, her voice was becoming clearer, even if her English remained strange. She sounded closer. Maybe he would finally discover what she wanted from him.

Come to me.

He looked around the chamber again, and the sense of her

presence intensified. The woman was very powerful and he prepared for battle with her.

By the fire, the air shimmered, as if gold dust danced on the air.

He stared, certain the flames were causing the air to sparkle. But the shimmering intensified; the gold dust began to congeal. Almost disbelieving, his heart thundered as the gold dust began to shape itself and form, so transparently he could see the hearth and fire through it.

Come to me.

He stood absolutely still. Her words were even louder now, but they still echoed oddly. He waited as the dust finally formed into a woman's tall, lush, truly perfect figure and strikingly beautiful face. He inhaled. In that moment, he wanted her to be real because he desired her so greatly.

If she were a flesh-and-blood woman, he'd end this soon enough with her immediate seduction. But he could see through her to the other side of the chamber. She wasn't mortal. He was disappointed but not daunted. Even if she was a goddess, he intended to triumph over her.

She stood before him, shifting and swaying, as if on a breeze, and her eyes were golden and mesmerizing. He could not look away. Their gazes had locked. "What do ye want?" He was careful now. He did not want her to vanish.

"Come to me."

Before he could ask her where she wished for him to go, the air between them visibly sizzled. Macleod tensed and felt the space around him lurch, putting him off balance. The chamber seemed to sigh—or was it a breeze from the sea? And then such a profound stillness came, with such an absolute silence, that he knew it was the lull before the storm, the interlude before the cataclysm.

Instinct made him seize his sword.

She vanished.

And he was hurled up toward the stone roof of his chamber.

In that instant, he thought he would be crushed against the ceiling and that he was about to die.

But the ceiling vanished and he was flung upward and there was only the ebony night sky, filled with stars, suns and moons, which he passed at dizzying speed. He gave into the pain and roared.

CHAPTER THREE

"MISS, WE'RE HERE," the cabdriver said.

Tabby was so distressed by what had happened at the Met that she'd zoned out the entire taxicab ride downtown. Now she saw the brick façade of the building where she shared a loft with Sam. As she dug into her purse to pay the cabbie, the Highlander's dark image remained engraved on her mind. Her pulse accelerated. He was hurt and he needed help.

She paid the driver, tipping him generously, and slid from the taxi. The Highlander had been in that fire at Melvaig. It was the only conclusion to draw. She assumed that amulet had drawn him to the Met. If she hadn't touched his hand, she might have thought him a ghost. But he was no ghost—she'd felt a man's strong hand beneath her fingers and it had not been her imagination.

She trembled. He had clearly traveled through time from the medieval world. Was he a Master, like Aidan and Royce? And why had she been chosen to see him? What did Fate want of her?

She inhaled, still shaken. Even if he was one of the brethren, he was hurt. She was not a Healer, but that didn't matter. No Rose would ever turn her back on anyone in need. She was beginning to think that she was meant to help him. She couldn't think of another reason to explain what had just happened.

He must have walked out of that fire. He'd looked as fierce

and savage as a warrior who'd just left a medieval battlefield after a bloody and barbaric battle. He was so huge and so muscular, so powerful, that even hurt and anguished, he had been daunting.

Of course, she didn't even know if her spell had worked.

Tabby wasn't hopeful. She was pretty good with simple, classic spells—like sleeping spells—but inventing a powerful spell to bring someone to her across time and having it work was a whole different ball game. She might never come face-to-face with him again. That would almost be a relief. On the other hand, their brief encounter was not that of two normal strangers passing on the street. Not when she was a Rose, and he, a Master.

The front door to the building had high-security locks. After glancing behind her to make certain no one was going to follow her inside, she unlocked the door and stepped into the front hall. Another locked door was there, which she unlocked. Inside, the lobby was spacious and modern, with green plants spilling over planters built stylishly into the travertine floors. At the elevator, she leaned her head against the burnished metal door while waiting for it.

It crossed her mind that he had looked at her as if he knew her.

Tabby jerked away from the elevator as the door opened. She had to have imagined that! But he had somehow seemed familiar—or was that because she'd become so obsessed with him? But almost every moment at the Met had felt like déjà vu.

There were twelve floors in the building; their loft was on the eleventh floor, because eleven was a master number. The Roses always looked at the numerology of everything that they did, and tried to choose appropriately. It was more tradition—and superstition—than anything else.

The moment Tabby opened the triple locks on her front

door—before she could even cross the threshold—she knew that something was wrong. She didn't know if she suddenly had a new sixth sense, one warning her of danger, or if it was mere human instinct.

She froze, staring wide-eyed into the large spacious interior of the loft. For one moment, nothing seemed out of place. An immaculate white kitchen was to her right, while a great room with a media area, a living area and two desks faced her, done in shades of beige and chocolate. The far wall was white-washed brick, as were two central pillars. She and Sam had chosen the furnishings together, and everything was sleek and modern, classic and timeless, right down to the pale leather sectional and the glass coffee table.

Her gaze slammed to the iron-and-glass table in front of the sectional and she inhaled. A huge bouquet of bloodred roses was in a vase in its center. It had not been there when she had left for the Met that morning. Sam had left at dawn to work for a few hours at HCU, and Tabby knew she hadn't been back since. No one had access to their loft, except for Kit. Tabby knew she hadn't stopped by, either—and certainly not with red roses.

Tabby said firmly, "Who's there?"

Only silence greeted her.

She hated weapons in general, and only carried pepper spray with her, except at night, when Sam insisted she arm herself with a .38. Tabby had been using a protective spell for years; it was one of the few spells she could summon up really quickly. It didn't afford total protection—madmen and demons could breach it if they were really determined—but most humans could not.

"*Good over me, good around me, good everywhere, barring dark intent. Circle formed, protecting me,*" she murmured swiftly. Then she stepped inside, straining to hear, aware of the white cocoon she was in. She had left the door open so she could run if necessary. "Who's there?" she said again, more loudly.

The loft was quiet and it felt vacant. Nothing felt awry or evil. She went to the kitchen drawer, took out her gun and went to the first bedroom door. It was wide-open and she glanced inside the room, which was filled with the gray light of dusk. Sam's bedroom had one dark, almost ebony wall, but the rest of the furnishings were beige. Still, she could see clearly and it was empty.

She checked the closet and the hall bathroom; they were empty, too.

Refusing to put down her guard, she checked her own blue-and-white bedroom—also empty.

Only somewhat relieved, Tabby put down the gun and locked the front door. Someone had left the roses. She walked over to the sofa and sat down, looking for a card. There wasn't one.

She pulled off her knee-high, medium-heeled brown boots and stared grimly at the roses, wondering what kind of threat they were. Had they been a romantic gesture, they would have been delivered to the front door. The roses were an omen—and not a good one. She'd call a locksmith tomorrow and have the locks changed.

The dark Highlander's image returned to her mind. Tabby hesitated, and then went to the locked chest at the loft's far end, set against the brick wall. She unlocked it with the key she wore on the chain beneath her pearls and took out the Book of Roses.

She was pretty sure that the spell she'd made up on the spot at the Met wouldn't work. The Book of Roses contained just about every spell ever invented. But the Book was almost two thousand pages long. Some of the passages needed translation—they were in a very unusual and ancient form of Gaelic. Although Tabby had been studying the Book for seventeen years, she did not know it thoroughly—only a very ancient Rose ever could. Her grandmother Sara had studied the Book for generations, and had been able to find spells in a heartbeat—assuming she didn't already know the spell by heart. But Grandma Sara had been an amazingly powerful and wise witch. She had died of old age in her sleep a few years ago, and Tabby still missed her—she always would. But she often felt as if Grandma was with her still, smiling with approval and encouragement. Just then, she desperately needed her guidance.

Because finding the right spell could be a huge challenge. Once in a while, Tabby could find a spell in a few hours, but usually it took days or even weeks to locate the exact spell she needed. She was almost certain she had neither days nor weeks to find the Highlander.

She prayed for some otherworldly help and began thumbing through the book, pausing to read bits and pieces and key words. As she did, his powerful image remained firmly implanted, front and center, in her mind.

The words began to jumble. Tabby stared at them, realizing she was exhausted from the events of that day, but she did not intend to quit. "Who are you?" she murmured, staring at the pages before her.

Of course there was no answer. She sighed, curling her legs up under her, telling herself she wasn't going to take a nap, not now, not when she needed to find him. But she could close her eyes just for a minute, she thought.

Her lids drifted closed. She cradled the Book to her chest. She refused to fall asleep; instead, she relived their brief encounter at the Met, hoping for a clue as to who and what he was. But nothing in her memory changed and she was so tired…

Suddenly he was looking at her—and the burns and blisters were gone from his face and body. He was gorgeous. She sat up, wide-awake.

Sheer disappointment claimed her. The Highlander was not standing there in her loft; she had been dreaming.

She tightened her hold on the Book. Her heart was thundering. At the Met, it had been impossible to make out most of his features. She had surely invented such masculine beauty. Real men did not look like poster boys for a romance channel version of *Braveheart*.

Someone knocked on her front door.

Tabby tensed. It was impossible for a visitor to get into the lobby and upstairs to her door without buzzing from the downstairs front hall first. But someone was knocking loudly and insistently on her front door. Someone had gotten through the building's locked doors. She became really alarmed, glancing at the red roses, her concern for the dark Highlander now taking a backseat to the intruder at her door.

"Tabby, are you home?" her ex-husband demanded.

Tabby jumped to her feet. *Randall was banging on her front door?* She hadn't seen him since the divorce, twenty-one months ago, except by chance one night, when he'd been out on the town with a nineteen-year-old Russian model—one of the many models he'd cheated on her with.

Her gaze slammed to the roses. No, it was impossible. He'd never start things up again—not that she would let him.

"One moment," she cried loudly, flustered and uncertain. Even though she had no wish to ever see him again, she felt a moment of distress. She had loved him. They'd been intimate, a couple; they'd been husband and wife. She'd given him two years of her life—and she'd thought it would be forever.

But their marriage had been a lie—one big, fat, long lie. Randall was ambitious and successful, on a fast track to the top, making millions of dollars for his clients and himself. He'd been smooth, charming, macho and charismatic, and she'd truly thought he loved her wildly, with all of his heart. While she'd thought that, he'd been out on the town with the city's most beautiful women—the kind of women he could brag to his cronies about.

As she went to the front door, she could not imagine what he wanted. "Hello, Randall. This is truly a surprise."

His gaze slid over her from head to toe, in a very familiar way. He smiled and shook his head. "Even barefoot, you're as elegant as ever!"

She felt herself bristle, but she contained the surge of anger. She did not want any flattery from him.

Now he said, dropping his tone, "You could walk out of a steam room in a towel, Tabby, and you'd never have a hair out of place."

"I highly doubt that."

"Aw, come on. You could be First Lady, another Jackie O."

"I hardly have that kind of ambition." She trembled. "What are you doing here, Randall?"

His brown gaze was warm as it met hers. "I've been missing you and I decided to do something about it."

She had stopped trusting him a long time ago. "We haven't seen each other in almost two years. How did you get in?"

"Do you like the roses?"

She inhaled, very taken aback. Suddenly she was angry. "Randall, what are you doing?"

"I wanted to let you know that I've been thinking about you. I'm glad you like them." His focus moved to the roses. "They're gorgeous. I paid top dollar. When I ordered them, I told the florist only the best will do."

"They're inappropriate, Randall."

He grinned. "I think they're really appropriate—gorgeous, yet classic."

It was hard to breathe. Randall had always admired her style, her sense of fashion and her grace. He had been so proud of how "elegant" she was. By the divorce, she'd come to hate that word. She vividly recalled a party on a humid day in the Hamptons. As they'd pulled into the driveway, Randall had told her again how elegant she was. It had suddenly bothered her. She'd wanted him to pull over, grab her and make love to her as if she was a sexpot. Sex was usually the last thing on her mind.

Tabby stared at him in dismay. "What happened to your Russian girlfriend?"

He didn't hesitate. "I've grown up."

She was beginning to have an idea of why he had come.

"I can see the skepticism on your face. Tabby, how many dumb models can a guy go out with before he gets it?"

"I have no idea," she said truthfully.

"You're still angry with me. I don't blame you. But I have great news and I want to share it with you!"

"Whatever it is, I'm happy for—" she began to say, but he cut her off.

"I meant what I said, Tabby. I have grown up. The truth is that we shouldn't have married three years ago—I wasn't ready. But things have changed." Excitement flared in his eyes. "I've been offered a top position at Odyssey, Tab. I mean top—as in my salary is doubling. With the clients I'll have, I could be making eight or nine mil a year! Not only that, in a couple of years I'll be in position to make CEO, if not there, at another major firm. This is it, everything we've always wanted!"

She'd never doubted he would make it to the very top of New York's financial world, so his news was hardly a surprise. But CEOs at firms like the Odyssey Group needed suitable wives—wives who knew how to charm the city's elite and their husband's clients, wives who knew how to graciously hold fund-raisers and dinner parties, trophy wives who were fashionable, attractive, charming and *elegant*. She felt ill, realizing what he wanted. "I am very happy for you. But it's late."

He approached, his eyes blazing with excitement, and he seized her hand. "We can go to the top together, Tabby, I know we can!"

She tried to pull away but he wouldn't let her go. "I can't do this again."

"I will never cheat on you again," he said seriously.

Randall had never taken no for an answer, she thought, dismayed.

"Beyond the impeccable manners, you are still the kindest woman I know. Everyone makes mistakes, even you. Won't you give me another shot? Because I am being sincere, Tab."

She knew she must not give him another chance, and she had meant it when she said they were done. But the truth was, everyone did make mistakes and everyone deserved a second chance.

The dark Highlander loomed in her mind, as he'd been at the Met, bloody and burned.

Randall suddenly let her go. He was smiling. "Just think about it. You're also the fairest person I know. Take your time. I'll call you."

Because she was proud of her manners, she walked him to the door, although she balked at allowing him a kiss on the cheek. When he was gone, she poured a huge glass of red wine and carried it to the sofa. She sipped, in absolute disbelief, her temples pounding.

She was angry. She hated being angry—anger had never worked for her. Anger made her uncomfortable. As far as she was concerned, it didn't work for anyone. Civility and compromise were always the best path.

But no matter how polite she intended to be, how gracious, how fair, Randall's return was unacceptable.

Besides, she had another man in her life, didn't she? The joke was a bad one, but Tabby smiled anyway.

Her telephone rang.

She hesitated, certain it was Randall, then saw Sam's number pop up on the ID screen. She seized the receiver. "Sam, we have to talk."

Sam hesitated. "Yeah, we do."

Tabby felt herself still. "What did you find out about An Tùir-Tara?"

"I got in touch with the foremost authority on the subject, a historian at Oxford in Britain."

Dread began. "What happened?"

"Well, he's the one historian who says the clan war between the Macleods and MacDougalls was not the real reason for the fire in 1550. There's nothing written down to support the theory, but there is another oral tradition."

Tabby had a bad feeling.

"Folklore has it the fire was a result of a war of witches."

Tabby cried out.

WHAT HAD HAPPENED? Where was he?

Had he just journeyed through the *universe?*

Macleod lay very still, afraid to attempt to move. Having landed on stone, there was pain, although he was aware of it lessening as he lay there. And there was so much noise, most of it unfamiliar. People had been screaming, although their screams were ceasing now. He bit back a moan, and realized that he could move his fingers and toes. *He had been hurled across the sky, past stars and suns. Was this the leap that MacNeil and the brothers spoke of?*

The torment was fading swiftly now and he became aware that the people standing around him were speaking the same strangely accented English as the golden woman. He opened his eyes. Some of the women wore the same fashion of clothes that the goddess had, their skirts knee-length. His thoughts sharpened. She had summoned him. But now, he wondered if she was a mortal like the other people crowding over him. Or perhaps she was a near immortal like him? She certainly seemed to be from this time.

Was she there? He certainly wanted a word with her now.

Somebody call 911… Is that a costume…?

He could not comprehend their words very well, but he clearly heard and understood their thoughts. Slowly, Macleod looked past the excited crowd.

Is he dead? Did he fall from the roof?

He shut out their thoughts, stunned.

The night sky was oddly starless, but still light and milky, as he had never before seen it. Hundreds of soaring towers filled it, the highest towers he had ever seen. He was in a huge city. *Where was he—and in what time?*

He forgot her and her summons. He gripped his sword and slowly began to sit up, realizing his body was not broken after all. The people who had gathered around him cried out and ran farther away from him. He noted that no one carried weapons but he did not relax his guard. Now, he saw that the golden woman was not amongst the crowd. He wondered what that meant and if it was some kind of trick. It didn't matter. He would find her sooner or later. He would make a point of it.

He dismissed them all, his gaze returning to the astonishing sights around him. What kind of people could build such tall buildings, crowded so closely upon one another? Were they impregnable? And the windows within the towers were strangely lit. They could not be illuminated so brightly by rushes and candles.

He stood up, looking warily around. The men wore strange hose and very short tunics. His eyes widened. Horseless vehicles were passing along the black stone street.

He became absolutely still, adrenaline rushing. No mortal could make a wagon or a carriage move without the power of a slave or a beast.

"He's alive!"

Macleod ignored the man. A screaming sound that did not come from any animal or human made him turn, seeking its source.

One of the horseless vehicles was speeding toward the crowd, passing the other carriages. Red, blue and white lights were blinking on the roof. The vehicle screeched to a stop and the whining noise ceased. Doors slammed as men in dark clothes stepped out of the vehicle. From the way they began to approach, he knew that they were soldiers.

Macleod tensed. He was in a strange world and he did not know what kinds of powers these soldiers had. He had never fled a battle in his life, but he was certain now that he had leaped through time. He had to be far in the future. He should try to learn the secrets of this world before any attempt at engagement. And he had to find the woman. He did not like being flung through time without his consent. He wanted to know why she had cast her magic upon him—and most of all, why she'd haunted him for so many years.

But he was not a coward. He stood absolutely still, shifting his weight so he was evenly balanced, his right hand on the hilt of his long sword. If he had to fight, he hoped his powers would not fail him—and he certainly hoped that the dark soldiers did not have immortal powers, too.

"What's going on?" a black-clothed soldier asked firmly, his intent gaze on Macleod. From the way he stared, Macleod knew he expected a fight.

The woman in the knee-length gown ran to him and began telling him that Macleod had fallen from the sky. As she gestured, he felt the icy cold fingers of evil chill the nape of his neck.

They had deamhanain in this time and place, too.

He hadn't taken his vows, but he had been able to instantly sense evil's presence from the moment he'd taken his first steps as a toddler. He had instinctively and passionately disliked evil ever since he could recall, and had been vanquishing evil since he was a small boy capable of wielding a child's dagger. Macleod gripped the hilt of his sword, slowly turning to face the deamhan. A tall, blond man stared at him, smiling with bloodlust. The deamhanain desired the death of the good and the godly every bit as much as the brotherhood wanted evil gone. Its eyes slowly turned red.

Macleod didn't bother to smile back.

"Hey, you, buddy."

Macleod knew one of the black-clad soldiers was speaking to him; he ignored him.

The deamhan grinned and blasted him with his black power, which flared crimson as it was hurled at him.

Macleod blocked the blast with his sword, using his other powers, and he was pleased when it blazed silver as it struck the demonic force. He hurled his power at the deamhan simultaneously and it went down, the people around it screaming and fleeing.

"Drop your weapon!" the soldier shouted at him.

Macleod ignored the command, advancing swiftly, sword raised. The deamhan leaped up and sent more energy at him, but he was weakened now and Macleod did not pause. He lunged, so swiftly and powerfully that his blade tore through the deamhan's power, running right through his chest and out the other side.

"Put the weapon down!"

Macleod withdrew the blade. The deamhan collapsed. Standing over him, Macleod breathed hard and slowly faced the soldiers. Both men were down on one knee, and had small, strange black weapons pointed at him.

Macleod glanced swiftly around. He was at a crossroads,

with lights that changed from red to green on all four corners. He glanced at the milky night sky—no moon or North Star could be seen. "I dinna wish to fight. Tell me, what place is this? Where am I?"

"Hands in the air, sonuvabitch! Weapon down!" The first soldier shouted at him, while the crowd behind them murmured in surprise.

No one had *ever* called his mother a bitch. It was an unimaginable insult. For one moment, he was in shock. And then rage rushed over him, through him, and he wanted to murder the soldier for his words. The fact that he was out of his time did not matter. But he somehow controlled himself. Breathing hard, he said, "Where am I, soldier?" But before he had even finished speaking, his power exploded.

Silver sizzled in the night and both men were hurled backward by the blazing light.

The remaining crowd screamed, fleeing. He saw two black-and-white vehicles with the red, white and blue blinking lights coming toward them at quick speed, making that high, whining noise. *We have an officer down... Code black... Armed and dangerous...reinforcements...*

He heard a hundred frantic thoughts, a dozen sharp commands, and he felt the fear, the hatred and anger. As jumbled as the thoughts were, he knew that more soldiers were coming—and they would hunt him now for what he had done to one of their own.

Macleod ran.

Sharp sounds followed him. As he passed a building with a large window, it shattered. He had seen stained glass once, in a great cathedral at Moray. As the shards bit into his arms, he was stunned to realize the window had been covered with clear, nearly invisible glass. Just as he turned the corner, something burned like an iron brand deep into his shoulder.

It was painful and he gasped, but it could not compare to the thrust of a sword. And now he saw the hundreds of vehicles coming toward him on the street. In the distance, behind most of them, was one that carried soldiers, with its blinking lights on top of the roof.

He paused and glanced behind. More soldiers had turned the corner and were in pursuit, on foot, their black weapons drawn.

A woman was stepping out of a building. Behind her, the interior was brightly lit. Most of the buildings were alight, but several were in shadow. Tonight the dark would be his friend.

He ran up the street, the sharp, popping sounds following him. The iron brand felt worse now but he ignored the pain and seized the door to a building that was not lit. It was locked, but he wrenched it open easily. Then he stepped into the blackness inside, barring the door by bending the locks back into place. It would only hold the soldiers back for a moment, but a moment was all he needed.

He swiftly checked the first three doors. The fourth door was what he was looking for. Macleod ran up the stairs, listening to the soldiers entering the small front hall below.

How the fuck did he break the locks?

Forget about it. He's heading for the roof—the fucking fool.

He smiled savagely to himself, running up the stairs, counting fifteen flights. He finally burst onto a large, square roof and ran to one end, looked down, and then to another. He did not hesitate. This way felt right. He chose the southern end and leaped to an adjacent roof, about two stories lower, and ran across that, heading in the direction he thought was east. He ran by pure instinct now. The next roof was higher but he leaped onto that, and then onto another, and another, until the soldiers were far behind him.

He began to become familiar with the strange sounds of the city night; he began to comprehend the city's noisy rhythm. He slowed to a walk. There was no reason to run now; for the moment, he was safe.

And he paused, listening to the night—feeling it.

Awareness began.

He opened a window and slipped into a dark vacant building, his pulse taking on a new rhythm. Aware that he was alone, he began to explore it, his eyes adjusting to the darkness. Within moments, he realized he was in a building meant to house children. The tables and chairs were tiny, and children's toys and drawings were on the walls.

He began to smile.

Her presence was everywhere.

Macleod settled down to wait.

CHAPTER FOUR

A HOLY HIGHLANDER WAS in the city, and he had just taken a demon down.

Nick Forrester decided this might be a really interesting night.

He was a tall, powerful man with rugged good looks, brilliantly blue eyes, and the kind of appeal no woman had ever refused. He was utterly devoted to his agents, the war on evil and HCU, in that precise order. Sitting in his corner office, on the phone with one of his contacts at the *New York Times,* he felt Sam Rose before he saw her. He turned to wave her into his office as Paul Anderson said, "They're breaking the story even as we speak."

"Motherfucking shit," Nick replied, slamming down the phone. He felt himself go into battle-ready mode. There was nothing he loved as much as a good battle, not even sex.

Sam's eyes were wide with interest, although a moment ago she'd been wearing a don't-read-my-mind poker face. And even while speaking with Anderson, he'd instantly known she had a secret. He did not like his kids keeping secrets, not unless they were personal ones. And then they'd damn well better keep secrets, because he didn't like his kids having personal lives.

Either you were in this war or you were a bystander, it was that simple. And if you were in, love, romance, family and all that shit was out.

He'd made a really smart move three months ago, when he'd lured Sam into HCU and his employ. She was a soldier in every way, right down to her kick-ass, martial soul.

"Goddamn it," he said, facing her. "There's been a sighting."

He eyed her as he picked up the blue phone, a direct line to his agents in the field. "There's a Blondie down on Thirteenth and Broadway," he said. The highest level of demons were beautiful, blond, blue-eyed and almost angelic in appearance. They'd been given a slew of appropriate—and inappropriate—nicknames.

"What's going on?" Sam asked.

"It's almost impossible to believe, but a Highlander has surfaced in the city. He took out a cop. I've got Angus bringing the goods to Five."

"Okay." Sam turned her back on him, walking over to a chair. She sat down. Even though she wore short skirts most of the time, and he'd seen her gorgeous and very strong legs hundreds of times, he stared at them while he thought about the night to come.

Being clandestine meant keeping a low profile. The press still thought the war was with crime, not evil. CDA had its own medical center. Shot-up, maimed and dead agents were all brought to Emergency there. Five had a morgue, too, and some very serious labs. Those were mostly filled with vanquished demons—if the demon could be brought in before disintegration began—and occasionally, the surviving sub.

She turned. "Do we know this one?"

"I don't think so," Nick said.

They exchanged a long and steady glance, and he didn't have to read her mind to know she was thinking about the trip they'd made into the past.

He turned and walked to the wall of windows that looked down on Hudson Street. Outside, it was dark, the streets icy and gleaming with patches of snow, sleet and slush. Winter in the city sucked for most people, but he actually liked it. His blood continued to rush.

He did not like losing an agent in the vast expanse of time. Every agent at HCU had been handpicked by him for their respective jobs. He considered each and every one his responsibility, and when one went MIT, he went ballistic.

And he also went back.

The holy, time-traveling Masters of Time rarely surfaced in this city. They seemed to prefer medieval periods. CDA had sightings of them as early as the eleventh century, but the more contemporary the period got, the fewer the sightings.

The Highlanders were not the only warrior society out there. CDA had evidence of two other secret sects dedicated to the war on evil, one ancient, one modern. From time to time he came across men who had some of the same extraordinary powers he had. These men lay low, revealing themselves only to vanquish the enemy, and then they vanished, like ghosts in the night. Pretty much the way he did.

The Masters were an interesting bunch. They loved and warred like any other medieval Scot, but secretly worshipped pagan gods, most of whose names no historian had ever recorded. They defended a set of three holy books, and came out of the medieval woodwork to defend the good and the innocent and kick the ass of a demon honcho or two. Then they vanished back into the local population and their particular time. Only an experienced agent could identify a Master from the average Highlander, whether on paper in HCU's immense database, or while in the field.

He'd lost count long ago, but over the course of the two decades he'd been at HCU, he'd probably traveled into the past a dozen times, usually on the heels of a great demon. He'd had exactly three encounters with Masters in all that time.

Maybe it wasn't that odd—he'd chased demons into the past all over the world, as far back as the first century, when the Romans were about to rule the world. The closest he'd ever come to a Highlander was last September, right there in the city. The Highlander had been turned against the Masters, and he'd taken his own agent hostage, vanishing into the past with Brie Rose. Nick had gone back to find her because there was nothing worse than losing an agent in time.

He'd found Sam's cousin Brie and dragged her home before he could chat with her holy friends—and she'd gone back to her Highlander anyway. Her case file might have MIT stamped across it, but he knew she wasn't really missing in time. She was just fine.

He'd had the chance to debrief her extensively, and now he knew more about the Brotherhood than anyone at CDA had ever known. Of course, encounters between CDA agents and Masters—and civilians and Masters—were as old as the agency and maybe, for the latter, as old as time. But the Masters remained secretive. They refused to talk about what they did; they simply fought evil when they had to, and were devoted to the war on evil in Scotland.

Except, a few hours ago, a Master had nailed a demon just a few blocks away from HCU.

Were they coming out of the medieval closet? And if so, what did that mean?

He refused to worry, but agency analysts were predicting the end of the world—literally. That was how dire the war had become. If it wasn't turned around, every high government agency in the free world would be infiltrated by demons and controlled by evil within another decade.

He'd taken Sam with him into the past to find her cousin. It was about the toughest test he could give any agent, new or not. She'd passed with flying colors.

So why was she looking really tense? Why was she worried?

He lurked and his concern vanished. He was not interested in a war of witches, although he knew her civilian sister was a witch.

"Why would you think the Highlander is someone we know?"

She shrugged. "No reason."

What wasn't she telling him? "What's wrong with you? Bad lay last night?"

She gave him a look. "There's no such thing. Maybe the Highlander followed the demon here."

He liked her arrogance—a lot. But her comment gave Nick pause.

He had decided well over a year ago that the witch burnings were not as random as most of law enforcement believed. He also disagreed with the agency's social anthropologists and shrinks who claimed the gangs were simply on a new demonic high, and it was cooler to burn people at the stake than to murder each other gangland style. He knew with every fiber of his being that there was a rhyme and a reason to the burnings. He was absolutely certain that there was one great black power behind all of the gangs in the country, if not the world, and that their leader was a medieval demon.

And he had made it his personal mission to nail the sonuva-bitch.

So if the Highlander had followed a medieval demon to New York, he'd jump for joy if the incident was somehow connected to the witch burnings. "We know nothing about our holy friend—although I intend to change that."

"It was too quiet this weekend, until now," Sam said after a reflective pause.

"Yeah, it was like a vacation." He hated vacations. "Let's not speculate. We have a priority. We need to find our medieval ally before someone else does."

"Why?"

Before he could tell her about the breaking news, the child screamed.

He knew that horrific sound inside and out. It was a part of his soul and he'd hoped to never hear it again.

The young girl screamed, and he heard the roar as the sedan went up in flames. He inhaled, flinching. He had no time for a flashback now.

But he saw the inferno on the night-darkened freeway and he heard the heavy, black laughter.

"Nick? You okay?"

He heard Sam, but vaguely, as if she was speaking to him from far away. He breathed hard and realized he felt sick. He'd just had a goddamned flashback!

It took him a moment to push the image away. When he had, he was at his window, staring down at the cars passing below on the slick city streets.

Holy shit. He'd vanquished the flashbacks about a decade ago. He couldn't understand why they were starting up all over again.

He'd pretend it hadn't happened—so it hadn't happened. He had the best secretary money could buy—and money couldn't buy Jan, only her own, personal demons could. Jan was classified Level Five at HCU and she'd been at his side through the best times and the worst times. Once upon a time she'd been his best field agent. If she ever learned he was having flashbacks again, she'd hound him so bad he'd cave and go to a shrink. Of course, by then, hell would have frozen over and the war would have been won or lost.

He got it together and faced Sam. "Here's the deal. The Highlander got Brad with his sword in front of a bunch of cops and civvies," Nick said.

Sam faced him, her eyes wide.

"The press got wind of it and they're going with it. I can't close it down. They're calling him 'the Sword Murderer'—original, don't you think?"

"Shit," Sam said. She was a bit pale, when Sam was usually the coolest cucumber he knew.

"He also took at least one hit from our city's finest," Nick added. "Of course, a teensy-weensy bullet probably won't bother him very much." He picked up the white phone and made a single call. It would stop the cops from hunting their Highlander down. He could do that much.

He smiled cheerfully at her after hanging up. "The cops will be put to bed shortly. But the story is breaking on the evening news right now."

"It will cause hysteria," Sam said, heading for the door. "We have to find him before one of the vigilante gangs does."

Normally, Nick didn't mind the dozens of violent vigilante gangs in the city. They were no match for the demons, but they sure as hell helped the war effort—even though their activities were against the law. CDA, the cops and the Feds all looked the other way.

He wasn't looking the other way now.

The Highlander was wounded—and from all accounts, on the run. He needed their protection. "Let's go find the holy warrior," he said. "And see if we can help our medieval friend."

HER NEWSPAPER TUCKED under her arm—she usually glanced at the front page in the teachers' lounge when her class was in fifth-period music—Tabby walked into the school where she taught first grade. She greeted a half-dozen other teachers as she strolled toward her classroom, still trying to get focused on the day to come. She loved children and she loved being an elementary-school teacher, especially in public school, where many of the kids so needed direction and guidance. But she'd slept badly last night. Her dreams had been anxious and stressful—they'd all been about the dark Highlander.

She'd awoken with the certainty that he was in trouble, more so than ever, and that he needed her.

One strange visit to the Met and her life had changed so quickly, she thought.

And something was up. Sam hadn't come home that morning. She worked at night—evil played after dark and hid in the daylight. But she was usually home at sunrise. Tabby knew she should assume whatever Sam was doing was routine, but her senses were telling her otherwise. Something was happening, and she wished she knew what.

Tabby entered her classroom and some of her anxiety vanished. The room's walls were covered with the kids' cheerful and colorful paintings and pictures, their latest spelling assignments, and maps of the city, the state and the country, with important landmarks flagged. Some articles they'd discussed from newspapers and magazines were also taped to the walls.

She always had a really good vibe when coming to class, and that hadn't changed. First period was current events, so Tabby laid her copy of *USA Today* down on her desk, and with it, the article she'd clipped for the kids from the *New York Times*.

She glimpsed the paper's headline and cried out.

Sword Murderer Threatens City. Tabby sank into her chair, scanning the article, somehow already knowing what she was going to find. A man dressed in a medieval Highland costume had murdered a man in Tribeca last night. He had escaped the authorities, but he was wounded, armed and dangerous.

Tabby began to shake. *He was in the city, and he was hurt.*

She closed her eyes and whispered, "I can help you."

Come to me, she thought, straining for him. *Come to me.*

"Hello," a cheerful voice called to her.

For one moment, Tabby was so focused that she heard the woman but couldn't move or open her eyes. Then the woman spoke again and Tabby came back to the present.

She got up, drenched with perspiration, and faced a woman she had never seen before. The woman had very fair skin and hair, and she was wearing a beige suit that gave her an oddly bland appearance. "Are you okay?" the woman asked.

"I'm fine—I was lost in thought," Tabby said, aware that she'd spoken the truth.

"I'm filling in for Marlene, and I just wanted to pop in and introduce myself," the woman said, smiling. "I'm Kristin Lafarge."

Marlene was vice principal, and she was on maternity leave. Tabby smiled in return, walking forward so they could shake hands. "Hi. I'm Tabby Rose, although you probably already know that."

"I do," she said pleasantly. "And I've heard great things about this school. I'm looking forward to my time here."

"It's a great faculty and a great group of kids, for the most part," Tabby said.

Kristin glanced at her desk. "Just what we need, a nutcase on the loose in the city, running people through with a sword."

Tabby smiled grimly. "I'm sure he'll be apprehended." *Please keep him safe,* she added silently, a prayer.

"I hope so. Although it's not in the news, it's all over the school that the victim was murdered eight blocks from here."

He had been so close. Tabby lived five blocks from the school. She breathed hard as Kristin left, promising they'd catch up in the teachers' lounge later. The vice principal was hardly out of the door when Tabby ran to her desk. She seized the newspaper. The murder had happened at eleven o'clock last night—when she'd been asleep, dreaming about him.

Had he come to her neighborhood because of her spell?

She inhaled, shaken. Was it possible that she had cast such a powerful spell? She had to call Sam. HCU would help him. Or was Sam already on the case? Was that what she'd been working on last night? But her first students began arriving, and Tabby couldn't linger on the phone. Instead, she sent Sam a text message.

Have you found the Highlander?

Then she began greeting her class. If she did not get a grip and focus on her students, it would be an endless day for her, and unfair to them. Besides, a medieval warrior with the power to travel through time could probably handle a few cops and a wound or two. But she was not relieved. As she greeted her kids, she almost expected him to walk into her classroom, but every time she looked up, a parent or a student stood there.

A tiny, pretty blond girl named Willa, who happened to be one of Tabby's brightest pupils, came into the classroom. "How are you, Willa?" she asked. Willa could already read and write at the second-grade level, and she was always asking questions that were amazingly insightful for a six-year-old.

Willa asked, "Can we have a spelling bee?"

Tabby laughed, and laughing felt good. "A spelling bee! You must have seen that show on TV over the weekend. I'll think about it." It was a foregone conclusion that if they had a spelling bee, Willa would win it.

More children filed in, greeting her with happy smiles, calling out to one another eagerly. It was a really good group of kids. But she couldn't relax and she couldn't stop worrying—or glancing at the door. When a few of the parents and caretakers expressed concern over the Sword Murderer being on the loose, Tabby reassured them all that the school was completely safe. *Was he nearby?*

If only she had a moment to focus, she would meditate and try to feel his presence.

Finally her last student arrived. Tabby shut the door, asking everyone to settle down so they could talk about the lame-duck presidency. "Does anyone remember what that means?" she asked. As she showed the class a picture of a duck, the kids shrieked and made outlandish comments. She let them carry on, her gaze drifting to the newspaper article.

"Ms. Rose? Ms. Rose!"

Tabby jerked, realizing the kids had settled down and were waiting for her expectantly. She heard her classroom door open, but did not turn. Assuming it was a staff member, she said, "Who wants to try to tell me what a lame-duck president is?"

Only Willa raised her hand. Tabby noticed that the kids were distracted by whoever had come into the room, but she said, "Willa?"

"Why are they locking the door?"

Tabby turned as she heard the lock click. Two teenage boys stood by the door, clad from head to toe in black, their complexions eerily pale and made more so by the application of pancake makeup.

Her heart began to thunder uncontrollably. The boys had the appearance of the subs that ran in the gangs burning civilians. She prayed the boys were Goths, not possessed humans. The sub gangs had always preyed on the Innocent in large groups— until last week's Rampage. As for her "new" sixth sense, the only feeling she was getting was that these boys were definitely looking for trouble.

She managed to feign a calm she did not feel as she slowly put the paper aside and stood up. "Hello." The children must not be alarmed. "Can I help you?"

The boy who had pitch-black hair with flame-colored streaks dyed in it grinned. "You sure can, Teach."

She didn't know if she finally had the power to sense evil

or not, but she knew these boys were evil. While she didn't know what they wanted, she did know their intent was purely malicious. How was she going to protect the children?

She turned from them and smiled at the children. "I have a great idea. Everyone sit down on the floor in a small circle, with the paper. Find as many items relating to the President as you can."

One of the teen boys snickered.

"Come on," Tabby said, wanting to gather the children into one tight group. As they all sat down on the floor, as far from the two boys and the door as she could get them, she handed Willa the article. "Willa, I want you to be the group leader and make a list."

Willa stared at her with her big, intelligent blue eyes. Tabby smiled more fully; Willa knew something was wrong. "Are they going to watch the class?" Willa asked.

"Maybe." Tabby smiled, when she heard the whirring of a drill.

She whirled and saw the blond boy drilling holes into the door. "What are you doing?"

"What does it look like?" the dark-haired boy said. He pulled out a long metal object from his backpack.

The blonde was now drilling a set of holes into the wall, and Tabby realized they were adding a bolt to the door to lock her and the children inside the classroom. She lowered her voice, aware of her fear rising. But she somehow breathed and tamped it down. "Whatever you intend, do it to me. But let the children go."

"Oh, don't you worry, pretty lady. We are definitely doing it to you." He laughed at her.

Tabby wet her lips, knowing she must hold her fear at bay for the children's sake. She sent a silent message to Sam—telepathy was huge for them. "What's your name?"

He bared his teeth and said, "Angel. You like that…Tabitha?"

They knew her name. Then comprehension flashed in her mind—her name was on the door. "You want me, not the children. Please, whatever you want, I won't resist. But we have to let the children go, now."

"We've got plans for the kiddies," Angel said.

"Ms. Rose?" Willa asked.

Tabby jerked, wishing Willa hadn't left the security of the circle of children, as false as it was. She took her hand. "Willa, go back to the other children."

Willa looked carefully from her to Angel and then to the blonde, who was drilling screws into the new lock on the door. "Is he locking us in?"

Before Tabby could come up with an excuse for what was happening, Angel said, "We sure are, pretty girl." He walked away and dumped the contents of a huge duffel onto the floor.

Tabby cringed as she saw the kindling.

He poured gasoline on it and grinned. "What's wrong, Teach? Afraid of fire?"

Tabby breathed. "Go back to the other children, Willa." But now she saw that every child had his or her eyes trained upon the drama that was unfolding.

Angel's hand snaked out and he seized Willa, who screamed. "Maybe we'll start with her, witch," he said to Tabby.

Tabby sent Willa a reassuring glance, and Willa fought her tears and stopped struggling. "Let my student go," she said, and it was not a request.

Angel nodded at his blond friend, ignoring her. The blonde produced matches and began to light one.

Tabby's heart thundered as he lit the match. Her mind raced with lightning speed. Willa was going to be burned at the stake, and perhaps the other children would, too. And then they'd burn her. She needed a spell.

Dear God, it *had* to work.

The pile of kindling burst into flames. The children screamed, except for Willa, who was deathly pale now. But she could not calm the other children. Tabby closed her eyes and murmured, *"Fire fears water, fire needs rain. Fear fears water, give us rain. Rain douse fire, give us rain."*

"She's casting a spell," the blonde said, sounding a bit alarmed.

Tabby opened her eyes. Nothing had happened; nothing had changed. Her students were crowded together by her desk, some of them crying, and all of them were staring at the fire roaring in the front of the classroom. The blond boy seemed nervous, but Angel looked pissed. Tabby was expecting the fire alarm to go off, but it did not. Surely they hadn't been smart enough to dismantle the fire alarms last night or that morning before school?

Tabby glanced at the ceiling and saw a wire hanging off the closest alarm, and her heart sank. The fire alarms had been tampered with. Then she saw a yellow mark spreading across the ceiling.

"Come on, pretty girl—girls get to go first," Angel said, grinning.

Willa screamed as Angel started to drag her toward the fire.

Tabby realized there was a water mark growing on the ceiling. As she rushed forward to fight for Willa, water dropped on her head—once, and then again and again. But a few drops of water weren't going to put out the fire. She reached Angel and Willa; the blonde seized her, restraining her. "Don't worry, you'll get your turn."

"Let her go," Tabby said furiously, struggling to jerk free of the blonde. She was wearing her usual two-inch heels and she ground down as hard as she could onto the instep of his foot.

He was wearing sneakers and he howled, releasing her.

Tabby seized the can of kerosene and flung it at Angel. He cursed, releasing Willa, wiping the few drops of kerosene from his face. The fire suddenly roared, turning into an inferno. Tabby seized Willa and shoved her closer to the children. "Run!"

"Like hell," Angel sneered. His eyes were black fire.

The next thing she knew she was in his arms and he had the blade of a knife pressed hard against her throat. She froze.

"There are many ways to kill a witch," he said softly.

Tabby didn't move, afraid he was going to sever her carotid artery.

"Do it and let's get out of here," the blonde said, "before she casts another spell."

"Sounds good to me." Angel grinned wickedly.

Dinna move.

Tabby heard the command, spoken in a heavy Scot brogue, as clear as day. Her fear vanished. Stunned, she looked across the classroom, past the fire.

The dark Highlander stood outside. He was staring at her through one of the windows. Their gazes locked. His was hard and ruthless, like his set face.

Tabby began to tremble.

And glass shattered. Energy blazed and the fire exploded, the heat intensifying. The children screamed, as did the blond boy, who was hurled backward into the bolted classroom door. Angel cried out as the Highlander bore down upon them both, sword raised. Panicking, Tabby pushed at Angel's arms, but he didn't release her.

The Highlander towered over them and smiled dangerously. "Release her or die."

Tabby stared into his ice-cold eyes and knew he meant his every word. She wanted to protest but could not form words. His power was so strong, she inhaled it. It wrapped itself around her, male and thick and potent.

Angel knew he meant it, too. He dropped the knife but did not release her, wrapping both arms around her now. "I'll let her go—outside."

Tabby failed to breathe. Angel meant to use her as a human shield, in order to escape.

"A foolish choice," the Highlander said softly.

She heard him again, although he did not speak. *Dinna move....*

Tabby met his dark blue gaze and knew he was going to free her somehow. He would triumph—this man never lost. Her life was in his hands, but she trusted him with it. She didn't move, obeying him.

The silver blade flashed.

Tabby wanted to scream as it arced down toward her. Watching that blade descend was the most horrifying moment of her life. *She had made a mistake; she was going to die.* But it was Angel who screamed, as the sword came between them.

For one more moment, he held her. Then, as Angel's head toppled away from his shoulders, she was in a headless man's arms. He collapsed and she was released. The children screamed. Tabby jumped away, shocked.

The Highlander had beheaded Angel while he held her. He could have taken her head, too!

Aghast, she met his gaze. Then she saw the blond sub pointing a big black gun at him from behind.

She gasped as it went off.

He turned, and silver blazed from his hands. The blonde was hurled back again, and this time, as he hit the wall and crumbled to the floor, Tabby knew he was dead.

And then Tabby ran to the children, urging them to crowd around her. "Don't look over there!" She had never seen a man decapitated before. Of course she hadn't. This was New York City, 2008, not Scotland in 1550. She choked back bile and fear.

Most of the kids were crying. Bobby Wilson wanted to go home. As they huddled tightly together, several in her arms, she tried to get past her horror and shock. He had saved her life. He had done what he had been taught to do. He was the product of his violent, barbaric times.

But he had beheaded Angel while she was in his arms.

"The fire is spreadin'," he said, and she felt him standing behind her. "Ye need to take the children from here."

Tabby turned to look at him, incapable of saying a word, her pulse soaring. She met his dark, intense blue eyes, eyes she had seen at the Met—and in her dreams.

"Ye dinna wish fer me to kill the boys?" His blue gaze chilled. "They intended fer ye to die a verra unpleasant death."

And that was when she realized he wasn't the same Highlander—not exactly. He was the same man she'd briefly seen and touched at the Met, she had not a single doubt. But he wasn't blistered and burned. His hard, determined face was scratched from glass, and he had a scar on one high cheekbone, but there were no burns, no blood, no blisters. In fact, he was damned gorgeous. His tunic was bloodstained, and there were cuts on his arms, face and legs from leaping through the glass, but he had not been in a fire recently. *This man had not been at An Tùir-Tara.*

Instead, he looked exactly as she had imagined he would before ever being in that fire.

"You're not from Melvaig or 1550, are you?" she somehow said.

His face tightened with obvious displeasure. "Nay."

She breathed hard, uncertain. Was he angry? If so, why? She wanted to back up, but she needed to get the children to safety. "Can you get the door open for us?" As she spoke, the school's fire alarms finally went off.

For one more instant, his gaze held hers, searing in its intensity. Then he strode to the classroom door and wrenched it off its hinges. Tabby somehow smiled to reassure the children and she began herding them quickly that way. Behind her, there was an explosion.

The children screamed but Tabby cried, "Walk, don't run. Everything is fine." The Highlander stepped to the first child and took his hand, restraining little Paul Singh from running, clearly understanding that they must proceed without panic. She glanced behind her and saw that pieces of pipe and the plaster ceiling had collapsed and fallen to the floor.

In the hall, faculty were evacuating the children, trying to maintain a calm and orderly manner, as if this were a fire drill. The principal, Holz Vanderkirk, and Kristin came running up to them. "Are you all right?" Kristin cried, seizing her arm, her eyes wide and trained upon the Highlander. Police sirens sounded, screaming.

Kristin and Holz were clearly assuming that he was the Sword Murderer and a threat to them all. Tabby wanted to explain that there had been an attempted witch burning and that the Highlander had saved her and the children. She turned to face him, instead. "It's all right," she cried, when she knew no such thing.

His blue gaze met hers. It was the gaze of a professional soldier, devoid of all feeling and all fear. Then he turned and hurried back into the burning schoolroom.

Tabby screamed, "Come back!" She was afraid for him.

He ran into the fire as the ceiling began to fall in. Plaster and pipe hit him, but if the debris hurt him, he gave no sign. She froze in horror as he skirted the blaze, heading for the shattered window. Suddenly the fire exploded again, and then a wall of fire separated them.

Her insides curdled.

Standing on the other side of the fire wall, by the window, he paused and looked at her.

Every horrific emotion she'd felt yesterday at the Met flooded her, incapacitated her. The feeling of déjà vu was intense. There was outrage, fury, there was horror and dread. And there was love—the kind of love she had never felt before, but had dreamed of.

She loved him.

An expression of bewilderment crossed his dark face.

The fire wall blazed between them.

Even if he wanted to, he could not cross it.

He turned and leaped out of the window; Tabby felt her legs give way.

CHAPTER FIVE

KIT MARS HUNCHED over her desk at HCU, staring at her computer screen. She was watching the tape of last week's Rampage, for the hundredth time.

She knew she'd missed something, and it was bothering her to the point that she wasn't going to eat or sleep until she figured it out. She wanted to nail the little bastards terrorizing the city. She'd never rest, not until every demon had been wiped off the face of the earth.

She owed it to her twin sister, Kelly.

As always, Kelly stood behind her, approving—or it felt as if she did.

Kit had been recruited by Nick last year, while she was at Vice. He'd been stalking her for a few weeks, turning up at crime scenes or in the precinct corridors. At first she'd assumed he was a Fed, working a case. Then she'd begun to realize he was after her. But he was clearly one of the men in black. Finally, he'd caught up with her in a bar at the end of a really lousy day. After buying her a few drinks, he'd asked if she wanted to spend her life busting drug dealers and porn traffickers—or if she wanted to get into the real action.

She'd known exactly what he meant.

And she hadn't thought twice about taking him up on his offer.

From her first day on the job at HCU, all the pieces of the

puzzle had begun to fall into place. She'd already been keenly aware of evil. It had taken her sister from her, and she encountered it daily on the street. So when the revelation came that evil was a race and that there was a goddamned war, a million times more important than the war on terror, she had not been surprised. It had almost been a relief.

The war on evil was her life.

Kit stared at the computer screen. Hidden cameras were installed in sixty-nine percent of the city, at traffic lights, in restaurants, hotels, department stores, groceries, in every major airport, on every bridge and in every tunnel. Only a handful of lawmakers on the very secret Committee for Internal Defense, a half-dozen generals at the Pentagon and the President knew about the hidden cameras. The Civil Liberties Union would have a field day if it ever found out.

The surveillance system was CDA's baby.

Kit tensed and leaned close. She watched the screen with absolute clinical detachment, as the two boys and a girl began starting the fire beneath their victim's feet. The kids were possessed; the tape was proof. Real demons only appeared as dark, ghostly shapes on film and could not be individually identified. Sub-humans—or subs, as CDA referred to the possessed—could be filmed just like any flesh-and-blood man or woman. However, they also cast dark shadows, even at night. Subs on tape were simply impossible to miss.

Five passing civilians had stopped, gawked, then fled, all one-hundred-percent human. She jammed the pause button, hit Rewind. A civvie was fleeing. Kit zoomed in.

There was an odd blip just behind the man's shoulder as he ran away from the gruesome crime—the hint of something grayish and almost oblong.

She hit Pause, backed it, then zoomed in on the civvie

again. She froze the screen, and zoomed on his left shoulder at the odd blip.

It wasn't oblong now. It was a shapeless form, becoming more and more indistinct the farther she looked from the center. She went back to the darkest part of the blip. A face began to emerge from the grayish light.

"What the hell?" Kit asked.

Now, she saw two eyes and a mouth—she would swear to it.

So someone had been standing there, watching the burning.

No, not someone—*something*.

TABBY SAT ON ONE OF the children's chairs, hugging herself, exhausted. CDA had been all over the scene for hours—she'd been interrogated by Nick and his agents *five* times. The children had been picked up shortly after the crisis. Now, Nick was seated with Kristin and the principal, sipping coffee. She knew he was questioning them, but his demeanor was so casual he might have been at Starbucks with a couple of friends.

Those last moments of the morning kept replaying ruthlessly in her mind. She saw the look in the Highlander's eyes just before his sword had flashed and he decapitated Angel; she saw the look in his eyes when he'd walked back into that school-room to avoid the police, his gaze hard and cold and devoid of all feeling, all fear. She trembled. Calling that man savage was an understatement—she couldn't find the right word to describe him. She had witnessed violence for most of her life—evil was cruel and barbaric and it was everywhere. But the Highlander wasn't evil—yet he had not had any conscience when he'd beheaded Angel. They could have tried to retrieve Angel's soul, but he hadn't hesitated. It was obvious that such brutality was second nature to him. He was a barbarian; he made Randall look like a saint.

She shivered.

But what really bothered her was how he'd stood on the other side of the fire wall, and how she'd felt standing across from him, the flames blazing between them.

For one moment, his hard face had changed, filling with surprise. Tabby wasn't sure what he'd thought, but he'd suddenly seemed reluctant to leave her. She had been terrified and desperate, afraid that it was the end for them.

But there was no "them."

Except, standing there with the fire between them, she'd felt as if she loved him.

Of course, she did not love him. He was a total stranger and as medieval as a man could be. She was a civilized, modern woman and a gentle soul. There would never be any kind of relationship between them, except for her helping him, if she could. But now, the idea that she might want to help a barbarian was laughable. It had to be a joke. As far as her feelings of déjà vu went, they were simply inexplicable.

Her temples hurt and she rubbed them. He needed medical attention, and then he had to go back to wherever he belonged. She'd feel better—safer—when he'd gone back to his primitive world. Maybe he'd left already—she would be relieved! She'd go back to the Met and try to figure out why that amulet had made her feel evil and so much more. Then she'd determine what she was supposed to do about it—and him.

Sam laid her hand on her shoulder, her face grim. "Nick said we can leave."

Tabby got up, relieved to be able to go home. At least the police had been called off. Sam had told her that. He was running from the cops unnecessarily. But maybe that was a good thing. Otherwise, he might be hanging around. "Sam, if he hasn't gone back in time, he needs medical attention."

Sam grimaced. "So you said, a dozen times. If he's still here, Nick will find him and have him taken care of."

Tabby looked into Sam's eyes, carefully shielding her thoughts—but not from her sister. Sam had told her she was certain Nick could read minds. Tabby thought it likely. She'd seen him in action once or twice and he was not your average mortal.

She had not told Nick what had happened yesterday at the Met. She wasn't sure why she felt the need to be secretive now—not that she worked for Nick, anyway. But Nick was a control freak and he had his own agenda, always. He would be on the Highlander's side, but she was oddly afraid of Nick's interference. Involving him now, before she knew what was really happening, felt wrong.

Because she'd been covered with Angel's blood, Tabby had borrowed an older student's gym clothes. She picked up her white wool coat, slipping it on, and her purse and tote. Sam gestured and they started for the door. Nick rose to his feet and approached.

"So when you want to tell me what really happened, you have my direct line," he said.

Tabby fought to control her thoughts and feelings. "I told you everything." She hated lying, but did so now with aplomb—or so she thought.

But he seemed amused. "You're lying through those pearly whites, Tabby." He sobered. "I want to protect him, too."

Tabby crossed her arms over her chest. Nick *would* protect him. She should come clean. "I didn't say I want to protect him, but I don't want to see him hurt." She hesitated, then added, "He needs to go back to wherever it is he came from, Nick. I don't think he should be here."

"And you think that because?"

Tabby tried not to think about her encounter with him at the

Met or the spell she'd cast. "Isn't it obvious? A medieval man running around the city will raise all kinds of questions." Tabby was aware that CDA's second priority after the war on evil was to remain clandestine. The agency had an entire department devoted to public relations, to spinning demonic crimes into acceptable criminal ones. The public would not be able to handle the truth, and general hysteria would ensue, leading to chaos and anarchy. And that was what evil wanted. "If a single reporter figures out what is going on, it's all over."

Nick was clearly skeptical of her. Then he leaned close. "Listen, Tabitha, everything that happened last night was not reported in the press."

Tabby tensed. She did not like the sound of that. "What do you mean?"

"He hurt a cop in the initial confrontation." Nick stared, letting that sink in.

It took Tabby a moment. "Please tell me the cop is all right."

Nick was grim. "I just got the call. He died an hour ago."

Tabby took a calming breath, aware of Nick's speculative stare, and Sam slid her arm around her. Nick said, "There are a lot of pissed-off cops in the city right now." His blue gaze slammed to Tabby's. "I wasn't kidding when I said I want to protect him. He needs protection, because orders or not, the men in blue are gunning for him."

Tabby knew the mind-set of the police. They were heroes— they defended the Innocent every single day—but they were merciless when one of their own went down. "He saved us today, Nick. He's a Master, and he would never hurt a police officer on purpose. It had to be self-defense."

"Don't tell me," Nick said. He patted her shoulder clumsily. "You look like hell. Go home and rest. Let us worry about the Highlander. And, Tabby, he's probably long gone by now."

Tabby couldn't smile back. The Highlander was in

trouble, and clearly he knew it. He'd fled at the sound of the sirens. On the other hand, he looked capable of surviving an apocalypse. But the police might shoot first and ask questions later. The Masters weren't immortal. Enough bullets could kill him. Even though the odds were that he was gone, she was worried, terribly so. "Can't you use your clout with the NYPD? Can't you insist he be brought in alive and unharmed?"

"I've already used all the clout I have," Nick said. "You know, you're so worried that I'm beginning to wonder if he's swept you off your feet. Remember your little cousin, Brie? She fell for Aidan of Awe in about two seconds, and Aidan was turned."

Tabby was aghast at the mere notion. "I am a human being," she cried. "I may be obsessed, but I am *not* in love."

His eyes widened, and his smile vanished. Sam was staring, too.

Tabby flushed.

"You see him again, you call me, ASAP. And that is not a request, sweetheart, so even if you are in love, I will expect that call." He walked back to Kristin and Vanderkirk.

Tabby had never really liked Nick Forrester. He was a hero, of course, and on their side, but she didn't like his type, especially after Randall. He was arrogant, powerful, macho and controlling, just like her ex. As they stepped outside into the frigid night, she looked at Sam. The Highlander made Nick seem soft and easy, she thought.

"What aren't you telling me?" Sam demanded.

It was too cold to pause, so their pace quickened. "I saw him at the Met yesterday," Tabby said swiftly. "He was bloody and burned, Sam. I know he came to me from An Tùir-Tara."

"You're telling me now?" Sam said, sounding upset.

Tabby looked at her. Her sister was never distressed. "Our

paths are clearly meant to meet. They've crossed twice now, at the Met, and at school." Her stomach churned with worry. "But he was not bloody and burned this morning. He had not come from the fire at Melvaig. What on earth could that mean?"

Sam glanced sharply at her.

"When you left me at the Met, I tried to cast a spell to bring him to me. Did my spell work? Did I bring him here, but from the wrong time?"

Sam's eyes widened. "You've never cast such a powerful spell, Tabby!"

"Sam, *if* it worked, it backfired." Tabby's teeth were chattering now, even though she spoke slowly and chose her words with care. "Why do I want to help him? Am I supposed to help him? The Highlander does not need me or anybody. He is a hard, dangerous soldier. He was conscienceless, Sam." Tabby shivered, but not from the cold.

"Tabby, he's medieval. It's do or die in that world."

"I know." She tried not to think about Angel.

Sam was silent. Tabby glanced at her and she said, "You're so worried about him."

Tabby hesitated. "I am worried about him, which is senseless. The man who rescued us today doesn't need me." She added, "He scares me."

"Are you sure?"

Tabby halted in her tracks.

"There's no such thing as coincidence. If your spell backfired, it was meant to be. If he came here, he was meant to help you." Sam shrugged. "Maybe you're meant to help him, too. You'll have to play this one out, Tabby."

Tabby felt her heart lurch. Sam was right. "What if I'm not up to this?" she asked slowly. It was the kind of intimate revelation she would only make to her sister, Allie or Brie.

"You're up to it." Sam was firm.

Tabby softened. Sam had more faith in her than she ever had in herself. "What are we going to do about Nick?" she asked, as they rushed through a red light, the street devoid of traffic.

"Nick won't mess this up. He's a good guy, remember?" Sam said. "I'm certain he'd like to debrief the Highlander, but he really means to protect him. As long as he stays in the city, he's in danger from the cops and vigilantes."

Tabby stared at her as they hurried down the last block toward their apartment building. "You like Nick." It wasn't a question.

"His courage and ambition outweigh his less than stellar personality. He'd die for any of his agents, Tabby. He'd die for any Innocent. And he has his own demons, I think."

Tabby had wanted to know something for a long time. "I know this is not my business, but I hope you aren't sleeping with Forrester."

Sam didn't even crack a smile. "I thought about it. He thought about it. But I like my job and you know how it goes— not a good idea to shag the boss." She added, "I do like Nick, Tabby, and that's the best reason not to sleep with him."

Tabby knew she'd never really understand Sam, who had never been friends with a lover and didn't seem to ever want friendship from a lover. "That is a relief." Tabby ran to their building's door, ripping off her gloves to find her keys. Her sister simply stood behind her, so she said, "Call me the moment you hear something."

"Yeah. Any news about your Highlander, I'll call."

Tabby hesitated, aware of how Sam had used the word *your*. She almost sounded unhappy. Something was wrong, and for the first time in her life, she simply couldn't deal with it. She hugged her sister. "Thanks."

"Sure," Sam said, and when Tabby was safely inside, she strode off.

SHIVERING, TABBY hurried into the elevator. A moment later, she was safely inside her loft.

She was chilled to the bone and before she even took her coat off, she put on a pot of water to boil. Then she began to tremble, partly in exhaustion, partly from the cold, and partly because she was worried about the Highlander. Her mind knew better, but her heart wouldn't listen. It never had.

The fire in the classroom had raised all those feelings related to An Tùir-Tara. She did not like that. She had never had any odd reaction to the sight of fire before. Even thinking about it now made her stomach churn. Was she picking up on his emotions? She was doubtful. She was certain he was not capable of the love she'd felt.

The kettle began to sing and as it did, someone knocked on her living-area window.

Tabby started and cried out. He was standing on her fire escape!

She froze. In the night, through the glass pane, their gazes locked.

He knocked again. Tabby came to her senses. He was wearing a thin linen tunic and a wool plaid; he was bare-legged in his boots. She rushed across the room, unlocked and opened the window. He climbed inside and with him came a frigid burst of air. She slammed it closed and turned, stunned. "You followed me home?" she cried breathlessly.

He towered over her. His face was hard and set, his shockingly intense blue eyes unwavering upon her. "Ye summoned me. Why?"

He was angry—and he reeked of male power. And they were alone in her loft. She was alone with a medieval warrior, one capable of beheading a man in a single second. Worse, she was suddenly aware of his huge, muscular body and his proximity to her. She didn't like it! "What? What are you talking about?" She backed up. She looked at his arm and the blood crusted there. "Are you hurt?"

He stepped forward, closing the distance between them, not allowing her to escape. "No one commands me, Tabitha."

She felt dread. "I still don't know what you are talking about!"

"Your power," he snapped. "Ye brought me to ye… Why?"

Tabby went still, dazed by his powerful presence and trying to make sense of what he was telling her. "My spell worked?"

"Aye. I ken ye're a witch. I felt yer powers strongly in the school, an' now. Why did ye bring me here?" he demanded.

Tabby began shaking her head. It was really hard to speak. "To help you," she managed to say, a hoarse whisper. "I wanted to help you!"

He cursed and strode away.

Tabby felt her knees buckle. He made every recollection of every bad romance novel she'd ever read about the Vikings and other conquerors return, full force. She could picture him dragging women off to his bed by their hair!

Then she went still. Her spell had worked?

He turned, hands fisted on his hips. "Aye, yer magic brought me here."

She was amazed and even excited. He stood across the loft from her, and damn it, as daunting as he was, the distance between them allowed her to really look at those high cheekbones, that square jaw and those stunningly dark blue eyes.

Her pulse escalated wildly. He was pure male.

His hard expression eased fractionally. Tabby had the unhappy notion that he was aware of her interest—except, she wasn't interested, not that way. But how could she not notice that face and that body? His attire was skimpy! The tunic clung to his huge frame, and the two belts he wore helped delineate his anatomy. The plaid pinned to one shoulder highlighted his broad shoulders and equally broad and muscular chest. The short sleeves of his tunic and his current posture revealed his huge, bulging biceps, but of course he was built—he wielded heavy, huge swords on a daily basis. The belts made it clear that he had a six-pack—no, a twelve-pack. Worse, she was pretty certain a huge amount of muscle was beneath that oddly drifting short skirt.

She decided not to look at his legs. She didn't have to. They'd been impossible to miss, bare between the top of his boots and the skirt and entirely corded with muscle. That man wasn't the product of the Zone Diet and steroids; he ran hills and rode horses.

What was she doing? Why couldn't she breathe? Why was he angry? She backed up. Putting more distance between them seemed to be a really good idea.

"Do ye fear me now?" He almost seemed amused. "Ye should fear me. I dinna take orders, not from anyone."

She thought of Angel. "Got it. No more orders!" Then she choked. This was not the time to be incoherent. "I wasn't summoning you. I thought you were hurt. I wanted to find you to help you."

His face changed. His eyes blazed, but with interest, not anger. He strode rapidly forward. Tabby cried out, backed up and hit the couch. "What are you doing?" she gasped.

"I willna drag ye off by yer hair," he said. When he halted, he had her trapped against the sofa.

He was telepathic. Great!

"I can't breathe," she said somehow. "Not with you standing over me like this."

He suddenly tilted up her chin.

Tabby went still. Her heart thundered. Pulse points she'd never known she had began firing off all over her body, one by one, and a very definite throbbing began as desire suddenly reared up in her body.

For one moment, his blue gaze changed, searching hers, and Tabby had the definite feeling that he knew and was pleased. Then he said tersely, "Ye've haunted me fer a century. Why? Did my enemies send ye?"

Tabby gasped. "Now what are you talking about?"

"Ye heard. I first saw ye when I was a boy. Ye wanted to help me. Then ye bothered me in my dreams. Sometimes ye even bothered me after battle. An' I saw ye yesterday, on the beach where I buried my family."

Tabby began to tremble. As unnerving as his touch was, this was stunning information. "Please don't touch me," she said.

His eyes widened. He dropped his hand.

Tabby had no choice. To get away from him, she had to slip past his big body and the sofa. It would be absurd to climb on the couch to avoid his body, even if that was what she wanted to do. So she brushed past him, escaping into the rest of the living area. As she did so, something she didn't want to think about bumped her.

He was aroused. She felt her cheeks flame, felt that surprising throbbing again. Before facing him, she hugged herself. How was she going to handle that? But her mind had just shut down.

"Tell me why ye continued to haunt me."

Slowly she pulled herself together and turned to face him, aware that she was still blushing. "I don't know anything about a haunting. First of all, I thought one had to be a ghost to haunt someone. Clearly, I am not dead."

He made a harsh sound but he was very still now, listening intently to her.

Tabby hugged herself harder. She decided not think about the two of them being alone in her loft, not now. "Are you sure it was me?"

He laughed without mirth. Even his laughter was frightening—no, disturbing. "Woman, t'was ye."

He was certain. He believed he'd seen her over the years, from the time he was a small boy. She'd felt that he was familiar the moment she'd seen him at the Met—and when she'd envisioned him as a boy, reading that plaque, she had felt that she'd known him, too. "I can't explain this. But I saw you yesterday, at a museum. There was an exhibit there, related to Melvaig, Scotland. And when I saw you, you seemed familiar and I wanted to help you."

His eyes were wide but hard. "Melvaig is the stronghold of my enemies."

"I know." Tabby knew better than to elaborate. This man hadn't been in a fire, which meant that An Tùir-Tara was in his future. She didn't need a Wisdom from the Book of Roses to tell her not to reveal his future to him. That was strictly forbidden. "At the museum, they mention a massacre in 1201. Only a fourteen-year-old boy survived. Was that you?"

His face became so hard she was frightened and alarmed. His expression seemed ready to crack—or explode? It was a moment before he spoke. "Aye. They have written about my family in yer time? About me?"

Tabby nodded. That boy had been devastated by the loss of his family. She almost wanted to go up to him and touch his hand, which was absurd. He wasn't that grieving boy now. Oh, no. He was the antithesis of that boy—he was the antithesis of just about everything good and proper with the world!

He cursed and suddenly her couch-side lamps shattered, a bowl and the vase of roses sliding off the coffee table.

Tabby froze. Clearly getting him angry was not a good idea.

"Why do they write about me?" he demanded.

"Historians write about history—anyone's history," she said helplessly.

He looked at her destroyed lamps. Only the shades were intact.

This wasn't going to work, Tabby thought. He had a temper; he was angry with her. He had to go back to wherever it was that he came from—immediately! Clearly, she wasn't the one to help him. She was simply not up to the task.

Carefully, she said, "What time, exactly, did you come from?"

"Ye dinna ken?" When she shook her head, he said, "Yer magic took me from Blayde in the middle of the night, on June the tenth, 1298."

Tabby tried to keep her shock from showing. He had come from the late thirteenth century—which wasn't even close to 1550! No wonder he was such a ruthless barbarian.

His gaze narrowed. "Tabitha, I dinna like being judged. I am the Macleod, an' those who judge me rarely live to tell of it."

Tabby trembled. Had he just threatened her?

"I saved ye. I willna harm ye. But heed my warnings."

Tabby somehow nodded. "Do not get me wrong, because I'm grateful for what you did today, but I'm not sure why you're here. The police want you dead. You really need to go back to Blayde in 1298."

A funny, small smile changed his expression.

Tabby tensed. What did that look mean?

"But ye want to help me."

She instantly knew they had entered extremely dangerous territory. "You clearly do not need my help right now."

His voice dropped to a murmur. He said, "But ye're grateful, aye?"

Tabby went still. "Wh-what?"

"Ye're a grateful woman. Ye owe me now."

Her mind went blank. Then, as comprehension came, her pulse exploded. He meant to seduce her! She was aghast—but her body was thrumming.

"Ye want me. I want ye. Ye owe me. I will gladly accept a night in yer bed."

She choked.

He simply looked at her, staring, his eyes distinctly smoldering now.

Tabby whirled, starting for the kitchen, tripping as she did so. She was grateful, true, but he expected her to pay him back with her body! She would never do such a thing! And what was wrong with her damned body, anyway? Why was she breathless, too warm…aroused?

How was she going to get him to leave?

She paused at the kitchen counter, clinging to it. Then she felt him as he approached, coming up behind her. "Ye dinna need to fear me."

She made an entirely incoherent sound. "You beheaded Angel while I was in his arms!" She twisted around to face him—a mistake.

She was almost in his embrace, and now, gods damn it, he was amused.

"I am a master with a sword."

"You could have beheaded me," she accused.

He lifted up a hank of her hair. "Never."

She went still. Their gazes locked. His was dark blue smoke. "You need to go back to your time, Macleod. Immediately!"

He smiled. It was seductive and sexy, but most of all, it revealed how shockingly handsome he was. And it made him seem almost human. "Why do ye fear my bed so much?"

"We don't know each other!"

"In my time," he said softly, "when a woman is as hot as ye, she takes her pleasure an' enjoys it."

Tabby was speechless. She felt dazed, and her body was doing all kinds of crazy and *inappropriate* things.

She closed her eyes to avoid that smoldering gaze. He was

coming onto her, and she couldn't handle either him or her own reaction to him. Everything was wrong! "Just go," she said hoarsely, opening her eyes. "Just go back to Blayde, back to your time, because this will never work!"

His stare became searching, intent. It was as if he was trying to figure her out. She knew he was reading her mind.

"I made a mistake," she added desperately. "You were supposed to come from 1550, not 1298!"

"I canna return," he finally said. "I dinna have the power to leap. Ye'll have to send me back." He smiled now, cool and confident. "When I am ready to leave."

CHAPTER SIX

TABBY KNEW SHE had misheard. "What did you just say?"

"I canna return."

He was joking, wasn't he?

"Ye look the way ye did when I took off Angel's head."

"Of course you can return!"

His expression hardened. "I dinna have the power to leap."

Tabby choked in disbelief. "You're a Master of Time... aren't you?"

He folded his arms across his chest. "I havena taken my vows."

Dread began. "Why not?"

He didn't bother with an answer.

And it struck her then. Macleod was not your everyday mortal, but he wasn't a Master—he hadn't taken his vows. Her spell had brought a very violent, very ruthless, very powerful medieval Highlander to her, one who could kill with a broadsword or a blast of otherworldly power. One who did not have much respect for life and, maybe, not much of a conscience.

A superpowered barbarian was standing there in her loft with her!

And he could not get back to his time—she was stuck with him.

Tabby studied his terribly beautiful blue eyes, set in an equally gorgeous but incredibly hard and definitely frightening face. Her gaze dropped. His Highland garb could not hide an equally beautiful, equally hard body. But that body posed a huge threat, because she was so impossibly aware of him.

He tilted up her chin. "Ye want me gone because ye fear being in my bed."

"Let go," she said uneasily. She did not want to provoke him in any way, and she did not want to continue the subject he seemed intent upon. She had no wish to be dragged off to his bed, and that was undoubtedly his MO. "How can this be happening?"

He did not release her. "If I wished to drag ye to my bed by yer hair, I would have already done so."

Tabby grasped his wrist to protest, hardly reassured. As she did so, he clasped her waist with his other hand, and the sensation of holding him, the feel of him holding her, was shocking.

For one instant, she knew she'd gripped him this way before. In that second, she saw herself on her back, grasping his arms as he moved over her, smiling in triumph, filling her. She was climaxing; he was controlling her—and enjoying her rapture.

No, she thought, shocked. Tabby somehow wrenched away from him. *She was imagining their being lovers—it was not déjà vu.* She would never take this medieval man to bed! He was the antithesis of her type—he was worse than Randall—more powerful, more controlling, more macho. There wouldn't be love, because there couldn't be love. She was too intellectual to get involved with him, which meant there wouldn't be sex.

But so much heat sizzled between them that she saw the red-hot current in the air.

He slowly shook his head. "I think ye want to be dragged to bed—an' I think ye want me to drag ye there."

Tabby backed away, trembling. "You are so wrong. I like gentle men."

He began to smile. "I dinna think so. But mayhap, ye believe so."

He was *wrong*, but she wouldn't argue. A long, heated moment passed. Tension was coursing through her body. This was untenable. But even as she decided that, she envisioned him as he'd been at the Met, bloody and burned, enraged and anguished.

He crossed his arms and stared coolly at her.

What was she going to do? He had insinuated that he wasn't ready to go back. She prayed that was not because he wanted her favors first. Her spell had backfired—she'd brought him from the wrong time. If she tried to send him to his home, was there any chance she could succeed?

She suddenly imagined his winding up in the middle of a Regency ball, with the guests screaming and fleeing. Then she imagined him winding up fighting a lion bare-handed in the Roman Colosseum. She trembled, suddenly at her emotional limit.

The man who'd been in that fire was very different from the man standing before her. Centuries separated them. The former might need her one day, although she was no longer certain if she was up to the task of helping him. The man standing before her didn't need her at all. But he was here because of her spell.

And he'd seen her for a century.

Tabby didn't want to try to figure that one out—it was too scary.

"Why would you want to stay here?" she asked, her mouth so dry now she had to wet her lips.

"I wish to comprehend yer world. An' I wish to go to the museum."

Tabby was shocked.

"Ye'll take me there," he added flatly.

Tabby didn't have to think about it to know that was a very bad idea. The police were looking for him, and even if she got him clothes, she was pretty certain he'd stand out like a sore thumb. And there was no way he should ever be told about his future.

"I saved ye," he flashed. The pots and pans on the stove rattled. "I saved the children. Ye owe me that much."

"Damn it," Tabby whispered. "The police want you dead!"

"I dinna fear yer dark soldiers." He gave her a dismissive look and walked away from her.

Tabby felt like collapsing. Instead, she sat down on a stool at the counter, breathing hard. He had saved her. He'd saved the children. She owed him. A gentleman wouldn't expect anything in return, but he, of course, was not a gentleman.

And it was her spell that had brought them to this impasse. He might very well be trapped in her time—with her—for longer than either of them wanted. She was afraid to try to send him back, which meant he was staying with her for a while. And that was the bottom line. So she was going to have to deal with that. With him.

"We need a truce," she cried, standing.

He sighed. "Do ye have hot water an' linen, mayhap?"

Tabby's gaze shot to his right arm, where dried blood crusted the short sleeve of his tunic and the area on his arm above his bicep. "I don't trust you. But I'm not powerful enough to send you back, and until we figure out what to do, we need an understanding."

He smiled without amusement but didn't speak.

"I want your word that you will leave me alone, that you will not try to seduce me or crawl into bed with me while I'm sleeping!"

He laughed. "Tabitha, before this night is through, you'll be in my arms an' verra pleased about it."

She'd come up against a macho brick wall. "My answer is no."

"But I dinna ask a question."

Tabby wondered if this man was capable of rape. He'd beheaded Angel, maybe force was a habit of his, too. But the moment she had the thought, she knew he would never use force. She didn't know how she knew, she just did.

He spoke quietly. "Barbarian that I may be, I have never forced a woman and I willna force ye. I dinna need to use force. Women beg to share my bed—all of them, all the time."

Tabby grimaced at his conceit. But she had little doubt that most medieval women lined up outside his bedroom door. She had the sudden, unhappy notion that he pleased every one of those women. They wouldn't be uptight like she was. She was the exception, but she decided not to say so. She just hoped he was a man of his word, and oddly, she had the feeling that he was. "Okay." She exhaled loudly. "I feel better now." That was a vast exaggeration. She'd probably be on edge until he went back to Blayde.

"Help me with my wound."

"You said you weren't hurt." She was really glad to be distracted now.

"I said I will live. One puny bullet canna kill me." He flexed his right arm and winced.

Tabby couldn't help but be concerned. She was going to have to get a grip on her composure. He'd promised her he'd behave, and immortal or nearly so, he had a bullet in his arm. "Sit down, Macleod, on the sofa. I'll clean your wound for you." She went into the kitchen and added, "You're probably hungry. I'll fix you something to eat, too." Cooking always relaxed her, but she was pretty certain it would not relax her now.

Tabby began gathering up first-aid supplies, trying not to think. It wasn't easy, because she was so acutely aware of him and the fact that he could not get back to the thirteenth century, not on his own. Her spell had really backfired. Maybe, one day, she and Sam would laugh about it, but it wasn't funny now. What should she do with him?

And where was he going to sleep?

Maybe she should stash him in a hotel room. Carrying a tray with bandages, soap and water and bacitracin, Tabby went back into the living area. "I'm sorry." She forced a smile. "We have gotten off to a bad start, and it's my fault. I've forgotten all my manners, but the circumstances have been extenuating."

He looked at her with skepticism.

Tabby sat down on the sofa, instinctively keeping an arm's length between them. She wished she could trust him and stop being so nervous. "I am known for being polite. I'm teased about it. I never lose my cool or my temper!" She threw another bright smile his way.

He studied her.

She smiled again but really didn't look at him, dipping a washcloth in warm water. She reminded herself that she would do this for any human being. The truth was, she didn't like being this close to him. His body was too big and it felt too dominant. And in the back of her mind, that shocking vision was now engraved of the two of them in bed as lovers.

"Sometimes I get so tired of people saying how nice I am! I'm always being told that I am too polite, too sweet, too kind— and oh-so-elegant." The cloth was soaking wet now. She held it, dripping water all over the sofa, finally looking up at his face.

He waved his blood-crusted arm at her. "French ladies are elegant," he said. "In velvet an' jewels. What garments do ye wear?"

She realized she was in a thirteen-year-old's sweaty, dirty track pants and T-shirt. Tabby felt herself blush. She was a wreck. When had any man ever come onto her so strongly, much less with her not impeccably attired and perfectly coiffed? She was hardly country-club ready now. "I borrowed the clothes," she said slowly, "from a little girl. They're dirty," she added unnecessarily. She touched her hair. It was in a ponytail, but strands were coming down everywhere.

"Aye—they smell."

Tabby set the cloth down, embarrassed. Her clothes did smell, like a stale locker room. He clearly did not think her very elegant, and that somehow disturbed and confused her.

Tabby soaked his sleeve, trying not to notice his arm, aware of his stare. When she could, she began peeling the linen from his skin as carefully as she could. She didn't want to hurt him—and she didn't want to touch him, either.

As she pried away the linen, her fingertips grazing his skin, she realized that he was right. She was aware of him as she'd never been aware of any man. She feared her desire…as she should.

Desiring a medieval stranger was insanity—and she must never act on it.

But damn it, her heart was skidding like a car on black ice. Why was he the one to stir her as no other? What could that mean?

"Ye willna hurt me, Tabitha," he said.

Tabby looked up. "Your arm has to hurt."

"It hurt before I removed the bullet last night…but not verra much."

Tabby went still. He'd removed the bullet *himself?* Then, of course he had—he wasn't a poster boy for Polo, he was a poster boy for *300*.

His mouth curved. "Ye're easy to play."

Tabby stared into his unwavering eyes. He'd stirred up her compassion. She couldn't help it. He'd probably been immune to the pain of extraction, but she hated the idea of his being alone and on the run and having to dig a bullet out of his own arm. "I am not very experienced when it comes to men. Even though I was married, I never dated a lot."

His eyes widened. "Ye were married?"

Tabby nodded.

"Ye act like a virgin."

Tabby flinched. "That is so unfair."

"But true."

Tabby put the wet rag down, affronted. "I am old-fashioned. I am morally conservative. Sometimes I wish I wasn't, but I am." She picked up the rag and started cleaning blood, dirt and debris from the bullet wound, a bit more callously than she should have.

He took her hand and held it to still it. "I dinna mean to insult ye, Tabitha. Explain old-fashioned. I dinna ken morally conservative," he said, his tone demanding.

She pulled away, his touch searing. Her insides felt so hollow now. She was careful not to glance up. "I do not sleep with strangers," she said. "Although many women in this time do."

He was silent.

She kept cleaning the wound, trying to stay entirely focused. Talking no longer seemed like a very good idea, either.

The emerging skin seemed pink and healthy. Of course his recuperative powers would be otherworldly, too. When he didn't speak—although she could feel his watchful stare—she looked up.

"So ye fear sex with all men," he said flatly.

She cried out. "Absolutely not!"

"Taking pleasure is natural."

Tabby stared. "Why are we on this topic again?"

"I have never met a woman like ye before. Ye fear me but ye shout at me, debate, speak yer mind. Other women fear me, but they never speak—they run from me when we're through."

Tabby threw down the rag and stood. "Are you telling me that you have never had a conversation with a woman? Are you telling me that all women fear you?"

"Aye, they all fear me and I dinna care."

Tabby didn't believe him. It struck Tabby that this man had to be incredibly lonely. No one could survive a lifetime without intimacy from a lover and the opposite sex.

He stood and reached for her, his expression becoming indolent and sensual. "Tabitha, in my bed, there's no need fer conversation."

His hand burned her wrist. She tried to pull away and he let her go. "We are stuck with one another until I can figure out what to do. You have to stop coming onto me." She was becoming angry, at last. "And you have to stop looking at me the way that you do," she said tersely. "It's not helping. There's so much tension in here, no one can breathe!"

He seemed surprised by her angry outburst. "But ye dinna have to be so tense, Tabitha. Ye choose to be so tense."

She refused to comprehend him now. "I owe you and I want to help you, if I can," she said in a rush. "But not the way you want. I am not going to bed with you, not now, not ever."

"Because ye fear sex with all men—or just with me?"

She flushed. He was a stranger and she did not owe him any explanations or her life story. On the other hand, maybe if she told him she was the queen of fake orgasms, he'd leave her alone.

"Tabitha? A wise word…never tell a man 'never.'"

Did he think her a challenge now? "We have a truce."

He just shook his head and said, "I need to bathe."

She went still, hoping she hadn't heard him correctly. Images of him in her shower struck her vividly, full force.

"I stink of blood and death."

Of course he wanted to bathe—he was hardly a caveman. It occurred to her that nothing was going the way she wished, but then he was alpha, so of course everything would go his way! "I guess I can't refuse you a bath. It's a fair request." She kept her tone light, as if she didn't care, and avoided looking at him. He'd bathe; she'd cook enough food to feed an army—that would help her relax. And then she had to figure out where he was spending the night. He could not stay with her. That had suddenly become really clear.

She would call Sam while he was in the shower. It was time to populate the loft, and Sam could bring him clothes; agents kept extras in their lockers. Sam would keep her big medieval secret. Maybe she'd help get him to a hotel. Or maybe they'd call Nick and let him in on the action. Nick could actually solve her dilemma, she thought. But her heart seemed to sink.

"I willna leave."

"Stop reading my mind!" she cried. "I am not referring to sending you back to 1298. I am referring to you walking out my door and spending the night elsewhere—alone."

He folded his massive arms across his chest.

Her heart lurched, but this time with a frisson of alarm. "You are not spending the night here."

"Ye dinna trust Nick."

Tabby almost cursed. "Obviously you're not reading my mind very carefully. Nick is a warrior and he's on our side. He fights demons and wins."

"Ye think he'll interfere in the Destiny we share."

"We do not share any Destiny!"

"Ye believe ye're meant to help me. 'Tis why ye've haunted me fer ninety-seven years, offering to help me."

Damn it, he might be right. "I'm not calling Nick. You can stay at a hotel—an inn."

"An' what about the dark soldiers?" He was smug, as if he knew he'd won.

In that moment, she knew he had won, too.

"Do ye wish to ken why I willna leave ye alone?"

Tabby stared at him, dismayed. "Not really."

He ignored her. "Ye need my protection."

She was instantly bewildered. "I don't need protection." Then she realized he didn't understand. "Macleod, this loft is fortified with my grandmother's spells. She was a very powerful witch. Evil has never been able to get in here. It's like holy ground. What happened earlier today won't happen again."

He shook his head, his face set now. "Evil hunts ye."

A chill swept down her spine. "Evil hunts everyone. Evil destroys whatever it can."

"No. Evil hunts ye, Tabitha Rose."

Tabby met his gaze and he stared back. He was so serious that her alarm became dread. "Why do you think that?" she asked slowly. But she was becoming uncertain. "It was a witch burning. It happens all the time, here in this city and in major cities around the country and across the world."

"The boys wanted ye. I heard them."

The chill churned in her gut. He could not be right. Why would evil hunt her?

Those boys had known her name—but that was on the classroom door. But the Rampage had been premeditated, because the fire alarms had been dismantled. Rampages were usually spontaneous and random acts. There had only been two subs intent on a witch burning, when they usually worked in large gangs. Except for the crime last week, when three subs had been involved. Maybe the attempted burning in her school was a part of a new trend…or maybe not.

But why would evil target her?

He was wrong, she managed to think. Evil hadn't targeted her. And damn it, now he meant to stay the night.

"Show me where to bathe."

They could argue about the intention of the subs all day and all night, and never figure it out, she thought. He was clearly determined to stay and protect her. "All right. You win. But I'll bet you always win, don't you?"

His expression never changed.

Tabby clenched her fists. "You can stay, but only for one night, and you sleep there, on the sofa." She pointed, her hand trembling. "And you will sleep there *alone*."

He murmured, "Then stop thinkin' about me without my clothes."

Tabby couldn't think of a suitable response to that. She marched to the linen closet and returned, placing a pile of towels in his arms. Her mind skidded back and forth between his theory that she was a target and the shower he was about to take—and the night about to come. It promised to be endless. "The bathroom is down the hall."

He walked away. She felt her body explode and it was inexplicable. She prided herself on her intellect. A Ph.D. turned her on more than a six-pack ever could. Her friends had crushes on actors like Brad Pitt and Colin Farrell; she had crushes on intellectuals like Tony Blair and Mark Steyn. She'd rather spend an evening at an exhibit like the Wisdom of the Celts, discussing the various finds, than in bed with a boyfriend, pretending to be something she was not.

But this man made her nervous and upset. Worse, this man made her body come alive in ways it never had—in ways she didn't even want to recognize. But Macleod was a walking advertisement for sex. Maybe all women went nuts around him. That was probably it.

Tabby opened the refrigerator, then closed it. *What was he doing in there?* How on earth would he know how to turn on the water faucets or even adjust the water temperature?

She groaned, then cursed. She stared at the chopped onion, waiting for her eyes to burn. *Had he taken off his clothes?*

Her knees felt weak. All those new pulse points were firing up. She must not go back there to help him!

She strained to listen, but did not hear the sound of the shower.

Her heart was thundering so hard now, she thought it might come out of her breast. Tabby realized she was already halfway to the bathroom. She gave up. Apparently she was incapable of self-control. But she was only going to help him. She repeated those instructions to herself.

The bathroom door was wide-open.

Tabby halted. He stood inside, still fully dressed...and she was incredibly disappointed. His back was to her and he was regarding his reflection in the mirror over the sink. In that mirror, she met his eyes.

They were lazy and indolent, sensual and hot, promising all kinds of unearthly delight.

She managed to say, "I came to turn the water on—not for anything else."

From the corner of her eyes, she saw his hands moving. He was unpinning the plaid he wore. He smiled knowingly.

She knew she should back away—no, run away. No decent woman would stand there while he undressed. She did not move.

The plaid fell from his huge shoulders and he folded it and laid it beside the swords he'd placed on the vanity before she'd gotten there. His hands moved to the heavy leather belt he wore, over the tunic. Tabby couldn't look up. Her eyes were riveted to the reflection of his strong, scarred hands. Heat suffused every inch of her face and body. Beneath his hands, that skirt was tented. She couldn't really breathe.

He made a soft sound and the leather belt joined the plaid and swords on her vanity.

She stared at the items, then stared at him. A huge silence fell. Tabby knew it was time to leave, *now*.

"I never drag women to my bed. They come gladly."

Of course they did.

His navy-blue eyes were so dark with desire they were the color of a Highland night sky—purple and black. He slowly turned to face her.

She breathed hard, aware of heat dripping down her inner thighs, and refused to take another look at the tented tunic. Her tension had spiraled to an impossible level. She could hardly think.

How could she go? How could she stay?

Why did she have to be so aware of him?

"Men like me because I'm elegant," Tabby said harshly. "I am not elegant now. I just don't get this."

His stare intensified. "In my bed, ye willna have to be someone ye're not."

She inhaled. "No. I'm really not into sex."

He smiled, as if he knew something she did not.

"I'm really hard to please."

"I dinna think so," he said softly.

He reached for the vee neckline of the tunic. Tabby watched his hands and her heart stopped. The tunic vanished over his head and fell to the floor.

Her body exploded. She looked at his huge, sculpted chest, then at his six-pack—and the hollow below it.

She went still. He was massive and hard.

"Do ye still wish to leave?" he murmured.

Medieval or not, he was the sexiest man alive—ever.

Maybe he was right. Maybe she wouldn't have to pretend to be the kind of woman she was supposed to be in bed. Maybe she wouldn't have to fake it to please her partner. Maybe her hormones would take over and she'd have a good time.

She finally looked up. She meant to look into his eyes, but

he was reflected in all of the bathroom's mirrors. His beautiful face and powerful body were *everywhere*.

She wanted him. She had never felt this way before. Her body was a mass of swollen, hurting flesh. But she didn't love him and she never would. She wasn't a liberated woman. If she gave in now, it would be the most sordid act of her life—and in the morning, she would hate herself.

"I dinna think so," he murmured. "In the morn, ye'll be verra pleased."

He was still reading her mind. "Don't," Tabby whispered, but she had the awful feeling that he might be right.

He suddenly reached out, took her hand and reeled her in.

CHAPTER SEVEN

TABBY CRIED OUT as she found herself in his embrace. He was naked, she was dressed, and she felt every inch of his huge, hard and very naked body pressing against her. His power, masculinity and heat made her feel dizzy and faint. Instinctively she pressed her hands on his chest, and the moment she did so, she went still, giving up.

His hands closed on her waist, pulling her up tightly against him. "Ye willna have any regrets," he said roughly.

His loins strained against her. Tabby felt herself move against him in response. She cried out, meeting his searing eyes. How could she be doing this? But she was trembling wildly now, every nerve she had begging for release. Instead of protesting, she slid her hands up his chest to his shoulders, using her nails to dig hard into his flesh as she did so. His mouth curled in triumph.

"Damn it," she said, breathing hard. She caught his shoulders and held him fiercely, his skin catching under her fingernails, and she moved her thigh up, over his.

He laughed. The sound was smug and triumphant. She didn't care. Clawing him, she tried to climb up him, not even realizing what she was doing. When she did, she was horrified, but only in her mind. Because her body was determined to ride his.

She wrapped her calf around his hip, digging her nails in deep. As she did so, their eyes locked.

He caught her hair, using it as a leash, and twisted her head backward. Then he whirled her around, until her back hit the door. He shoved his huge thigh between hers, and Tabby moaned, throbbing wildly all over him. Still holding her hair, anchoring her so she couldn't move, pressing his leg into her, he brought his mouth down on hers.

His lips were hard and aggressive, possessive. He forced her lips open, took them over, moved his tongue deep. Tabby felt all those new pulse points explode and she surrendered. She let him kiss her so hard he was probably drawing her blood. It didn't matter. She was in a vortex, spinning toward that usually elusive brink, shaking wildly in his arms, her blood roaring in her veins, her brain. Every inch of her was on fire. Now, she clung and begged. "Oh, God, hurry."

He wrenched down her track pants, ripped apart her panties. With one hand he lifted her leg and pushed his huge throbbing length hard and deep inside her. Then he paused.

Tabby gasped, the wave of rapture beginning. He strained inside her, filling her impossibly, almost painfully, so much so that she couldn't move, not this way. It was too much to take— he was too much to take. He wasn't moving, but she felt him pulsing inside her, every single drop of hot blood roaring in his phallus, in her. She was vaguely aware that he was watching her, but she didn't give a damn. She was about to break apart and she wanted to go there, as she'd never wanted anything before.

He began to move, slowly, sensually, once, twice, three times.

Tabby broke. She shattered, clinging to him, as he drove hard now, brutally, intently, and she clawed him, demanding more. She wept in more pleasure than she'd dreamed possible. Her back found the hard floor. He suddenly went still, buried deep inside her.

She was still spinning away. Her orgasm seemed to be impossibly endless. And then he slid away from her.

"Tabitha."

It took her a moment to realize that something was wrong. Tabby opened her eyes, a semblance of coherence returning, and glimpsed Macleod, starkly naked, impossibly hard and so beautiful, on his hands and knees, posed over her. *What was she doing?* "What are you doing?" she gasped helplessly. "Come back!" As she seized his arm, she became aware of the door buzzer.

His gaze turned cold. "Yer husband."

His words were like ice water. All insanity vanished. Randall had come back? Tabby stared at him, aghast.

"He has keys," Macleod murmured, but now he looked dangerously pleased.

And Tabby heard the locks turning.

"CLOSE THE DOOR," Nick said.

Sam did so.

"How's your sister?" he asked.

"Upset. Can you blame her?"

"She's a lucky lady," Nick said. "Imagine that, a Highlander showing up just in the nick of time."

Sam scowled unhappily at him.

He knew why she was upset. "Jumping to conclusions?"

"What do you think?"

He stared. In September when he'd gone back in time with Sam, they'd bumped into her sister and her husband. Tabitha had been living in the past for over two hundred years. It was her Destiny to go back, and it would be very easy to conclude that the man she was meant to go back with had finally come to the city for her. That would explain his sudden appearance, both in the Big Apple and at school. "If Mr. Tabitha is our Highlander, there's no stopping either one of them."

"I know. I'm cool."

"You look like you're losing your best friend."

Sam's face tightened so impossibly he expected her skin to crack. "If it's Macleod, I *am* losing my best friend." Then she shrugged, forcing a smile. "I fight better alone. I won't have to worry about Tabby and her spells going awry."

"Bullshit. And, kiddo? You're not alone."

She met his gaze. "Don't bother feeling sorry for me. I like being alone."

He liked the lip; it was better than her mourning her sister, who was going back in time sooner or later. "Why not? You're feeling sorry as all hell for yourself."

"Fuck you, Forrester," she said. She turned and seized the doorknob.

"What do you make of Kristin Lafarge?" he said to her broad shoulders.

She opened the door, closed it and faced him. "Evil. But so is half of this city, and she's not demonic."

"Really? Because I'm not sure she's human."

"It's one or the other."

"Is it? I've been at HCU for a long time, Sam, and I've seen my share of twisted, strange entities...and things."

Sam absorbed that. "What do you want to do? Today was Lafarge's first day at school. The fire alarms were dismantled before the boys took Tabby and the kids hostage. They knew her by name. This was planned. The burnings are never planned."

He'd already reached the same conclusion. "Why would some demon-run subs hunt your sister?"

"I don't know. You think they're hunting her?"

"Mr. Tabitha will protect her—if he *is* Mr. Tabitha. And I think there's a big fat chance she is being hunted, but not by brainless subs."

Sam stared. "You know, because of what we learned about my sister, almost anything from any time might be after her."

"Yeah. She's a bit of a sitting duck. Because she has no idea that her life teaching little kiddies in Manhattan is about to change…drastically."

"Why don't I bring Lafarge in?" Sam said furiously. As she spoke, there was a knock on Nick's door. "I don't mind grilling her a bit."

He felt Kit outside and told her to enter. As she did, he said to Sam, "Let's play this out, see if we can use her. But let's play gentle. We'll tail her twenty-four/seven," he said. "Leave her be, see where she leads."

"Okay," Sam said. She smiled grimly. "Being as you are the boss."

He didn't mind the acknowledgment, not from her, because when she was in the field she often ignored his very specific orders. However, she had great instincts, and this far, had managed to avoid his wrath.

Nick looked at Kit, who was clad in black pants, a black turtleneck and black boots. As always, her dark hair was drawn back in a ponytail. She was very fair, and even without makeup, she was striking. Now she was holding a huge stack of what seemed to be enlarged glossies under her arm. "Boss, I've come across something really weird."

He had to crack a smile. "Life is weird."

"No, it's major. I've been going over the videotapes of last week's Rampage, the one on Eighty-first and Madison," she said.

He knew which Rampage she meant. "And?"

"I found someone—or something. Something was there, during the entire event. It showed up as a really small, grayish blip. I zoomed in and the shadow got larger—the size of a small person. When I zoomed into the center of it, I actually saw two eyes and a mouth. Human eyes and a human mouth." Her green eyes were wide.

Sam came forward. "Demons don't show up on any kind of film except as black shadows, that we know of. If you could make out features, it wasn't a demon."

Nick felt chills begin. "What's with the photos?"

"I fed Big Mama the features, to see if she could come up with a composite." Kit grimaced. "But she was in a creative mood and she came up with a million or so possible faces."

Big Mama was the agency's supercomputer.

Sam said, "Ghosts photograph really well with the film we're using. If it was a ghost, the entire face and body would be visible, but you'd see right through it." That was because ghosts were the energy of dead humans, and they were trying to slip back into their human forms and lives.

Kit said, "I know. I've seen ghosts now and then, and not just on tape. They're pretty cool."

Nick knew she was referring to her dead sister. He'd actually caught her talking to Kelly a few times. Still chilled, he said, "Let's see the goods." But he knew what he'd find.

She handed Nick the top photo and Sam leaned close to look at it, too. "Well? It's not human and it's not a ghost. It's not a demon. It's not a sub. Subs cast shadows, without the sun. What the hell is that?"

He stared at the malevolent eyes, which stared back at him. Even in print, the eyes were filled with energy and hatred. "Oh, it's a ghost, all right," he said. "But not a human one. Just what we need—a demon that forgot to go bye-bye."

TABBY JERKED to sit up, overcome with dismay. In that exact moment, she realized that she was half-naked on the bathroom floor, having just had sex with a stranger. No, with a medieval barbarian. Shock paralyzed her.

Macleod was standing, calmly wrapping his plaid around his waist, in no rush. He looked smug and pleased.

What had she done?

"Tabby?"

Randall had let himself in. Clearly he was in her living area. Tabby came alive. She jumped to her feet, hopping into the track pants, setting a world record. "Do not come out of the bathroom," she whispered furiously.

"I willna hide from yer husband."

Tabby straightened in disbelief. Had he just snarled at her? He was cool, calm and poker-faced, but his eyes glittered dangerously. She inhaled. No good could come of Macleod and Randall meeting! "Just wait in here!" she snapped.

"Why?" he asked. "Because ye dinna wish fer yer *husband* to see ye with a mostly naked man?" His eyes were dark. "I thought ye a widow, Tabitha. I dinna realize yer husband remained alive."

Tabby became even more alarmed. "In my time, women can leave and divorce their husbands—and vice versa. I have to go and I am asking you to wait here."

His smile was sudden and mocking. "Did ye love him, Tabitha?" he asked softly. "Ye never had sex without love— until now. Ye must have loved him, otherwise, ye'd have avoided his bed."

Did he know everything about her? She was stunned and incredulous.

"Do ye love him still?"

Macleod was not keeping his voice down. "Be quiet," she muttered.

"Why? What do ye care if he sees ye with a lover?"

She trembled, angry and distraught now. "Stay put, damn it! I am asking you to stay put!"

"Tabby?" She heard Randall walking toward the bathroom.

Tabby raced out of it, slamming the door closed as he turned the corner from the living area. He halted the moment he saw her, his eyes widening.

Tabby felt her color increase. She'd been having sex on the bathroom floor. Did she look like a woman who'd just had a huge, almost endless orgasm? Impossibly, she felt herself flush even more—and not with guilt.

"Are you okay? I just saw the evening news!" Randall hurried toward her.

Tabby was acutely aware of Macleod in the bathroom and what she had just done. "It's surprising that you care," she began. Now, the fact that he'd let himself in with her keys—for the second time—hit her.

Randall strode to her and crushed her in his arms. She tried to press away from him. "You look like hell," he said. "And of course I care." But the words weren't even out of his mouth when he stiffened—at the exact moment Tabby heard the bathroom door open.

She tensed impossibly as Randall released her, his face turning pale with shock. "What the hell?"

"Hallo, a Rhandaill."

Tabby whirled and groaned. Macleod stood there smiling, clad only in the plaid, which was wrapped around his waist. He looked smug and satisfied.

Randall's eyes popped. "Oh, my God," he said. "I don't believe this!"

She didn't owe him any explanations, but Tabby flushed with shame. "It's not exactly what you think," she tried. But it was exactly what he was thinking. What had happened to old-fashioned, morally conservative Tabby Rose?

Randall looked at Tabby, incredulous. "This is what you're doing? Shacking up with a steroidal illiterate jock?"

Tabby covered her face with her hands. She did not have any

reasonable explanation. "My personal life is not your business. We were done almost two years ago. I can sleep with whomever I want." His eyes widened impossibly. Tabby trembled, amazed that she would be so harsh with him. "You can't barge in here, Randall. And you can't call Macleod names." Oddly, that last dig really bothered her.

"What did he just call me?" Macleod asked her very softly, but his stare never wavered from her ex.

Randall whirled and took in his mostly naked body. "I called you a steroidal illiterate jock."

Tabby cried out. "Macleod, ignore him!"

But Macleod had seized Randall and was spinning him roughly across the room. "Ye ken I kill men fer such insults."

"Macleod!" Tabby cried, aghast.

Randall fell and Macleod towered over him. "Yer little wife has no more use fer ye. Ye can give me the keys."

Randall scrambled to his feet.

"Can ye understand my English?" Macleod asked softly.

He flushed, thrusting Tabby's extra keys at him. Then he began backing away. "I don't believe this." He looked at Tabby. "I want to marry you again, and you're playing around with that moron?" He looked at Macleod. "I'm slapping you with assault charges, bud!"

Macleod's mouth curved and he seized Randall by the shoulder. "Tabitha isna foolish enough to marry ye a second time. She wants ye gone. I want ye gone. Leave afore I cut yer throat an' give yer carcass to the dogs."

Tabby cried out. "Randall, you had better go."

"Holy shit," Randall cried. "He's a psycho! He means it!"

Tabby nodded desperately. "I think he does mean it."

"Then you're crazy, too!" Randall cried. "A crazy, lying whore!"

Macleod reddened. It took Tabby one moment to realize he

was furious, and by then, lightbulbs were popping, pots and pans were rattling and her curtains were flying around the windows. Macleod pushed Randall toward the door so violently that he fell to the floor again, face-first. Tabby cried out. "Macleod, stop!"

"I can manage insults from such a womanly man," Macleod spit. "I dinna think ye deserve his insults, Tabitha."

"They don't bother me," Tabby cried, lying.

"He's insane," Randall cried, getting up, his face pale. Blood trickled from his nose as he ran to the front door. "He's got damned 'roid rage!"

"What is 'roid rage?" Macleod demanded.

This was going to escalate, Tabby thought, panicked. She seized Macleod's arm with both hands and held on for Randall's life. "It doesn't matter! He is leaving, Macleod. Just let him go."

"It means that shit you take to make all that brawn is melting down your brain," Randall spit. "Tabby might like going to bed with you, but intelligence is what really turns her on. I mean, can you even read?"

"Please don't," Tabby cried.

Macleod pulled away from her and started to cross the room, slowly, like a big cat lazily and confidently stalking its prey. "Only Latin," he said. "An', Randall? With me, she dinna fake it."

It took Randall a moment. "What?" he said, turning to look at her, disbelieving.

Tabby felt her cheeks flame and she didn't respond.

Randall choked, realizing she hadn't been all that honest with him while in his bed.

Macleod was almost at the door. Randall seized it, flung it open and rushed out. He didn't even go to the elevator, where he'd have to wait for it to arrive at the eleventh floor. He ran desperately for the stairs and vanished into the stairwell.

Macleod actually laughed. "What a puny man! What a coward!"

Tabby backed away, sinking down on a chair by the couch. She covered her face with her hands. She actually felt sorry for Randall. But he had called her a lying whore.

She heard her front door close. She felt Macleod approach, although she didn't hear him—he was too skilled and his steps were soundless. Through her hands, she saw him holding out her keys. "Go away," she whispered. Her mind was blank now, and she wanted it to stay that way. She was pretty certain that in a moment, she was going to think about every damned minute that had transpired in the past quarter of an hour or so.

He didn't move. "Ye wanted him to leave."

Her head ached terribly now. Don't think, she begged herself. Just go to sleep and deal with this—with him— tomorrow!

"Ye despise him. He treated ye horribly when ye were his wife. Ye wanted him gone," Macleod said flatly.

Tabby looked up. "Okay. I wanted him gone. But not that way."

"Then what way?"

"I was going to ask him to leave politely!" Tabby screamed at him.

Macleod's eyes widened.

Tabby covered her mouth with her hands. *What had happened in that bathroom?*

He had touched her and she had gone insane. One touch, the feel of him beneath her hands, and she'd been frantic and desperate and sexually crazed. She'd had a violent orgasm, right off the bat.

It always took her hours to climax, usually during gentle, thoughtful sex, with a good and very private fantasy thrown in. *What was she going to do?*

He said, "He doesna respect ye and he wouldna leave if ye asked nicely."

Tabby stood up and her knees buckled. Macleod reached out and steadied her. She struck his hand away, so hard it hurt her own wrist. His eyes were wide, wary, and he kept his hands to himself. "You treated him terribly! Rudely—violently. You acted like a…a thug!"

He was silent, but his eyes flashed with displeasure. Then he said, "I dinna like him verra much. He called ye a whore."

She was close to tears. Now, images from their very brief encounter in her bathroom were replaying wildly in her mind. She'd tried to climb up his body! She'd clawed his shoulders— literally! His skin had to be under her fingernails. And had she begged him to do it? What was wrong with her?

"It doesn't matter what he called me. You are violent, savage…bestial!"

He crossed his arms, his face hard and tight. "But ye liked it a moment ago."

Tabby struck him across the face as hard as she could.

He didn't flinch, when her blow would have made another man reel. His eyes widened—and then narrowed.

Tabby could barely believe she'd hit him. She'd never hit anyone or anything in her life. She did not retreat, however. "Violence is the way you live. I get it. But here, in my time, in my home, we don't abuse guests!"

He made a harsh, disparaging sound. "So ye wish to treat him as a guest when he insults ye?"

"That's right!" she screamed again. Her stomach was churning. Why didn't he get it? He had rescued her, but they could never be friends, much less lovers. Their values were too different. He lived by the sword, when she used magic to help others. But she had just had raw frantic sex with him on her bathroom floor. And now, damn it, she could not forget it. She would never forget it!

But it wasn't shame or guilt that was foremost on her mind. It was shock.

She'd been uninhibited and passionate. She'd taken, instead of given. The more she kept recalling it, the more dismayed she was—and the more her body was quickening with the memory. It was so hard to breathe!

"If ye were a man, ye'd die fer that."

Tabby hugged herself, just looking at him. "Then I'm lucky, aren't I? Go away. I need to be by myself."

"Ye dinna care fer Randall. Ye dinna even like him now."

"Go away—far away!" she shouted.

"He has no respect fer ye. He thinks to use ye fer his own gain."

He was right on that last point. "Like you respect me?" she cried. "Because I do believe that you were using me a few minutes ago!"

She heard him exhale harshly. He said, "We used each other. Ye wanted me, I wanted ye. 'Tis natural. And I gave ye pleasure." He added, "I enjoyed yer pleasure."

She so wanted to hit him again. But he was right—it had been mutual. She stared at him furiously and he stared back impassively. The memory of their brief encounter made it hard to think clearly.

But she did know one thing. "This will never work."

His brows slashed upward. Then his expression changed, becoming cold and speculative, at once.

"It will never work!" she repeated, pointing at him. Did men die for that rather rude gesture, too? Of course they did!

His hands had fisted. "Ye said," he said low and carefully, "that many women in yer time take their pleasure when they wish. Now ye're like most others."

"I am not like other women. I am a prude, and if you don't know what I mean, look it up!"

A bewildered expression crossed his face and Tabby simply didn't care. She pointed at him again. "I am sorry I cast that spell to bring you here. It backfired. You were supposed to come from An Tùir-Tara, all bloody and burned and grief-stricken, so I could help you! Instead, I get this murdering warrior without a soul or a conscience!" She could not control her tone. She was probably hysterical and she didn't care. "I don't know why I had to be the one to see you at the museum, damn it! I don't know why you think you've seen me haunting you for a hundred years! *And I don't care.*" She stopped, panting.

"Ye care."

"No, I do not! In fact, tomorrow I am sending you back to Blayde, and we can both say a little prayer and hope you wind up where you belong!"

He folded his arms and stared coldly at her. "Like hell."

Tabby finally became silent. Their gazes locked.

"Someone has to protect ye."

"Not you. My sister can do that."

He scoffed at her. "A woman? I dinna think so."

"Sam is a warrior. You cannot stay here. You do not belong here. That is really obvious."

"I will stay until I vanquish the evil behind the boys."

"Shit!" Tabby cried. He wasn't going to budge. She didn't even know if she could send him away. If he refused to go, she had a terrible suspicion that he might be able to resist any spell she might cast. "You haven't taken vows, but now, suddenly, you're a protector?"

"Ye're the woman sharin' my bed."

She inhaled so sharply it hurt her ribs. She saw his strained face as he loomed over her, his hand in her hair, holding her still, so he could kiss her the way she'd never been kissed before.

He intended to continue this.

What was she going to do?

Image after image came, brutally and erotically now. His huge body, driving up into hers. Her back against the door, on the hard floor. And the incredible ecstasy…

Her blood was so hot she thought her skin might start smoking. She swallowed. "We're from different worlds," she said slowly. "Your world is violent and savage—too violent and savage for me. Being together makes no sense. Surely you can see that?"

"I live by my word…an' my sword, Tabitha. If I dinna destroy my enemies, they will destroy me." His gaze was hard, but it was also searching.

"I know. And that's the bottom line—our worlds are too different." She turned abruptly, her back to him, and reached for her bedroom door, tears finally forming. They burned her eyes. She didn't know why she was upset. She didn't know why she wanted to curl up and cry. She prayed he wouldn't come after her. If he did, she was really afraid of what would happen next.

"Our worlds are nay as different as ye'd like to believe."

His tone was bedroom soft. Tabby rushed into her bedroom and slammed the door closed, shaking. He was wrong; she was right! Then she covered her face with her hands, giving into utter despair and utter exhaustion, her head feeling explosive.

They did not share any Destiny. It was a mistake, or one big fat celestial joke; it had to be.

The sooner he went back to 1298, the better.

They had nothing in common except for the war on evil.

But what about the desire that raged between them?

Maybe, just maybe, it had been a shocking abnormality— one single instance in her life that would never be repeated, an event that had come out of the terrible trauma of that day.

Tabby felt her tears start to fall. She wanted to be that wildly passionate woman—just not with a medieval man who callously beheaded his enemies at whim! She stumbled over to her bed and collapsed on top of the comforter there. She was so tired she couldn't move, not even to get under the covers. But she knew she'd never sleep.

Because now, instead of seeing him roughing Randall up or beheading Angel, she saw him in the bathroom, stripping down, naked, absolutely immodest and too physically perfect for words.

Tabby wanted to moan. Her attraction to him hadn't changed, and she didn't know what to do about it. She suddenly wondered if she simply thought about him and what he could do to her, she might find that rapture again. She blushed.

Her bedroom door opened abruptly.

He'd been listening to her. Tabby lay very still, her body suddenly inflamed. He was going to come onto her—and she was probably going to let him.

But he knelt beside her bed, and his large, strong hand covered her mouth.

Tabby tensed, alarmed.

"Dinna move," Macleod whispered. "Evil," he said.

CHAPTER EIGHT

Tabby met his gaze, alarmed.

He removed his hand and leaned over her. "Evil is close by, an' tryin' to get inside."

His breath feathered her. She sat up, shocked. "Here?" It was impossible. The loft was fortified with her grandmother's powerful spells. Evil had never gotten inside. Slowly, with growing dread, she looked past him and into the living room.

He'd left the lights on. Tabby stared into the living area, only able to partially glimpse her kitchen. If she'd been developing a sixth sense for evil, she did not have it now, because her loft looked exactly as it should have. Nothing felt awry.

She glanced at him. "Are you sure?"

He was crouched by the bed, one hand on the mattress by her hip. He nodded. Their arms touched, bare skin against bare skin. Her body began to vibrate in response to his. Just as she was about to ask him how he could tell that evil was close by, someone rapped on the living-room window.

The loft was on the eleventh floor, but the fire escape was outside.

A new tension began. Tabby looked at him and he nodded. She understood him completely. She slipped from the bed and went to the threshold of the bedroom, Macleod behind her, his hand on her waist.

Outside, the city night was bright and illuminated. The rapping continued on the same window she'd opened earlier to let him in. There was no one standing on the fire escape.

The rapping ceased.

Tabby looked at him, a sick feeling beginning. "What is that?"

He kept his focus on the window. "A ghost, I think."

"Ghosts can be seen—even if only partially. They haunt us in their human form," Tabby said. The words weren't even out of her mouth when whatever was out there began rapping on the other living-room window, this time more insistently.

A chill went down her spine as the knocking intensified, as if the thing was angry. She saw the windowpane shudder.

Tabby tensed. Macleod was right. An entity of some kind was trying to get into her loft. But surely it would not be able to get past her grandmother's spells.

Glass shattered, exploding into the room.

Tabby cried out, Macleod shoving her behind him. The other window exploded, as well, and Macleod flung a blast of energy at whatever was out there. Power sizzled from his hand, but it was a weak blast, nothing like what she'd seen at school. The glass seemed to hang in the air. He blasted the perimeter of the room again. This time, silver danced along his fingertips, but nothing else happened and the suspended shards of glass finally fell.

Macleod cursed. He spoke in Gaelic, and Tabby did not have to know the words to comprehend them. "What happened to your power?" she cried as the last window began rattling so vibrantly it was almost visibly moving.

"The gods," he said flatly. He blasted the window again. This time, not even silver shone from his fingertips.

For some reason, he was without his power. A veil of calm slipped over her as a furious knocking on the remaining glass window began. Tabby closed her eyes and concentrated with all of her power on the evil being trying to get into her loft.

"Evil get out, evil be gone. Grandma's spells grow stronger, evil is here no longer."

Sweat poured down her body. She tried to feel the "thing." But Macleod was standing in front of her, his power like a shield, interfering with her senses. She felt Grandma Sara's concern and presence so strongly that she smelled her rosewater scent. But she was a distraction, too. Tabby focused as hard as she could—harder than she ever had. The evil was vicious in its hatred, she thought. Its malice began to entrap her, as if an invisible web was twisting around her and drawing her in. It became frightening in its intensity. She strained for the entity, for its evil lust. Tabby began to feel lost in a cycle of hatred, and feel that she was spinning in it, but she repeated the spell again and again. She did not dare stop.

Suddenly there was only her and the evil's vicious desire to destroy her.

And Tabby was shocked out of her trance by the extent of its hatred.

As her eyes opened, she saw the third and last window shatter. Macleod turned to embrace her, pushing her down to the floor and shielding her from the flying projectiles of glass with his huge body.

She could not lose her focus now. She tried to slip back into the evil. She felt the web of sticky clawing tentacles grasping at her. She felt the terrible, hellish pull. There was only her and "it" now. And "it" wanted to destroy her—or them.

"Evil get out, evil be gone," she chanted, as the evil pushed at her, battering her. And suddenly she was blown back against the wall by a huge wind, in spite of Macleod's grasp as he cradled her. *"Evil get out, evil be gone. Grandma's spells grow stronger, evil no longer. The Rose will triumph here!"*

Lamps crashed to the floor, chairs were blown over, pots flew from the stove, dishes from the sink, and papers whirled everywhere from her and Sam's desks. She kept chanting the spell, the hatred of the thing filling her, trapping her. And then the hatred began to fade and suddenly the web that felt like a prison was gone.

An absolute stillness filled the room.

Tabby felt her body give way and she collapsed in exhaustion in Macleod's arms. Instantly she was acutely aware of being in his powerful and protective embrace. She recalled how he'd held her and tried to shield her during the attack. She began to tremble, fully lucid now. He had refused to take his vows, but this was the second time he had protected her fiercely, giving no thought to himself.

And they were on the floor. His body was huge, inherently and blatantly male. Her pulse was already high; it soared. She couldn't move away—she didn't want to move away. Now, no matter what had already happened between them, his body had become an incredibly safe harbor. Stunningly, his embrace felt powerful and right.

Slowly she raised her face. The danger gone, his blue eyes were glittering with heat. She tried to ignore the way that look affected her. It sent a fist through her belly, causing an aching need. She looked over his shoulder at the devastated loft. Had a hurricane swept through, it could not have been worse.

His large hand closed around her arm. "'Tis gone, Tabitha."

She shivered, aware now of the frigid cold blasting through the loft. The cold went right through her. She met Macleod's steady and reassuring eyes.

She wasn't going to even try to deny that she was really glad he'd been with her just then. He had enough courage for an entire army, she thought.

Tabby rose to her feet, still shaken. Macleod let her go and he stood, too. She looked at him grimly. "What just happened?"

He didn't answer, but she hadn't expected him to. She left Macleod and walked over to her laptop, which lay on the floor, at least ten feet from the coffee table where she'd left it. She picked it up and held it tightly to her chest. Macleod touched her shoulder.

She hadn't heard him come up behind her. "Is it broken?"

"I don't know." What had tried to get into her loft? She shivered. "If it's broken, I have a desktop over there." She pointed at the desk at the other end of the loft, where her Mac was, and stiffened. The computer lay on its side, and the monitor that had been on her desk was on the floor. "I can buy a new laptop first thing tomorrow, if I have to. All my files are backed up."

"Ye're brave."

She went still. In that instant, she knew how important courage was to him and she had the inkling that he did not toss praise about lightly. She smiled grimly. She wasn't brave, not really, but she wasn't about to reveal how scared she'd been. She was a Rose, and she'd done what she'd had to do. She thought of how unflappable he'd just been—even without his powers. She couldn't help but respect and admire his courage, too. But clearly Macleod would never panic, especially not in battle.

She put the laptop on the coffee table. She powered it on, and then went to the kitchen for a garbage bag. "My sister is a warrior—she likes nothing more than to slay demons. She's the really brave one. You'll probably meet her in the morning." She was not going to think about the rest of the night, she decided.

He took the garbage bag from her and their hands brushed. Fire felt as if it sparked between them. Tabby dared to meet his gaze. A long night lay ahead. Evil had tried to get into her loft, and she was glad he'd been with her. So where did that leave them? "Ye need servants to clean this up," he said.

A very safe topic, she thought in relief. "Our cleaning lady comes once a week. She would die if she saw the loft like this—and she'd quit."

"I'll see that she cleans the loft."

Tabby started. "She's not a servant, Macleod, or a serf. I pay her with coin for her services and she can leave my employ at any time." Tabby realized she was blabbering and her composure was starting to crumble. An attack on her loft, after that interlude in her bathroom, was more than she wanted to think about. Abruptly she sat down on the sofa.

What had that thing been?

When had she ever faced such hatred?

Did it hate her?

"Ye're tired. Ye used up too much power chasing the ghost away. Can ye rest?"

"I was tired before that ghost appeared," she said carefully. He wasn't really concerned about her, was he? He was a ruthless barbarian who used women, right? He had one interest when it came to her—getting her back into his bed.

Except, he kept saving her life. Or trying to do so.

His eyes changed, taking on the indolent and sensual look that choked up her breathing and made her feel dizzy. "I'll find wood to cover the windows while ye sleep."

Her insides vanished completely. No matter how cold it got inside, if she let him sleep with her, they wouldn't be cold at all. Unable to move, she stared at him, her mind treacherously thinking about having that big body beside hers in her bed. She flushed everywhere, became acutely aware of how late it was and what they had just gone through together. Most of all, she knew what would happen if she let him sleep with her.

She'd shout and weep in pleasure while he filled her.

Tabby Rose would vanish, leaving a wildly passionate stranger in her place.

And if that ghost came back, she would rather be in his bed than alone in hers.

She had to rein in her feelings. He was a powerful warrior, but she had to remind herself of their differences and not allow herself to be seduced by his courage, heroism or power. He was ruthless and savage, and she had to remember that. If she decided to sleep with him again, she had better keep her head on straight. It would be a one-night stand.

Tabby almost choked on her thoughts. In the span of twenty-four hours, she was thinking like a stranger—no, her sister. "You're a helluva partner in a demonic crisis," she said carefully.

His eyes flickered. "Yer magic was strong. Ye're a warrior like yer sister."

She wasn't certain her magic had helped. "What happened to your power, Macleod?"

"The gods are angry with me because I have refused to take vows to serve them. They aggravate me whenever they can." A cold smile arose and vanished as quickly.

"Please tell me you are not in a battle with the deities?" Could he be that arrogant?

He was amused. "I dinna fear such a challenge, Tabitha. I am one of them."

"It would be stupid to go up against the gods—even if you're related to them."

He simply smiled at her and she knew he was doing just that.

This was not her affair, she reminded herself. If he wanted to aggravate and anger the Ancients, he would eventually pay. Suddenly she wondered if he'd paid the price of such arrogance at An Tùir-Tara. "Why won't you take your vows? You were born to defend the world from evil, weren't you?"

"My duty is to Blayde."

What did that mean, really? "You can serve your people and take care of your lands while serving the gods, can't you?"

"I fight evil every day," he said flatly. "But my word is sacred. If I took vows, those vows would have to come first—always. I canna turn my back on Blayde."

She could not figure him out. He'd been so heroic a moment ago, but now, his mind-set was incredibly narrow and medieval. Did it have something to do with having lost his entire family in the massacre? That might make him determined to cling to all that was left—Blayde. Maybe he wasn't even destined for the Brotherhood. For all she knew, guys with überpower were running around the world in every century—guys like Sam's boss, Nick. Maybe that kind of power was a genetic glitch. But then, why would the gods be angry with him, enough so to interfere with him? The old gods never bothered with mankind anymore. Or, they didn't bother with humanity in the twenty-first century. It was probably really different in 1298.

"Where can I find wood? I dinna wish to break yer fine furnishings to cover the embrasures."

She stood up. "No, we are not hacking up the furniture. We'll use garbage bags…plastic." She walked across the room, suddenly thinking about his age. He'd been fourteen years old in 1201, and in his time, it was ninety-seven years later. He looked a few years younger than she did—like a young man of twenty-five—but he was over a hundred. He'd lived an entire lifetime. He was a very experienced and worldly man for his time. He'd been in hundreds of battles. He'd slept with hundreds of women—at least.

She shouldn't care, not about anything other than the fact that he could have taken his vows since coming into manhood, and he'd refused to do so for decades. His mind was obviously made up.

It was a waste.

"Why do ye care about those vows? Why do ye care how old I am or what women I keep?"

She took a box of garbage bags out from under the sink. "Rose women have been helping the Innocent survive evil for generations. It's our Destiny. We've met a few Masters and we've thanked the gods they exist. You'd probably make a great one."

He made a disparaging sound. "Ye're worried about how many women I've had."

Tabby knew she turned red. "I hate this one-sided invasion of privacy!"

His regard moved over her face and then returned to her eyes. "Ye worry so much. But then, all women do."

She could happily add chauvinistic jerk to his list of character traits. She began pulling plastic bags from the box, wanting something to do. "Being as you're so into my *mind,* I hope you've been listening closely to all my thoughts."

"I dinna need to *look up* chauvinistic jerk, Tabitha. I can feel what ye mean."

She slammed the garbage bags down on the counter between them. "Good. Meanwhile, a ghost just tried to get in here—an evil, hateful ghost. We have a lot to worry about. So if you are too proud to worry, have no fear, I'll do enough worrying for us both."

He suddenly tilted up her chin with one of his strong, magic fingers. "Ye're brave, even with yer fear."

She felt herself nod. Of course she was afraid.

"I'll worry," he said.

She went still, stunned. *It would be so nice to let him worry for her. It would be so nice to let him shoulder this.* Of course, she'd do no such thing. She was a liberated, strong and independent woman, and sooner or later, she'd be on her own again. In fact, that evil thing might still be hanging around after he'd gone back to his time.

"I will worry, Tabitha, an' plot, an' ye can rest with ease."

She slowly pulled back, so he wasn't touching her face. "Why would you do that?"

He half smiled. "In my time, men war an' worry. Women bake bread and bear babes."

His chauvinism was a vast relief. "Got it." She didn't want him acting concerned or caring toward her.

"Tabitha? I willna go back while the ghost an' the boys hunt ye."

She'd almost forgotten his theory about the incident at school that morning. Tabby wet her lips. "Macleod, I recognized the evil. It came from An Tùir-Tara."

SAM RANG THE BUZZER on Kristin's apartment door at almost a quarter past eleven at night. Kristin used the peephole before opening the door, her eyes filled with surprise.

"I am really sorry to bother you at this hour, but before I call it a night, I have one or two more questions about what happened at the school today." Sam continued to smile smoothly as she lied.

She had a powerful sixth sense for evil, which had saved her ass a lot, and she wanted to hone in on Kristin now. She had decided she wasn't demonic, merely the lowest form of evil that there was, a human filled with the basest emotions and ambitions—greed, jealousy and envy, the desire to see others fail and fall, the ability to gloat over it. But Nick was certain she wasn't one-hundred-percent human. He'd explained to her that humans with a low percentage of demonic DNA could take on demonic traits but escape detection as demons. Sam was intrigued. She'd only been at HCU for three months, and hadn't realized a hierarchy of sub-humans could exist. Her world had been divided into demons, possessed humans or subs, and humans. Adding a mixed breed of partially demonic humans would explain a lot, like people with more power than they should have. So now she would carefully check Kristin out. Tailing Kristin was starting then and there.

"It's late, and I'm usually asleep by now, but the truth is, after what happened today, I am dreading bad dreams." Kristin smiled grimly. "Come in. Let's go into the kitchen. My roommate's asleep."

Sam followed her inside. Kristin still felt both entirely human and entirely evil. Her smile hid a multitude of hatred and sins. Now Sam was excited. What if Kristin had a drop or two of demonic DNA? If she had set Tabby up, she was going to wind up dead.

Kristin offered her water, which Sam refused. "Would you tell me one more time exactly how you became aware of the fire?" She smiled, as if friendly by nature—which she was not.

As Kristin answered, Sam stared, not really listening. At first glance, one saw Kristin's platinum hair, her pale skin and blue eyes, her even features, and the assumption was that she was an attractive woman in her late twenties or early thirties. Now, as Sam really looked at her, she decided she wasn't attractive, or even pretty. She was oddly bland—almost a generic version of a blond, blue-eyed woman. But what better way to hide her evil nature than under such an understated façade?

As she spoke, she gestured and Sam noticed the fine blue veins in her hands. Young women did not have visible veins, not even when as fair as Kristin.

She looked at her neck.

There were creases there.

She did not have the hands or the neck of a woman in her twenties or thirties. But plenty of women went under the knife. Maybe she'd had her face done. Sam studied her again and noticed some fine lines around her eyes and mouth, wrinkles no average person would really ever see. Kristin Lafarge had an oddly timeless quality to her appearance, neither the look of a mature woman who'd had a bit nipped here and tucked there nor the youthful and beautiful appearance of a demon.

Demons lived for centuries, but their DNA came from Satan. Under a microscope, the difference between human and demonic DNA was obvious.

"Is that it, Agent Rose?"

Did this woman have *entirely* human DNA? Sam had thought so, but as much as she hated admitting it, Nick was usually right. Something was off, and she was good enough at what she did to leave no stone unturned. "Yeah, that's it. I'm really sorry to bother you, but I always follow my gut."

"That's all right." Kristin stood. Her smile was polite, almost friendly. There was no sign of relief in her eyes, as if she didn't care that the brief interview was over.

If she was hiding something, she was damned good.

"Can I use your bathroom?" Sam asked, thinking about the fact that the apartment was a one-bedroom flat. The sofa was already pulled out, which meant Kristin slept on the sleeper. It was an old building, the only full bathroom would be attached to her roomie's bedroom. Kristin probably used the powder room more than she did the other bathroom.

A moment later she was inside the powder room and she knew she was right. Because there she found Kristin's makeup, hairbrush and toothbrush.

Perfect, Sam thought.

TABBY STOOD IN THE steaming hot shower, the water pouring over her, trying not to think about Macleod. The shower was long overdue, but her body had a mind of its own and was not quite enjoying the shower as she intended. The drops seemed to agitate her breasts and nipples, and her belly was tight and quivering with tension.

She closed her eyes, trying to keep a grip on the desire she seemed incapable of escaping, desire for a man she hardly knew—a man terribly inappropriate for her—a man she'd already had sex with.

Images danced, of Macleod walking into the bathroom and taking off that plaid, his smile slow and suggestive.

She swallowed and thought she heard the door, but when she looked at it, it remained closed.

She needed to finish showering; she needed to think about something else.

She pushed her heavy hair back, closed her eyes and let the water pour on her face, determined to ignore the weight of her body. It was almost impossible, because she could feel him inside her, filling up every inch of her, the pressure immediate, inescapable and shattering.

Whatever was haunting her—or them—from An Tùir-Tara, she didn't want to think about it now. She *wanted* to think about him, about his courage, his strength and how protective he was of her. Just then, she did not want to acknowledge his savagery, his barbarism or his chauvinism. If she kept this up, she'd leave the shower, open the bathroom door and call him to her.

Come to me, Highlander.

It would be so easy.

In fact, if she spent the night with him and was as unbridled and as passionate as she'd been for those few minutes in the bathroom earlier, she might actually believe herself to be a new and different woman. She opened her eyes, dismayed. The truth was, a part of her was afraid that she'd never experience that passion again.

That she was still the old, conservative, uptight Tabby.

But she hadn't been uptight or conservative earlier. They'd had rough, hot, animal sex—the kind of sex only two crazed strangers could have.

She thought about everyone always saying how elegant she was, how proper and genteel, how she was held up as the perfect lady, and she started to laugh somewhat hysterically.

Was that woman forever gone? Or would she reappear when Macleod went back to the Middle Ages?

If he came to her now, which woman would climb into his bed?

She wanted some of that perfect lady back. She wanted the grace, the good humor, the confidence, the unflappable composure. She even liked being so preppie! But she really, really wanted to be able to continue to enjoy a man in bed. If she could hold on to one thing, it would be her newfound passion.

She never wanted to fake it again.

She slowly turned.

Macleod stood on the bathroom's threshold. She hadn't locked the door. Of course she hadn't, because she had wanted him to come to her. Without turning, not taking his eyes from her, he closed the door behind him and pulled the plaid away from his tense body. He tossed it aside. "Be careful what ye wish for."

She inhaled.

He started forward, stiffly aroused. "Ye dinna need to pleasure yerself, Tabitha, when I am here to do it fer ye."

She dropped her hands, aware of her resistance crumbling, and whispered, "Macleod…I'm frightened."

He took her hands in his, and his long, strong fingers closed over hers. For an instant, as he looked into her eyes, she thought that there was something possessive in the action. She thrilled but her fear increased.

"Maybe I can't do it again."

He began to smile. "Ye can do it, Tabitha, ye may trust me on that."

"I was frigid, Macleod, until you. Do you know what that means?" she cried desperately.

"I ken." He laid her hands on his shoulders. "It means ye faked it every time."

"I've had, like, two orgasms with a man in my entire life. I have been dead inside!"

"But now ye're with me." And he tilted up her chin before running a finger down her body, from the hollow of her collarbone to the tip of her breast, her navel and then to the most swollen aching part of her pubis.

She gasped, tears forming, because she'd wanted him to touch her again so badly ever since the first time. Tabby seized his shoulders. His finger pressed low and deep, then high and she stiffened entirely, throwing her head back, the wave of pleasure rapidly building, releasing the raging torment.

"I canna bear yer pain," he said bluntly, clasping her waist. His fingers tightened there. She tried to protest. His eyes gleaming, his face hard and determined, he pulled her abruptly forward. She gasped as the long, solid ridge of his manhood was crushed between them.

The shower started to spin.

She cried out. She couldn't stand it. "Make me come, Macleod."

He gave a sexual sound, seized that hank of her hair again, tilting her face upward, toward his. Tabby couldn't breathe. Their gazes locked. Pleasure mingled with pain while he throbbed hotter and harder against her. She couldn't stand it. For the second time in her life, she did not want foreplay and she did not need it. "You win, I lose. Hurry, Macleod," she said harshly.

For one moment, he looked at her, his face determined, his eyes ablaze with lust and desire, his huge manhood pressing against her belly. Then he smiled and moved.

He abruptly lifted her leg and wrapped her calf over his hip. Tabby climbed up on him and he helped her, lifting her other leg. He spun her around as she locked her ankles against the small of his back, clawing him mercilessly and pushing down onto him. She realized she couldn't impale herself, not until he allowed it, and she started to weep against his huge shoulder, the friction between them mind-blowing.

Her back against the tile wall, he tugged on her hair, hard. "Look at me, Tabitha."

She did, furiously. "Damn you…damn you."

Anchoring her hips, holding her back to the wall, he thrust upward.

She choked as he stabbed his entire huge length into her. She was shocked to feel so much pleasure. She hadn't imagined it the first time. She began to spin out of control, yet she was desperate for more. She clawed him. Ecstasy blinded her. She soared off the precipice, into a zillion stars, shattering in more pain and pleasure than could possibly exist. "Harder," she wept. "More."

She seemed to climax again, blinded by him now, his mouth tearing at hers, her mouth tearing at his. Each climax was more intense than the previous one. She whirled in so much ecstasy she couldn't stand it and she screamed in release after release. His skin shredded under her nails.

She became aware of his cries, his semen burning inside her. She became aware that she was on the bathroom vanity, but otherwise, in the exact same position, her legs locked around his hips. She blinked and realized she had a death grip on his shoulders, and he remained embedded within her. Having him inside her was sheer heaven. She didn't know how long they had been going at it, nor did she care.

He had paused and some coherence crept over her. She saw his slight, smug smile. The shower was still on. "Don't stop."

But he pushed her heavy wet hair behind her ear, bent and nuzzled the lobe. He whispered, "Ye'll always have this with me."

She did not want to think clearly and analyze that statement. She didn't want to consider that she was seated on the bathroom sink, sweaty and breathless, her legs still locked around him, as he throbbed hugely inside her. She was clasping his shoulders; she saw the myriad nail marks there, all bright red. She tightened her grasp anyway. "I don't want to talk, Macleod."

His smile widened, dimples came. "I ken." He moved away from her, making her incredulous, but then he began deliberately stroking her with his shaft. Tabby seized his shoulders and leaped onto him.

Macleod laughed.

THE PLEASURE WAS DIFFERENT this time.

It was filled with triumph as he held her.

She had haunted him for decades, but he was the victor. It almost felt as if he owned her now, body and soul, and that somehow gave him greater pleasure. But there was more. He could not get enough of her bright power. Her rapture seemed to fill him with that stunning white light. It made him insatiable.

And then he heard the intruder. He jumped from the bed, reaching instinctively for his sword.

It was in the other room.

Simultaneously he felt the intruder's white warrior power. He jumped into her mind and knew she was the sister and he dismissed her as irrelevant. He did not care about her warrior sister.

He slowly turned to look at her. Tabitha gasped, breathing wildly, clutching the covers high. She had plenty of passion, for him and him alone. He was very pleased. But he'd never had any doubt about the outcome of any sexual encounter with her. He couldn't ever recall feeling as satisfied. His smile faded. *She was different from the others.*

Her eyes turned lucid. "It's my sister."

"Aye." He folded his arms and became thoughtful. He had been very angry to be brought to her time without his permission, as if a hostage or a prisoner of war, but he was no longer angry with her. Yet he was a Highlander; forgiveness was rare. Grudges were usually kept to the death.

He decided that he could forgive her for the terrible trespass of abducting him across time, because she desperately needed his protection. He might have never met her in the flesh otherwise—or had her in his bed, either. No, he did not mind forgiving her.

But one astounding fact remained. She had struck him. It was unbelievable. As unbelievable was the fact that he hadn't struck her back.

He did not beat women or dogs or any other creatures. But he did not know any man who would let that slap pass without retribution, and he hadn't had even the slightest urge to hit her back. In fact, he did not like the mere idea of hurting her.

There were very few subjects he brooded upon, and they were usually related to war and the MacDougalls, but he'd thought about her almost constantly since meeting her. He wondered if she'd cast a spell upon him. That would raise his ire as nothing else. Macleod became uneasy.

Tabitha sat up, hugging herself, her eyes wide upon him. "It wasn't a hallucination, that first time," she said hoarsely.

He understood. She'd been afraid that the passion he'd stirred in that first brief encounter had been a mistake and would never occur again. "Ye'll always weep with pleasure in my bed."

She grimaced. "You look really smug."

"Do I? Ye look verra well pleased also."

She flushed. "Not to get into semantics, but that word *always* is bothering me."

He sighed. God, she thought so much! She was debating what would happen between them, if they would have sex again. He felt like laughing out loud. Of course they would share his bed. Why would they *not* do so?

"Yer sister wants to speak with ye. She doesna want ye with me," he said sharply, now noticing the sister's unhappy thoughts for the first time.

Tabitha began to worry about her sister's reaction to the devastation in the loft—and to Macleod.

He wrapped the plaid around his waist, deciding to ignore her thoughts. Tabitha had been haunting him for a century and she hadn't even known it. He had lurked, and he knew she told the truth. He wanted to know what that signified.

She'd meant to bring him to her from Melvaig in 1550, after a great fire. The evil that had attacked them last night had come from that fire, or so she thought. He was concerned. His enemies were at Melvaig now, and undoubtedly they remained there well into the sixteenth century. But he'd felt the evil, too, and its hatred had not been directed at him. Like the possessed boys, it had wanted to harm and destroy Tabitha.

She wasn't safe in this time, he thought. And that meant that when he left, he'd take her with him. The prospect was rather pleasing. She would probably object. Come the night, he'd end her objections.

He looked at her. She'd left the bed, dragging the covers with her, as if he didn't know every single inch of her body. "I need clothes," he said.

Her eyes widened. "I can wash that tunic, but you're right. We don't know how long you'll be here, and we'd better get you in clothes that don't stick out." She opened a closet door and began jerking clothes from the rack. She was still nervous and distressed. She couldn't decide what to do next with him or what to really think about him. She was worried about the kind of woman she was becoming.

He did not mind the words *savage, violent* or *ruthless,*

because every warrior should be those things. He was starting to dislike the word *medieval,* and he was becoming tired of being called a *barbarian.*

"When will ye get the clothes?"

She faced him. "Is there a rush?"

She knew what he wanted—and he always got what he wanted. He had told her last night, and she was very clever, so he knew she hadn't forgotten. "I will go to the museum, Tabitha, to see the display ye keep thinking about. An Tùir-Tara."

Tabitha paled.

CHAPTER NINE

HE WOULD BE at An Tùir-Tara—in another two-hundred-and-fifty years. Bringing him to the exhibit and showing him a slice of his future was a dangerous idea. It was even more dangerous than the chance of their running into the cops. She didn't dare do anything that might affect his future.

She had no idea what to do or say next.

She clutched the sheets to her chest, trying to sound composed. "Macleod, it's a terrible idea to go to the exhibit. Seeing as you keep invading the privacy of my thoughts, you know I think you were there—or rather, that you will be there." Why was he staring? Had her sheet slipped? "But no one should ever glimpse a part of their future. It might change your Fate."

"I will go. Ye can show me the way or I'll find it myself," he said flatly.

Tabby inhaled. She was butting heads with a medieval brick wall—again. But this time, after last night, she was dismayed. "I won't let you go alone." As she spoke, she heard Sam knock on her door. If he intended to go, she wouldn't be able to stop him. But she could try to keep him safe from the cops—and himself.

He nodded, clearly having expected her answer. "Good. We'll go together."

Sam said tersely, "I take it you're all right—and not alone?"

"We'll be out in a minute," Tabby said. She thought her voice sounded hoarse—probably from her screaming. "I'm fine."

Trying to be nonchalant when she was very modest, even after all they'd done to each other, Tabby put on her velour pants and a T-shirt as quickly as she could. She was pretty certain that Macleod watched. She faced him and said, "Could you *not* go out of the bedroom dressed like that?"

His lashes lowered. "Can ye kindly bring me my leine?"

Tabby nodded and hurried from the bedroom, closing the door, as if she didn't want her sister seeing Macleod more naked than not. That, of course, was absurd. Sam was in the kitchen—amazingly, making coffee. Sam never made coffee, not even when it was instant. "I guess I missed the party," she said, turning. Her face was serious.

"It was an extraordinary night," Tabby said, rushing into the bathroom where he'd left his tunic. She returned to the bedroom and handed it to him through a crack in the door.

He took it, shrugging it on. "Yer sister doesna want ye with me."

Tabby barred Sam's view with her body, wondering if she had lost her mind. "Sam just doesn't understand what happened, because she knows I don't sleep with strangers."

He simply looked at her.

Tabby realized she was barring his way, too. She left the door and turned to face her sister, who was staring at them both. She tried to smile at her but Sam scowled back.

Tabby shivered, approaching, as Macleod strolled out of the bedroom, nodding rather dismissively at Sam. Sam seemed to bristle. Tabby didn't get it. It was as if they disliked each other, but they didn't even know one another. It was freezing in the rest of the loft. Last night, Macleod had taped garbage bags across the windows, but they didn't seem to be helping. Sam began taking mugs down from a high cabinet.

Damn it, Tabby thought. Sam probably thought her a victim of seduction, and that was not the case. "I'll do that," Tabby said, joining her in the kitchen and smiling at her.

Sam didn't smile back and she ignored Macleod. She was probably the only woman in the city who could resist looking at him. "So what happened? I mean, what got in here last night?" Sam still refused to look at Macleod, but she cast a worried look at Tabby now.

Tabby flushed, feeling guilty. Sam had every right to demand what was up, because they were sisters, but clearly she was avoiding the subject. "There was an intruder—an evil force. Macleod helped me banish it. I'm fine," she said grimly. "I decided to live life, for once."

"Really? Because you don't look very happy. You look upset and worried. No, you look scared."

Tabby felt her smile slip away. "I don't know what's gotten into me."

Sam made a sound. She turned and finally looked at Macleod—scathingly. Tabby saw him tense, as if preparing for battle. She was alarmed as Sam said, "I know who's gotten into you. You're frigging head over heels in love."

Tabby was so surprise she stuttered. "Th-that is not the case!"

"You don't sleep around, Tabby," Sam said. "So if you are not in love, you will be soon. And that, my dear, must be Destiny." She jerked the coffeepot from the coffee machine, but it was still brewing and coffee went all over the counter.

"I'll do that," Tabby said, shocked that Sam was so upset. "I'm not hurt," she whispered. "I'm fine. I...had a good time." She felt herself blush.

"Well, that proves my point."

Tabby turned to Macleod. "Can I speak to my sister alone for a moment?"

"She doesna like me and she doesna want ye to like me." He walked over to one of the patched-up windows, taking a piece of it down to stare outside at the bright morning.

Tabby started. She knew her sister, and she wasn't that way. In fact, she'd be happy for her, if Tabby was happy, too. She lowered her voice, then realized how ludicrous that was—he was telepathic. "What's up?"

"Nothing," Sam said. Then she said, "He's not good enough for you!"

"It was one night," Tabby cried. Sam gave her a look indicating that was simply impossible. "I am not in love," she tried. "I mean, he is medieval, Sam. I've seen him in action. He is very violent and you know I can't handle that! But I owe him and I let him stay the night. And I slept with him. So what?"

"So you paid him back with your body?" Sam was disbelieving.

"I would never do such a thing!"

"Yeah, no kidding!"

"Why are you upset? It was out of character and I can't explain it, not really, but I needed last night... I'm sort of confused."

"You're in love with Macleod. It's the only way you could possibly go to bed with him and enjoy it."

Why was Sam insisting that she was in love, when it was not even on her mind? She became adamant. "He is a million times worse than Randall." When Sam didn't speak, appearing doubtful, she cried, "I watched him behead a boy—but you already know that!" She stopped. "How do you know his name?"

"I work at HCU, remember?" Sam said, turning away.

Tabby knew her sister was lying to her. They never lied to

each other and she was shocked. She said carefully, "He's not a threat, Sam, not to us."

Sam snorted.

Her sister was more than a Slayer. She had the instincts of both the hunter and the pursued, and she was usually right. "He's not a threat," Tabby insisted. She suddenly turned. Macleod watched them, not bothering to pretend not to hear. She faced Sam. "What aren't you telling me? Why do you dislike him? He saved my life." Could Macleod represent some kind of danger to them? No, Tabby refused to believe it.

"I know you better than anyone. You're incredibly romantic. You'll probably follow him back to medieval times, the way Allie did Royce and Brie did Aidan."

Tabby was horrified. "That's a joke, right? I am a modern woman. I couldn't possibly live in the Middle Ages—not for a New York minute—and not with a man who beheads his enemies without even blinking his eyes!" *Sam was afraid she would leave her and go back in time with Macleod.* "We're all that's left of the Rose women. I'd never leave you here to fight evil alone."

Sam smiled grimly. "Of course you wouldn't."

She didn't believe her. "Sam." Tabby hugged her briefly, hard. "I am not going back to 1298. Trust me."

Sam sighed. "I can't fight Fate, Tabby. What's meant to be is meant to be. So what happened here last night?"

Tabby glanced at the destroyed loft. "The same evil that I felt at the Met tried to get in here last night. But we couldn't see it. It was an energy filled with hatred and malice, like a malevolent ghost. It had enough power to break the windows."

Sam was silent. "Do you remember the Rampage last week, the one that Kit hasn't been able to stop thinking about? A demonic spirit was there. It was caught on the video and Nick identified it."

"What do you mean, a demonic spirit?"

"I mean a demon that was vanquished but did not go to hell," Sam said sharply.

A chill swept Tabby, from head to toe. "Macleod called it a demonic ghost, too. But demons don't have ghosts."

Sam was grim. "According to Forrester, once in a while they do."

MACLEOD DID NOT LOOK like a modern man—not one single bit.

Tabby had run to the closest shop and bought him Lucky Brand jeans, a black long-sleeve T-shirt and a bomber-style, faux fur-lined leather jacket. Even dressed in contemporary clothes, he looked frightening and dangerous—as if he was a pissed-off, badly damaged returning Special Ops vet or, worse, a ruthless mercenary. The clothes could not hide the savage quality of his nature.

But he looked really good, otherwise.

In fact, every woman they'd passed that morning on their way uptown, from prepubescent girls to blue-haired grand-mothers, had looked at him at least twice. Women Tabby's age had smiled and tried to flirt. To his credit, he'd been oblivious to them all.

They stood three or four people away from the security guard and the metal detector at the Met. Tabby wrung her hands. Being with him was no easy task, not after last night. She was acutely aware of his virility and power, and her own body. She simply could not reconcile the woman she'd turned into with the woman she'd been her entire life.

What did last night mean? Had it been a shameful and amazing one-night stand? She was not capable of a meaning-less affair, was she? But, until Macleod, she hadn't been capable of raw, animal sex, either.

Worse, she had sex on the brain now, like a sixteen-year-old after her first time.

But it *had* been her first time. She discovered passion last night at the age of twenty-nine.

The cops were looking for him, so their outing to the Met was a dangerous one. Tabby knew it, but she was nervous more because of his masculinity than because the cops might recognize him and decide to gun him down. Every time their eyes connected she felt like jumping out of her skin—or into his arms. And it was hard keeping her eyes off him—those jeans fit perfectly. She wished she knew what she should do about him and them, but she didn't have a clue.

"What's that?" Macleod asked.

She kept her voice low. "We have to go through a metal-detector machine, and all bags go through an X-ray. No one is allowed to bring weapons into the museum."

His eyes flickered. His mouth curved ever so slightly.

Tabby became alarmed. He had a weapon? "Macleod?"

"Aye, a wee dagger in my boot."

Her temperature soared. She was wearing a skirt, a cashmere turtleneck and her boots, but she wished she were in a thin jersey dress. She had her coat over her arm, and she held the turtleneck away from her throat. But it didn't help. They were probably going to get nailed the moment they reached the security guard and the metal detectors. "We need to leave and get rid of it and then come back," she whispered.

"Ye even worry like a shrew," he said calmly. "When will ye trust me?"

Tabby was taken aback as his dark blue gaze held hers, and she realized that she did not want to trust him—not ever. Trust might complicate matters. Except, their relationship really couldn't be more complicated.

Tabby felt him stiffen.

Alarmed all over again, she followed his glance. A civilian stood beyond the security line, already inside the museum, with a cup of steaming coffee in his hand. He was with a woman—probably his girlfriend—and although she was chatting to him, he wasn't paying her any attention. His dark eyes were casually scanning the huge lobby. Macleod had him in his sights.

To distract him, Tabby plucked his sleeve. That man looked like a cop or some other kind of government agent.

As she did so, the man looked at them, apparently aware of their stares. Instantly Tabby dropped her eyes, only to realize that Macleod stared back with a cold, ruthless stare that was a challenge and possibly the prelude to violence. She jerked on his arm. Only one person was ahead of them now. "Who is that?" she asked.

"A soldier."

Tabby went still. "Please don't tell me he's a cop?"

"Aye, he's off duty, but he's thinkin' about work tonight. He's thinkin' about me."

Tabby inhaled and said unnecessarily, "Are you sure?"

"Oh, I can hear his evil thoughts verra loudly."

She tensed. "Is he evil, or are you simply mad?"

He gave her a look. "He may be a soldier, but he's evil."

There were good cops and bad cops. It was just their luck to be standing twenty feet from a bad one—who was thinking about the Sword Murderer.

"Hey, you two lovebirds. Move it. You're holding up the line."

Although Macleod's expression never changed, Tabby seized his hand. He probably never allowed anyone to speak to him in such a way. She glanced up at him and he gave her a lazy look. She realized he was in absolute control, and not about to blow up. He was not even worried. Maybe, for him, this was a walk in the park. Relieved, Tabby stepped forward, and then realized that she was still holding his hand. She released it as if burned and handed the inspector her purse.

Macleod never noticed. He was too busy staring at the inspector. It took Tabby one moment to realize he was using his otherworldly powers of persuasion on him.

The inspector opened her bag but then looked up instead of going through it. He stared at Macleod, perplexed, then riveted.

But enchanting him wouldn't stop the metal detector from going off. And the bad cop was still hanging around, although he seemed to be checking everybody out. Hopefully, it was just a habit of his nature.

The inspector now handed her bag back to her, not having looked through it. "Go on," he said, waving them through the metal detector.

Tabby went through first, her heart thundering. When she was on the other side, the metal detector suddenly rocked wildly, as if struck by a huge force. She saw Macleod's power blazing.

She cringed.

The people in line behind him gasped, moving back from the blazing machine.

Macleod stood innocently on the other side, awaiting his turn to go through.

The metal detector was still.

Her heart pounding, Tabby looked at everyone present. Yes, a few people were whispering and staring with wide eyes at Macleod. How could he use his powers so openly? It was too dangerous!

Macleod was still as a statue. Even his impassive expression was set in stone.

"What the hell?" the security inspector exclaimed. The cop ran over, as did two other museum security guards, but their attention was on the machine, not Macleod. One of the guards started calming the crowd. Tabby glanced at Macleod as they began trying to figure out if the machine still worked or not. Someone suggested it had been shorted. The cop revealed his shoulder holster and gun, and went through. The metal detector did not go off. Macleod looked at her, his blue eyes satisfied. Tabby gave up. She shouldn't have doubted his ability to get by a simple metal detector. He had known what he was doing. She couldn't help admiring him. In a crisis, he was as cool as a cucumber.

She hated to admit it, but he would make a terrific partner for anyone in the war on evil. It was a shame and a waste that he hadn't taken his vows. With that kind of courage, he should be on the streets, defending the Innocent, every single day.

"Oh, great. Now we have to frisk everybody," the security inspector said. He turned. "Call Mel and tell him what happened." He waved at Macleod. "Come here, buddy. We have to do it the old-fashioned way."

Tabby held her breath, certain that Macleod would keep the inspector enchanted, and she was right. The balding inspector patted his chest and thighs and said, "Go on." It was the worst frisk job ever.

Macleod smiled pleasantly at him and walked into the museum lobby.

Tabby breathed. Then she turned and saw the off-duty cop staring at her closely—no, he was watching Macleod as he joined her, and suspicion was written all over his face.

Her heart skipped too many beats to count. "He's onto us," she whispered.

"Aye, he suspects me, but I can destroy him easily enough," Macleod told her softly.

"What if your powers fail you?"

He looked at her. "I could choke his life from him with my bare hands."

She stared into his cold eyes. He meant his every word. If push came to shove, he'd break that cop's neck as swiftly as he'd beheaded Angel.

She'd spent most of that morning thinking about having sex with him. What was she doing? The fact remained that he was a medieval man. Last night she had forgotten it. There would not be evenings at wine bars and trendy restaurants. There wouldn't be movies or ice skating. There wouldn't be weekends at a cozy cottage in the Hamptons. She almost laughed at the idea of his doing any of those activities! The only relationship they could possibly share was a sexual one—or a martial one.

Suddenly she was depressed. "Come on. The exhibit's upstairs."

His gaze turned searching as they started across the lobby. "Ye should stop thinkin' so much."

"I wish I could." She realized she meant it.

It was too early for a line, and it was Tuesday, so the museum was quiet. Macleod left her behind, heading rapidly to the display case. Tabby hurried after him. She wasn't surprised when she saw that he was staring at the gold amulet. Disbelief and shock were written all over his face.

"What is it? You recognize the talisman, don't you?"

He began to tremble. Tabby was stunned by his agitation— and by the grief that flickered in his eyes and the anguish that crossed his face. Her head ached. She saw the fourteen-year-old boy, covered in blood and choking on grief, standing not far from an inferno.

"I am so sorry for what you went through," she said softly, thinking about how terrible it must have been to lose your entire family and be the only one to survive.

He turned to look at her. For one more moment, she saw him as that grief-stricken and enraged boy. Then it was Macleod standing there, the grief replaced by fury. Behind them, the display case rattled. "The amulet is mine."

Tabby went still and then dread arose swiftly. "Macleod, no! The pendant was found in the ruins of Melvaig quite recently. Apparently it was in the fire of 1550. It belongs to the British government."

His expression was ruthless. "'Twas my mother's. It belongs to me."

She clung to his hand with both her hands now. "Don't do anything rash. Please, let's go and calmly discuss this."

His smile was chilling. "There's naught to discuss, Tabitha."

This was not going well, Tabby thought. Then, out of the corner of her eye, she saw the off-duty cop and his girlfriend across the room, wandering about the adjacent exhibit. Her unease escalated. Had they followed them? "Macleod. Let's go. Let's grab a coffee and talk about Melvaig, your enemies, the fire, and try to figure this out." She hadn't even finished speaking when a security guard rounded the corner.

Macleod turned. The display case shattered. Alarms screamed.

"Damn it!" Tabby cried.

Macleod seized the pendant through the broken glass case.

"Hey, you! Halt! Put your hands up!" the security guard cried, training his gun at them.

"Let's go," Macleod said calmly to her.

"Put your hands up!" the guard screamed.

Tabby closed her eyes and thought, *Good over Macleod, good around him. Good everywhere, barring dark intent. Circle formed, protecting him.*

Macleod seized her arm, ruining her concentration. "We have no time fer magic now!" he said, already hurrying her toward the hall and staircase.

The guard began speaking on his radio, behind them.

"Halt right now, before I blow your fucking head off."

Tabby knew it was the bad cop and she was horrified. She tried to halt. Macleod tightened his grasp on her, saying, "Come!" He started to run, dragging her with him.

Tabby screamed, "He'll kill you!" She was certain he could not survive a bullet to the back of his head.

"Fuck you," the cop snarled, behind them.

Macleod roared, turning, flinging his arm as the gun fired, but no power blazed. Tabby cried out as the bullet hit him high on the chest, but he only flinched, when a mortal would have gone down.

The cop's eyes went wide. "One of them," he said, about to shoot again.

Macleod moved faster than the human eye. His dagger, which had been in his boot, beneath the jeans, landed in the cop's heart as the gun went off again. The bullet went astray, hitting the wall, as the cop collapsed.

The guard shouted, "He's killed Frankie!" He ran up the hall toward them, gun in hand.

Macleod marched forward, his face savage. Tabby thought he meant to murder the guard with his bare hands. She screamed at him. "He's an Innocent! Don't!"

But then he tore his dagger from the cop and straightened, staring at the guard. The security officer hesitated, his face pale, his gun trained on Macleod.

She had to save him.

And suddenly the morning became still, silent. Suddenly she was so calm, so detached. *"Good over Macleod, good around him. Good everywhere, barring dark intent. Circle formed, protecting him,"* Tabby chanted. The air shimmered around Macleod. Vaguely she heard the sirens outside and booted steps pounding madly up the stone stairs.

Tabby focused her entire being on the spell as the guard pulled the trigger. Only a loud click sounded.

The guard blanched, clearly in disbelief.

Had her spell worked? "Macleod, we have to run," she said, trying to shake herself free of her trance.

Macleod lifted his arm and, this time, his energy blazed, hurling the guard backward. As Macleod strode back to her, a man materialized between them in a whoosh of golden dust that formed into a huge, towering golden Highlander. Otherworldly power filled the hall.

"Ye took yer time," Macleod said.

"Aye, I wondered how ye might manage this crisis," the golden Highlander said calmly. He nodded at Tabby as if he knew her.

"I willna go back without Tabitha," Macleod warned.

Tabby tensed, coming fully out of her trance now. Only two things were clear—Macleod was leaving and she could not go with him. "No, wait. I am *not* going back to Blayde with you." *He was leaving.* She forced her dismay aside. She could not go back in time with him!

He reached her, seizing her hand and pulling her hard to his side. His gaze locked with hers. "Hold on verra tight."

Panic overcame her. "Macleod, no!" She had never meant "no" more.

But he nodded at the golden Highlander and suddenly Tabby was crushed to his chest and they were hurling toward the high ceiling above. She screamed.

Blayde, Scotland
June 10, 1298

TABBY COULDN'T BELIEVE she would survive the pain. She had gone through the universe, probably at the speed of light. Maybe she wouldn't survive—maybe she was dying, even though she lay on the damp ground in Macleod's arms, moaning. Every bone in her body had been shattered into a zillion pieces, or that was what it felt like. If the pain didn't stop, she would explode and die.

He spoke against her ear. "'Twill pass soon, Tabitha."

Tabby didn't think the torment would ever pass. She wept against what felt like wet grass, grateful that his arms were around her.

"Will she survive?" Macleod asked, sounding worried. He didn't release her.

"Aye. If ye let me touch her, I can heal her quickly enough."

The golden Highlander could heal her. Tabby somehow moaned.

Tabby felt strong but gentle hands on her and great warmth began seeping into her, through her. She continued to cry, but started to realize that the pain had become tolerable. In fact, her broken body began to throb with the force of a headache. She was no longer crying. She dared to try to take a breath and it felt like a miracle when she could breathe deeply.

More warmth filled her, a powerful healing light. "Take yer time, lass," the golden Highlander said softly.

"Ye can take yer hands off her now," Macleod said.

The pain vanished. Tabby opened her eyes and saw the brightest, bluest wildflower she had ever seen, inches from her nose. She inhaled and the most amazing, freshest scent of earth, grass, flowers and pine filled her nostrils, so strong it could have been a perfume. Then she identified the tang of the sea. Her mind clicked into high gear. *She was in the Highlands.*

No, she was in the medieval *Highlands...because Macleod had brought her back with him.*

Tabby slowly sat up. Macleod steadied her, but she didn't look at him. The tall golden Highlander stood behind them, and her gaze veered past him, too. *She was in medieval Scotland. Oh, my God.*

As dark as ebony, Blayde was situated above them on a

stark hill, its walls and towers butting up against the sky and the sea.

And it was familiar. *She knew Blayde.*

The headache began. The fortress changed, flames shooting from the parapets, the towers, the ramparts. Men, women and children were shouting, screaming, crying. An inferno blazed and she saw Macleod as that skinny fourteen-year-old boy, stumbling down the hill, away from it.

Tabby inhaled and blinked. Blayde became a dark shadow on the hilltop again, silhouetted against the Highland skies. Nothing should be familiar, not Blayde as it was just then or as it had been in 1201, when it had been razed to the ground, but it was.

She inhaled again, shocked at the fragrance of the summer afternoon. She could smell every blade of grass, every petal of gorse, every pine needle and cone, every wildflower. But then, there was no pollution in 1298.

And the afternoon was filled with birdsong. Dozens of different types of birds were chirping, and she heard the buzzing of insects, too.

A rasping sound made her turn her head and she saw a magnificent young buck, rubbing his immature antlers on a tree. There was no noise pollution here, either, she thought. Being in historic Scotland would be incredible—under other circumstances.

She trembled and turned, meeting Macleod's gaze. "So you brought me back to 1298."

"Aye," Macleod replied, his gaze holding hers. "With MacNeil's help."

Now Tabby recalled every moment they'd spent at the Met. She trembled with anger, getting to her feet. She had said no. She had told him that she would *not* go back in time with him. But he hadn't listened. Of course not.

She looked at Macleod's chest. Now he was an incredibly incongruous sight, in his sweater and jeans, standing in front of a castle in thirteenth-century Scotland. The blood on his sweater had already dried, perhaps from the speed of time travel. The sweater was torn from where the bullet had struck him. "Are you hurt?" she asked tersely. She thought she knew the answer.

He shook his head, his expression a bit wary. "MacNeil healed me, too."

"Good." With that established, she saw red. *She did not want to be there! He had ignored her completely.* Her hand lashed out, as hard as she could, and she struck him across the face.

His eyes widened as the slap resonated like the crack of a whip in the quiet afternoon.

"How dare you!" she cried, shaking with fury. "I was very clear. I said in plain English that I would not go back in time with you!"

He rubbed his jaw. "'Tis the second time that ye've hit me."

"So what?" A part of her was shocked that she had struck him again. But mostly, she was so angry she didn't care—even though the ground seemed to shift a bit beneath her feet. "Oh, wait! You're a savage brute so now you'll beat me for my sins? Because that's what big macho medieval jerks do to their women, right?"

The ground moved violently beneath them. "'Tis nay safe in yer time."

"Like it's safe here?" she shouted. She simply didn't care that his temper was igniting.

"I dinna wish to leave ye behind to fight the deamhan ghost alone," he snapped.

"And that makes you my hero? I don't think so!" He darkened. A wind kicked up. "I am not a piece of baggage, to be shipped here or there at your whim! I am a modern woman, and modern women control their choices, their lives, their

Fates. Damn it, Macleod, I do not want to be here. I do not belong here. Send me back."

He folded his massive arms across his huge chest and glowered steadily at her. "Nay."

That single word, spoken in an uncompromising tone, was like ice water. She did not speak, panting and breathless, staring at him. He had abducted her and he wasn't going to send her back. She saw it in his eyes and in every set line of his face. It was unacceptable.

But maybe this was what she deserved for going to bed with him! She'd known all along that doing so was *wrong,* that it was like opening a Pandora's box.

She turned to the golden Highlander. Tabby knew she should take a few deep breaths and find her inherent good manners, but she said abruptly, "In my time, men are imprisoned for what you did. It's a felony and we call it kidnapping."

The golden Highlander looked as guilty as a twelve-year-old boy caught red-handed with the neighbor's pretty daughter. "I'm very sorry, lass," he said softly. "But Macleod needs ye fer a bit. An' no one decides their own Fate."

Tabby really looked at him. She remained very angry, but she did notice that MacNeil was drop-dead gorgeous and massively built. Like Macleod, he had the powerful body of a warrior-knight. But she didn't care. "Who are you? The dispenser of wisdom? An oracle, a seer—a Gypsy fortune-teller?"

"I ken ye're very angry. I dinna blame ye, lass." And as he sent her one of the most disarming and seductive smiles she'd ever received, Tabby became slightly less angry. His mouth curved with good humor. "Sometimes, when the gods allow it, I see a great many things."

She became still. He meant it—he had wisdom that came from the gods. Macleod couldn't leap, but this man could. "Are you a Master?"

"Aye." He shrugged nonchalantly. "I am very pleased to meet ye, Tabitha Rose. I knew yer grandmother, once."

Tabby gasped. "Are you kidding?"

His beautiful smile vanished. "Sara was a powerful woman, an' ye remind me of her greatly. I wouldna jest."

She inhaled. Her grandmother had time-traveled. It was mind-blowing. "Do you know why I'm here? Do you know why my spell to bring Macleod to me in New York worked?"

"But ye ken the answers, Lady Tabitha. Macleod needs ye an' ye need him."

Tabby started and glanced at Macleod, who was grim. He'd rescued her at school and had been at her side during the ghost's attack, but she refused to admit that she needed protection from him. But she thought about that boy again, and the older man who'd suffered in the fires of An Tùir-Tara. "I don't think he'll need me until 1550," she said. "Which begs the question, am I in the right time?"

MacNeil smiled. "I dinna claim to keep all wisdom, lass, just some of it."

Tabby looked at Macleod, who was staring at her. She felt his sharp interest. She was going to have to forget about his needing her in another two-hundred-and-fifty years. She had better stay in the here and now—which was 1298, with a super-macho, supermedieval protector she didn't want and was mad as all hell at. And he certainly didn't need her now—except, maybe, for sex.

Both men looked at her.

She instantly had the awful feeling they were reading her mind, and she blushed. "Don't you dare invade my thoughts now! And I am speaking to the both of you!"

She saw on Macleod's face that he'd been lurking. It was the slightest glint in his eyes that gave him away. "I canna comprehend a single word ye speak otherwise."

"Great!" she cried. "How perfect is that—we don't even share a language!"

He made a sound of disgust. "We share many languages," he snapped. "Tonight I'll show ye how many!"

"Do not bring up last night," she warned. "Tonight, we are having separate bedrooms."

For one instant, he seemed puzzled, and then he gave her an incredulous look.

He intended to continue their affair. Tabby felt the unbelievable ache in her midsection, at once hollow and intense. "You abducted me," she cried.

"I had but a moment to decide what to do," he shot back. "How many times must I say that I wish to keep ye safe?"

She trembled. Then Tabby looked at MacNeil, who seemed rather entertained. Her focus moved past both men, to the stark splendor of the castle set high above them. Why was it familiar? There was a reason for everything, although just then she hated admitting that. She was at Blayde in 1298. If that was meant to be, then her spell bringing Macleod to her hadn't backfired at all. But then why had it all begun at the Met? What was the role of An Tùir-Tara?

"If ye let yer anger go, ye might find yerself pleased to be here," MacNeil chided softly.

Tabby tore her attention from the castle. First Allie, then Brie and now her. "Why am I here?" she demanded.

"I told ye already. Ye need him and he needs ye."

She folded her arms tightly across her chest. "Have I been here before?"

"Never," MacNeil said.

Tabby was shocked. She'd expected him to say yes, and to possibly tell her she'd had a past life at Blayde in the thirteenth century. "Are you sure? Because everything is so familiar."

"I am very certain," MacNeil said. "The soul is a strange

entity. It moves an' feels in mysterious ways. I wouldna question yer feelings, Lady Tabitha."

Tabby was aghast. "If I haven't had a past life here, then my soul knows *nothing,* damn it." Was he suggesting her soul knew this place? That it knew Macleod?

MacNeil said softly, "Ye must play this out, Tabitha. I would never bring ye back if I dinna think it wise to do so."

You'll have to play this out, Tabby. First Sam, now MacNeil. Tabby stared grimly at MacNeil, whose eyes were kind, and then at Macleod, who was filled with tension. Too late, she thought about the fact that she'd promised her sister she wouldn't leave her. Not only had she done that, she hadn't said goodbye. Her heart sank. "MacNeil, is there any way I can convince you to send me back to New York?"

Macleod darkened. The wind caused the firs to whip about and the earth rumbled. "He'll do no such thing."

Tabby ignored him.

"Macleod isna as dark an' dangerous as ye think, lass, an' it will serve ye well to remember that," MacNeil said simply.

And Tabby knew he was about to vanish into time. "No, wait," she cried frantically.

MacNeil disappeared into the golden sunlight.

Tabby cried out in frustration, "You're both outlaws!"

"When will ye finish yer insults?"

Total comprehension began. They were alone. Not only that, she'd been hurling insults at him—not to mention that she'd hit him a second time. She was in thirteenth-century Scotland. Every medieval woman needed a man in order to survive in the Middle Ages. She knew that much.

She was stuck, really stuck. "I'm sorry."

His brows lifted. "Ye're nay sorry at *all.*"

"I want to go back and you can't take me and your partner in crime won't. I am pretty much a prisoner."

"Ye're my guest." He was harsh. "Let's go up to Blayde."

Suddenly Tabby balked. Tears came to her eyes. She swiped at them. She was not going to feel sorry for herself now and she was not going to become a weak, cowardly woman. She was a Rose. If Allie and Brie could survive a leap back in time, then she could manage this predicament.

Besides, if her Fate was helping Macleod, she was not going to be able to resist it or fight it. "You win."

Before he could respond to her sarcastic quip, she felt the ground move under her feet.

Tabby jerked, because she couldn't imagine how she'd set off Macleod's temper now, but he was listening to the afternoon. The ground continued to vibrate. Her mind slammed into gear. They were about to experience a landslide or an earthquake.

He took her arm. "Riders."

Tabby's alarm crested. A few riders could not make the ground shake. It was at least a fifteen-minute hike up to the safety of Blayde's stone walls.

Thunder filled the day.

Blayde's bells began ringing.

A shapeless mass appeared on the top of the ridge that was closest to them. Tabby squinted and saw the mass rippling, undoubtedly the movement of restless warhorses. Like a pale landslide, it began descending.

"Damn it," Tabby said. "That's an army, right? A medieval army?"

Macleod nodded.

CHAPTER TEN

THE ARMY HAD HALTED. Tabby could make out the horses and their riders, as well as three banners in the front ranks, which waved in dark, dangerous colors against the bright sky. Tabby inhaled. It appeared as if a few hundred medieval warriors were facing them. Her heart felt overloaded with fear. Had she landed in the middle of a war?

A lone horseman left the army and thundered toward them.

She stepped even closer to Macleod's big body, aware now that she was the only woman present among so many savage fighting men. The concept of human rights didn't even exist in this world. "Now what?"

"Ye can rest easy, Tabitha. 'Tis Ruari Dubh—a friend."

She was relieved, but barely. Treachery was the name of the game in medieval Scotland. "You are sure he's a friend?"

"Aye." Macleod put his fists on his hips and waited.

The posture was not reassuring. She was going to have to start trusting Macleod. This was his world, and he was most definitely a survivor. She intended to be a survivor, too. She had to get home to her sister and her life.

But an odd frisson swept her. She did not know why—it wasn't really alarm or unease, and she couldn't identify it.

A Highlander as massively built as Macleod halted his gray charger before them. Her eyes widened. He had tawny hair, a hard face, and wore mail over his leine and a gold cuff above one huge bicep. He was ridiculously good-looking, but he wore the same frighteningly ruthless expression she'd seen on Macleod and she knew that he was heartless.

Tabby was confused. She had the feeling that they'd met—which was impossible. Wasn't it?

But his power, which wafted out to her, seemed so familiar. And the gods felt closer, somehow.

"Who is that?" she whispered. Even as she spoke, the thought drifted through her mind that he was not just a Master, but a soldier of the gods.

"Black Royce," Macleod said.

Even the name was familiar, and her heart lurched with surprise.

"What happens, Ruari?" Macleod asked brusquely, stepping forward.

Ruari replied in Gaelic, his granite expression never changing. He gave her one brief dismissive glance. Clearly he was not taken aback by her modern clothes or Macleod's sweater and jeans. As he spoke, Tabby stared at him in growing excitement.

Her best friend in the world, Allie, was at Carrick in Morvern—but in the fifteenth century. Her soul mate was a Master named Royce. Shortly before Allie had vanished, Tabby had read the tarot cards for her. Royce had been a powerful golden warrior, a soldier of the gods—so much like this man.

Their conversation stopped. "Is he from Carrick?" she asked Macleod.

He gave her a piercing look. "Aye."

It was Allie's soul mate, it had to be. Surely she had recognized him because of that reading. But he hadn't even met Allie yet—and he wouldn't, not for more than a century.

Royce was now staring at her. Tabby realized he could undoubtedly read her every thought. She prayed he hadn't done so. Then he gave her a look which stripped away her every garment, as if appraising her body for his future use, and he whirled the gray and galloped back to his army.

"I'll kill him if he ever looks at ye again," Macleod said harshly.

Tabby's excitement vanished. She hadn't liked that utterly objective look. It had been the look of a man who only wished to use a woman's body—there had been nothing admiring about it. Allie was going to tame *that?*

"Who is Allie?" Macleod demanded.

"Allie is my friend. She's a Healer. And she's at Carrick Castle in 1436."

He was disbelieving. "With Ruari? I dinna think so."

Tabby decided not to argue. "What did he want?"

"I dinna wish ye to bother yerself with Highland politics."

"Macleod!" Her newfound temper blazed. "I am here against my will and you tell me not to bother with the lay of the land? I don't think so! Do you want to get along with me or not? I need to know what's going on. I have no intention of walking into the arms of your enemies by mistake."

He folded his arms across his chest. "Ye can hardly do so if ye dinna leave the safety of Blayde."

"So I am a prisoner."

"Ye debate like a man!"

Tabby started. "That's a compliment."

"To be called manly?" He shook his head and sighed. "I dinna wish fer ye to stay angry with me, Tabitha. Ye ken Melvaig belongs to my enemies. The laird of Melvaig has been caught stealin' my cattle. But he is in my tower now."

"That's it?" She was incredulous. Then she said softly, "What did Royce want?"

"The lady of Melvaig seeks revenge upon me. She has vowed it. Ruari came to warn me."

"Nice of him," Tabby said. But she did not like the way he was regarding her now. It sent a shiver up and then down her spine. "Okay, what is it? Have I grown a third ear *and* warts?"

"Tabitha," he said quietly. "She is a black witch."

The shiver became chills.

HE MUST NOT LET Tabitha war with the witch of Melvaig.

He entered his great hall, with Tabitha at his side. She was also grim, but for more reasons than what he'd just told her.

She hadn't liked the human bones she'd seen in the dry moat, bones left on purpose as a warning to his enemies not to dare try to breach Blayde's walls. She had skipped quickly over the trapdoors beneath the floors of the entry hall, as if afraid they might open, and he knew that she was aware that lethal objects lay below in the cellars, objects that would impale her if she fell. She had not liked how heavily armed his men were, neither the watch on the ramparts nor those coming and going in the barbican. She was very familiar with his time—apparently she had read many books on the subject of Scotland. He understood her interest. Her ancestors had come from Narne.

At least her anger had vanished. Now, she was anxious, thinking mostly about the black witch and the war of witches that would come in two-and-a-half centuries at An Tùir-Tara, but also worrying about just how violent his time was. She would never find out. She was the gentlest woman he had ever met, in spite of her temper and inclination to hit him, and he would keep her from all harm.

His most trusted warrior had met him before he and Tabitha were halfway across the inner ward. He gave Rob a look which told him to pause. He turned to Tabitha. "Do ye think ye can take a moment or so to rest?"

Her attention was on the hall, not him. It flew back to his face. "I doubt it."

"Ye're safe within Blayde's walls, Tabitha," he said. "My enemies willna attempt treachery here."

"Except that the lady of Melvaig has sworn revenge and the threat is serious enough that Royce thought he should warn you of it."

She was so clever. "Revenge is our daily bread," he said flatly.

"She's a witch. And either she's still around in 1550, or her progeny is. In any case, Macleod, if she's the witch we read about at the Met, then that means she wins all your wars now."

He stiffened. "If she decides to cast her black magic at me, I will go to Melvaig an' vanquish her."

"Maybe you'd better take your vows so you can count on your powers."

Now he was annoyed. She was becoming as opinionated as MacNeil on the subject of his vows. "I can choke her with my two hands—or take her head with my sword."

She paled.

He nodded at a serving maid and walked away from her, Rob hurrying to catch up.

She called after him. "What will you do now? Interrogate the cattle rustler?"

He did not look back. "My prisoner doesna concern ye."

"Tonight we're going to discuss the Geneva Convention," she said.

Tonight he was going to pleasure her as never before, and there would be no time for talk. He smiled slightly at the notion.

Let me help you.

He tensed, whirling, but she was walking away from him and she hadn't spoken. Why had he just recalled her soft, garbled tone, the voice he'd heard that day so long ago when he'd buried his family at sea, the voice he'd heard numerous times, in his dreams or after a long and difficult battle? It was strange.

She hadn't known him—and he wasn't even sure she'd been alive when he was fourteen years old—but somehow, she had reached out to him, from wherever she was, trying to comfort him.

He reminded himself to tell her that he did not need comfort, not from her or anyone. He never had, and he never would. He would also tell her to stop pitying that boy. In fact, she should stop thinking about him entirely.

"Guy, what manner of fashion do ye wear?"

Macleod looked at him. Very few men called him by his first name—he'd been named after his father's best French ally in a time of war—but Rob did so and he did not mind. They were too close, having fought side by side too often. More than once, Macleod had refused to let him die in a bloody battle and had summoned MacNeil to heal him. They had never spoken of Macleod's Destiny or lineage, but Macleod knew Rob had guessed who and what he truly was.

Many at Blayde feared him because they did not know the entire truth, but had heard of or seen his powers. He was aware that the gossip about him was fierce. Some even suspected that he belonged to the Brotherhood, but the existence of such holy warriors was also mere rumor. No one knew for certain, other than those like himself. But Rob suspected the truth.

"'Tis a fashion from a faraway land," he said. He could not tell Rob that he had been to the future.

"Those garments look uncomfortable, but the woman is very beautiful." Rob gave him an odd look. "She speaks back to you."

She certainly did. "She is verra brave."

"What land does she come from?"

"A city called New York. 'Tis across the ocean. Their women are different, Rob—they try to live like men."

Rob laughed. "No woman can live like a man."

He happened to agree. "She is clever, though, an' she is a witch."

Rob started. "Then 'tis a stroke of good fortune ye have her here, to use her in yer war with Melvaig."

He shook his head. "She willna war with us. I willna allow it. I met Ruari on the hill. He told me that he happened upon Coinneach as he tried to steal three cows." They started up the narrow staircase, Rob behind him. "We both ken Coinneach dinna come to Blayde to steal cattle—he came to murder me."

"I dinna think he'll admit it," Rob said. "But the guards have heard him swearing revenge fer Alasdair."

Macleod pounded up the steps. "Let him try." His entire being became calm and focused—as it should, before confronting the enemy.

"He's brave," Rob said, behind him.

Rob would never dare suggest mercy, even if he might think about it. "He'll be an example to all who think to trespass on Blayde's land with foul intent." He reached the highest landing.

Rob joined him, his blue gaze searching. "Ye'll do what ye must," he finally said.

"Aye." The boy was a fool to come to Blayde alone, seeking vengeance, but Macleod would have done the same.

One of his men was standing guard in front of the closed tower door. The guard stepped aside and Macleod pushed inside the square room, his hard eyes moving to the boy.

Coinneach MacDougall was shackled to the wall by one ankle. His eyes blazed with hatred. He spit toward Macleod's boots.

Macleod paused, hands on his hips, unmoved by the foolish act of defiance. "Ye think yer spit will bother me?"

"My spit shows ye I think of ye as I do a small, worthless bug."

"Do ye think it wise to taunt me?"

"Murderer!" The boy's blue eyes were brilliant in his pale face. "Heartless murderin' swine!"

And Macleod envisioned the boy he'd once been, kneeling on the beach, watching the funeral galleys drifting away. The memory was acute and intense. What was this?

For not only could he recall the moment in utter detail, he suddenly felt a flash of hatred, a flash of rage, of grief.

Let me help you.

He whirled, but Tabitha did not stand in the doorway.

"Are ye ill?" Rob asked.

He shook his head, turning grimly back to Coinneach now. That boy had become a man overnight. Coinneach was sixteen, and he had become the MacDougall.

Let me help you.

Was she haunting him now from his own home? He quickly found his composure. "Aye, I murdered yer father, an' his father, an' his father afore that. An', Coinneach? Ye'll be next."

Coinneach writhed against his shackles like a wild animal, filled with fury and desperation. "Go ahead, murder me, too! Lady Criosaidh will destroy ye with her powerful magic, an' my uncles will destroy Blayde! She has vowed it."

Criosaidh had undoubtedly already unleashed her spells, intent upon avenging the death of her husband. Over the years, he had avoided most of her spells with the help of MacNeil and an occasional god or goddess. She was powerful, but her spells could not reach him at Blayde, they never had yet.

He spoke coldly and quietly. "Let Criosaidh do as she wishes. Let yer uncles attempt to destroy Blayde. 'Twas foolish to come to Blayde to steal my cattle."

"I meant to put a dagger in yer black heart," Coinneach cried, "but ye were not here!"

Macleod had wanted a confession and now he had it. But there was no satisfaction. Instead, there was an odd confusion.

"Had I been here, ye'd already be dead an' rottin' in my moat with my blade in yer throat."

"Had ye been here," Coinneach said, "ye'd have the blade in yer black heart, an' yer head would be on a pike at Melvaig."

"Believe as ye will, fer it surely comforts ye," Macleod said.

Coinneach spit again.

Macleod was done. He had no interest in continuing the pitiful debate. The boy would die, as soon as he commanded it. Criosaidh would cast her spells; his uncles would launch their armies. Nothing was new, nothing would change.

Let me help you.

He glanced at the doorway again but Tabitha did not stand there. Was she trying to interfere with his prisoner?

"Yer day will come soon," Coinneach shouted, twisting against the shackles. "If not by my hand, then by another."

"Yer father should have taught ye tact an' diplomacy. But ye're nay a coward like he was, I will admit to that."

Coinneach cried out, struggling to rush forward, as if believing he could pull the shackle from the wall.

Suddenly Macleod felt a touch of regret. Not for what he must do, but for provoking the boy as he had. But it was the truth—Coinneach's father had been a coward and the boy knew it—he had watched. Suddenly Macleod realized he had something in common with the MacDougall boy. He'd helplessly watched his father being murdered, too.

He was uncomfortable, and he did not like it. "Ye'll break yer leg," he said flatly.

Panting, Coinneach subsided, sliding to his knees. "I'll kill ye," he cried. "I swear, I will find a way!"

He refused to compare himself to Coinneach another time. "Put him in the stocks in the bailey so all my people can see the Fate of thieves and those who think to murder me. He'll have no food, no water…an' we'll see how long he lives."

SHE TURNED TO WATCH Macleod vanish into a dark stairway. Tabby decided she had enough to worry about without getting involved in Blayde's business. He'd undoubtedly taken many prisoners over the course of his long lifetime and this one had only rustled cattle. The lady of Melvaig was a witch. She could barely adjust to that startling and ominous piece of information. If An Tùir-Tara had resulted from a war of witches, did it mean that the current MacDougall lady would be one of the witches in the battle two hundred years from now? There were spells for longevity, although Tabby had never found one or known anyone who had used one. But hadn't MacNeil said he'd known Grandma Sara? She'd been ancient when she passed. She and Sam had assumed she was about a hundred years old, but now Tabby was uncertain.

Her head was hurting again. To survive, she needed Macleod. If she was not mistaken, she was cruising along just as Fate had planned. Tabby grimaced. She did not want to ever decipher MacNeil's comment about souls.

The serving maid tugged on her sleeve but Tabby wanted to look around. "One moment," she said, smiling at her.

Macleod had left, but Tabby felt him everywhere. Now that she was resigned to having gone back in time, she could not believe how she'd shouted and vented at him, much less hit him. She'd angered him—of that, there'd been no mistake. She was lucky, she decided, that for some reason, he hadn't hit her back.

It crossed her mind that maybe he wasn't as brutal as she'd assumed. Or at least, he hadn't been brutal with her, not yet.

She intended to keep it that way. No more un-Tabby-like temper tantrums. Tabby gave the great hall a cursory glance and nodded at the maid. "Let's go."

They crossed the room. It was barely furnished, with a massive fireplace, and exactly as one would imagine a medieval great room to look like. The ceilings were high and timbers crisscrossed them. There were rushes on the floor.

The history books were all wrong, she thought as they left. The chamber was clean. Dogs were not present. The rushes were fresh and smelled great.

Tabby paused before starting up another spiral staircase. The huge room should have felt cold and uninviting, but it seemed almost welcoming. She didn't mind it being so spartan, not at all—frankly, it suited Macleod. And suddenly she saw herself curling up in one of the two chairs before the hearth with the Book of Roses.

She cried out.

What on earth did that fantasy signify? She was never going to sit before that fire and work on her spells! The only place she would do that was at home. And she didn't have the Book there, anyway.

Real dismay began. The Book was always in a Rose woman's keeping—always. It was her responsibility, and it was at home, with Sam. If she needed a new spell, she might be screwed. But hopefully, she'd be at home before that ever happened.

She followed the maid upstairs, uneasy, thinking about the black witch of Melvaig.

A moment later she was on Blayde's third and uppermost floor. Facing her was an open tower room. She saw stairs that went to the ramparts, where the watch were. The maid went to the only door on the landing and showed her into a large bed-chamber.

It was Macleod's. As it had in the hall, his power and presence filled the chamber. Here, his mark was so strong it made her feel faint, stirring her body pleasantly. Tabby looked at the fireplace briefly as the maid knelt before it. Then she looked at the bed. It was heavily carved, the wood almost black.

A dozen embroidered pillows were piled up against the ebony headboard, and red and blue wool blankets, a fur and a red-and-black plaid were at its carved foot. Ralph Lauren would love this bed, she thought. It could be in one of his showrooms.

Now that their terrific argument was done, her body was starting to make demands on her. She hadn't forgiven him for treating her like baggage—and she wasn't going to, either. So she had to rein in that sudden and intense wave of desire.

She looked past a rustic table and two carved chairs set against the wall beneath a pair of shuttered embrasures. Because it was a beautiful summer day, the shutters were open, revealing an expanse of sparkling sapphire-blue sea. She walked over to the narrow window. The sea below was so large she assumed she was looking at a part of the Atlantic Ocean. It was a view no one could ever tire of.

She reminded herself not to get too comfortable. Her new plan was to stay at Blayde for a few days and gather information on Melvaig and its witch.

She looked at the bed. When Macleod apologized to her—with sincerity—and made it clear that he understood the error of his ways, she'd join him there. Otherwise, it was hands off. A major principle was at stake.

The maid was having trouble lighting the fire. Tabby told herself to focus. The first order of business was to put a protective spell on the bedchamber. She could not possibly sleep there otherwise, not with a witch a few miles away at Melvaig. But it was very cold inside the room. Tabby closed her eyes and focused on the wood.

Fire obey me, fire burn. Fire obey me, warm the room.

Tabby spent a few minutes casting the spell, and she opened her eyes. The maid turned, sending Tabby a helpless look. Then she said something and left.

Not even an ember glowed, and Tabby sighed. She'd been

able to stop that guard's gun from working, but she couldn't get the wood to burn. However, her protective spells were habitual. She walked over to the bed, sat down there and closed her eyes. *"Good over this chamber, good around it. Good everywhere, barring dark intent. Circle formed, protecting us."*

Her focus sharpened. She intensified her desire, until it tingled through her flesh and bones, chanting the spell again and again. Perspiration began. When she thought it likely she'd finally succeeded, she sat back in the bed, drained.

Tabby started.

A small fire was burning in the hearth.

Had she started it? She murmured, *"Fire obey me, fire burn. Fire obey me, warm the room."*

The fire danced merrily, but it did not blaze.

Suddenly one of the open shutters slammed against the wall.

Tabby sat bolt upright. It was a still summer day. How would a sudden gust of wind cause it to lift away from the wall where it rested and then slam down?

The shutter slammed on the wall again.

It was entirely unnatural. As a terrible comprehension arose, another shutter slammed against the wall, too. So did the next shutter and the next one, as if someone was walking from shutter to shutter, lifting each from the wall and banging it down.

Hatred and malevolence surged closer—the same hatred and malevolence she'd encountered in her loft. *It had come back.*

And then the fear and shock vanished. Calm slipped over her. She did not take her eyes from the windows, where she could feel the evil lurking. *"Evil get out, evil be gone. Protection spells of mine keep you far from here."*

The shutters all began slamming on the wall at once in a fit of fury and hatred.

Tabby was aware of the open bedroom door. It was tempting

to leave. Instead, she started to repeat the spell, her eyes on the door, and it slammed closed. *"Evil get out, evil be gone. Protection spells of mine keep you far from here."*

But she wasn't a fool. Tabby went to the door and seized the handle but the door didn't budge. Fear surged again. She willed it away. *"Evil get out, evil be gone. Protection spells of mine keep you far from here."* She used all of her strength to pull on the door.

It suddenly opened.

She hurried from the room, chanting the spell. An ice-cold blast of air struck her with a huge force from behind, coming not from the chamber but the tower or the window at the end of the hall. She stumbled, stunned.

The ice-cold air pummeled her from behind.

"Tabitha!"

Tabby fell, hard, to the floor. She heard his heavy booted steps as he ran up the stairs and she tried to get up, but the icy blast was pushing her down. She looked up, and saw Macleod, still in his jeans, his face a mask of rage. Silver energy blazed from his hands. "A Thabitha!" he roared.

Tabby heard stone shearing, and as it crashed to the floor from the ceiling, the pressure pushing her increased. She strained against it. *"Evil get out, evil be gone,"* she cried.

She thought she heard laughter.

Macleod cursed. Tabby looked at him and saw his power blazing, while more stone sheared off the walls from the tower. He was trying to blast the energy coming in from the window, but clearly, his power was meant for a far more physical entity. If she didn't send the evil away, it would break her back.

"Evil get out...evil be gone."

The vicious hatred pushed at her so hard Tabby thought it had finally snapped her bones. As viciously, Tabby fought back with her magic. And as she did, the terrible pressure suddenly vanished. Tabby cried out, gasping in relief, getting to her hands and knees.

Macleod knelt, his huge hands stunningly gentle, and he pulled her into his arms. "Are ye hurt?"

Tabby slowly sat up, amazed that she wasn't broken, and she leaned against him, meeting his wide blue eyes. Shock vanished and she looked toward the end of the corridor, where an open window embrasure and the stairs to the ramparts were. She began to tremble. "Macleod. It followed us here from New York."

CHAPTER ELEVEN

New York City
December 9, 2008

HER PAGER WOKE HER UP.

Sam was a light sleeper. She shot upright, looked at the pager and dialed Nick. As his cell rang, she realized she'd had less than two hours of sleep and she cursed. Why in hell was Nick bothering her in the middle of the day?

"Where's your sister?" Nick demanded.

"Hey, good morning to you, too." Sam was instantly uneasy. "I assume she's out and about."

"You helping her keep secrets, Rose?" Nick sounded pissed.

Sam could not read minds, but she didn't have to. Nick knew all about Macleod. She was certain. "What's up? Because I need my beauty sleep and I am a bitch when I don't get it."

"A really big man, who might be a magician—because he seemed to create lightning with his hands—robbed the Met."

Sam went still. "Shit."

"Oh, and another cop is dead. And a priceless friggin' necklace is gone. So where did you say your sister is?"

Holy shit, Sam thought. "I'll call you right back."

"Rose," Nick shouted, but Sam hung up. She jumped into her jeans and was pulling on a crewneck tee as she ran barefoot into the loft. She didn't even bother to call her sister's name, because she knew she was gone and so was Macleod. The loft was empty.

She breathed hard. There was no way Tabby had left the city and gone back in time without saying goodbye. She would never do such a thing. It sounded like Macleod had robbed the museum. If so, they'd probably walk through that door at any moment.

She breathed harder, shaking. She never trembled; she had nerves of steel. But now, she stared at the garbage bags taped across the living-room windows. Her cell rang.

She had it in her back pocket and she picked up. "I don't know where Tabby is. But, Nick, something tried to get in here last night. Tabby swears it was a demonic energy."

Nick was silent. "First some demonized kids, and then a demon ghost?"

Sam wet her lips. "Can a demonic ghost command subs?"

"How the hell would I know?"

"Gee, I don't know, you seem to know just about everything," Sam said, suddenly furious.

"Have you seen Macleod, damn it?"

"Yes," Sam gritted, "and I lied. Tabby asked me to keep it quiet, so I did. Fire me. Like I give a fuck." She realized she was choking, as if on the verge of tears.

Nick's tone softened. "I might suspend you, but I'm not firing you. Come into HCU so we can figure this out. And, kid? You'll hear from her."

Nick was being *kind*. Sam's rage knew no bounds. "She didn't leave—she's coming back!" She almost threw her cell across the room, but at the last moment, jammed it back in her pocket, instead.

The doorbell rang.

Sam was instantly wary. No one could get up without buzzing up from the exterior lobby first. She went to the door.

Halfway there, she felt evil—and recognized it. Her surprise vanished as she opened the door and stared at Kristin Lafarge.

Kristin smiled, holding a bag from a nearby French bakery in her hand. Her attention went to the garbage bags on the windows and back to Sam. "Hello. I hope I'm not disturbing you. I couldn't sleep last night because of what happened. I tried to call your sister this morning, but she didn't answer. I became worried. I thought I'd drop by on my way to school."

"It's noon."

"Vanderkirk told me I could take a half day. At first I refused, but this morning, I changed my mind. Is Tabby here?"

"Come on in," Sam said, smiling. But inside, she was ice-cold. This bitch was going to talk before she was allowed to leave and Sam did not intend to play nice. "Neighbor let you in?"

"Yes, the sweet elderly lady who lives on the second floor." Kristin set the small paper bag on the kitchen counter. "Is Tabby here? Is she all right?"

Mrs. Morris would never let anyone in whom she did not know. She'd been mesmerized by Kristin. "As you can see, we had a bit of an altercation last night—the good, old-fashioned, horror-movie kind."

Kristin sighed. "Sam, should we get to the point?"

"Oh, yeah," Sam said, licking her lips. "Why are you after my sister?"

"Payback is a bitch," Kristin said softly. Her eyes glowed and a dark wave resonated from her body. "Bitch get down, in so much pain."

Sam felt a knife go through her stomach. She gasped, "I should have known—a witch from hell." She flung her power at her.

Kristin was struck so hard she slammed against the kitchen counter.

Although her stomach still hurt, enough that she was afraid she might be bleeding, Sam smiled. "You can't mess with a Rose." She struck her again and Kristin cried out, going down to her knees. Then Sam advanced. "What has Tabby ever done to you?" she demanded, standing over her. "Why are you hunting her?"

Kristin closed her eyes and began chanting silently. Sam tensed, fully aware that Kristin was trying to cast a spell on her. She steeled herself against it. If Kristin was as powerful as her mother or grandmother had been, she might be toast. "Answer me, bitch!"

Kristin opened her eyes, which glowed eerily again, like incandescent opal. "Where is your sister, Sam?"

"She's at Blayde, in Scotland." Sam was horrified—she'd just told Kristin where her sister was!

Worse, she was confused. Suddenly she didn't know what she wanted from Kristin, or why she was filled with so much urgency. And the moment she became aware of her confusion, she knew she had been mesmerized.

She had to fight the spell. She hadn't told Kristin the year in which she could find Tabby.

"Is she there now, in the present? Or did she go into the past?" Kristin asked, approaching.

Sam struggled against the witch's hypnotic eyes, knowing she must not answer, but replied helplessly, "She's in the past."

"What year, exactly?"

"1298." Crap, Sam thought, as she spoke. Kristin had dark power and she was after Tabby, and Sam had just told her where to find her. But she'd get out of this spell and go back in time, somehow. She'd protect her sister, to hell with Macleod.

Kristin smiled and said, "Don't move, darling, not yet." She turned and went into the kitchen.

Sam felt as if she was caught up in an invisible vise. She

knew she had to act—she had to destroy Kristin—but her will would not obey her mind.

Kristin returned, holding a butcher knife. "Take the knife, Sam."

Sam knew what Kristin intended. *I am a Rose,* she thought, furious, and suddenly she lifted her hand and to her relief, her power blazed. The knife was struck from Kristin's hand.

"Bitch get down, in so much pain," Kristin hissed.

The invisible knife stabbed through her, but Sam strode forward, fighting the pain. Kristin paled and turned, rushing for the door. Sam picked up the knife, gasping in pain as she did so. Kristin murmured in a strange language Sam had heard before. Shocked, she held her abdomen with one hand, the knife in the other.

She was chanting in the ancient tongue of the demons.

Kristin seized the moment and ran out of the loft.

Sam breathed hard, slowly sliding down the wall to the floor, and eventually, the pain lessened. How did the witch know a language that only the oldest, most ancient demons still used?

"ARE YE HURT?" Macleod repeated, his gaze piercing.

Tabby inhaled and started to get up. He put his arm around her, helping her to her feet. "I'm fine." She was still shaken. He had been at her side in another crisis and she was glad. Of course, there was no way of knowing whether she would have been attacked again if she'd remained in New York, where she was supposed to be.

But it was hard to hold a grudge now. She smiled wanly. "You appeared in the nick of time."

"I was leavin' the tower an' I felt the evil, Tabitha." He was subdued, too. "It dinna follow *us.*"

Tabby felt her insides lurch with dread. "Okay, you may be right...*may* being the operative word."

"I *am* right. Do ye wish to sit down?"

His face had that hard warrior expression now, and she felt his impatience. He wanted to fight the evil spirit. She just knew it. "I'm okay. I feel a bit battered and I might even be bruised, but I'll live."

His face tightened impossibly. "Evil dared to breach my walls!" He erupted, and the walls shook. Small pieces of stone and mortar fell from the ceiling. Tabby ducked and Macleod pulled her close.

She looked up, instantly aware of him in every possible way. He was courageous, powerful, sexual and a gazillion-percent male. "I think you should control your anger—not that I blame you for it—so the whole wing of this castle doesn't come down on us."

He released her. "Aye."

"Macleod, I feel certain that evil came from New York. It was the same evil that came from the Met. It is the evil associated with An Tùir-Tara. But is there any chance I am wrong? Could it be the Melvaig witch, sending us a little present?"

"Criosaidh is a witch, Tabitha, but a mostly human one. There are rumors one of her grandfathers was a deamhan, but I dinna ken the truth. But she lives an' breathes as we do. She canna put herself into the air as evil." His expression changed. "Or I dinna think she can."

Tabby hugged herself. Now that the attack was over, the ramifications were suddenly sinking in—all of them very bad for her and Macleod.

"I'll protect ye."

She met his steady regard. "Why? Because we're sharing a bed?"

"Aye...an' ye're Innocent."

"But you've refused to take your vows."

His dark blue eyes glinted. "MacNeil has harped on me like

a shrew for almost a hundred years. Dinna start, Tabitha. Ye're Innocent and ye have power. I wish to protect ye an' I will."

"I have a news flash." Tabby grimaced. "Your power is meant to stop our flesh-and-blood enemies. You can't stop a spirit, apparently."

"But ye can."

"Maybe, but my powers are erratic!" Tabby cried, really worried now. "One day they will be strong, I think, but I can't depend on them. If we're counting on me, we're in trouble, Macleod!"

"Yer magic is stronger than ye believe." He left the hall and Tabby followed him into the bedchamber.

"We still don't know why a vanquished demon would hunt me," she finally said.

"Ye have enemies," he said flatly, staring down at the locked chest at the foot of the bed. His expression became thoughtful.

"As far as I know, my enemies are dead. Every time we've fought evil, we've vanquished it—otherwise, we'd be dead right now."

"But the evil has come back from the vanquished, aye?" He gave her a look over his shoulder and knelt, taking keys from his belt.

She suddenly recalled something he'd said to her—if he didn't kill his enemies, they would kill him. Maybe their worlds weren't as different as she'd believed. "Macleod, I don't think it got in here. It was at the embrasures, and really mad that it couldn't get in. But it pushed the door closed, sending its energy from the window." She sobered. She'd barely been able to open the door. And she had been afraid that the spirit would break her back.

Macleod darkened. "'Twas in the hall with ye, Tabitha, right there, outside this chamber door. I felt it strongly."

"I put a protective spell on the bedroom, but not the hall." Tabby shivered. "She hates me—or us."

He shifted to look at her. "She?"

"Remember the Met?" When he nodded, Tabby said, "My first visit there, I saw your mother's pendant and instantly felt a woman's dark evil. This spirit is a woman."

He stared. "Ghosts dinna haunt the past, they haunt the future."

He was right. It was one thing for a ghost of any kind to haunt her in 2008, coming from 1550. But this ghost had gone *backward* in time. Slowly, she said, "Well, if we can time-travel, I guess it can, too." Then she added, "What are you doing?"

"Hold this," Macleod said, reaching into his jeans' pocket.

Tabby started as he handed her the amulet he'd stolen from the Met. It was ice-cold in her hand. "I forgot about this entirely."

He gave her a look and unlocked the chest.

Tabby felt her tension soar as she realized what he was doing. He had told her that he'd left his pendant in a chest at Blayde. But she had the same pendant in her hand, and she didn't know what to expect. There couldn't be two of a single object, could there?

She wet her lips. Time travel changed everything. If she traveled back to the future, but to a few days before she'd ever met Macleod, what would she find? Would she encounter a slightly younger version of herself? Would she come face-to-face with herself? Was it even possible? "I need the Book," Tabby said suddenly. "Every Wisdom you can think of is in that Book. I've never been without it, not in my entire life." She became uneasy. "The Book is always guarded by a powerful Rose witch. My grandmother left it to me. I don't know if I can manage without it."

His glance was steady. "The Masters live by many rules, Tabitha. Over the years, I have learned a few of their laws. 'Tis forbidden fer a Master to leap forward or backward an' encounter his self in another time. 'Tis one of the most sacred parts of the Code."

"Why?" Tabby asked with some dread.

"I dinna ken, but the consequences are dire—or so I have been told."

Tabby looked at the pendant in her palm. The moonstone was flat and lifeless. "This has lost its power. It had magic, Macleod, but it's gone."

He had heard her but he didn't respond. He reached into the open chest and, to Tabby's shock, produced the identical pendant. Even though he held it, she instantly felt its warmth and power, its protective magic. The entire talisman glowed. She looked more closely; the moonstone was as bright and alive as a star.

Suddenly she cried out, dropping the pendant she held. It had become so cold it had burned her hand. Incredulous, she looked at the patch of frostbite on her palm. Then she saw the pendant on the stone floor, turning into white-gold dust…and it was gone.

Macleod seized her hand. "Ye'll be fine. A wrapped rag with loch water will take the chill from yer hand."

"That was pure physics. One object cannot be in two different places at the same time."

He said, "Take my mother's amulet, Tabitha. I want ye to have it."

Tabby went still. "What?"

"Elasaid was a priestess an' a Healer. She had great white power—like ye do. She dinna cast spells, but her power an' faith made the Innocent strong. My father used to tell her she'd be lost without the amulet. She dinna deny it." Suddenly his face hardened and he looked away from her.

Tabby felt a surge of grief coming from him but as suddenly

as she had felt it, it was gone. She touched his bare arm. He still had pain deep within him, even ninety-seven years after the murders of his family, and that anguish had to be faced and released. Suddenly she wanted to help him, comfort him, as urgently and passionately as she had when she'd first glimpsed him at the Met. It felt like the most important thing in her life.

She was shocked by the powerful feeling.

"What happened to Elasaid, Macleod?" she asked softly.

He said, "Ye dinna ken? I have the amulet…she is lost."

Tabby started. He pulled away from her. He spoke dispassionately now, the way a curator might recite facts to a museum audience. "She died in a fire here at Blayde, an' her body was never found."

"I am so sorry," Tabby whispered. Suddenly she wondered if she'd been unfair to him from the first moment they'd met in her loft. She'd been judging him and condemning him incessantly. He was a product of his times, but he was a good man and he had suffered terribly in his life—and more suffering was to come.

"I want ye to have the pendant."

Their gazes locked. What did such a gesture mean? She could not fathom why he'd give her a family heirloom, especially a magical one. She did not delude herself by thinking that it had anything to do with their personal relationship. "Macleod, why? Why give it to me?"

"'Twill keep ye safe. It has power, Tabitha, power ye should have. An' with the pendant, ye'll never be lost."

Tabby shook her head. "I can't take it, Macleod. It's all you have left of her."

His face darkened. "Tabitha, I dinna think ye ken how grave the attack was."

She didn't like the sound of it. "No, I do. She almost broke my back."

He said softly, "She dinna wait fer the night."

THE GREAT HALL WAS FILLED with Macleod's men and their women, the evening meal concluding. Voices were raised in mild debate, laughter, song and conversation. The hounds had been let in and they were scrounging for leftovers, but they were big, beautiful dogs, and they only added to the unusual warmth of the medieval scene. Tabby sat alone at the table, near its head, where Macleod had been seated while they were eating. She had been starving, but she'd eaten rapidly and mindlessly, too upset to enjoy the wild salmon.

She was exhausted. She was worried about Sam, and about what was going to happen later that night—and she was not thinking about sex, she was thinking about evil. At least it couldn't get into the bedchamber, even if it could slam a shutter and keep the door closed.

Demons only came out to rape, murder and maim at night. But this vanquished demonic spirit had attacked her in broad daylight.

She felt sick. Okay, she was afraid. That thing could appear at any moment, at any time, in the broad light of day. She would have to be on guard now all the time—there was no respite.

Tabby was sipping red wine and staring at Macleod. She couldn't help herself. He had turned into her anchor, in a way. If she had to be back in the past, in this kind of predicament, then she was sort of glad he was with her. It was sure better than being alone when the thing came back.

Macleod stood before the fire with several of his men, and firelight emphasized his sculpted features and impossibly muscular body. He'd changed his clothes and was dressed in his leine and his red-and-black plaid—which she had learned was called a brat—and he had come to dinner fully armed. But he was smiling and pleasantly relaxed, a mug of ale in his hand, apparently enjoying being with his friends. It was as if an evil ghost hadn't just assaulted her inside his home—or assaulted them last night in her New York City loft.

Would any battle of any kind ever unsettle him? Tabby didn't think so.

Tabby knew that he knew she was staring. He hadn't looked her way since leaving her at the table, but she knew it. Stories seemed to be exchanged. The conversation was in Gael, so Tabby only caught the occasional word. The men gathered around him were eager for his company and attention. He was well liked, even admired, and he was certainly respected, she thought grimly.

She didn't particularly like his arrogant attitude, but there was no denying that she admired him once in a while and she certainly respected him.

She was trying to be calm, composed and objective about him and her circumstances, but her elevated blood pressure was a dead giveaway that nothing was normal now. She didn't want to be in the Middle Ages, but there she was. She didn't want to be Macleod's current meaningless affair, but she'd already been there and done that—and her hot, aching body was so insistent she was almost certain she wasn't going to be able to send him away that night, even if he thought her chattel. She did not want to go home and find her life devoid of passion, returning to her existence as perfect, proper Tabby. But she had a terrible inkling that would be the end result of her jaunt to historic Scotland.

If she survived that hateful woman's ghost.

It was too bad he was so good-looking. It was even worse that she knew every inch of his powerful body. Thinking about that made her flush everywhere.

He suddenly approached, his stare direct and penetrating. Tabby inhaled. She knew what he wanted. It was time to stand her ground.

There was a principle at stake. He had to understand that he was not her owner or even her boss. He did not have authority over her. Tabby got to her feet, her blood roaring. How was she going to resist him? She didn't want to resist him, not now. Only a very foolish woman would sleep alone when her other option was a night with Macleod.

"Damn it," she said as he came up to her. "This is still wrong. It's frankly insane."

His mouth curved in amusement. "Pleasure is natural, Tabitha, an' I canna stop thinkin' about pleasuring ye."

Her insides vanished. Every private inch of her quivered violently. "You do that on purpose," she accused softly, pressing her palm to his chest to hold him back. Touching him only made her light-headed.

"Aye, I do." He had a lazy light in his eyes now, one promising all kinds of sensual delights. It was too damn sexy.

Tabby realized her mouth was watering. "I am worried about my sister," she said, somewhat desperately.

He started.

"Macleod, I've been here maybe eight or nine hours. But is it eight or nine hours later in New York in 2008? Or is it days later, weeks later, months later? How does time travel work? Is it the parallel continuum that some say it is? Is Sam a wreck because I've been gone all day, or by now, have years passed, without her having heard a word from me? I have to go back. I can't just vanish from her life forever."

If she had vanished without a trace, she knew her sister would never quit searching for her. Sam would find a way to track her down—or die trying.

"Tabitha, I hardly have the answers ye seek, except I swear I will make certain ye see yer sister again."

His words cut through the terrific sexual tension sizzling between them. Did he think she would stay in medieval Scotland forever? Because that was not even a remote possibility. "You mean that I will see Sam again because in a few days I am going home."

He laid his large hand on the small of her back, fingers splayed low. He pressed her forward, ahead of him. "I said what I mean."

Tabby inhaled, his touch causing her to tighten. "I am not chattel," she said, starting for the stairs. He did not remove his hand and, dazed, she didn't really want him to.

"Aye, ye're nay chattel. Ye're my guest," he murmured.

His sexy tone washed through her. How could he set her body on fire so easily? "Guests leave when they wish to."

"'Tisna safe fer ye to leave, so why argue?" He laid his other hand on her waist as they moved into the narrow spiral staircase.

Tabby felt her mind start to go blank. Both of his hands held her hips now. She knew how strong he was and she sensed he wasn't going to let go of her, not anytime soon. "We will finish this discussion tomorrow," she said thickly. Arguing now, when her body was raging, making it hard to think clearly, was ridiculous.

He suddenly halted her in her tracks and his mouth moved to her neck. He pulled her backward, toward him, and Tabby went still, her heart slamming, as his huge erection burned against her skirt, over her buttocks. They were halfway up the spiral staircase, which was too narrow to accommodate anyone else, and eerily lit with rush lights. "What are you doing?" she gasped—the stupidest question of her life.

He wrapped her hard in his arms from behind, throbbing heavily against her. "I dinna wish to wait."

They were on a public staircase. She wanted to protest—didn't she?

He growled and wrapped his huge arms tightly around her, holding her for one moment so she could not move. In that moment, she felt that entire solid length, escaping the tunic, pulsing urgently against her buttocks, over her skirt. She felt his thundering heartbeat, his savage excitement. *She could not stand it.*

He lifted her skirt and that heavy length butted hard against her bare thighs. He ripped her bikini apart, sliding his fingers over her wet, throbbing flesh. Tabby cried out, pressing her face to the stone wall. Tabby felt him coming, massive and slick, and he embedded himself in her.

She gasped, vibrating in pleasure, wrapped in his arms. He moved his mouth against her neck repeatedly, small, hard kisses, while he thrust, again and again, hard and determined. She went over the brink, pleasure becoming rapture. He laughed and then groaned loudly, joining her. He slid his hands lower. He held her there, murmuring to her. His excitement seemed to merge with hers and became unbearable. Tabby wept his name.

HE COLDLY LIFTED his sword as Alasdair cowered on the ground on all fours, begging for his life. But he didn't hear him. Instead, he glanced at the river below. Coinneach was there, running hard toward them, screaming, "No!"

He started, as Coinneach came rushing up the hill, filled with fury, desperate to save his father. But he could not stop what must be. Macleod sent his power blazing at him and Coinneach fell.

He lifted his sword, glancing at Alasdair, who was trembling at his feet.

"No!" Coinneach screamed, struggling to get to his feet. Macleod blasted him lightly again. This time he was annoyed.

The MacDougall boy went down, writhing wildly. Macleod almost felt sorry for him. Then he froze, incredulous, because the tall, blond boy writhing on the ground changed. Suddenly he was dark-haired and twisting in absolute futility against a deamhan's embrace. He fought furiously, desperately, as

Blayde's halls rang with screams and sabers, as wood dropped away from the ceilings, falling to the ground, ablaze.

"Nay! Father!"

Macleod wanted to step back, away... Where was Alasdair?

But he couldn't move, he could only watch himself—an impotent struggling boy. And William looked up as the two Frenchmen began stabbing him repeatedly in the back....

The boy screamed and screamed and screamed.

Macleod awoke abruptly. He was breathing hard, and for one moment, he smelled the fires consuming Blayde's great room. He was in shock. He had been dreaming of the boy prisoner, Coinneach—and the boy had turned into him.

Coinneach had been helpless to prevent his father's murder.

He had been helpless to prevent William's murder, too.

The rage took him by surprise. It suffused him and the entire bedchamber shuddered. And with it came so much hatred, not for his enemies but for that damned fourteen-year-old boy!

That boy had failed everyone!

Her hand covered his clenched fist.

He jerked, aware of Tabitha for the first time, as she lay in bed beside him, their bodies touching. Her golden eyes were wide, warm and concerned.

Let me help you.

He knew he was recalling that long-ago voice. He jerked free of her, sliding from the bed.

"Are you all right?"

"I am fine," he lied, too late realizing that he was covered with sweat and trembling. *Damn that stupid boy. He had failed....*

Tabitha sat up, holding the covers over her chest. "That must have been a nightmare."

The room was still shuddering. He took a deep breath. "I dinna ken. I dinna recall."

"Do you want to talk about it?" she asked softly.

He paced to the fire. *Let me help you.* He whirled. "Are ye usin' yer magic on me now, Tabitha?"

She tensed with alarm. "No, I'm not."

Perhaps her soul was familiar with his. Too much was strange in this world, and he did not dismiss the idea. "I dinna need help."

Her eyes widened. "Okay," she said carefully, pulling her knees up to her chest. "But you do seem upset. Are you sure you don't remember that dream?"

"Women dream," he snapped. "Men dinna bother to do so!"

"That is such bull," she said as softly.

He whipped his brat from the chair and wrapped it around his waist. Coinneach was bothering him, he decided. Maybe he should be hanged tonight to end this insanity instantly.

"Why are you angry?"

He trembled. The shutters rattled. "I said I dinna need yer help."

She was silent for a while, and he was relieved. He poured two goblets of wine. When he handed hers to her, her golden gaze played over his features, lingering on his eyes, searching there. "I can imagine you're dreaming of war and death," she said. "This is such a violent time. You've probably lived through hell, many, many times."

He actually spilled wine on the sheets as he jerked away. "War doesna bother me."

"I can't believe that. War is horrible. Nobody likes war."

He faced her now. "The Highlands would be better without war."

She smiled just a little at him. "But war doesn't frighten you, does it?"

He almost smiled because, finally, he was somewhat amused. "I fear naught, Tabitha."

"Everyone fears something."

He drained the wine, feeling better, the disturbing dream receding now. "I fear women who speak too much."

She gave him a look. "You're afraid to share your nightmare with me."

He tensed, dismayed. The dream he'd just had returned full force. So did the pain, the despair, the rage—and now, the guilt. "'Tis nay fear."

"Really?" She smiled skeptically at him. "I think you cannot control your dreams—and that must be a bit frightening, to a big, bad, macho man like you."

He twisted and writhed and the deamhan laughed, urging him to watch his own father's death. Helpless, he screamed....

"Ye need to stop," he shouted at her.

She sat up straighter.

He fought for composure. It eluded him. "Aye, I had a dream—a nightmare, as ye say. 'Tis done."

She wet her lips. "I keep seeing that fourteen-year-old boy—you were dreaming about him."

He was disbelieving. "That boy is gone, Tabitha, an' I am sorry ye keep thinkin' about him. Mayhap he needed yer help that day. But ye werena there—except as a spirit or an apparition. He chased the intruders away. He buried the dead. He did what he had to do." He spoke so harshly and swiftly that he couldn't breathe.

"I think that boy lost more than his family that day," she said softly, sadness in her eyes. "It sounds like he lost his childhood—that overnight, he became a man."

"Leave the boy alone!" he roared.

And he thought of Coinneach again.

He thought of Coinneach's cowardly father, who had died begging for his life. He thought of Coinneach's fear and bravery. He suddenly imagined the boy's head on his pike and his face changed—he saw his own head there.

Tabitha stood up, taking a cover with her. "Maybe you're too tough and macho for me to help, but damn it, I want to help that boy."

He whirled, irate as never before. "Then ye'll have to use yer magic to go back to 1201, aye?"

She shook her head, paling.

He became wary as never before. "Tabitha?"

"I think that boy is here, now, standing right in front of me."

It took him a moment to understand her. And when he did, his rage erupted and the timbers above their heads started cracking. Stone fell from the ceiling but Tabitha stood as still as a statue. He did not move, either. "That boy isna here, Tabitha. That boy is dead!"

She cried out.

"Ye leave him buried, buried at sea with the rest o' them. God damn ye!" He stormed from the room.

CHAPTER TWELVE

TABBY OPENED HER EYES. It took her an instant to comprehend why the ceiling above was dark stone and wood rafters, instead of white plaster.

Slowly she sat up in Macleod's bed. His power wafted from the sheets and filled the bedchamber.

She tensed, hugging her knees to her chest. It had been almost impossible to fall asleep after he'd left her in that rage. His anger was so obviously a disguise for his pain, and it went deep. She would never forget him shouting at her that the boy was dead. She shuddered. What a terrible and tragic thing to say.

He remained a complicated and medieval stranger, but indifference toward him was impossible. He had done some things she would not condone, but he had protected her several times and made love to her as if the earth was ending. Now, she understood that he had never gotten over the massacre that had taken his family in 1201.

How could she not be filled with compassion for him? No matter how often she thought about Angel or being taken into the past against her will, she could not stop herself from wanting to soothe him and help him. Most ordinary children would be traumatized by witnessing the murders of their family. As extraordinary as he was, it was clear now that Macleod was no different.

She hadn't ever suffered as he had. Although her mother had been murdered by demons in a pleasure crime, she'd been at ballet lessons when it had happened. It was Sam who had witnessed the violent murder. Like Macleod, her sister had refused to ever speak about it.

Was that why she was with him in 1298? Was she supposed to help him deal with that tragedy? Maybe it didn't matter, because Tabby couldn't leave it alone. She knew that intimacy was a terrible idea for them, and her compassion was a form of intimacy, as was the sex. But she was here and she intended to help, no matter how he might roar and rage at her—no matter how it might connect them further. She was compelled.

When he'd stormed out of the bedchamber, he'd been furious with her. She hoped he'd calmed down since then and decided to try to be a bit more subtle the next time she pried into his past. But there would be a next time. Now, though, she realized it would be hard to get him to open up. Men didn't discuss their feelings in the thirteenth century. She'd probably made him really uncomfortable.

A knock sounded lightly on her door. Tabby called out for the housemaid to enter. A young, pretty redhead came bustling in, crying out because the room was so cold. Immediately she knelt before the hearth, trying to start the fire.

Tabby stared out of the closest window. The shutters had been opened and it was a gray morning, heavy with clouds, indicating rain. The bedchamber had been cold last night, when Macleod had risen from the bed.

The maid jabbed the fire again, but the flames seemed ready to go out. Tabby looked at the fire, threw her mind into the task at hand, and murmured, *"Fire obey me, fire return. Fire obey me, warm the room."*

The maid looked at her, her eyes wide with surprise. Behind her, the fire burst into flames, and the maid jumped to her feet.

Tabby pulled the covers chin-high. "Good morning." There was no answer. "Do you speak English?"

"Aye, my lady…a bit."

Tabby smiled. "Thank you for the fire. It's so cold in here."

The maid stared. "Are ye a witch?"

Tabby knew just about everything there was to know about the history of witches and witchcraft. The great witch hunts of Europe would not begin until the middle of the sixteenth century. No one was burned or hanged for sorcery in this time. "A little magic can be useful," she hedged.

The maid smiled. "Can ye help me with yer magic?"

Tabby laughed. "Do you need a love spell?"

"Aye, I do. I'm Peigi," she added. Her brows lifted. "Ye're still in the Macleod's bed, so ye dinna need a love spell—or maybe ye put one on him."

Tabby tried to decipher that comment. "I have never tried to cast a love spell. Why wouldn't I be in his bed this morning?" She slid from the bed, seizing the red-and-black plaid at the foot.

"No woman has ever stayed the entire night with the Macleod," Peigi said.

Tabby thought she'd misheard. After all, he was over a hundred years old and he'd had lots of women. The thought was too disturbing, so Tabby said quickly, "What did you just say?"

Peigi repeated herself.

Tabby stared in surprise. "That makes no sense," she stammered. Ridiculously, she was somewhat pleased.

"The women he takes to bed are too afraid o' him to stay the night. 'Tis why he's never married, I think. They would have to be dragged to the altar, kickin' and screamin'."

Abruptly Tabby sat down. Macleod had never married. That was highly unusual in this time period. "That's terrible," she said softly. "Women use him for sex and then hurry away?"

"Aye, as far as they can get and as swiftly."

"I don't think he's that bad. Does he beat them?"

Peigi started. "He canna beat a dog, lady, so how could he beat a woman?"

She had laid a colorful bundle on a chair. "He told me to find ye garments." She shook out a dark blue velvet gown.

Tabby blinked at the beautiful velvet dress. Clothing her was a necessity, she reminded herself. But his sending her a gown felt terribly intimate, as if they were really lovers.

"'Twas his mother's." Peigi gave her a sly look. "Ye're the first woman to stay in his bed till sunrise, an' now he gives ye such a costly gift. Bein' as ye did not cast a love spell, ye must have truly pleased him."

Tabby was incredulous. "I don't think that's a gift."

"He willna want it back. I ken his lordship well. He's pleased with ye, but he'll never say so."

Tabby swallowed. She didn't want Macleod to be pleased with her—to start feeling some form of medieval macho affection for her. Did she? He might never let her go home if he cared for her. But he wasn't capable of that kind of relationship, was he?

And she didn't want to become fond of him, not in any way—she simply wanted to help him out. Disaster and Destiny had brought them together, not rational choice. Her choice of lover would be an intellectual from the twenty-first century.

She fingered the dress, certain it was a necessity, not a gift. But this was costly medieval finery, not the clothes worn by every other woman she'd thus far seen. The sleeves were long, bell-shaped and would trail to the floor, a sign of great wealth, and the cuffs, hem and neckline were embroidered in gold thread. It was a truly beautiful dress, and incredibly refined for the period.

Tabby fought her soft spot for well-made, elegant and beautiful clothes. She didn't want to like the dress.

"This might be getting too complicated," she muttered.

"I beg yer pardon?"

First desire, then compassion, and now a really nice dress. "Nothing. The gown is lovely."

Peigi smiled. "Mayhap he put a love spell on ye, lady."

She was surprised, but she felt her cheeks warm. "Peigi, I am not in love. I do not go for big brutes who wear swords to dinner—and they're not even dress swords! However, I owe Macleod for his protection, and I am a bit worried about him. Do you know about the massacre that took his family?"

Peigi sat beside her. "O' course I do. Everyone knows. His father was a great man who had made peace with the MacDougalls after a hundred years of war. There was a great day and night of celebration. But when the Macleod clan was asleep, they opened Blayde's doors to mercenaries. The family was murdered afore his very eyes. Fifty-eight kin died that day. He fought wildly, they say, but what could a single boy do? He was only fourteen years old when he became the Macleod."

Tabby closed her eyes, and the instant she did so, she saw that boy wildly heaving a huge sword at violently fighting men, hacking at their legs and hips, tears and blood mingling on his face. He was screaming incoherently, a combination of rage and grief—she could hear him! She could hear the ringing swords, the shouts.

She shivered. Had she just seen into the window of time? Had she just seen Macleod as a boy, in the midst of the massacre?

In the previous incidents, she hadn't heard a single sound. But each time she'd seen him as a boy, his image had become clearer, his emotions had felt stronger and more tangible. And now, she'd heard all of those terrible battle sounds.

"Lady, are ye ill? Ye're as white as a sheet."

Tabby trembled, suddenly sickened, perhaps from his grief

and despair. But maybe it was because she had just seen unbelievable violence and brutality. Blood had been running across the floor like a high tide. She was filled with anguish for that boy. It had been even worse than he'd let on—or than she had imagined.

"I'm just a bit dizzy," she said.

What fourteen-year-old boy could survive that massacre and ever have a normal life? He'd become laird that day. "Peigi, did he really become chief of this clan after the massacre, or did someone else run things? Was he laird in name only?" She heard the tremor in her voice.

Peigi was surprised. "He was laird, lady, in every possible way. The Macleod went to war against the MacDougalls that very spring. He led his armies even though he was a boy—an' he led them to victory." She was proud. "Our bards still sing of his revenge."

No wonder he was so cold and ruthless. Then she regarded Peigi, who didn't seem to think anything of the fact that her laird looked all of twenty-five years old although he had to be one hundred years and counting. "I feel very sorry for him."

Peigi stood, surprised. "Why would ye feel sorry fer the Macleod? He's a powerful man, with land and titles, an' he's not the first to lose family here in the Highlands." Peigi shrugged. "'Twas a long time ago. In the Highlands, ye must never trust yer friend—or yer foes. Can I help you dress?"

Tabby was thoughtful as she declined. He had lived through hell. She would always despise such a brutal and violent life, and the way he lived would always frighten and repulse her. But he belonged in the Middle Ages; he was a part of the culture, the times. It was time to stop judging him according to her modern standards. That was simply unfair.

But he obviously needed her help. Now, she knew why she was at Blayde.

THE MOMENT TABBY WENT downstairs she knew that Macleod was still angry with her. He stood at the trestle table with ten men, not speaking, as a debate of some kind raged. Maps covered the table. It almost looked as if they were plotting a war. Macleod stared at her while his men argued. He did not smile.

Tabby sighed and crossed the room. Couldn't he let bygones be bygones? She was ready for a truce. But of course, she had an agenda. She had been governed by the need to help others her entire life, and realizing that she was there to help him made her feel like herself again. It even felt good. It certainly felt right.

He strode to her, his gaze moving slowly down the blue velvet gown before lifting. "She gave ye a dress that was my mother's."

He hadn't known. She'd been right, it hadn't been a gift. "Good morning."

"Have ye enjoyed yer mornin' with Peigi?"

Tabby was dismayed. "Did you eavesdrop?"

"I dinna ken why I can hear ye from downstairs, across two chambers."

Great, she thought, becoming angry herself. "I'm not allowed to ask questions?"

"'Tis the past, Tabitha, but ye've decided I need yer help an' ye willna leave it alone."

She crossed her arms. "You do need help, Macleod. You are an angry man, and it's justifiable. But no one should have to live with so much anger or, worse, so much repressed grief and guilt." It suddenly crossed her mind that this was why he hadn't taken his vows—he was too scarred to do so.

"I dinna ken what ye speak of. I laid them all to rest and gave up mourning that verra day. The boy I was died that day, too."

She reached out to touch his cheek and he jerked away, eyes dark and angry. She said, "He fought as hard as he could."

Macleod started. "He did not die. He grew up to be the man standing before me—a determined and courageous warrior."

"He died that day," Macleod spit. "I became the Macleod that day—but Peigi already told ye so. Ye choose to harp on it. Dinna even think to press me on the subject of my vows!"

Wow, Tabby thought. Behind him, the fire roared in the hearth. None of his men seemed to mind. While she was a bit taken aback, she wasn't frightened. He would never hurt her, no matter how irate—she had no doubt now. "I have been judging you really unfairly."

"Ye feel sorry fer me!"

"Yes, I do." The fire briefly shot out of the hearth. Tabby ignored it, as she did the jumping chairs. "I am not giving you a pass on things you've done—like bringing me here against my express will—but I will never judge you again as I have been doing, Macleod. We're from different worlds. I understand why you live as you do."

His eyes shot to hers. He finally said, "Yer accusations have annoyed me. I dinna like bein' judged, not by ye or anyone. But—" he paused for emphasis "—I have given ye a pass, all o' the time, because I like havin' ye in my bed."

She flushed. "Did you have to ruin our conversation with that rude and sexist comment?"

"'Tis the truth. No woman likes an angry man." He was sneering. His face remained dark.

He wouldn't back down. He wanted to offend her. "I hate to tell you, but you don't frighten me and you can't offend me with sexual references." He stared. "Macleod, I am sorry. Can we start over? We have this odd tension, but maybe we can sort of be friends. I actually don't mind being here for a while, and we do have a common enemy which we need to dispatch."

His eyes widened. "We're lovers. Ye're my mistress."

She bit back a retort. Slowly, she corrected him. "In my time, very few women would like being called a mistress. It's pretty insulting."

"Aye, because women in yer time dinna want their men strong or to take care of them."

Tabby was going to dispute him, when she realized he was right. Women liked metro over macho and they were hell-bent on being independent. Which was positive, right?

He began to smile. "Ye're the most independent woman I have ever met. But I'll still take care of ye. I dinna need a friend, though I need a mistress."

She would never admit it, but it was almost tempting to accept having a big strong man to take care of her. Almost... "Think of me as your mistress if you will. But you need a friend, of that there is no doubt. I think I'm qualified. After all, I'm the first woman to spend the night and challenge you, right? I'm the first woman to stand up to your every angry stare and all those autocratic commands?"

He crossed his massive arms. "Ye challenge me to no end. Ye annoy me, Tabitha," he warned.

She smiled at him and it was genuine. The warmth unfurled in her chest. "Well, I guess that leaves you with one option—taking my head off." She started to stroll past him. "I thought I'd explore the grounds."

He was red-faced. "Ye're my guest. Ye can walk freely about Blayde." He turned away, then swung abruptly back. "Ye look French."

It took her a moment to realize what he meant. As he walked back to his men, she stared in surprise, recalling how he'd said that Frenchwomen were elegant, not her. But she'd been in a kid's dirty gym clothes. He liked her in the blue velvet dress. He thought her elegant. She'd thought herself sick and tired of that word. But she hadn't been elegant last night—and she was warming rapidly from his praise now.

Tabby smiled to herself as she walked out of the hall.

She was elegant *and* passionate. The good part of Tabby Rose was back; the bad, well, it seemed vanquished. She was warm and fuzzy inside her chest. She almost felt happy. Tabby told herself to slow down. If she wasn't very careful, she might start to care about him. She was firm with herself. Caring was not allowed. The only thing worse would be falling in love, and that would never happen. She could allow herself to feel some affection and friendship—and desire—but nothing more.

Outside, a drizzle had begun, but Peigi handed her a plaid as she went outside. Using it like a shawl, Tabby paused, breathing in the scent of the crisp morning. It was great. Then she hid a smile and headed for the stairs that led up to the ramparts. The view would be incredible from the crenellations.

She went up slowly, the stones slick and wet, starting to think about her sister. She and Sam had always had amazing telepathy. From the time they were toddlers, she would know what Sam was thinking and what she wanted, and it had been mutual. Even after they'd begun to speak, she'd been able to hear her thoughts when she wanted to. It wasn't unusual for Rose women, sisters or not, to be so in tune with one another.

If she focused, maybe she could let Sam know where she was and that she was all right. It was probably impossible, considering the gulf of centuries that separated them, but she intended to try.

And then she had to figure out how to gather information in medieval times. She wanted to research Melvaig and its witch. Peigi seemed in the loop, and Tabby would start with her.

She reached the ramparts. A big, handsome and young Highlander with dark hair smiled at her, but he was clearly just being friendly. Tabby felt certain that no one at Blayde would dare flirt with her, considering Macleod's temper and power. She walked to the edge and stared over the crenellations, then gasped at the sight of the steel-gray seas, frothing against the equally gray skies. It was stark and desolate but it was magnificent. This side of the fortress was perched on the edge of the cliffs, right over the ocean. Blayde was set in an unusual position, on an atoll of land with the Atlantic Ocean sweeping in from the north, facing the Western Isles. Melvaig lay somewhere to the south.

Tabby stared in that direction, dread slowly forming. It did not help that the sky in the south was black with storm clouds. She hesitated and almost thought she felt a finger of evil, beckoning to her. She shivered.

It began to rain.

The Highlander gestured at her, indicating that she should go back to the hall. Tabby smiled at him. "You're right." She turned, lifting the plaid to hold it over her head like a hood. That was when she saw the prisoner below.

For one moment, she stared. *Was that a man in stocks?*

It began to pour.

Her concern was instantaneous. The prisoner was on the far side of the bailey, almost behind the hall. It was hard to see clearly from this distance, but it appeared that a man was on his hands and knees, restrained by stocks. That was inhumane—it violated the Geneva Convention and her own personal code of ethics. Outrage began.

Tabby lifted her skirts and started to hurry toward the stairs. The Highlander seized her arm, shaking his head, and for one moment, she thought he was warning her not to go over to the prisoner. *"A'coiseachd."*

It took Tabby a moment to realize he was warning her to slow down. She tried to smile, realizing that he was right. Running would mean a certain fall. She went slowly down the stairs, which were dangerously slick. When she reached the ground, she lifted her skirts and ran.

She had been right. A man was in stocks. He was on his hands and knees, his neck locked in a vise made of wood, making it impossible for him to move. There were shackles on his wrists and ankles, as well. He looked at her, his eyes blazing with anger.

Tabby cried out, horrified. *He wasn't a man—he was a boy.*

He could not be more than fifteen or sixteen years old. She rushed to him and knelt. "Are you all right?"

His eyes widened. "Are ye English?"

She hesitated. "No." Her gaze flew over him. He was soaking wet and his face was bruised, but otherwise, he did not seem hurt. "Who did this to you?"

He laughed at her, the sound hard for such a young man. "The laird o' Blayde put me here, lady. Can ye help me? He means to leave me here until I die."

For one moment, Tabby refused to believe it. Macleod couldn't have done this. One of his men had done this. Then she turned off her rising dismay and the terrible comprehension she did not want to face, focusing on the boy. "Of course I'll help you. What's your name?"

"Coinneach MacDougall," he said flatly.

Her mind raced. The MacDougall laird had been rustling cattle—but surely this boy was not the laird. No one would put a boy in stocks and then leave him there until he died! But she already knew the answers she was going to get as she spoke. "Are you the laird?"

"Aye," he said, his face a mask of rage. "The day he murdered my father was the day I became laird!"

She couldn't breathe. "He murdered your father?"

"Before my verra eyes, as God is my witness!" He began to writhe against the stocks. "My da was on the ground, askin' fer his mercy, but he took his head and then flung it into the river!"

She was going to be violently ill, she thought, her stomach churning. "Stop, you'll hurt yourself. I am going to help you."

"Help me an' ye'll be next to die, no matter how pretty ye may be."

Tabby choked, staring into Coinneach's blue eyes. Coinneach stared back. Macleod had done this. He was violent and ruthless—cruel, even. She'd just been so happy and she'd just promised herself not to judge him. She understood him and wanted to help him, but this was inhumane. This was horrifying. It was unacceptable.

She had to fix this.

"Help me," the boy said, but he wasn't begging. He seemed determined. "Ye seem kind an' clever. Help me escape an' I'll repay ye handsomely—if ye live to receive the coin."

She fought for composure. The one thing she did know was that Macleod wouldn't murder her or put her in stocks. "Of course I will help you. You will be freed or I will die trying." She had never meant anything more. She was a Rose, and this was what Rose women did—they gave selflessly to others.

Tabby stood. "I'll be right back," she promised.

The hall was warm, the fire blazing, a truly obscene contrast to the wet cold outside. The men remained, still arguing over the maps on the table. Macleod turned and stared, unsmiling and wary.

He knew. He was in her mind, reading her thoughts, as he always did.

She halted, holding her head high.

He approached her, his face set. "Ye said ye willna judge me anymore."

She wet her lips. "There's a boy in stocks. One of your men must have put him there. He needs to be released before he catches pneumonia and dies." She prayed he would be surprised.

A moment passed, but it felt unendurable, until he spoke. "I put him there."

"He's a *boy!*"

"He's my enemy."

She trembled, disbelieving. "What has he done to you? And do not tell me that this is how you punish a cattle thief!"

Macleod hesitated, grim, eyes ablaze. The hall was absolutely still. "He lives... He breathes..."

Tabby cried out, the reality too much to bear. "Did you murder his father while he watched? Did you behead him and toss his head away?"

Macleod darkened.

She choked, sick at heart. She had spent last night in this man's arms. She had decided to heal him, save him from himself, but it was the rest of the world that needed to be saved—from him.

But hadn't she known that they were worlds apart? Hadn't she known that he was ruthless, a barbarian—and that she should not sleep with him? Her life was about giving. His was about taking. He was selfish. He had no interest in serving the gods or the Innocent. He served Blayde. And this was how he did so, by mercilessly sentencing a young boy to death.

"Cease yer judgments," he warned.

Tabby closed her eyes for a second. She had promised herself she wouldn't judge him. But she had never been so outraged. She was going to have to break that promise. "He's a boy. You're supposed to serve the gods and save the Innocent. Instead, you murder his father in the name of some stupid clan war? And I don't care that his last name is MacDougall!"

"But I care, Tabitha. He is my enemy," Macleod said harshly. "'Tis my duty to destroy him."

"No, he is Innocent. It's your duty to protect him!" she shouted.

"Dinna dare interfere," he warned. He whirled away, effectively dismissing her.

In the back of her mind, Tabby knew that she should be really careful now, because his temper was still in check—nothing was shaking or falling down. She sensed that meant something, but she could not stop. She ran after him and seized his arm, causing him to face her. "If you care for me at all, if you are really the grandson of a god, if your mother was truly a priestess and a Healer, you will let him go. I am *begging* you to let him go."

He stiffened, incredulous. "Dinna dare mention Elasaid!"

She inhaled. "She would tell you what I'm telling you!"

He shook visibly. The floor seemed to tilt. Then the absolute stillness came again. "No mistress tells a laird what to do." With that, he walked away from her.

His condescension actually hurt. Tabby began to shake uncontrollably. She had deluded herself into thinking that they had more of a relationship other than a sexual one. She had deluded herself into thinking that he needed her in any way, outside the bedroom. And he didn't care about her, not at all. "He is Innocent." He did not look back at her. "No Innocent should die and especially not by your hand."

Tabby became aware now of the silence in the hall. Every pair of eyes was upon her except for Macleod, who had his back to her and had joined his men at the table. It was hard to think. She wasn't just horrified and appalled, she was so hurt, too. "I don't know you at all."

Macleod pointed at a map and Rob said something. Macleod responded with a brief shake of his head.

The interfering mistress had been dismissed. Macleod was going to let the boy die. Clearly, he had no heart. She had to stop this, no matter what it took. "Macleod!" she cried sharply.

He didn't even look at her. He said something to Rob in Gaelic.

"If you do this, we are done," Tabby said loudly. As she spoke she heard her pulse roaring in her ears. It was deafening.

He slowly turned, a chilling smile beginning. "Ye threaten me?"

Her heart began to break, and too late, she wondered if she'd already fallen for him. "No." She could barely get the words out. "I am telling you."

His eyes widened and the men at the table shifted uneasily. "I decide, Tabitha, when we are done."

A frisson of fear went through her. "I can't let you do this," she heard herself say. She whirled, heading for the front doors.

"Stay away from him," Macleod ordered.

Tabby stiffened her spine and went out into the rain.

HE KNEW WHAT JAN wanted even before his intercom buzzed. He could feel Sam outside his office, seething with anger, with impatience.

"Nick? Can you see Sam? She seems a little...disturbed." Jan was wry.

Nick grimaced. Sam was more than disturbed; she was ready to blow a gasket. "Send her in. And, Jan? Go easy on her, okay?"

Jan made a sound that meant *never.*

He was used to their deep dislike for each other, but no man could expect two of the sexiest women on the earth to get along, especially when they were intent on being rivals, although only God knew why. They might look as different as night and day, but they had more in common than not. Sam looked as tough as nails, while Jan resembled a sex kitten, Marilyn Monroe style. Sam screwed around; Jan had decided she'd mourn her deceased partner until she died. Jan had been one of his best field agents, a long time ago, and Sam was one of the best now. If they could ever stop disliking one another, he'd love to put them in the field together.

It was a fantasy.

He rubbed his temples, knowing he was overworked if his fantasy was about putting those two out in the field and not in his bed. Sam strode in, flushed.

His eyes widened as he felt her pain, most of which was emotional. "She's gone?"

Sam breathed hard and slammed down into the chair facing him. "Not only is she gone into the past without a word—Lafarge paid me a call." She touched her gut. "She's a witch, Nick. A powerful one."

"What happened?"

"She put a spell on me and I told her where to find Tabby. Oh, I forgot. She's after my sister—and it's some kind of payback."

He had never seen Sam so out of control. "Cool it, kid. I don't want to find you laid out on a slab, covered in white."

"I am friggin' worried!"

No kidding, he thought. Jan poked her beautiful face inside, a file in her hands. "I have something for you, Nick."

Sam turned in the chair, her eyes shooting daggers. "Nick is busy."

"He'll want to see this," Jan said, her expression going from warm to cold in less than a nanosecond.

"Can you two sheathe the claws?" Nick waved Jan over.

Sam ignored her and said, "What if Lafarge can time-travel?"

Nick took the file from Jan. "Can I assume this is about Lafarge?"

Jan smiled. "You sure can. Unfortunately, it's generic."

And that meant it was as authentic as a cubic zircon. Nick opened the file and said to Sam, "Your average witch can't time-travel." He looked up. "We'll have that DNA comp back by this evening." He'd ordered a comp as well as the standard test. If she was one-ten-thousandth something inhuman, he wanted to know. A small genetic dose of demon, beast or "other" wouldn't show up on a standard DNA test.

"She isn't average. I also think she's really, really old," Sam said. She stood, hands on her hips. "I need to ask you something. Can I have a moment?"

He already knew what she wanted. He said casually, "If you think I'll let you go back in time, the answer is no."

Sam cried out, "Why the hell not?"

With inimitable timing, Kit poked her head into the door. "Can I bother you guys for a minute? I found something on An Tùir-Tara that is really interesting."

Nick gestured her in. "Join the party."

Kit entered, casting a worried glance at Sam. "You'll want to hear this. I found this quote in a first edition from Oxford University Press. The pub date was 1922. It's only one reference to An Tùir-Tara, but I will try to back it up." She had memorized the sentence. "The great rivalry between the ladies of Melvaig *and Blayde* ended that day in the fires."

Sam stared, paling. "I knew it. I knew she was there." She faced Nick. "Tabby is a gentle soul. She abhors violence. She is going to have a really hard time adjusting to life in the Middle Ages. I have to go back and help her through this—and I have to protect her from Lafarge. She doesn't even know Lafarge is out to destroy her."

She was too involved. "You're not going back. And that is final."

"Nick, this is really important to me."

Nick closed the file. He stared at Sam. "Rose, we both know your sister will be just fine. We both know she had to go back sooner or later. You're not going back—but I am."

Sam jerked. "Without me?"

He sighed, because she was spitting fire, and turned to look at Jan. Jan started. Instantly understanding, her eyes widened.

"I am not going back with you," she said flatly. "Never again!"

"You're taking *her?*" Sam cried. "Are you kidding?"

"Don't worry," Jan said. "I am *not* a field agent." She walked out.

He was sorry she was upset, but she'd have to get over it, because his mind was made up. "I'm going after Lafarge," he said. "But I'll check in on your sister while I'm at it."

"I don't believe this." Sam strode out.

Kit hesitated. "I'm more than happy to do the dirty and go down under."

He gave her a scornful look. "You're a rookie, you haven't finished your PST, goodbye."

Kit kept her face impassive but he saw the disappointment in her eyes, and she left his office.

He got up and went to the door. Jan was on the phone and she ignored him. He felt her distress.

He decided to remind her that they weren't going back to the days of the Roman Empire, and that in the Middle Ages, torture did not include crucifixion.

She lifted her green eyes. "I am not going back… It's a miracle you and Sam made it home in one piece and you know it. Forget about going back, Nick. Forget Lafarge."

"You know I don't give a rat's ass about Lafarge," he said easily. "But I can feel that she's the lead to the real bad boys. You can start packing."

She stared furiously, trembling.

"At least you won't need lipstick," he said.

"Damn you to hell!"

He thought about the flashbacks and didn't bother to tell her he might already be there.

CHAPTER THIRTEEN

As ABRUPTLY AS IT had begun, the rain had slowed to a mist.

Tabby didn't notice. She stumbled outside, the ground in the bailey now muddy, clutching the plaid like a hood to her head. A pair of dogs rushed over to her, tails wagging, but she ignored them. A knifelike pain was going through her breast, and it felt suspiciously like heartbreak. But that was impossible. *Macleod was going to execute that boy—unless she stopped him.*

He was horrible, cruel, heartless and terribly violent…and she had justified and rationalized it so she could have a torrid affair and live with herself afterward. Well, she couldn't live with herself now.

She had to save Coinneach. It wasn't an option; it was her priority. She had no right to this acute sense of loss. She was not suffering; Coinneach was suffering.

She paused, still unable to get enough air to adequately breathe. But it felt as if she had lost so much—her lover, and maybe the new, passionate and unbridled Tabby Rose.

Well, that was just tough luck, she told herself harshly.

She did not want to think about Macleod saving her and the children, or defending her from the ghost. She did not want to think about his rare smile, or the way he looked at her, once in a while, during lovemaking, when his eyes changed and almost softened. Instead, she reminded herself to think about their arguments. The truth was, she had lost a lover and a partner in war, but not a friend. She had no right to feel upset for herself. It was Coinneach she must focus all of her attention on now.

But Macleod was suffering, too.

Tabby tensed. She did not want to think about how he had fought as hard as he could to save his family during the massacre. She did not want to remind herself about how he had grieved and raged while burying them at sea, a boy suddenly required to become a man.

Tabby sank down onto a small wood bench. She began to tremble, overcome with despair. She could no more turn off her compassion for him than she could send herself back to New York. She hated what he'd been through, the grief he kept repressed inside himself. But so what? Coinneach was going to be murdered by his command if she didn't do something.

Maybe she wasn't at Blayde in 1298 to heal Macleod after all. Maybe she was there to save an Innocent. Or maybe, just maybe, she was meant to do both.

She felt the morning still.

How could the man who made love to her so passionately, who looked at her with so much concern, who was determined to risk his life for her, be one and the same with the man she'd just argued with in the hall?

How could he insist on protecting her, but intend to execute Coinneach the way he'd beheaded Angel—without blinking an eye, without a drop of remorse?

The answer was simple. That cruel, violent side was a direct result of his having survived the massacre.

She sat up even straighter. Macleod was the product of the most extreme and arbitrary injustice and violence. And that was exactly what he was meting out.

I can't hate him, she thought grimly.

Coinneach had to be saved, but Macleod had to be saved, too.

As Tabby sat there in the mist, a soft warmth flooded her. She jerked, glancing around. "Grandma?"

Her grandmother's reassuring and powerful presence was so strong and comforting that Tabby expected her to materialize before her. But she did not appear. It didn't matter. Tabby knew she was smiling.

And that meant she had reached the right conclusions. "Thank you," she whispered. "Would you mind staying around for a while? I am feeling a bit lost and lonely."

Of course there was no answer.

"Lady, come in out of the rain," Peigi said softly.

Tabby turned, realizing Peigi had heard her talking to her grandmother's spirit. Her expression was one of pity. It was hard to believe that only an hour or so ago, she and Peigi had been joking about her having cast a love spell. It was surreal. The stakes had dramatically changed.

She realized she was not ready to confront Macleod again. In fact, considering she was preparing to blatantly defy him, avoiding him was a really good idea. He could read her mind, after all.

"Ye'll catch yer death," Peigi warned.

She glanced across the compound. "No, that boy will catch *his* death."

"Aye, he'll die, but thieves must be punished. We dinna have enough cattle to feed all o' Blayde, lady," Peigi tried. "The Macleod canna allow thieves to go free. He must set an example."

Tabby stared. Peigi did not find this punishment unusual or excessive. It was a bit of a slap in the face. She was a modern woman, applying her standards to a very different world. She might be the only one at Blayde sympathetic to Coinneach, she realized.

She suddenly wished she could convince Macleod that her

values were right. But she had no doubt that he could not be transformed into a man with modern sensibilities.

"Ye canna question the Macleod, lady. Besides, ye ken the boy came here to murder him."

"Oh, I can question Macleod, and I will." Tabby stood up. She was back to her earlier position, she realized. "That boy will die because his ancestors betrayed Macleod's father. Do you really think that's right, Peigi?"

"'Tis our way. Here, yer brat's soakin'." Peigi handed her another wool plaid, her expression grim. "Please come inside."

"I think it best to avoid Macleod. He's angry, and I am determined to stop him from executing Coinneach."

Peigi paled. "I'd prefer the blood feud to be put to rest, lady, but I would never cross the Macleod. Ye shouldna do so, either."

Tabby simply looked at her.

"He'll never forgive ye if ye go against him," Peigi warned.

In that instant, she knew that Peigi was right. Macleod was not the kind of man to forgive betrayal. He would see her defection as sheer treachery.

Peigi left.

But that was okay, because they weren't friends—she was his ex-mistress. Tabby felt a new tension arise. She hoped Macleod would remain so angry with her that he would not even think about trying to entice her to bed. She was not up to that battle. Worse, she didn't want to recall being in his arms. It was a dangerous idea.

Shaken all over again with the enormity of what was at stake, Tabby hurried across the bailey. Coinneach remained in the stocks, soaking wet now. His face was riveted on her as she approached. She took off the dry brat, wrapping it over his thin body. "We have to keep you warm."

"I told ye he wouldna free me." He was bitter.

He was so young to hate. "This isn't over yet," she said. "I will help you. I won't let you die."

Coinneach appeared satisfied. "Then ye'll have to be very clever. Otherwise Macleod will discover ye and put ye in the stocks next to mine."

Her first thought was that he would never do such a thing. But how on earth could she know what he would do to her? As far as she was concerned, their affair was over. He might be ruthless toward her now, as well.

"Who has the keys to the stocks?" she finally asked.

"Macleod."

She would have to steal the keys, somehow. "Does he wear them on his belt with his other keys?"

Coinneach nodded. "Afore his men see ye here, can ye bring me water?"

Tabby started, dismayed. "When did you last drink or eat?"

"It's been a full day, lady. The well is over there."

Of course he hadn't been fed or given water, she thought. Macleod meant for him to suffer and die.

Tabby went to the well, managed to lower a pail, and when it was full, she lugged it back to him.

As he drank, she stared at the hall, the mist becoming so fine now that the air was damp. Blayde loomed, glistening darkly against the heavy gray skies. Macleod wore the keys on his belt, and he only took off his belt when he undressed before sleep— or rather, he only undressed to make love to her. She was almost certain he slept in his clothes otherwise. A lover could so easily retrieve those keys after he was satiated from lovemaking and had fallen asleep. But that was out of the question. She didn't know how she was going to get those keys off Macleod's belt, but she would. "I am going to free you," she said.

"How will ye get the keys?"

"I don't know. I have to think about it."

She tried to imagine herself sneaking into his bedchamber while he slept, and removing the keys from his belt. Her sleeping spell was a good one; she had used it a lot with Randall, before their divorce, to keep him away from her. But Macleod was very powerful and she did not know how susceptible he would be to any of her spells, even one she was adept at casting. On the other hand, she'd cast a spell on him across centuries, and it had worked. She was going to have to take a chance and try it on him. There was no other choice.

She was also going to have to find a way to block him from her mind. Otherwise, her efforts to free Coinneach would be in vain—he would know her every move.

She was resigned. Her shock over finding a boy in stocks, left there to slowly die, had dissipated. Resolve had arisen instead. But she did not like going up against such a powerful opponent. And that was what he was.

It all sank in. She was very much alone in the thirteenth century, and the man who had brought her there was her adversary now.

SHE HAD SAID SHE wouldn't judge him anymore. But she was judging him now.

And she meant to free Coinneach.

He was furious and disbelieving.

He did not know of any Highlander who would ever let a woman betray him. Even a disloyal mistress must suffer the consequences of her actions. Such a mistress would be summarily punished and then exiled—or worse. Neither man nor woman could be allowed to set the precedent of unpunished betrayal.

Listening to her plot and plan against him, Macleod paced his great hall, having sent all of his men away. He remained incredulous.

He did not want to go to war against her. He had brought her back in time to protect her—and of course, to share his bed.

What was he supposed to do now?

Macleod paused before the hearth, staring into the flames but not seeing them. He could not believe he had asked himself such a question. He was a decisive man, and he had two choices. Stop her or punish her.

He recalled her striking him, not once, but twice. Not only had he not hit her back, it hadn't even crossed his mind to do so. He did not want to ever put his hands upon her in an act of violence. He had no desire to hurt her.

If she crossed him this way, he would have no choice but to punish her. It did not matter that Tabitha was no ordinary mistress. She was from a future time, one so very different from his own time that he could barely comprehend it. And he was not thinking of horseless automobiles and underground tunnels and subways; he was not thinking of museums filled with history. He was thinking about women who lived alone, without men to protect them. These modern women provided for themselves, thought for themselves, obeyed no one but their government, and were proud of it.

Tabitha was just such a woman. She was soft and gentle, kind and caring, more so than almost any woman he knew—but these were traits a woman was expected to have. He liked that womanly side of her. But he also liked her courage, determination and independence. In fact, he admired her greatly.

But he still hated her judgments, accusations and condemnations.

His head began to ache, an unfamiliar sensation. His mind was going round and round uselessly. If she became his enemy, he would have to deal with her as he did all of his enemies—ruthlessly, without mercy. But how could he do that to the woman he wanted in his bed?

He already knew he cared about her Fate; otherwise, he would have left her behind in New York City, an easy prey for the evil hunting her. Now, he started to wonder if he cared about her. He had never had any concern for a woman before, not in any way. They had come and gone quickly, a parade of nameless women sharing his bed. But Tabitha had a name, her own thoughts and feelings, and she had grave concerns for him as well as for others. He wasn't sure what to make of this newfound discovery that he might be fond of her.

But she wasn't fond of him. Women did not betray the men they cared for.

Could she really betray him?

It almost *hurt* to think that she could.

Someone touched his shoulder. He was so deeply in thought, he hadn't heard his approach. He flinched and met Rob's intent gaze. "Ye let her speak against ye."

He stiffened. "'Tis her way."

"The men are whisperin' she has ye bewitched."

His tension soared. "They dinna ken the truth about her."

"They ken ye want her so badly, ye let her rant an' rave without respect or discipline."

Rob was right.

"Will ye let her betray ye, as well?"

"Of course not," he snapped. But he felt uncertain—and he was never uncertain.

"A woman should make a man strong, not weak." Rob walked away.

He was incredulous again. Rob thought him weak? But if he let her plot against him, if he did not punish her, then he was very weak, indeed—and Blayde would eventually fall victim to his enemies.

He had to end this before she did the unthinkable.

His mind was made up. He strode to the front doors and flung them open. She was still trying to put her magic on him. She hoped to block him from her thoughts. Every time he felt her magic pressing on him, pulling him into its vortex, he willed it far away. He intended to be the victor in that contest.

He saw her on the ramparts, silhouetted against the clearing skies. *If she cared about him, even a small bit, she would not be doing this.*

He glanced at his prisoner. The MacDougall boy was cloaked in his red-and-black colors. He choked. Then he turned and shouted, "Rob, get my brat from the boy."

"I wouldna wish to be her now," Rob muttered, hurrying past him.

Macleod strode across the ward. He started swiftly up the stairs. As he came up to the ramparts, he saw that she was in a deep trance, her eyes closed, her face lifted to the emerging sun. Sweat shone on her skin, making it almost translucent. Her arms were extended, palms up and oddly limp. She did not notice him.

For one moment he stared, aware of her beauty, her power and her grace. In that moment, he thought about how she had wanted to offer him comfort, which he'd refused. Her desire to somehow heal him and erase the past had annoyed him dangerously. Now, he would dearly love to have her harping on him that way. Then he glanced into the bailey. Rob had stripped the boy of the wool.

Macleod noted the pail. Tabitha had brought him water. His displeasure increased. So did his resolve. "Tabitha."

She did not hear him.

"Tabitha."

She started, her eyes flying open and, when lucidity appeared in her gaze, she paled.

"Will ye come inside an' dine?" he asked flatly.

She was breathing hard, trembling, and the fine gown he'd given her clung to her lush curves. Even as angry as he was, his body stirred. She did not answer, starting to rise. He reached to help her, but she flinched at his touch and jerked away. "Don't."

He truly tried to check his anger. "Ye begged fer my touch this dawn."

A flush appeared. "Yes, I did."

He hadn't expected such an answer. "I can make ye beg again—right now—right here." She would not be his enemy when she was weeping in pleasure and release.

"No, you can't," she warned.

He was tempted to show her that the attraction which raged between them, the desire which made him insatiable, remained.

She breathed hard and said, as if reading his mind, "No, Macleod. Don't think it. It's over now."

"'Tisna over, Tabitha. 'Tis only ended when I say so." And he meant it.

"I cannot allow you to abuse Coinneach, and I will not let you execute him."

Didn't she know how provocative those words were? "Yer courage amazes me. Ye dinna give the commands here."

"What you are doing is wrong," she said. "In my time, there are rules which govern the treatment of prisoners. Do you want to hear them?"

He was actually interested, but he shook his head. "I willna war with ye, and I willna allow ye to war with me."

"The reason there are rules is not to protect the enemy's soldiers as much as to protect your own soldiers. Of course, in my time, we value all human life."

He stared at her. Coinneach's mother was a witch, but he was certain that Coinneach was not evil or inhuman.

"Has it ever occurred to you that if you showed mercy to a MacDougall, they would show mercy to a Macleod?"

"O' course," he said, suddenly angry. "But there wasna mercy in 1201. I dinna start this feud."

She inhaled. "I know. It was awful. I am so sorry!"

He was stunned. She still wanted to help him! She thought to free Coinneach and help him with his pain. He softened his tone. "Come down and dine before ye get sickened. We can converse about yer rules—an' about the massacre."

Her eyes widened. It took her a moment, but she said, "Are you trying to distract me? Because it won't work."

"So ye refuse to come to the hall with me?"

She hesitated and, grimly, she nodded.

"I canna free him," he exclaimed, all patience gone. "He will return, an' next time, mayhap he'll put his dagger in my back while I sleep! Do ye wish me dead?"

"Of course not. But someone has to take the high road and stop this insane war."

His tension soared. "This war will go on forever." It was actually a dismal thought. "I'll war until I die. I owe my father that much. Why canna ye comprehend my world?"

"I do comprehend your world. It is a world of violence, where might makes right—only the strong survive. It is a jungle, with no value for human life! What will it take to end this bloody feud? How many boys and men must die first? Isn't it enough that evil claims so many innocent lives?"

"My father made peace with the MacDougall, an' it was a great mistake. While he slept, while we all slept, they came inside Blayde an' murdered everyone except for me. Children died in their beds that day, Tabitha, Macleod children."

"You have suffered terribly, Macleod. I wish you had been spared all that you have lived through. And your father was a great man, to attempt to make peace. Whatever you think you owe him, you've paid—overpaid! I have no doubt he would want you to be happy."

He jerked. "Happy? What kind of word is that?"

"He'd want you to be at peace!"

"My duty is revenge."

She shook her head, her color high now. "What happened here in 1201 was evil. Many innocent men, women and children died. But you're not evil, and Coinneach is Innocent."

"An' now ye'll harp on me?"

She nodded, her face strained. "I refuse to believe that you are not destined to be a Master. You were born to protect Innocence, not destroy it. I know that massacre made you hard and vengeful. I know you think it your duty to war on your mortal enemies. But you have a much higher calling in life. Why won't you consider that?"

"Ye sound like MacNeil!" he exclaimed.

She suddenly touched his arm and he felt her compassion flowing from her. "Have you ever considered forgiving the MacDougalls and starting over with them?"

He was disbelieving. "Ye ken naught o' this world!"

"Others will suffer as you have, both Macleods and MacDougalls, if this does not end. Do you want your son to spend his lifetime beheading MacDougalls to avenge you?"

He trembled with absolute rage. The ramparts shuddered beneath them, around them. "Cease! I willna have a son!"

Her eyes widened. "Of course you won't. You're too smart. You would never wish this life on your child."

He could not allow her to continue this way. He seized her shoulders. He ignored her stiff, resistant body and pulled her closer; she gasped when his manhood brushed her. "Ferget the MacDougall boy," he snapped. She was very still in his arms, while he pressed fully up against her. "Come with me now, to my chamber. I want this war over…an' I will win."

She pushed against him, but she was breathless. "No, stop. I will not be seduced—this is too important!"

He ignored her and wrapped her in his arms. "This is much better, Tabitha, dinna ye agree?"

She trembled violently and it was a surge of desire. He felt a moment's pure triumph, looked down, and their gazes locked.

Hers was clouded with tears, pride, passion and fierce determination. "Even if I give you my body, I will come back here and free Coinneach." A tear fell. "Then, even if you beat me, starve me, abuse me, I will stay and help you find a way to get past the massacre."

He released her. "Even in yer defiance, ye're the most annoyin' shrew!"

She hugged herself, rocking on her heels, another tear falling down her cheek. But she didn't back up or try to flee. "There is something strong and powerful between us," she whispered. "I saw you across time and you felt and saw me. Not just once but for a century. And the desire, well, it's obviously still there." She wiped the tear away. "I'm a Rose. I am proud to be a Rose. Fighting to protect, defend and to help others, is what we do. I am fighting for Coinneach, and I am fighting for you."

He almost told her he could fight for himself. Instead, he was silent. He was certain he had never encountered such conviction before.

"Macleod, please, let the boy go. His *great-grandfather* caused the deaths of your family. He is an *Innocent*."

He tensed, almost tempted to surrender to her. But the moment he realized that, he knew he had become dangerously weakened. This woman had weakened him. He had to fight her powerful allure. He spoke without passion. "Will ye come down to dine?"

"Can you really watch him die, day by day? Can you?"

Not only could he do so, he would do so. "Come down to dine," he said again. "This matter is closed." And if she tried to raise it later, when they were alone, he would change the subject and use his powers of sexual persuasion if he must.

She shook her head. "We won't be alone later, Macleod. I thought I made that clear."

His hard body told him otherwise. He crossed his arms and stared. He never spent the night alone and he had no intention of starting now.

"I can't ignore what you are doing. I will help you, but I can't share your bed again, and that is that." She trembled.

He was almost amused. "I never sleep alone," he finally said. "If ye refuse me, I will send for another woman." He was merely stating a fact.

She cried out.

He was surprised that his use of another woman would be so hurtful to her, but he did not dwell on that. It was hardly important. Instead, he said, "I suggest ye think long an' hard on whether ye choose the boy over me."

He turned to go but she stopped him in his tracks. She said, very softly, "If you sleep with another woman, you will never have me again."

He faltered, incredulous. As he faced her, he knew she meant it. His next words were a warning. "Tabitha, ye must choose to ignore my affairs."

"I can't," she said simply.

His heart lurched, hard. "Then we are at an impasse."

"Yes, we are," she said.

KRISTIN LAFARGE'S SENSES told her her roommate was out as she unlocked and entered their small apartment. She was pleased, because the woman was getting on her nerves.

Her mother wasn't there, either.

Kristin was alarmed. She hadn't seen her mother for almost twenty-four hours. Where was she? "Mother? Can you hear me? I need to speak with you."

Kristin took off her coat, crossing the living room, which was sparsely furnished. She'd left the front door unlocked—she did not fear evil, and why should she? When she heard the door open, she turned, thinking it her mother. Then she sensed her roommate, Liz.

Liz smiled at her, then ducked her head and rushed into the kitchen. Kristin smiled. Her roommate was afraid of her. Liz was starting to speculate—and pretty soon, she might even figure things out.

Kristin laughed. She wasn't worried, not at all.

"Mother, would you please get back here?"

There was no response, and Kristin sat down on the couch, taking her small laptop out of her briefcase.

Liz poked her head out of the kitchen. "Are you talking to me?"

"No, I'm not." Kristin smiled sweetly. Liz paled and returned to the kitchen. She went online. "Well, if you're listening, she went to Blayde in 1298," she continued. "And guess what? I am going to get the powers I need to follow her there. Don't worry. This will be over very, very soon."

Liz came out of the kitchen, staring at her in alarm.

"Looking at me that way is not a good idea."

Liz flushed. "Look, Kristin, this isn't working out. I think you should find a new place." She shifted uneasily.

Kristin sighed. If only the bitch had minded her own business. She simply stared at her, forming her black power into a noose. She slipped the noose around Liz's throat. Liz touched her neck, obviously feeling something. Kristin smiled, pleasure beginning. Her mother had told her that one of her ancestors had been Satan's grandson, centuries ago. It would explain why she could take so much pleasure in torture and pain.

She murmured, "Tighten, noose."

Liz gasped, her hands flying to her neck as the invisible rope began to strangle her.

"Tighten, noose," Kristin said, now breathing hard.

Liz reeled, trying to pull the invisible noose from her neck.

She staggered across the room, choking. Her eyes were wide with panic and terror, and they begged Kristin to stop. Kristin wet her lips. "Tighten, noose," she cried.

Liz fell to the floor, her face turning blue.

Kristin stood, panting. "Tighten!"

And she heard Liz's neck snap.

She closed her eyes and let the pleasure wash over her, moaning softly. Then she imagined that it was Tabitha Rose, the bitch, who lay on that floor, broken and dead. Her pleasure renewed itself.

It took her a moment to calm. And then she sat down at the laptop and booked the presidential suite at the Carlisle Hotel.

CHAPTER FOURTEEN

THE SUN WAS SETTING. The occupants of the castle had finished dining some time ago. Tabby had been able to hear the dinner conversation from her new bedchamber. Macleod had been angry when she insisted on a separate room, but he hadn't taken a stand and tried to force her into sharing his room. She had decided not to go downstairs to eat, not because she had no appetite but because she did not want to sit with Macleod—it was far too tense between them now. A small girl had brought her meal up to her, although she hadn't had to ask for it. Unfortunately, she knew Macleod had sent it.

She wished he hadn't done that. She did not want to see him as thoughtful, but the gesture had been exactly that. Of course, she'd been given a full meal—while Coinneach starved outside in the stocks.

Tabby hugged her knees to her chest. She was seated on the pallet she would sleep on. The chamber she'd found was in Blayde's south tower, directly across the hall from the north tower where Macleod slept. It was the size of a prison cell, but it had a window, which Tabby thought was a plus. There was no furniture, just a small stool and the pallet.

Downstairs, a silence had fallen, as everyone settled down for the night.

God, she was feeling so sad now. She felt sorry for Coinneach, who was physically suffering, and she felt sorry for

Macleod, who was a prisoner of his duty, his anger, his grief and, apparently, even his guilt. She was starting to realize why he wanted that boy dead. She was suspecting he wished he had died in the massacre, too. Instead, he had survived, and now he lived for revenge.

It made her feel even sadder. He was so courageous and so powerful. If he would walk away from that revenge and take his vows, he would be a hero. Wanting to help them both made her feel as if she was walking a very precarious tightrope, with no net below to break her fall.

Tabby was acutely aware that she could not stop thinking about Macleod. It was almost funny. She'd become obsessed from the first time she'd seen him at the Met, when he was hurt and burned from An Tùir-Tara—when it was obvious that he needed her. But when she'd seen him at school, she'd been so certain that the dark, dangerous warrior didn't need her or anybody. She had been completely wrong. But the real irony was that from the moment they'd met, she'd wanted to avoid getting close to him, yet every encounter had deepened their intimacy. Their moral conflict was keeping them apart, but it was also making her see him and understand him as never before.

Why will ye nay comprehend my world?

Do ye wish to see me dead?

Ye said ye willna judge me.

She laid her face on her knees. She had to free him from his past. She felt certain he would become a changed man if she could accomplish that feat. If he gave up his revenge, he might even take his vows.

Think long an' hard on whether ye choose the boy over me.

She had promised Coinneach she would free him that night. To do so, she would have to use her magic against Macleod. The only way she could get those keys was if she put a sleeping spell on him—and if it worked.

She was wondering if her spell to block him from reading her mind had worked. He hadn't mentioned anything, but she had cast her spell with care. Hopefully any thoughts she had about Coinneach were now impossible for him to hear.

Tabby glanced at the chamber's sole window. It was dusk now, the sky a dark shade of lavender, a few stars emerging in the purple sky. Right now, if they weren't in this terrible predicament, she'd be in his bed, in his arms. She did not want to let her mind go there, but being in his embrace had felt incredibly right.

She flushed. She had ended their physical relationship, but a part of her knew it wasn't over. How could it be, when she was so determined to help free him from his bondage? When she was so damn attracted to him? When he was the only man who had ever thoroughly and completely aroused her?

She stared at the darkening sky, sick with dread. *Was he alone?*

She couldn't imagine him refraining from sex, now that she knew how virile he was. But if he had taken another woman to his bed now, she would never forgive him, not if she went home and not even if she saw him again at An Tùir-Tara after two-hundred-and-fifty years had passed.

Her heart hurt, but she refused to acknowledge it. She had to stop thinking about him. She had to mentally shut down and forget about what he was doing, and with whom. Coinneach was outside in the bailey, shackled and in stocks. It was too early to try to steal Macleod's keys, so she had to wait.

Resolved, Tabby got up, putting one of his red-and-black brats over her shoulders. She'd eaten exactly a third of her meal, saving the rest for Coinneach. She picked up the trencher.

Think long an' hard on whether ye choose the boy over me.

She went downstairs. Most of his men were asleep on their pallets, but a handful of men were at the table, gaming. They turned to stare at her, seemingly disapproving and suspicious. Macleod was not present; he had retired for the night.

Do not think about it.

She straightened her spine, ignoring them all while mentally daring any man to try to stop her. No one did. She crossed the hall. But at the front door, she heard someone behind her. Tabby turned to face Rob.

He shook his head. "No good will come o' this battle, lady. Ye canna win. Ye dinna wish to turn him against ye."

"If I win, Rob, he wins, too." Tabby pushed her shoulder against the door, slipping outside.

It was a purple night, still cloudy, and only a few stars were illuminating it. She crossed the bailey swiftly, being as careful as she could be not to spill the ale. Coinneach had been sleeping, his position an awkward one, and Tabby realized he must be exhausted. Her heart went out to him. As she knelt, he heard her and awoke. He looked up and relief filled his eyes. Then he started.

Tabby felt Macleod's huge, powerful presence looming behind her. Her heart skidded and she glanced up over her shoulder at him.

He reached down and hauled her to her feet, the ale spilling. Without releasing her, he took the trencher from her and flung it to the ground.

She had thought him preoccupied with another woman. She had been caught red-handed trying to succor his prisoner. "He is starving."

His gaze was searing. "Aye, he is."

She didn't bother to try to pull away. His grip felt like a brand. She trembled. "He needs to eat. He needs water."

"Ye've defied me again."

Tabby tensed. Why did his power have to be so consuming? "Are you surprised? You know where I stand. I cannot compromise my values or my beliefs."

His mouth curled mirthlessly. "Nor can I."

They were at an impasse.

"Come," he said.

Before she could answer, he was pulling her with him back toward the hall, his strides long. She had to run to keep up with him. "Where are we going?" she cried, alarmed.

He didn't answer.

When he started toward the north tower, she realized where they were going. She dug in her heels; he did not stop and he pulled her with him. "I am not going upstairs to your chamber with you!"

He didn't look at her, but his grasp tightened. "I've had enough o' this war. 'Tis madness."

"I cannot stand by and watch you torture and execute that boy while sharing your bed. I can't do it, Macleod," she cried as he dragged her up the stairs with him.

He did not answer her.

"Macleod!" she cried, as he shoved open his bedchamber door. "Are you going to force me against my will?"

He finally let her go. Tabby turned to run past him, out the door and into the corridor, but he slammed the door closed in her face, caught her arm and whirled her back around closer to the bed.

She paused in the center of the room, shocked.

He folded his arms. "There will never be force."

He meant to seduce her. Tabby was already acutely aware of him—she was always acutely aware of him. His words made her stiffen and vibrate. It made all those newly discovered pulse points come to life.

He slowly smiled.

She shook her head, her heart thundering now, her mouth dry. "Don't do this. I will be furious in the morning."

He stripped off his tunic, revealing his hard, scarred, aroused body, and flung it aside.

Tabby meant to look anywhere but at him, but her gaze had a will of its own. "I will not forgive you," she warned. Her tone was unyielding.

"Ye'll forgive me. If ye insist on war, we'll war in the day. But not in the night."

She was disbelieving, but she couldn't stop her treacherous body from responding to the mere idea of a nightly truce and all that it entailed. Her skin was burning and tight.

"Or would ye rather I seek comfort elsewhere?" he murmured, and he was finally amused.

Tabby looked down. She tried to breathe and failed. He slowly walked over and she lifted her eyes. "I *hate* the idea of you with somebody else."

"Then offer me comfort, Tabitha."

They could argue tomorrow. Her hand strayed and found his rock-hard hip where his hip bone protruded. He went still, except for that huge, quivering length. Tabby slid her fingers lower.

When she touched him, the desire was acute, blinding.

He laughed and pushed her down onto the bed.

Tabby cried out, seizing his hair, pulling his face forward. As she kissed him, he drove deep.

THE CHILD'S CHOKED SOBBING awoke her.

Tabby jerked upright. The sun was high and bright, pouring through the closed shutters of the windows. For one moment, she didn't move, recalling every impossible, frenzied detail of last night.

She had surrendered to Macleod with more than her body last night. She flushed. She'd been the insatiable one. And it had been wilder and more intense than ever—perhaps because of their differences, their war. He'd been so triumphant and he'd let her know, repeatedly, who was in control and who had won. But she hadn't minded, oh, no.

In fact, she'd been so insatiable that she'd forgotten to steal his keys when they'd finally calmed. She'd fallen asleep, not even thinking about Coinneach.

She had missed the perfect opportunity to steal those keys, and she didn't know how she felt about that—just as she wasn't at all certain how she felt about giving in to him last night. It was late in the morning, a new day. She probably shouldn't have succumbed to him last night, but she had. Had their truce only applied to last night? She wouldn't mind a rational debate in the broad light of day. Maybe making love last night could be turned into an opportunity to discuss their differences.

Tabby slowly got up, opening the shutters. Outside, it was a magnificent day, the skies azure and cloudless. The ridges to the southeast were thick with forests, and glittered as bright as emeralds in the sun. Now what? she wondered. Last night, he had wanted sex and he'd gotten it. The problem was, she had no regrets, not on that score. But what she did regret was his ignoring her express wishes and refusing to discuss Coinneach and his Fate.

And then she heard the soft childish crying, again.

Alarmed, Tabby went to the door and flung it open, expecting to find a small child there. But the hall was empty.

Tabby hesitated, uncertain. Was her mind playing tricks on her? First she had dreamed about a crying child, and now, she'd heard him. Except no child was nearby.

Or was she sensing a child who was somewhere else, the way she'd sensed Macleod as a boy on the beach? Suddenly she heard the child crying again.

Very concerned, she lifted her skirts and started down the hall. The sound seemed to increase slightly in volume, as if she'd find that small girl or boy weeping on the stairs. But when she reached the narrow staircase, it was empty.

She tensed. Last night, the spirit had not made an appearance. Tabby did not know what that meant, but she was certain it was the lull before a huge storm.

And her mind was playing tricks on her now. She was certain that someone—or something—was behind those tricks. Was it Criosaidh, Coinneach's mother? What about that spirit from An Tùir-Tara? Was it involved in this mischief?

Tabby started downstairs. Peigi was cleaning up the hall with two other women. "Did you hear a child crying?"

Peigi shrugged. "Maybe 'twas young Seonaidh. He was here a moment ago."

Tabby did not know who Seonaidh was, and she found herself going to the front doors of the hall, which she pushed open. There were several little children playing in the bailey, but no one was crying and they were too far away for her to have heard any one of them. As she watched them tossing stones at a stake, she heard the child again.

And he or she was closer.

Tabby stepped outside, wide-eyed, scanning the bailey, the crying louder now. She saw two toddlers with their mothers, the women leading a pair of milk cows, but she did not espy a crying child. *I am being enchanted,* she thought uneasily.

But the sound shifted, and her concern escalated. She glanced up at the ramparts, starting for the stairs leading to them. Then she realized that the child was in the arched gateway, leading to the drawbridge. The drawbridge was down, but that did not seem unusual so early in the day. She hurried to the gated entrance of the stronghold.

Tabby paused inside the dark, cold tunnel, searching the shadows there. No child was present, but he or she was crying harder now. Suddenly she worried that the child was in the cellars below.

"Lady?"

She turned. It was the handsome young Highlander who had been on watch yesterday. "Do you hear that?"

"I dinna ken…I dinna speak…English," he said haltingly.

The crying had stopped. Tabby strained to hear. As she did, the child began to cry again, but this time, most definitely from outside the keep. Over the drawbridge and past the moat, she saw the rutted road she and Macleod had climbed up to the stronghold the other day. Beyond the road, the forests seemed thick and impenetrable, the kind of wilderness that did not exist in her time. Between the forests and where she stood, no child was in sight.

The young Highlander spoke abruptly to her. Tabby did not have to understand Gaelic to know that he was telling her not to leave the keep. She ignored him, vaguely aware that she was enchanted and this was treachery, but too worried about the child now to think clearly. She had to find this child. There was simply no choice.

She rushed through the arched gateway and across the drawbridge. The crying became louder. The child was terrified.

The young man shouted at her.

Tabby lifted her skirts and ran toward the road. The sound of the crying shifted. Tabby veered off the dirt. The child screamed as if it was being murdered. Tabby ran harder, branches scraping her face, her breasts. And then there was a shocking silence.

She halted, confused, panting hard. The fog lifted and she stilled, shocked.

She had just been lured away from Blayde with powerful magic. There was no child!

For her senses had returned, as clear and as acute as ever. "Highlander," she cried, turning. And she did not know where she was. Huge, towering pines surrounded her. She was in the forest, where it was dark with shadow and brush. She could

barely see the sky through the canopy of boughs above her—
and she could not see Blayde.

Comprehension stabbed through her. She was lost.

Branches rustled, snapped.

More comprehension came. She was not alone.

Alarmed, Tabby fought the sudden fear. The calm that
always preceded evil came. Becoming still, she put a protective spell on herself, finally turning to the sound.

Five darkly cloaked figures emerged from the forest, their
appearance shocking. They were adolescent boys, all fair in
complexion, with black, empty eyes. They were obviously
medieval boys. As Tabby was surrounded, the comprehension
was even more stunning now.

There were sub gangs burning witches in 1298, too.

They began to smile, their expressions evil, approaching.

Tabby turned to run.

Her heart thundered as her arms were seized from behind.
She struggled but it was futile and she was dragged back. She
heard someone else approaching, but she was pushed hard to
the ground. She cried out, landing on the rough ground on her
hands and knees, her face. *They wanted to hurt her.*

How far would they go?

The possessed always had unnatural strength, and she did
not have the power to escape them, she thought, carefully
getting to her hands and knees. Begging would accomplish
nothing. Evil did not know the meaning of mercy.

"Bind her and start the fire."

Tabby cried out at the sound of Kristin Lafarge's voice. She
was dragged to her feet and she whirled, incredulous. Kristin
was striding into the small glade, grinning at her maliciously,
her eyes overly bright. She was clad in medieval Highland garb.

Tabby's hands were jerked behind her and tied with rough rope.
Her fear vanished and calm descended. "You enchanted me."

"Yes, I did. Hello, Tabitha." Kristin approached, clearly relishing the moment.

Tabby straightened, ignoring the pain of the cord. "Are you from this time or my time?"

Kristin touched her cheek lightly with her nails. "I'm hardly a medieval woman. Do I appear to be?"

She didn't have the slightest trace of a Scot brogue, Tabby thought. "You could pass for a Highland woman in those clothes."

"I have *relations* at Melvaig."

"Are you a MacDougall?" Tabby asked swiftly. Everything was tied to An Tùir-Tara, she thought.

"You ask too many questions. And how are *your* relations, dear?"

Tabby went still. "What?"

Kristin grinned. "How is your warrior-bitch sister? I wonder."

The calm vanished. Icy fear returned. "If you have hurt her, I will kill you."

Kristin laughed. "And how will you do that? Fire, arise," she said smoothly.

Tabby heard the flames crackle and she whirled. The boys had gathered up a huge amount of brush and a fire instantly blazed in the center of the glade. Fear slithered through her. "What did you do to Sam?"

"Sam survived my magic, but she probably still has a tummy ache."

Sam was okay, Tabby thought, relieved. She reached out for the calm and it came swiftly to her. "What do you want? Why did you follow me into the past?" And then she wondered at the coincidence—two evil things had followed her into the past from New York City. "Wait a minute. Was it you at the Met? Did you try to get into my loft? Did you attack me the other night in Macleod's chamber?"

"I wish I had that kind of power. Unfortunately, I have to be present to use my magic on you."

Tabby began to shake. She believed her. Not because of what she had said, but because this woman did not have the same imprint of evil as the woman from An Tùir-Tara. Kristin was a diluted version, somehow. "How are you related to An Tùir-Tara?" she demanded.

"Isn't it obvious?" Kristin's pleasant smile and demeanor vanished. "I was there."

Tabby stared, surprised. "And I'm going to be there, too, aren't I?" She didn't know how she knew. Or maybe she did— all those emotions were just too intense not to belong to her.

Kristin grinned. "Hmm, how shall I answer? No, you will be there… Wait! Yes, you *were* there."

Tabby felt ill. And she knew suddenly that if she looked at the fire, she was going to feel all of the evil and hatred, the rage and outrage, despair, loss and love associated with An Tùir-Tara all over again. She kept her eyes on Kristin. "What happened?"

Kristin gave her a disparaging look. "It doesn't matter. What matters is I am going to destroy you, Tabitha. And I just can't wait to feel your pain." She licked her lips.

Tabby inhaled. Kristin was demonic. Not completely—but somewhere in her genes, she was tainted with Satan's blood.

Tabby prayed for courage and strength. Then she dismissed Kristin and dared to look at the fire. She stared into the flames, feeling sick, beginning to feel the hatred, the evil, the rage— the love. The sight blinded her. Sweat trickled from her brow. She could not let the emotions paralyze her now. *"Fire obey me, fire go out."*

The fire hesitated, and then it began decreasing in size.

"Fire obey me, fire go out!" Tabby cried.

As the fire shifted, becoming even smaller, Kristin hissed, *"Fire arise."* And the flames blazed.

Tabby realized Kristin had great power—more than she did. She breathed hard and fought the dizziness brought on by those terrible feelings, and said, *"Fire obey me, fire go out."*

The fire subsided into a few small flames, and then into embers. Tabby was surprised and relieved, but Kristin seized her by the hair, crying, *"Fire, arise."*

The fire blazed and she shoved her face toward the flames. "Who is stronger, bitch? And don't you want to know where your *protector* is?"

Tabby tensed in alarm. She reminded herself that Macleod could take care of himself.

"He went out with his men this morning. Not only is he far to the east, he is under my spell."

"I don't believe you," Tabby gasped. "He's too powerful for a petty magician like you."

Kristin hissed, *"Fire arise!"*

The flames roared, becoming a bonfire the size of an entire room. Tabby began to struggle, because if she was pushed into that inferno, she was dead. Kristin laughed and the five boys grabbed her and started dragging her closer to the bonfire. Tabby clawed at them. Heat engulfed her, and she was so close to the flames Tabby thought her dress and hair would catch on fire.

"Fire obey me," she panted. *"Fire go out!"*

The fire wavered, its hesitation clear.

The boys pushed her closer.

Thunder sounded.

In confusion, she looked upward as the thunder rolled more loudly, but the small patch of sky she glimpsed through the boughs overhead was brightly blue. And then the ground beneath her feet moved.

The thunder stopped.

She was abruptly released and she fell, hard, flames not far from her hands. Tabby rose. On the other side of the bonfire, she saw a woman on a horse.

She went still. Behind her, she heard the boys running away into the forest. She glanced back. Kristin stood as still as a statue, her expression livid.

Tabby looked back at the woman. She was dressed like a male medieval Highlander, in a belted thigh-length tunic and a royal-blue and black brat, and she held a full-size sword effortlessly in one hand. She rode her gray charger slowly forward. Hundreds of riders filled the forest behind her.

Branches snapped.

Tabby jerked—Kristin was gone.

Tabby looked at the fire. *"Fire obey me, fire be gone."*

The fire became the size of a large man.

Tabby repeated the command, and the fire was reduced to a few dancing flames and embers. Tabby glanced back at the woman.

The woman returned her stare. She had long, curly reddish-blond hair, a striking face and searing eyes. She looked as if she lifted weights and ran triathlons. Her power came from the other side, white and bright. It was very much like Sam's. But Tabby didn't have to feel that to know that she was a Highland warrior.

"Macleod is here," she said in heavily accented English. She turned the horse and galloped into the forest, her vast army following her.

As the thunder subsided, Tabby began to shake, collapsing against a tree.

Kristin had followed her through time; Kristin wanted to kill her; Kristin would be at An Tùir-Tara.

Hoofbeats sounded. Tabby looked up, feeling Macleod's power. Relief made her weak. He galloped through the trees, a handful of mounted men behind him. He leaped from his black stallion before it halted, reaching her in a stride. He clasped her, pulling her forward. Tabby went into his embrace.

"Kristin followed me from New York."

"The deamhan-ghost?" he demanded.

"No, she's a black witch—and a powerful one."

His intense gaze moved over her face. "I felt her, Tabitha, an' I felt yer fear. I followed yer fear until I found ye. What are ye doin' so far from Blayde?"

Tabby breathed deeply. "She cast a spell and lured me out. Macleod, a warrior woman with great white power appeared in the nick of time. Kristin was afraid, and so were the subs. She chased them away. Who was that?"

"The Lady of An Roinn-Mor," he said abruptly. "Some say she's a goddess. I dinna ken, but she can rouse two thousand mortal men an' each one will die fer her."

Tabby absorbed that.

"Are ye tellin' me Kristin is more powerful than ye?" Macleod asked. His hands moved to her face.

Tabby didn't hesitate. "Way more powerful." His eyes darkened. "Macleod. She seems to be allied with Melvaig and she wants me dead."

His eyes burned with anger. "Then I will ha' to kill her."

"There's more." She clasped his arms tightly. "You're not the only one who will be at An Tùir-Tara. I am going to be there, too."

TABBY SIGHED AND CURLED her toes and sighed again, smiling. It was late. The sky outside was gleaming ebony, but spangled with a billion stars. She stared at Macleod, her smile widening. He knelt naked before the fire, which he was starting with a tinderbox.

She leaned up on one elbow, so she could admire every inch of his body. Starlight illuminated him, highlighting his bulging muscles and powerful build. *"Fire obey me, fire begin. Fire obey me, fire come in,"* she said.

Macleod turned, sending her a slow and sexy, very satisfied smile. Behind him, the fire started, a few small flames crackling. He glanced at it and stood.

Tabby actually felt herself blush. "More?"

"Aye, if ye can manage to match me."

"A challenge I can hardly refuse." She wet her lips, trying not to stare, but then she decided to give up. Why not stare when he was so magnificent? She glanced at the fire. *"Fire obey me, fire rise up."* The fire grew, its flames filling the hearth.

Macleod sat beside her. "A useful spell. I wish a word, Tabitha."

His tone was somber and she tensed. Macleod was not inclined to conversation much less discussion. They had been making love ever since he'd found her in the forest. She straightened. They certainly had a lot to discuss.

"This war betwixt us is over," he said, and it was not a question.

That feeling, which was half satiation and half anticipation, receded. Dismay rose up. She searched his gaze and thought it softened almost imperceptibly. She would never accept his treatment of Coinneach or any other such prisoner, but she did not want to resume warring with him, either. So much had happened in such a short time, it felt as if they had been together for ages, not days. And most importantly, he had been so concerned when he had found her in the forest—as if he did care about her as a woman, not a sex object.

Her heart opened. Comprehension came slowly. She was starting to really care about him, too. She couldn't help but admire his courage, his determination, his power. Sure, he was medieval in a lot of ways. But that was to be expected, and his heroism made up for it. And they were more than lovers now.

They were partners in this life-and-death struggle against evil. She needed him and he needed her, as MacNeil had said. Their Fates were so clearly intertwined.

And they would both be at An Tùir-Tara.

It was a frightening thought. Tabby hugged her knees to her chest, aware of his watchful stare. Going through all that they had, even the conflict over Coinneach, had increased the intimacy in their relationship. Their relationship felt as if it was growing in leaps and bounds. She wasn't afraid of him anymore, either. He wasn't as daunting and intimidating as he'd first seemed. They might even be on the path to becoming friends, because friends looked out for one another; friends cared about one another.

It felt huge, eternal and irrevocable.

But of course it did. Otherwise she wouldn't have seen and felt him across centuries, as he'd seen and heard her. And she wondered if he was her soul mate.

It would explain everything. But how could that be possible when they were still worlds apart? When Kristin and the evil from An Tùir-Tara were vanquished, when Coinneach was freed, she would be going home—wouldn't she?

Suddenly Tabby did not want to think about the future. It was distressing.

"Being with you feels so right," Tabby said softly. "I know you think so, too."

"Ye need to bend to me," he said. "I must do my duty, Tabitha. Ye need to trust that my decision is right."

He was referring to Coinneach, she thought, but the pang she had wasn't half as huge as it had once been. There was no question in her mind that his decision was wrong. Now, she thought that there might be hope for him to change his mind and see the light. "I trust you. And I know you are doing what you think is right. But I am not going to approve. And by the way, your ancestors—the gods—won't ever approve, either."

He flinched and stood, his hard body rippling.

The gods were such a sore subject with him, she thought.

His face tightened. "Then ye'll disobey me, even now?" He was disbelieving.

Going against him, behind his back, suddenly seemed unbearable. She knew she had no choice but she didn't want to think about it. She spoke slowly, carefully. "Doesn't your feud with Coinneach seem paltry after what happened today with Kristin? Shouldn't the war on evil—all evil—take precedence over all mortal affairs?"

"The murder of my family wasna paltry. I willna allow ye to weaken me, Tabitha."

She inhaled. "I'm sorry. That isn't my intention. And I believe that if you ever took your vows, you'd become stronger than ever." She slipped from the bed.

She'd remained impossibly modest until that precise moment, and his eyes widened. Tabby moved to stand between his legs, taking both of his hands. His eyes darkened instantly. "Your revenge diminishes you, but let's not beat a dead horse."

He tugged his hands from hers and cupped her breasts. "Will ye use yer body now to sway me?"

It crossed her mind that if she could, she would. "I know you can read my mind, so you know I am starting to care for you. I want what is best for you, Macleod, not for me." He started. "We remain at an impasse." She touched his face tenderly. "But at least we are discussing it. That is a step in the right direction. It is civil."

"And bein' civil pleases ye, aye?" he asked softly, clasping her waist and pulling her forward, his face pillowed against her breasts.

She inhaled. "It pleases me almost as much as you do."

He lifted his face and smiled at her, his eyes hot.

And that was when she saw the woman standing in the fire.

CHAPTER FIFTEEN

THE WOMAN SEEMED to be standing inside the hearth, on the other side of the fire. Tabby could see her clearly, even if she could see through her. She was dark-haired, and clad in medieval finery. Her hatred and evil filled the room.

Tabby cried out, jerking upright.

Her protective spell had been breached.

The fire became a wall, roaring between them. She was horrified, outraged, consumed with dread, with fury. The emotions made her reel, all conflicting. *She had to triumph over her.*

The woman smiled and suddenly Macleod was standing on the other side of the fire behind the woman, his eyes wide, and it was déjà vu. In that moment, Tabby knew how much she loved him—and she was terrified.

But so was he.

And then she saw herself.

Tabby went still as her heart lurched with absolute dread.

The woman and Macleod stood on one side of the fire wall and she was on the other. And now, the fire raced toward her, encircling her.

And she went up in flames.

"Tabitha!"

It took Tabby a moment to realize that Macleod had seized her, was shaking her. And then she realized she was staring at a simple fire in the hearth, and that the woman was gone.

Macleod held her arm, his eyes wide with concern. Tabby felt the evil receding the way a wave rolled from the beach, vanishing into the ocean.

The fire blazed furiously now, and the open shutters were rocking on the walls.

But she was gone.

"Sit down," he said, putting his arm around her.

She reached for him. "It was the evil from the other night," she began. "The bitch from An Tùir-Tara. She's trying to manifest." She realized she was shaking wildly in his arms.

"I saw her, too, Tabitha."

Tabby started.

"'Twas Criosaidh."

Tabby was surprised—or was she?

"Tabitha?"

She just looked at him, still shocked by what she'd seen, and let him read her mind.

Macleod cried out.

"OUR LOVELY FRIEND is not at home," Nick said.

Sam stood with Nick outside the apartment Kristin Lafarge shared with her roommate, Elizabeth Adler. Neither one had bothered to draw a gun, because they could both sense that evil was not present. A bullet would work well on the bitch—unless she could cast a spell to deflect it. Sam would not be surprised. Kristin's power was dangerous. She would still love to see what a bullet or another weapon could do to the witch. Sam believed in grudges, revenge and payback.

She wasn't surprised that Kristin was gone. "GTB," she said grimly. *Gone to Blayde.* She didn't bother translating, because she damn well knew Nick could read her mind.

Which was why she was so carefully controlling her thoughts. He was taking that dumb bimbo Jan back in time, when Tabby was in so much trouble. Her plans were none of his damned business now.

"Let's see if anyone has read the mayor's Home Safety Code." Nick reached for the doorknob, and it turned.

They saw Elizabeth Adler at the same time. She lay on the floor, not far from the front door, her eyes wide and sightless. Sam hurried over to her, already knowing her neck was broken and that there would not be a pulse. Nick beelined for the laptop he saw on the coffee table, sitting down with it. Sam knelt. She was careful not to feel anything for the victim. Feeling only got in the way of war. She had learned how to shut out and shut off her feelings a long time ago. Compassion was always a bad idea.

She now noticed how pristine Adler's throat was. Sam closed Adler's eyes, aware that Adler was about her own age and too young to die. They were always too young to die, she thought without emotion. Then she checked her arms, wrists, hands and nails. "Not a scratch, much less a bruise. Doesn't look like there was a fight."

But of course there hadn't been a struggle. Kristin had killed her with her black magic.

She stood and walked over to Nick. "I thought you'd be GTB by now, too." She guarded her thoughts really tightly, but she let her anger seethe. She'd never forgive Nick for this.

"This is Lafarge's," he said cheerfully, seated on the sofa. His blue eyes gleamed as he looked up. "School calendar. Looks like she's missing a day."

"What did you find?" Sam asked, instantly interested. As far as she was concerned, Kristin was her quarry, not Nick's—and certainly not Jan's.

"Look at her screen saver," he said.

Sam walked over and saw a landscape with ruins and she knew instantly it was Scotland.

"That's Melvaig," Nick said, pleased.

"And you know that how?" But Sam's nape prickled. She couldn't help being excited. If Nick was right—which he probably was—Kristin was connected to An Tùir-Tara, too. Which begged the question, just how old was she?

They'd gotten back the DNA comp results and Nick had been right. Kristin's blood was tainted. She was only ninety-two-point-three percent human.

"It's in our new Macleod file. He warred with the MacDougall clan for the first century of his life." He glanced up at her. "I wonder if your sister domesticated him a bit. In 1325, he actually went to war as an ally of the MacDougalls." He tapped the keys, opening Kristin's Recent Items folder. His eyes widened. "Well, well."

Sam leaned over. "She booked a suite at the Carlisle. For last night."

He closed the laptop and picked it up as he stood.

"Why would she do that? My sister is at Blayde."

"She must have met someone before she made her trip," Nick said. His stare was penetrating. "Whatever you're planning, don't do it. I'll check on Tabitha when I go back. Meanwhile, you're on this. Find out who she met and what she wanted."

"Okay," Sam lied smoothly. She was good at lying. She had to do it on the streets all the time, like any undercover cop. Sometimes she played vigilante, and sometimes just mean, almost evil and ready-to-be-turned tough ass. Either way, lying was a good way to get in with the wrong people.

"I mean it. You're too involved. Jan and I will nail Kristin. And your sister is *fine*."

"She's not fine. She's in over her head. She'll be fine in a few hundred years, when she's superpowerful—assuming she makes it through the fires of Melvaig. And you damn well know it." Sam was furious. "Nick, may I say that you are the most heartless SOB I have ever met?"

"I'll see you at HCU." He handed her the laptop and walked out, already on his cell, dialing CDA's Medivac unit.

Sam breathed hard. As if she would take orders from Nick when she knew what she had to do. She knew how to get back. Or rather, she knew someone who could take her back—if he could be persuaded to help her.

He was a bastard and more heartless than her boss, but she knew exactly how to convince him.

Sam had already booked her flight to Glasgow under an assumed name. And she knew that Ian Maclean was in residence at his fine home on Loch Awe.

TABBY SANK ONTO THE BED. She was still feeling sick from the onslaught of so much hatred and rage. It had been even more intense than what she'd felt at the Met and at school. But mostly she was feeling sick because she was certain she had looked through the window of time again—and she had just seen herself die.

She would die at An Tùir-Tara.

Kristin had said she would be there. But she had already known it, hadn't she? The déjà vu had been too strong. Somewhere in the back of her mind, in the depths of her soul, she had known that those feelings were hers.

But she'd assumed that the evil woman had died—not her.

Macleod sat beside her and seized her hand, his eyes blazing, his face hard. "Ye think too much! Ye imagined it! 'Twas nay yer death ye saw."

Her temples pounded now. She was ready to throw up. "It's okay," she lied, trembling. "That's two-hundred-and-fifty years away."

He exploded. "Ye canna die in the fire! She dies!"

Tabby stared. "Are you sure it was Criosaidh that we just saw? She wasn't crystal clear—"

He cut her off. "'Twas Criosaidh."

Tabby looked at their clasped hands. Realizing how tightly he held her hand, he released her and stood. He began pacing like a caged tiger, restlessly, with repressed rage. Tabby wished she could read his mind.

Maybe it was better not to think about her death. It was a long time away. If it was Fate, it couldn't be changed anyway.

But time travel made an infinite number of scenarios possible. She didn't want to think it, but she did. *She could be taken to the fires of An Tùir-Tara at any moment. She could die there tomorrow or the day after or the day after that.*

She looked at Macleod. He needed her. She couldn't die anytime soon, not until she'd helped him let go of his past, not until he took his vows and became the kind of man she knew he could be.

"Ye think of me now?" He was incredulous.

Tabby nodded, but even as she did, that fiery vision returned. She would never forget seeing herself become a human inferno. She shut off her thoughts. She told herself she was not going to throw up. She could and would handle what she knew. She was a Rose! And if she was lucky, Macleod was right—she had imagined what she'd seen.

Except, she'd smelled the smoke and she'd heard her own screams.

He whirled to stare at her, his face twisted with revulsion and dread.

He cares about me, Tabby thought. She pushed herself to sit up straighter, too tense to feel any joy. "Macleod, let's focus on what we do know. That woman is the evil that came from An Tùir-Tara and followed us here from New York. It attacked me twice so far. How can it be Criosaidh? She's alive and at Melvaig. Right?"

Macleod said slowly, "Criosaidh is alive an' well at Melvaig,

Tabitha. But if her ghost has come here from the sixteenth century, I think it verra dangerous fer them both."

Tabby tried to think about Criosaidh being alive and just to the south, with her future spirit, having time-traveled into the past to stalk them. Macleod had to be onto something. The pendant he'd brought from the twenty-first century had imploded when it came into contact with its thirteenth-century self. What would happen if that ghost met itself before it had died?

Tabby's tension escalated. "In the Book, there is a Wisdom that every Rose is taught early on. It's in Gaelic, but translated it says, 'Seek it in the sands of time and you will find it in the light of eternity.'"

"That can mean anything."

"The entire passage is long and convoluted and hard to comprehend, but my grandmother said it means that every moment in time is continuously occurring—that it's eternal. Until my friend Allie went back in time, I never really understood it, but I do now. Or I think I do. Time is a continuum," Tabby said slowly. "Every moment exists, for everyone, at every possible point in time, like a sliding ruler. Slide into the future and there we are—at Melvaig, in the Burning Tower in 1550. Slide backward, here we are. Slide forward—we're dead. Slide back—we haven't been born."

His stare was sharp. "But only fer those who can leap. If ye can leap, ye can find anyone at any time."

"I wonder," Tabby said thoughtfully, "if the spirit is *allowed* to move backward?"

"Satan is probably pleased." He shrugged and Tabby thought about the bottom line—evil wanted chaos and anarchy. Evil followed no rules.

"You told me that the Masters aren't allowed to go backward or forward in time and encounter their older or younger selves. I think we both have an idea of why that rule exists."

He confronted her, fists on his hips, reading her mind. "No."

"I have barely conceived my plan," she cried. "But maybe we can lure the ghost to Melvaig and get it into contact with Criosaidh."

"By usin' ye as bait? Never!"

Tabby stared. If she went to Melvaig, ostensibly to make peace with Criosaidh, maybe the ghost would follow her there and implode. "It can't hurt to try."

He was disgusted. "She'll kill ye then an' there. There willna be conversation, just yer death at her hands!"

"Because of her vengeance for her husband and her son?"

His expression hardened. "Ye blame me now fer the ghost? Mayhap ye're right. Mayhap my war started this."

Tabby hurried to him. She touched his face. "I don't blame you. I would never blame you. And placing blame right now is pointless."

He breathed hard. Tabby had the strongest certainty that he was blaming himself.

"This is not your fault. But freeing Coinneach might be a really good idea—and returning him would be the perfect excuse to go to Melvaig."

"Ye willna be bait."

In a way, Tabby was relieved, because she wasn't all that brave. "And Coinneach? Keeping him prisoner can't be helping."

Macleod's expression became hard enough to crack. "She'll gloat if we return him. 'Twill be seen as a sign o' weakness. Her revenge against me will continue."

He was probably right on all three points, Tabby thought. But she suddenly sensed that fourteen-year-old boy somewhere close by. "It can't hurt to free him. It might appease her, even if for a moment."

His tension seemed to escalate. "I will think on it."

Tabby blinked in surprise.

"Maybe it will appease the ghost, too," she whispered, stunned that he might see reason, after all.

He spoke harshly. "She has to be the woman who dies in that fire, Tabitha. 'Tis when she becomes a ghost. Ye dinna die there—she dies there."

He was distressed and not trying to hide it. "She is associated with that fire and that is all I am sure of. If the fire did result from a war of witches, maybe it was me and Kristin." Tabby didn't think so. "Maybe she dies afterward." Meaning that Tabby had died first. Macleod made a hard sound. Tabby tried to sound casual. "Maybe she hates me so much that her ghost takes up the war where we left off." That was a dismal thought.

He stared at her. Tabby felt his mind racing.

"I hate not being able to read your mind!" she cried.

"This needs to end now. I will go to Melvaig."

She inhaled. "To kill her?"

He smiled coldly. "It's long overdue."

"Do you even have the power?" Tabby's worry escalated wildly. "And what is that going to accomplish? Her ghost will be born in the thirteenth century, instead of at An Tùir-Tara?" She realized what murdering Criosaidh would do—it would change a future historical event if she died now. She would not be at An Tùir-Tara in 1550. "This isn't a good idea! We can't mess around with history and you know it."

He was thoughtful now.

"Macleod…how powerful is she?"

"I dinna ken."

That was not the answer she had wanted. "If you go, I am going with you! And what if you fail? What if you can't destroy her?" Tabby thought that a likely possibility.

"I need the power to leap," he said softly, more to himself than to her.

And Tabby knew what he meant. "To do what? To leap to Melvaig to go after her? And when that doesn't work, to go to An Tùir-Tara to protect me? To make certain she dies, in one time or another?"

"Damn the gods," he said softly, his eyes blazing.

"That will hardly help! And changing the future is as bad an idea as changing history!"

"I willna let ye die! I will get the power, if I have to beg fer it or steal it!"

The gods were already angry with him. They'd be furious if he went to Melvaig now to interfere in their handiwork—and just as furious if he went to 1550 to intervene in An Tùir-Tara. "Changing Fate is not allowed!"

"Do ye think I care?" he raged.

"If I am meant to die there, it's over, Macleod!"

"I willna let ye die—not now, an' not at An Tùir-Tara," he said. "An' if the gods dinna like that, to hell with them all."

MACLEOD WAS DOWNSTAIRS in the hall, brooding over wine. Tabby hoped he wasn't trying to bargain with the gods for the power to leap.

Tabby couldn't sleep either. They'd just made love again—frantically, as if their time was running out. She lay in his bed, staring up at the dark ceiling. She was going to have to admit it. She was scared.

She was afraid to die in that fire and she was afraid for Macleod, too.

It was so much easier worrying about him. He was so reckless, so arrogant—so defiant! He wanted to change Fate and she had to stop him. She couldn't imagine what his Fate would be if he dared to make that attempt, either at Melvaig now or at An Tùir-Tara.

Harmless shadows drifted across the ceiling. Outside,

wolves howled and the moon was high and full. She tossed and turned restlessly. It felt as if they were in over their heads, with no way out. But Macleod was becoming reasonable. He was considering releasing Coinneach to ease tensions. Maybe she could convince him to go along with her plan to lure the ghost to Melvaig. The only problem was that the plan scared her a lot. But his idea of hunting Criosaidh was even worse.

The shutters scraped the wall. Tabby's tension soared but it wasn't Criosaidh, it was the wind. Either plan would be worth it if they vanquished her damned ghost in the process. But destroying her ghost wouldn't necessarily change An Tùir-Tara. Getting rid of that spirit would buy them some time…maybe. Macleod's plan to simply kill Criosaidh and prevent her from ever being at An Tùir-Tara could save Tabby's life—if she was the witch Tabby would fight there. And Tabby was certain that she was, although she wished she had doubts.

She closed her eyes and felt hot tears. Tabby realized she wanted time with Macleod. Wanting two-and-a-half centuries was absurd—she didn't think she had that kind of life span—but she wanted time to really get to know him, to talk to him, spend time doing all kinds of silly things like ice skating and picnics and pizza while watching John Wayne movies.

She felt like crying now. Macleod wasn't going to go ice skating at Rockefeller Plaza, but he might like a John Wayne movie and he'd love pizza—except he belonged at Blayde and she did not. Her heart thundered, trying to tell her something. "Not now," she whispered.

They were in trouble—or, she was in trouble, and a few things were clear. Getting rid of the ghost was a great idea and freeing Coinneach wasn't a bad one. But she had to stop Macleod from going to either Melvaig or An Tùir-Tara. Not allowing him to interfere in history was the biggest priority of all. Even if it meant she would die.

It can't be soon, Tabby thought desperately. Just thinking that made her feel selfish. But she was thinking about Macleod. She had so much to do. He needed her so much.

But Fate could be very cruel, and bad things happened to good people all the time.

The chamber's open door slammed closed.

Tabby sat bolt upright as evil and hatred swarmed into the room.

Criosaidh had come back.

Even as she knew that the witch's ghost was present, the evil closed in on her like quicksand. Tabby slowly stood up, everything except her adversary forgotten. *Just how powerful was the ghost?*

Her evil filled the room.

Tabby felt herself slip into a sea of calm. Focused as never before, she said, "Show yourself, Criosaidh."

Nothing happened. Instead, Tabby felt the hatred growing.

She closed her eyes as several shutters began banging, casting a spell to reveal the spirit. Its anger and hatred intensified. When Tabby opened her eyes, a dark and sultry woman shimmered in the chamber, her eyes burning with hatred, so transparent that Tabby could see through her. And then she smiled.

Against the wall, Tabby tensed, preparing for a terrible onslaught. She began to put a protection spell on herself.

But Criosaidh vanished.

Stiff with tension, Tabby looked around the interior, and the shutters slammed open, a huge blast of frigid air gusting into the room.

It was so strong that Tabby was hurled across the entire chamber and against the far wall. She cried out as she was smashed against the stone, and then the energy died.

On her knees, Tabby straightened slowly, her eyes wide,

every hair on her body standing on end. Even though the chamber was absolutely still, she felt the spirit's evil and hatred gushing about her. She couldn't see Criosaidh, but she was still present.

"Evil get out, evil be gone. My white power, keep you away," Tabby murmured.

The energy returned with blazing force, crushing Tabby against the wall. She gasped, but focused on the spell. The force beat her there, battering her as an insane man might with a stick of wood. *"Evil get out, evil be gone. My white power, keep you away!"* But even as she chanted, she knew that Criosaidh's ghost wasn't harmless after all.

The energy shifted.

Tabby collapsed to the floor. *"Evil get out, evil be gone,"* Tabby cried.

And suddenly Criosaidh took form again, standing there in the center of the chamber, murderously enraged. They faced each other.

"Evil get out, evil be gone!" Tabby screamed.

She vanished and a hurricane force swept into the chamber as the shutters blew off the windows, and her pallet slammed into the wall. Tabby braced herself, but she was hurled backward, and then Criosaidh's energy pinned her brutally to the wall.

In that moment, she thought of Macleod, and knew death would take her now if he didn't save her.

HE WOULD NEVER LET Tabitha die in the fires of An Tùir-Tara. He would do whatever he had to in order to change her death. And damn the gods, because the knowledge of her death by fire was so familiar to him, as if he had somehow known all along that this was how she died. But if Kristin had spoken the truth, they would both be there.

She could not leave him.

It was a terribly dismal thought.

Was he coming to care for her?

Did that make him weak?

He was actually considering freeing his prisoner, but it had nothing to do with giving up his vengeance. Tabitha might be right and Criosaidh might be momentarily appeased. He saw no reason why he couldn't protect her and fulfill his duty to the dead at the same time. Coinneach would live another day, but not for much longer after that. And returning Coinneach gave him the perfect excuse to get inside Melvaig—so he could murder Criosaidh and end this once and for all.

Where was Ruari? Hadn't he heard him? He needed the power to leap to An Tùir-Tara, just in case he was incapable of destroying Criosaidh now.

Macleod sighed, his head hurting—his heart hurting. An Tùir-Tara was two-and-a-half centuries away. But the deamhan ghost was there in the present with them. He should not stay downstairs for too long. Criosaidh's ghost had breached Tabitha's protection spell, even if she hadn't tried to use her black power. The failure of the spell was ominous; it did not sit well with him. He had the instincts of a hunter, but now, he almost felt like the hunted. And to make matters more dire, he sensed that the sands of time were running out.

He heard a sob behind him—or he thought he did. He whirled.

A thin fourteen-year-old boy faced him, standing before the hearth, crying in despair, weeping in rage, wanting to know why. *Why?*

He couldn't breathe. He couldn't look away, incredulous that the boy would dare to make his presence known at such a dangerous time. He wanted the damn boy gone.

It was so clear that the boy was terrified, but not of evil or his enemies. He was afraid of being alone.

Macleod had forgotten that.

The boy fell to his knees, crying. Mixed up in the fear, there was rage. That boy was furious with the world, but instead of ranting and raving, he wept. When he was finally done, he had to take that rage and bury it at sea with all of his loved ones, so he could become a man and do his duty and live a life of soulless revenge.

He had forgotten that, too.

The boy stared at him as if bewildered. Why?

Why? Every man had his duty, his burdens, his responsibilities. Macleod strode to the boy, intending to kill him with his bare hands, because he did not want to recall any of this, ever! But the boy vanished, so he seized the chair and hurled it at the wall with all of his strength. It struck the stone above the hearth, splintering into a thousand tiny pieces.

That boy was pathetic. He pitied him—hated him. How dare he question his life!

And then he heard Tabitha call him.

Too late, he felt the evil and her pain.

CHAPTER SIXTEEN

"ARE YOU ALL RIGHT?" Nick asked. He did not bother to lower his voice, as they were in the midst of a thick forest and entirely alone. He glanced upward to locate the sun. Although he saw slivers of blue sky, he gave it up and reached into his pack for his GLD, a palm-size device that would instantly tell him where they were—but not if he'd made it to the right time.

Jan was also clad in camouflage, carrying a small pack with her gear, and she stood, brushing dirt and pine needles from her thighs and seat. She had resisted going back until liftoff, arguing that she was needed at HCU to hold down the fort. But, never one to hold a grudge, she said, "I'm fine. Where are we?"

He smiled. The best thing about Jan, other than the fact that he considered her family, was that she was all business when it counted. He glanced at the LED screen. His smile vanished. "Motherfucker. We're just north of Loch Gairloch."

Jan didn't bat an eye. "You know how hard it is to pinpoint a landing. How far are we from Blayde?"

He tapped the screen and a moment later, an estimate had come up. "About twenty miles. And there's a few big puddles between us and them. I don't know about you, but I don't have an inflatable raft in my pack."

Jan folded her arms, appearing cross. "Come to think of it, considering the high percentage of water in the Highlands, why didn't we pack one?"

"Last time I flew by Scottish Air, I landed right on target." He tapped the screen. "We're really close to Melvaig."

"Tabby's at Blayde. Or that is the most likely scenario. My money says Kristin's wherever Tabby Rose is."

"What would I do without you?" He grinned. He liked going back in time, especially to medieval Scotland, even if this was only his third trip back. The air was so damned invigorating. And he loved the fact that he couldn't predict what the hell they would encounter. Now they'd have to borrow a vessel from Melvaig.

Jan said, "You should have told me about the flashbacks."

He shrugged as if he didn't give a damn, even though his gut clenched. There'd been four—when he'd hoped that first one would be the last one. They were getting more intense and closer together.

"You need a psych evaluation. You should *not* be here, now, damn it," Jan said, her beautiful green eyes flashing.

She'd been arguing about the mission when he let the information slip. She kept telling him to take Sam or MacGregor or the new Russian guy. She'd had that steely look in her eyes that meant she was never going back in time again, not for anyone, not even for him. And that was when he'd told her he was having flashbacks.

They'd almost killed him once.

They'd killed an agent instead.

He couldn't do this alone and he couldn't tell anyone. They'd put him back in psych. And he had HCU to run.

"No one has ever been able to determine how long a leap takes. For all we know, it takes years."

"You should not be in the field! You cannot afford to have a flashback in the middle of hand-to-hand combat with some six-foot medieval demon. We both know you are *incapacitated* during a flashback."

"That's why you're here, sweetheart." He glanced at his GLD again. "I know you'll take care of your old boss."

"Don't you dare *sweetheart* me. I can't stand this."

He became concerned. What looked like static covered the screen. What the hell? He looked up. "You went through hell, Jan, but you made it, and that last trip was a long, long time ago. Time to move on." He glanced at the screen. "Shit. Look at this."

Jan came to stand beside him and her eyes widened. "I'd say an energy source is nearby."

He slid the useless GLD into his vest pocket. "Yeah, but is it friend or foe?" He looked upward. There was no way to discern where the sun was. He knew they should head down the forested ridge toward Melvaig and Blayde, which lay to the north, but without guidance from either nature or the GLD, they would probably lose their way.

Jan pointed at the towering pine behind him. He got it. They decided on a patch of black far below, and started in silence down the ridge, using both markers to keep going in a straight line. Suddenly shadows consumed the forest. Clouds had blown in, and their black object was gone.

He tried the GLD again. Nothing.

"We're going to get lost," Jan said, stating the obvious.

"Not if I can help it." Nick was determined. He was going to nail Kristin, no matter what it took, and make her talk about her unholy connections.

They started in silence down the ridge, brushing branches out of their way. Above them a deep-throated owl hooted. Birds sang. It was actually a helluva pleasant day, except for the fact that they were not alone. Nick kept checking his GLD every few minutes, but the static remained. A source of energy was nearby—and it had lots of power. But Nick didn't sense evil. Neither did Jan; she'd say so otherwise.

When he looked at the screen again, it was a frenzy of static activity. "We have company," he began, when thunder boomed. Not from overhead, but from up the ridge, behind them. The earth moved beneath their feet.

There was power, lots of it, but it was the good kind.

Her eyes sharp with interest—Jan was rarely afraid—she touched his arm as they turned to face the slope above them. He was damned curious, too. The forest was dark now, silent, unmoving. The snow on the GLD screen continued to dance like crazy.

The trees shifted and branches parted. Nick watched a rider on a horse emerge from the shadows and his eyes widened.

A woman sat a white stallion, her reddish-gold hair falling down her back, a huge sword in one hand, her muscular arms ripped. He took one fast look at her face and his heart lurched hard. She was shockingly beautiful. He quickly looked at her bare muscular thighs, wrapped around that horse—he couldn't help himself. She was dressed the way the Highland men dressed, which meant she was showing a helluva lot of leg, and she had frigging great legs.

Jan breathed, "Chill."

He caught himself. The woman was a warrior and she had power—lots of it. She halted the horse a dozen feet from them, unsmiling. Her eyes were green, he realized, and unblinking. Her demeanor could not be called friendly. In fact, it was cool and wary.

He smiled to disarm her and said in Gaelic, "We're lost. Can you help us?" She'd know that they had power, too, so there was no point in stating the obvious, that they were all on the same side.

She did not return his smile. "Aye. Ye wish to go to Blayde," she said flatly, in Gaelic. Her horse moved restlessly but she did not seem to care.

"Yes, we do." Now he became a bit perturbed. He was

acutely aware of her but she was as cold as ice. Not that it mattered, except that he was used to stopping women in their tracks. He lurked and was shocked when he couldn't get into her thoughts. His gaze returned to her.

She stared, and he thought the corners of her mouth had lifted ever so slightly in triumph.

So she meant to keep him out of her mind. Two could play that game. He envisioned her stark-naked on that stallion, really liking the mental image, and then blocked his thoughts from her.

He could have sworn that a hint of a flush came to her face, but it was hard to tell, because her eyes turned to ice. "Ye're goin' east, Outsider. Ye need go north. There's a trail that will take ye toward Melvaig and on to Blayde." Her power seemed to seethe. "The witch is at Melvaig," she added.

A new excitement began. "The witch from my time— Kristin Lafarge?"

She gave him a look of pure disdain. "I dinna ken her name. I dinna care fer yer future time. She's evil—an' great evil is with her."

"I need a guide. I'm sure there's something I can offer you in return." He did not want his thoughts to zip into the bedroom, but they did.

Jan jabbed her elbow into his ribs. "Cut it out," she said.

"You have nothing to offer, Outsider." She tightened her reins, flushing. "Domnhal!"

A huge, dangerous-looking, very human Highlander rode out of the woods.

She finally smiled at him, coldly. "Domnhal will show ye to Melvaig so ye can vanquish the witch an' go back to yer time. Outsiders are nay welcome here."

Their gazes finally held. Nick smiled slowly at her; she did not smile back. He reminded himself not to alienate her. "I appreciate it," he finally said softly. "But you should know that you are welcome in my time."

Although her eyes were ice, her color seemed to deepen. But he wasn't having entirely dirty thoughts. He wanted to know who she was and what she was capable of and her part in the war—and if she was somehow associated with the Masters. But she whirled the horse, galloping into the forest, before he could try to entice her into a dialogue. It thundered as her army joined her.

He became thoughtful. That woman was a warrior and she seemed fearless, but he'd had the odd notion that she just might be afraid of him.

"What is wrong with you?" Jan cried. "Do you have to come onto everything in skirts?"

"That wasn't in a skirt," he said thoughtfully. His blood continued to pound. She was *hot*. "She has a lot of power. I wonder what, exactly, she can do. She is one of us. She needs to lighten up, though." His mind couldn't help moving back to the medieval bedroom.

"Oh, and a few hours in your bed will do the trick?"

He had to smile. "Probably." In fact, he had no doubt he could ease her mind, among other things. He looked at Domnhal. "Who was that?"

"The Lady of An Roinn-Mor…a daughter of the gods."

MACLEOD REACHED the chamber's threshold. In horror, he saw Tabitha pinned to the wall.

A huge, vicious demonic force had her imprisoned there. Her feet did not even touch the floor. That force had every item in the chamber on end. The shutters had been ripped from the window and were in bits and pieces, thrust against the ceiling; the chest, table and chairs were in broken pieces, too, and plastered to the walls. Even his bed was upside down and broken, affixed to one wall. And Tabitha was in agony.

He instantly understood that it was as if she was caught within a terrible vise. Her face was deathly white and strained, her eyes were bulging, and the sheer force that had her pinned to the wall had her clothes pasted to her skin. Her pain struck him, pierced through him.

He roared in fury, attempting to battle through Criosaidh's energy, but it was so strong it was an invisible wall and he could not get inside the room.

Her terrified eyes met his. *I love you.*

It was déjà vu—he'd heard her before—her last dying words.

"Nay!" he roared, blasting the chamber with his power. The room shuddered but the cyclone only intensified and Tabitha screamed in more agony.

His power would do nothing. Macleod pushed against the wall of wind, determined to get past it and inside. Tabitha's screams kept sounding as he fought to get into the chamber. He somehow pushed across the threshold, the effort so monumental, his own tears fell. He grunted, refusing to give up, fighting his way through the demonic force—and Tabitha's screams abruptly stopped.

He didn't dare look up at her. He fought his way through Criosaidh's power, step by painful step. And suddenly the shutters that had been on the ceiling came raining down in pieces around him. The bed fell to the floor from the wall, as did the tables, chairs and chest. The wind had vanished; she had vanished.

Macleod looked up as Tabitha fell to the floor, eyes closed, as limp as a lifeless corpse.

He rushed to her and knelt, terrified now. "Tabitha!"

She was so badly beaten, so bruised, her neck at such an odd angle, that he was afraid to touch her and take her in his arms. Worse, her magic and power, her life, suddenly felt weak and fragile—and by the moment, it seemed to be ebbing. Slowly, he reached for her pulse.

She lay unmoving, as if dead. "Ye willna die," he said fiercely. "I willna allow it!"

He thought her lashes flickered.

He tried to stay calm so he could find her pulse. And then, finally, he felt the slow, faint beating of her heart, barely fluttering in her chest. And now, below her breasts, where the velvet dress clung to her torso, he saw that her ribs were broken.

"Tabitha." He had never been this afraid. How badly was she hurt? She was so pale but the skin around her eyes was turning black and blue. *She could not die.* He found his will. "MacNeil can heal ye. I need MacNeil." He was frantic. He dared to clasp her hand. "MacNeil!" he roared.

She moaned.

He jerked. "Ye will be fine, Tabitha. MacNeil will come an' heal ye an' I will kill Criosaidh!"

She lay so still, so beautiful and so fragile, her power slipping further away.

"Fight to live," he begged her. He raised his head. *"MacNeil!"*

And then, suddenly, he felt her weak grasp on his hand as he held her palm, and the shockingly brutal waves of her pain. She was becoming conscious. MacNeil should be on Iona. He needed the power to leap to him because he could not simply stay there and watch her die. He did not know if MacNeil had heard him. It crossed his frantic mind that MacNeil journeyed often and he might be in the past or the future. Macleod did not know if he was even in this time, or if he was able to hear him and come to them. But MacNeil was the only healer he knew of!

And then he recalled something Tabitha had said to him. Her best friend was a Healer, and she was at Carrick Castle with Ruari—but in the fifteenth century.

The gods had denied him the power to leap for his entire life.

Damn it, he must have it now! But should he try to find that woman or find MacNeil?

"Help us," he gritted, looking up. "Help her. Tabitha is good an' she deserves to live!"

There was no answer. Not only that, he did not feel a single god or goddess anywhere close by. Damn them—they did not care!

If ye dinna take yer vows soon, the gods will turn against ye.

Continue to displease the gods an' they will take from ye what ye cherish most...

Nay, he thought, trembling in fear. MacNeil could not have foreseen this moment. The gods could not be so angered with him that they would destroy Tabitha, who was kind and gentle and good.

He jerked. The fourteen-year-old boy knelt beside him, eyes wide and filled with tears. *Why?*

I dinna ken.

He had never felt so helpless.

Rob ran into the room. He took one look at her and said, "Her neck looks broken. Is she alive?"

He hadn't wanted to think it. Was her neck broken? The angle did not look right. "She's alive, but barely." She could not die—he could not live without her.

He had done this to her.

"Can ye use yer power to summon MacNeil?" Rob asked. But now, he was looking wide-eyed at the utter destruction in the chamber.

She was in so much pain. "Ye will live, Tabitha. Ye have some broken bones an' they will heal." He meant to reassure her. "I ken ye can hear me. So fight, Tabitha, fight to get well." Where was MacNeil?

He felt the slightest pressure on his hand and then he heard her.

Allie...

She wanted him to get the Healer.

I love you.

"Ye willna say goodbye!" he cried, aghast.

Take your vows...be my hero...

And the pressure on his hand disappeared.

"Nay!" He realized his tears were falling. "Tabitha, dinna give up, damn it!" But she was still now. Her life felt distant, as if it was getting farther and farther away by the second.

"MacNeil!" he shouted, and for the first time in his life, he felt powerless and lost. But MacNeil was not coming. Because if he'd heard Macleod, he would have already come to them.

He wanted to hold on to her tightly, forcing her to stay with him. "Ye will live. I will make certain," he whispered to her. Getting to his feet and leaving her was one of the hardest moments of his life. "Rob, ye willna move from her side."

Rob nodded. "An' how will ye do what ye've never been able to do?"

Macleod stood, ignoring him. He pushed his fear aside. He was the grandson of a great god and the power of the leap was his *right*. He pushed his awareness of Tabitha aside. He could not think of her now. He had to find the power, before it was too late and she died.

Everything in the chamber faded, blurring. He closed his eyes. He strained. There was only the struggle to go inside himself and grasp the power that had eluded him his entire life.

And as he delved, the crux of his life became crystal clear. It was all meaningless without her. It was his need for vengeance which had done this to her. In the end, the vengeance he was sworn to was going to destroy her.

And he hated the vengeance.

It served no one now.

The chamber became stunningly still and he felt their presence.

Light was pouring through the chamber's single window: white, bright, shimmering light. He inhaled. The figures in the light were vague and indistinct, like ghosts. The power was so bright, so holy, so fierce, so majestic, power he had never encountered this closely before, that he was mesmerized. He could not look away, even as the light intensified, hurting his eyes. "She canna die," he cried.

There was no answer.

His life flashed before his eyes. The massacre at Blayde in 1201—the day that he had lost everyone he loved, the day that had changed his life. The first time he had seen Tabitha, when she had come to him through her spell, an apparition summoning him with her magic to her time. And then he saw the face of every MacDougall he had ever murdered in the name of vengeance.

There was so much regret.

The brilliant white light became blinding.

He could not find the power because the gods were furious with him.

And he was furious with himself. Why had he fought this war for so long? Yes, his father had been betrayed and murdered, and it had been his duty, but he had had more than enough revenge. Had he given up the clan war against the MacDougalls long ago, she would not be dying now. He was certain that Criosaidh's ghost would not be stalking her so obsessively.

Tabitha was more important than his damned war of vengeance.

"Fine," he screamed at them. "I will give up my vengeance. Ye have my word. But give me the power to leap!"

And the gods briefly became visible—a handful of powerful immortals, male and female, in long, flowing gowns, all striking in power and beauty. And then they vanished.

The white light faded.

Silence fell.

He jerked his gaze to Tabitha, who remained still and silent on the floor. He could not feel her life now.

Horror consumed him anew. *This was how he would feel at An Tùir-Tara....*

The floor tilted.

The air moved.

Macleod cried out as he was hurled through the stone ceiling, through the clouds, and past this sun and too many other ones to count.

CHAPTER SEVENTEEN

TABBY SLOWLY BECAME conscious, swimming in pain. Crio-saidh had hurt her this time, she managed to think. She had almost died. But as she opened her eyes, warmth began seeping through her entire body. With the warmth, there was so much relief.

"Don't move, don't speak, just let me heal you."

Tabby blinked and saw Allie Monroe kneeling beside her. Her surprise vanished. She was so happy to see her best friend in the entire world. She wanted to hug her and hold her, hard.

"Do not move yet," Allie murmured. She was a tiny, beautiful dark-haired woman, who was now radiating intense white light. Tabby smiled at her, but Allie was entirely focused.

She had never been this powerful when she had lived in New York. Tabby was stunned by the intensity of her healing power, her pain already easing. As it receded, her recall of the recent attack returned. As excited as she was to see Allie, she instantly thought of Macleod. As Allie hovered over her, pouring her white healing power into her, Tabby started to sit up. But Macleod wasn't in the room with her. Instead, she saw Royce standing behind them, watching them carefully, his massive arms folded across his powerful chest, that gold cuff glinting.

"Hey, I'm good, but not that good," Allie said with a cocky smile. "Can you relax and give me another moment?"

Tabby looked at Allie. She realized she was worried, but

couldn't quite pinpoint why. And now she saw that Allie was wearing tight jeans, high-heeled boots and a tiny leather jacket. But of course she was. "Are you a medieval fashionista now?"

Allie grinned. "That would be you—no longer the country-club hostess but lady of the manor! I *hate* medieval clothes. I refuse to dress like a medieval woman and that is that."

Tabby was hardly surprised. She glanced at the velvet gown she was wearing, thinking of Macleod. "I love this dress."

"You would."

They smiled at each other.

But the prickling of worry came back. "Where's Macleod?"

Allie sat back, apparently finished, the radiant light diminishing. "He brought us here and then he left. He was very upset."

Tabby thought that she recalled his absolute and abject fear for her. Had she hallucinated his making a pact with the gods? Had she heard him swear he would take their vows and give up his vengeance? "How did he find you?"

Allie seemed puzzled. "He found me at Carrick, Tabby, in the fifteenth century. Since we don't know each other—yet—I assume you sent him to me."

"I did." Tabby wet her lips. "But he can't leap."

Allie slowly smiled. "Uh, honey, he can leap, and if he's said otherwise, he's telling a big fat lie, although I cannot imagine why."

Tabby collapsed back onto the pillows, tears forming. He had made a pact with the gods and they had given him the power to leap. He was going to take his vows and become a Master, giving up the dark and bloody life he lived. She was thrilled.

"What is going on?" Allie cried. "Those are tears of happiness, aren't they?"

"He has been suffering so," Tabby whispered unsteadily. "And, yes, I'm happy, considering all that has happened."

"Welcome to the world of big, bad and oh-so-sexy medieval men." Allie grinned. "Oh, and did I forget to mention how superstubborn they are?"

Tabby looked at her, her tears falling. She had survived Criosaidh. She wasn't sure how that had happened. Criosaidh had been far more powerful than she, Tabby, had been. Had she simply decided to leave, with the plan of coming back again to finish what she'd started?

But she was supposed to die at An Tùir-Tara. Tabby tensed in dread.

"What is it?" Allie asked quickly.

No, she told herself. Macleod had made a pact with the gods. He would not go to An Tùir-Tara to change history and defy them another time. But she cringed inwardly, because he was so reckless and arrogant. She didn't think his character would change overnight. When he made up his mind to do something, nothing would stand in his way—not even a god.

She turned to smile grimly at Allie. "So they're all impossible?"

"Honey, they're *medieval.*"

"No kidding. The first time I met Macleod, he beheaded a sub—while I was in that boy's arms."

Allie winced. "Ow. I bet that did a ton for your romantic relationship."

Tabby started to laugh. Allie grinned with her. Automatically they both reached out and held hands, clinging. "I love it," Allie said softly. "You are the gentlest soul I know. And he's one of the hardest of souls. Life with him won't be easy," she warned.

"I never said we were going to make a life together," she began, then stopped. Her heart shrieked at her.

Allie gave her an "are-you-crazy" look. "So you're going to walk away and leave him hanging around here without you? When another woman looks at Royce, my claws come out!"

Tabby sat up straighter. "I can't *stand* the idea of him with another woman."

"Good!"

"Why are you cheering for us?"

"Because you love him. Because he obviously loves you."

Tabby stared.

Allie's brows lifted. "I am meant to be with Royce. He is my other half. I couldn't live without him—and he certainly couldn't live without me. We are a team, Tabby, in every way, even the silly ways, and certainly in the life-altering ones. It is meant to be."

Tabby nodded, wondering if she and Macleod could ever get past their differences and become partners and soul mates like that. She sobered. He was giving up his vengeance and taking his vows. It was a step in the right direction.

"Why do you look so uncertain?" Allie exclaimed. "Because he can behead his enemy without blinking?"

Tabby smiled grimly. "He can be cruel and he is ruthless."

"He's a Highlander, girlfriend. And in case you haven't figured it out, grudges are carried for life around here, his mortal enemies are as cruel and as ruthless, and given a choice, these machos *like* using their swords. Hey—they are real men."

Tabby almost smiled. *Ye need a real man*...."You're so cool about it."

"I want Royce alive, Tabby, and at my side."

Leave it to Allie to find the bottom line, Tabby thought. "He put a boy in stocks, without food and water, intending to let him die there. I couldn't allow it, Allie. But I could barely reason with him."

"I never said the medieval-modern thing was easy, but it's worth it. But you already know that—and I know it." Her grin was saucy.

Tabby sighed, thinking about all the good times and all the

bad times—and all the nights they'd shared. "He cares about me and he's proven it time and again. He's even sworn off vengeance. At first it was just sex." She blushed. "Maybe it is worth it."

Allie said softly, "Yeah, Tabby!"

They'd had many late-night talks, discussing their love lives and Tabby's problems. "I don't even know how this has happened, but I really care about him, too. I care so much." Her heart thundered. "I love him," she whispered, and the moment she'd spoken, she realized it was true.

Allie touched her arm. "You are his better half," she said softly. "And, Tabby, gentle soul that you are, he is your other half."

Tabby bit her lip, wondering exactly how much Allie knew about her future.

Royce came forward, his gray eyes hard. "Ye canna divulge the future, Ailios," he warned. "Not even to Lady Tabitha."

Tabby looked back and forth between them, wondering what his words meant, exactly. Did he know her, too, in the fifteenth century? Was she going to choose to stay with Macleod in his medieval world? It sounded absurd! But leaving him felt crazy, horrible…and impossible.

Allie smiled. "Royce is uncompromising. Before I came along, the Code was his love and his life."

Royce gave her an annoyed look. "We have overstayed our welcome."

Tabby started, alarmed. "You are totally welcome!"

Allie took her hand and gave Royce a dark look. "I am not ready to leave her yet, when she is confused and upset."

Royce said softly, "Macleod would confuse an' upset any lass, even Lady Tabitha. He confuses ye, most o' the time! She an' Guy need to help themselves—as we did."

Allie gave him a long look and he flushed. "I will make this up to you, Royce," she finally said, very softly.

Tabby looked away, but not before she saw him hesitate. Then he sighed and stalked from the room. Tabby looked at Allie. "How long have you both been together?"

Allie laughed. "Almost sixty years, and, yes, I can still manipulate him with sex! He is supersexed and the promise of my best behavior in bed always gets me what I want." Then she became pensive. Her dark stare was direct. "I love him so much."

"I can see that. And I am so happy for you." Tabby stood and paced to the window. Her smile faded. She wished Macleod would walk through the door so she could go into his arms. Was he the love of her life after all? Was it possible? She was never going to forget how frantic he had been when she'd been dying. And he'd given up his vengeance so he could leap to get her help.

Tabby wondered if she was remembering that correctly. It was such a blur of pain and fear. And where was he?

She turned. Allie and Royce were a super couple. There was no doubt in her mind that they were attached at the hip, the heart and the soul. There was something obvious, powerful and natural about it. Suddenly she wanted that bond for her and Macleod.

Allie stood and came over to her. "So what's going on here? What attacked you?"

Tabby shivered. "A ghost...that came from the sixteenth century."

"Great." Allie smiled, unperturbed. "Is it human?"

"Actually, its corporeal self is a fairly immortal witch that is living at Melvaig right now, even as we speak."

"Interesting. How are your powers?"

"Better." Tabby smiled. Being with Allie again was great. She hadn't changed—she remained unflappable and fearless.

"I wonder what you did in the sixteenth century to piss the witch off, other than kill it?"

Tabby froze. "Is that what you think?"

"Tabby, you just said it's haunting you."

"Allie, I've been seeing into the window of time."

Allie's eyes widened. "From that serious expression, I'm almost afraid to ask."

Tabby wet her lips. "It all began at the Met. There was this exhibit about a great fire in 1550 at An Tùir-Tara. I felt the ghost's evil and saw Macleod. He was bloody and burned. He'd been at the fire and it all felt like déjà vu."

"What do you mean?"

"I felt that I knew Macleod, and I knew that witch. I felt that I'd been at the fire. In fact, when I first came to Blayde, it was familiar, too! But MacNeil said I've never been here before."

"Maybe you're having a flash forward."

"What on earth is a flash forward?" Tabby cried.

"It's that moment when your soul recognizes its Fate."

Tabby stared, stunned.

"It's actually that simple—a flashback in reverse. Your soul can recognize what will happen, as if it has already happened, and it feels familiar and right. Some say it happens because a soul feels itself across time, in another moment. Does it matter? Soul recognition is soul recognition. We've all had flash forwards at some point. I've had them with Royce—and it always ends with the feeling that it's familiar and right."

Tabby breathed hard. Was it possible that her soul had recognized Blayde, Macleod, their love—and whatever would happen at An Tùir-Tara? "Do you know anything about An Tùir-Tara, Allie?"

Allie shrugged. "I haven't lived that long yet. You know it's awfully risky business to zip around time—one slip and Fate is all messed up. Royce and I try really hard to mind our own business—except, of course, for protecting and healing Innocents."

"You never mind your own business!" Tabby smiled and then she sobered. "I die at An Tùir-Tara."

Allie paled. "Like hell you do! Royce died in my arms, do you remember? But I never gave up on him or us, and I went back and changed it! Macleod will not let you die!"

"I hope you're right." Tabby didn't state the obvious. Allie knew the rules as well as she did. She knew all about Fate.

Tabby looked at the door again. "Okay, I'm getting worried. He was flipping out when I was hurt. Why isn't he here?"

Allie hesitated. "He can be really difficult. As far as he's come, he will still be a challenge for you for a long time."

Dread began. "Where did he go, Allie?"

"I know you said he swore off vengeance, but he walked out of here like a man bent on revenge."

Tabby felt her heart stop. In that moment, she suddenly knew what he intended—she knew it as if she was in *his* mind. "Oh, my God. He's going after Criosaidh to kill her!"

THE FRONT GATES TO THE baron of Awe's home were closed. Sam stared at the closed iron gates, set between two stone pillars, from the front seat of her rental car. She saw the intercom but ignored it. The gates began to open, a simple enough task to accomplish.

She was filled with tension, so much so that her grip on the steering wheel of the Jag was white-knuckled and her entire body was vibrating. She took a breath as the gates swung wide enough to admit the car. What was wrong with her? Not only was she unusually tense, she had a damned headache. But of course, she expected a hellish confrontation with Ian Maclean. She would never let him best her. The truth was, she had hoped to never set eyes on him again.

She hit the gas and the tires screeched, kicking up gravel. She'd met him in Oban last September, just a few months ago, when she and Brie were trying to figure out Aidan's Fate. They'd exchanged a dozen words and he'd taken Brie back in time to find his father, leaving her standing on the corner alone. She'd disliked him immensely, instantly. And why not? He was drop-dead gorgeous, reeking of virility, power and wealth—and he knew it. He knew he was handsome, rich and mega-powerful, one of the world's elite. His arrogance had been obvious and so had his disdain. He didn't like women— he simply liked sex. Sam had felt it. He was an oversexed, over-powered user. It had been obvious that he expected women to fawn over him, chase him. It was as obvious that he didn't give a damn about anyone or anything.

And why should he? He could buy whatever he wanted, destroy whatever he wanted, fuck whomever he wanted, whenever he wanted. And he expected it to be that way.

He was a bastard and it was that simple. He'd looked at her, clearly thinking about all of the things he'd like to do to her in his bedroom. *Ha-ha,* Sam thought. If push came to shove and she took him to bed to get what she wanted, it would be exactly that—*her* taking *him* to bed. However, she hated the idea. She was not going to be one of a thousand forgettable women, not ever. She needed to go back in time, but she had a bargaining chip or two. She knew he'd never help her just because they were both good guys on the same side of the battlefield. But he could surely use her connections at HCU.

He'd never do anything for nothing.

Sam braked in front of a huge, centuries-old ancestral home. She got out of the car, a short skimpy dress beneath her wool coat. She was wearing stilettos and she had to navigate the stone path leading up to the front door. She felt his power coming from within the house in huge hot waves, and she felt the power of two more men, as well.

A butler greeted her at the front door, his eyes wide with

surprise. "I'm afraid I did not realize his lordship was expecting another guest."

He had a *butler.* It was so absurdly classic that it was funny. Sam stepped past the man, handing him her coat. "He's not. I opened the gates with my superpowers. So where's his *lordship?*"

The butler paled. "Your name, madam?"

"Madam Butterfly." Sam smiled. "I'll find his lordship myself." She started across the entry hall, acutely aware of the coat of arms on one wall and the multimillion-dollar masterpieces on the other walls. She heard voices and the tinkle of glasses. Great, a party. She loved parties.

"Please wait, madam," the butler cried, chasing her.

Sam strode to the threshold of a living room, instantly dismissing the two other men and three beautiful women in the elegant, old-world room. Ian stood in front of a massive stone hearth, clad in an impeccably tailored tuxedo, a flute of champagne in one hand. A solid gold watch was exposed, as were sapphire cuff links. His eyes were on her as she paused. He'd felt her, too, and was expecting her.

"It's all right, Gerard," he drawled in a heavy Scot brogue. "The more, the merrier." He tipped his flute at her, his blue gaze gleaming with male interest.

Sam breathed hard. Well, she hadn't imagined the lust—or how frigging hot he was. He was looking at her long, strong, bare legs, undoubtedly speculating about how it would feel to have them wrapped around his waist. *Dream on,* she thought silently.

He started.

Great, he thought to read her mind. Two could play this game. "Your lordship, I hope I am not imposing," Sam mocked. She thought about curtsying but decided that would be overdoing it.

His eyes gleamed even more brightly. "I was wonderin' how long it would take ye to find me."

She smiled coldly at him. "In your dreams," she murmured.

"I'm very fond o' dreams."

"I'll bet."

A beautiful woman in a long, slinky red dress stood, moving to stand possessively beside him. She had a *Playboy* centerfold body, a perfect face and endless legs—but so did Sam. She did not have lethal blades concealed in her high heels or a laser-edged DVD in her purse that could sever a man's head from his body. "I didn't realize you'd invited another guest to Lord Ross's."

Ian didn't look at her. He sauntered forward and Sam tried not to inhale. His stride was sensual and suggestive, the gait of a man in slow pursuit, a man absolutely certain of the evening's outcome. "Hello, Rose." He paused by a dry bar and poured champagne into an untouched flute. He handed it to her. "Welcome to my lair."

"But your father was the wolf." Sam batted her lashes at him.

"Like father, like son," he murmured, his gaze dipping to her cleavage.

The champagne was Cristal, of course. Sam took the flute and knew he meant for their fingers to brush. Her body was very hot and very tight, but it didn't matter. She was never giving in to him—unless it was on her terms. "In the mood for a proposition?"

His mouth curved. "I've been in the mood since Oban."

"I'm so flattered." Sam nodded toward a pair of closed doors. Ian took her arm and looked at his guests and obviously expendable date. "We have some unfinished business to conclude. We'll only be a moment."

Sam glanced at his guests. The two women were affronted, but the two men seemed amused. She glanced at him carefully.

His eyes were almost silver now, and directed at the woman in red. He was mesmerizing her to his will.

She turned and sat down with the other women, an obedient little slave. She even smiled at them.

Ian opened the pair of doors, gesturing, as if a gentleman. Sam slithered past him, very deliberately, brushing her hip against him as she did. She entered a dark room. She heard him close the door; the lights came on. He smiled with relish at her. "I expected more of a hunt, Samantha."

"No one hunts me. And no one calls me Samantha."

Ian's mouth curved. "Ye've never had a real man."

Sam laughed with disdain at him. What a jerk! She sat down, crossing her legs, making sure her short black dress rode up precariously high. He looked. She leaned forward to set her flute down, aware of his focus on her full, mostly exposed breasts. She straightened, pleased. "I like toys," she said. "Oops, I mean *boys*."

"No wonder ye're so hot an' bothered around me." He smiled, hardly perturbed.

Sam bristled inwardly. "I am always ready for a good time."

His mouth curved again. "Then come here."

She sat back. *Not in a million years.* She lowered her lashes and said, "I need your help."

"O' course ye do. Ye need to go back in time to find your sister."

She jumped to her feet. He'd been reading her mind well before she'd arrived at his home on Loch Awe and that set her off balance, when she was almost never surprised. "I am not asking for a favor, Maclean."

He laughed at her, approaching, his gait slow and unrushed. "Of course not. Ye think I'm Santa Claus."

Sam tensed as he touched her bare shoulder, and his touch went through her entire body, causing a thousand tiny pulse points to explode in delight. "Santa wears a red suit and he's fat and gray. Have no fear, I know you helped Brie only to save your father."

"Take off the dress."

She started.

His eyes smoldered now. "Ye don't have to share my bed tonight. 'Tis yer loss, not mine. But I want to see the goods."

Sam seethed. He hadn't even given her the chance to make a deal. "You are an unbelievable bastard."

He laughed. "I've heard it a thousand times. Can't ye come up with something a bit more original? What's wrong? Are ye afraid of the bright lights?"

She didn't have a drop of cellulite on her body. Furious, Sam said, "I never refuse a challenge."

"Good."

Sam lifted her spaghetti straps and slid the dress down her otherwise naked and very flushed body. His gaze narrowed and his smile vanished. There was no laughter now. "Take a good long look, because it's your last one."

His thick lashes lifted. His stare was gray and sizzling. "'Tis my first one, Samantha, an' not the last."

"Delusions are always so sweet."

His gaze moved down every inch of her body then lifted. "Do ye really wish to prolong the agony?"

Unfortunately, every inch of her body seemed to be expanding and hurting. Sam stepped out of the pile of silk, leaving it at her stiletto-clad feet. "Send me back in time and I'll think about playing nice with you when I get back."

His mouth curled. It was a moment before he spoke. "I don't want ye to play nice," he said softly. "I want ye to play *bad*."

She inhaled. Desire dripped, pooled. It was a huge blow to her gut. "What's wrong? Miss Goody Two-shoes bore you? Oh, wait, let me guess. She only knows three positions."

He slid his hand over her breast. "She only knows two positions."

Sam bit off a gasp, refusing to make a sound of pleasure. Then, with the speed of a striking snake, she reached down, popped a four-inch stiletto from her heel, and pressed it against his jugular. "I so want to spill your blood."

He smiled. "Go ahead an' cut me. I don't care. I like blood. But we both know ye want me deep an' hard inside ye."

She was furious. "Drop your hand."

He did, only to stroke the curve of her cheekbone. "Good luck to yer sister," he said, turning away from her.

Sam was disbelieving.

Ian Maclean walked out of the room, leaving her standing there naked.

And he left the doors open, too.

MACLEOD DID NOT KNOW if he would ever become accustomed to the leap through time. He straightened, breathing hard, his head still exploding with pain.

"Ye fuckin' bastard," Coinneach gasped, moaning as he rolled in pain on the ground. "What kind...o' torture...have ye devised?"

Macleod breathed hard, not certain he could speak coherently yet. They had landed within Melvaig's central courtyard, the huge tower soaring almost directly above them—the tower from which Criosaidh practiced her magic, or so it was said. It was the tower that would be destroyed in the fires of 1550. If he had leaped correctly, it was but minutes later in the day.

He was going to kill Criosaidh. And while he was at it, if the other witch was there, he'd kill her, too. Tabitha would be safe from her enemies—unless the damned deamhan-ghost somehow survived.

His gut clenched so tightly it hurt. Tabitha had almost died that day. He would never forgive himself for what had happened to her. He would never forget how she had suffered. And it was his fault—he knew that now.

He would end this today. He would destroy Criosaidh, and then use his powers to go to An Tùir-Tara, if necessary, to save Tabitha from death. And when he was done, when she was safe, she could go back to her time, if that was what she still wished to do. He had brought her to Blayde against her will and he was sorry he had done so. Tabitha hadn't deserved such treatment. He would never force her to his will again. Now, he wished to atone for his behavior and for all that he had done, even if it meant sending her back to her time.

He could not bear the idea of life without her.

If he was truly fortunate, she would forgive him and wish to stay with him in his world.

The boy was afraid to be alone.

Cries began sounding from the watchtowers.

Coinneach sat up, his eyes widening as he realized where they were. "We're at Melvaig?" His befuddled glance blazed at Macleod. "'Tis true. Ye're one of them."

Macleod reached down and lifted him to his feet. "Bring yer witch mother to me."

Coinneach snarled, "I dinna think to obey ye, Macleod. An' if ye think I'll show ye mercy, think again. Ye'll die here, today, by my blade, at my hand!"

Macleod stared at Coinneach. Suddenly he pitied him. His life would be one of bloody revenge and it would never change—unless he found a great lady like Tabitha.

Let me help you.

He flinched. Now he understood what she had been trying to do for the past century.

And Coinneach jerked, as if he sensed a change in Macleod. He tightened his grasp on him anyway, as dozens of soldiers began rushing toward them from the ramparts and the hall. He would use Coinneach against the witch if he could. There was no other choice, even if Coinneach was an Innocent. He felt her evil approach.

He tensed. Thunder rumbled—but it wasn't Criosaidh, it was the gods. Surely they were not displeased now?

And as the evil intensified, as the hatred welled, as the fury rushed toward him, he slowly looked up.

Criosaidh stood in a tower embrasure, staring down at him and her son. Even from this distance, her black eyes blazed.

Then he felt a frisson of surprise trickle through him. Sensing an unfamiliar white power, he glanced at the soldiers surrounding them. Either a Master was present or someone very close to the gods. Whoever it was, he did not know him.

Behind several soldiers he saw a tall, dark-haired man, whom he instantly recognized. They had never been introduced, but he had observed Nick from his hiding place outside the school after the hostage crisis, during the hours Tabitha had been forced to remain there, answering his questions. He had learned his name and determined that he toiled to fight evil. He was clad as a Highlander, as was the beautiful blond woman with him. His ambition seethed.

Their gazes locked.

Nick sent him his thoughts. *I am hunting Kristin.*

Mayhap I will leave her fer ye.

I want her alive!

Macleod didn't care what Nick wanted. A big MacDougall man stepped forward. "Coinneach, are ye all right?"

Coinneach smiled coldly. "I've been starved an' beaten like a dog, but Macleod willna live to see the night fall. We'll have our revenge, Douglas."

Douglas's eyes hardened. "Ye're a fool, Macleod. Ye come alone? Ye think we will accept Coinneach's return an' feast with ye? Thank ye? Release him now. Ye're outnumbered here. Yer day is done."

"Bring me Criosaidh," Macleod said.

And suddenly the wind blasted through the courtyard, stirring up leaves and dirt, tunics and skirts lifting. "Release my son."

Macleod looked up at the tower window where Criosaidh stood, haloed in a dark mist on a bright sunny day. "Come down an' ask me nicely."

He felt her rage. The wind blasted him this time, causing dirt to strike him in the eyes. But even though briefly blinded, he did not release Coinneach. Instead, he sent his power at the tower, intending to strike stones from it.

But his powers failed him entirely.

He was furious and disbelieving.

The gods would dare to interfere *now?*

He had sworn off his vengeance against the MacDougalls, and his revenge now was against the evil hunting Tabitha!

But he was trying to change history, and it was not allowed.

Criosaidh laughed and this time, her black magic brought hail upon him. He withstood the onslaught somehow, refusing to cower, refusing to release Coinneach, who remained untouched by the debris. When it was over, he was bleeding and breathless and furious.

"You dare to fight me?" she called down to him. "I am the most powerful here!"

He looked up, wiping blood from his eyes. And then he saw the other witch at her side, pale, blond and diminutive in size.

Furious and aware of being weakened, he flung his power at them both—with no results.

Criosaidh roared and lightning cut across the bright blue skies. Macleod tensed. If she could strike him with the lightning, he would become very mortal, he had not a doubt.

Leap away.

Macleod looked past the Highlanders at Nick and the woman. Nick was telling him to flee like a coward. He wasn't a coward but he needed his power to vanquish Criosaidh. There was no other possible way.

"Macleod!" Tabitha screamed.

Stunned, he turned. In doing so he accidentally released Coinneach, who ran into the safety of the MacDougall soldiers. And he saw her standing with Royce and Allie, her face pale with fear, her expression imploring him to run and hide.

"Get her gone!" he shouted in alarm. He was afraid Criosaidh would try to destroy her again and, this time, succeed.

The words were hardly out of his mouth when the lightning bolt came.

He saw it come from above, veering toward him. And as its fork sizzled toward his heart, he knew he was going to be struck and that he would die.

Tabitha screamed in horror.

The lightning blazed into him, fire meeting flesh, searing it, and going through tendon, muscle and bone.

Macleod fell.

Blue flashed before his eyes—the bright blue Highland sky—and then there was only darkness.

CHAPTER EIGHTEEN

TABBY SAW THE LIGHTNING bolt go through Macleod's chest and she screamed again as he collapsed. It was Royce who reacted first; he flung his power at Criosaidh. As the tower where she stood began to collapse, he rushed forward, heaving Macleod onto his shoulder, a feat impossible for a normal man. He shouted at Allie, already running for a sally port. Allie seized Tabby's hand and as they started for the exit, a man standing there slammed the small door closed.

"Dinna let them escape," Coinneach screamed. "Seize them!"

More power blazed and the man fell over, but two other Highlanders had reached the sally port. Tabby had never cast a spell while on the run, but as the man seized the door, she did so now. *"Highlander stand aside,"* she gasped, *"mindless and let us pass!"*

He whirled and Tabby cried out when she met Nick's blazing blue eyes. He flung the small door open as a hail of arrows began. Tabby cried out but Nick seized her, jerking her past him and into the small doorway, Allie on her heels. A moment later they were all outside Melvaig, and Allie was kneeling over Macleod. Royce flung his power back at the men on the ramparts, and Tabby saw a dozen men fall from them.

She rushed to kneel by Macleod. He didn't appear to be breathing. He was white as a ghost when he was normally a swarthy man. *He could not be dead.*

A strong hand clasped her shoulder, pulling her to her feet. "Stand back an' let Ailios heal him."

Tabby looked up at Royce, terrified. How could he die? He was larger than life, and he meant everything to her! "He won't die, will he? Allie can save him, can't she?"

"I dinna ken."

That was not reassuring. Tabby trembled wildly, sick with fear, as Royce went to stand behind Allie, guarding her so she could heal Macleod. He lay unmoving, his pallor deathly. Tabby could not control her fear now; it was consuming. And she wondered if she'd ever told him that she loved him.

But he had to have known. He was always invading her thoughts—and she'd give anything for him to be doing so now.

Suddenly Tabby felt an intense and vicious hatred aimed at her. She glanced up warily at the ramparts. Coinneach stood there.

She tensed, dismayed. He'd been released and returned to Melvaig but the feud had drastically escalated, she thought uneasily. And she recalled Allie's insights. In the Highlands, grudges were held for life.

Then two women appeared on either side of Coinneach.

They were some distance away, but one was dark, the other petite and fair. There was no mistaking Criosaidh and Kristin. The sense of their hatred and rage escalated impossibly.

"Damn it to unholy hell."

Tabby turned as Nick paused to stand beside her. What on earth was he doing in the thirteenth century?

He flashed a brief, chilling smile and stared at the witches silhouetted above them. "I want that bitch," he said.

"You're hunting Kristin?" She glanced back at Allie and Macleod and cried out. Macleod was visibly breathing now and the color was rapidly returning to his face. He was going to make it!

Nick seized her arm before she could rush to him. "Mr. Tabitha is fine. How are you holding up?"

Tabby was trembling, tears flooding her eyes. She needed to go to Macleod and tell him that she loved him. She had never been so relieved. But even as her heart exploded with the power of her emotions for him, his lashes lifted slowly and their gazes met. When he saw her, he seemed relieved, too.

"I'm okay," she whispered, instantly understanding his concern for her.

Macleod sat up, rubbing his chest, Allie still kneeling by his side. His focus was on the ramparts, where Coinneach stood with the witches.

"Tabby?" Nick drawled, sounding impatient. "We need to talk about your little adventure."

She jerked to meet his very direct and intense blue gaze. "Do you want the short version or the unabridged one?"

His mouth tilted up at the corners. "Got some sass at last, Tabby?"

"Kristin followed me here from New York. And that demonic ghost is after me, too. As it turns out, it's Criosaidh." She nodded at the women on the ramparts, but glanced at Macleod, still thrilled he was all right. "She came from An Tùir-Tara and she's gone back in time to haunt me. We're trying to figure out how to get rid of her."

Nick's gaze moved from Criosaidh and Kristin and then back to Tabby. "It looks like the Middle Ages have done you some good. Got you out of that straitjacket you were so fond of."

Tabby gave in to the urge to let him have it, once and for all. "I have always respected you, Nick, and I have no idea how you got back here, but I don't like you."

"I know—I'm too macho and controlling for sweet little you." He actually chuckled and glanced at Macleod, who was standing and having a rushed conversation with Royce. "What an amazing match, huh? The gentle schoolteacher and the big bad barbarian."

Tabby flushed. "Macleod is difficult, but he's a product of his time...and he's evolving."

He leaned close. "Not that anything I say matters, but never think you can change a man. You're stuck with him." His grin vanished. "I need a debrief, kiddo."

Tabby was annoyed. Her relationship with Macleod was none of his business, but even Allie had said that Macleod would be a challenge for a while. It didn't matter. She didn't mind. Challenges were great! He was alive and that was what mattered. "Later, Nick."

She started to walk away from him, but he said, "Sam has been worried."

Tabby stopped in her tracks and turned. Thinking about her sister, whom she might never see again, hurt. "When you see her, tell her I'm fine and that I miss her. Is she okay?"

"She's a winner, Tabby, and a survivor, but you know that." Nick nodded at the two women standing on the ramparts. "Ten minutes, Tabby. That's all I need."

She sighed.

"WE HAVE TO GO," Allie said.

They had leaped back to Blayde. Allie and Royce stood with Tabby by the front doors of the hall. Tabby couldn't look at her, and not because Nick and his agent, Jan, were wandering around Macleod's hall with great interest. Or rather, Nick was roaming the hall with interest—Jan seemed really uptight. But MacNeil had appeared on their heels, and he and Macleod seemed to be having a very intense and mostly one-sided argument. In fact, MacNeil was doing most of the speaking. It was obvious that he was deeply angry with Macleod.

Tabby thought she knew why. He had gone to Melvaig for the wrong reasons. He hadn't gone simply to hunt evil and protect Innocence. He'd gone to destroy Criosaidh, in the hopes that she wouldn't be Tabby's adversary at An Tùir-Tara. He knew exactly what he was doing, and he didn't care about history or Fate.

If only he could be more cautious, more circumspect!

Tabby realized she was still staring at Macleod, who was poker-faced, and MacNeil, who was furious. Allie plucked her sleeve. "It's a really bad idea to mess with time. He knows better—but he doesn't care."

Tabby gave her best friend her full attention. "You're so right. I thought his giving up mortal vengeance would change him, but I don't know, Allie. I'm worried."

"You should worry. Fate is written by the gods for a reason—their reason—and we're not allowed to interfere."

She inhaled. She knew where Allie was going with this tangent.

"Which of the witches belongs to the ghost?"

Very defensively, Tabby folded her arms across her chest. "Criosaidh. If I had known what Macleod intended, I would have stopped him."

"Really? Tabby, I am going to take a chance and tell you something but I hope I don't pay for it. In my time, you and Criosaidh are arch enemies."

Tabby stared, surprised but not shocked. The fact that she would be around in the fifteenth century made her exult, but she understood the point her friend was making. Criosaidh wasn't meant to die in 1298. But she already knew that, because she knew her ghost came from An Tùir-Tara. And Macleod had known it, too.

He had chosen to destroy her before her time so he could protect Tabby.

"He's so strong-willed," Tabby whispered. "Maybe the gods don't know what he's done."

"They're pretty benign most of the time, but when push comes to shove, they make their wishes and feelings known. Guy is impossible when he makes up his mind. I've never seen MacNeil like this," Allie said, appearing uneasy. "He's mad as all hell, and his usual approach is logic and persuasion. Not only that, MacNeil thinks of Guy as a little brother, because he took Guy under his wing, so to speak, after the massacre. I have a bad feeling about this."

Tabby did, too. "We have to be through the worst," she said. But she didn't believe it, not for a moment. Criosaidh was alive and enraged, just to the south, and so was her son; her ghost hadn't been vanquished, so it was undoubtedly preparing another attack; and An Tùir-Tara was in their future.

And just how was she going to live for a couple of centuries?

"Tabby, you have to persuade Macleod to obey some of the rules! He can't decide to change history, no matter how much he loves you."

Tabby's heart lurched with dread, but there was joy, too. Did Macleod love her? "When I first met him, I assumed him incapable of love."

"Ha," was all Allie said.

Tabby turned to glance at him. He was brooding by the hearth, alone. "Sometimes I'm afraid he's a train wreck waiting to happen."

"He is. But he's strong, powerful and blessed—he just needs a guiding hand." Allie smiled at her. "Good luck."

Suddenly Tabby clung to her. "Allie, I wish you didn't have to go!"

Allie stroked her hair, reaching up to do so. "But I do have to go. Royce and I belong in the fifteenth century, and you know the rules. Before you know it, we'll be drinking wine and fighting evil together again! And you're not alone, not anymore—not ever again."

Tabby couldn't smile. Allie was right—she wasn't alone. And while she wanted to know how she'd wind up in the fifteenth century, she decided not to ask. She could be flung there in five minutes, but Allie had said she'd been with Royce for almost sixty years—and she still looked twenty-five.

Maybe time travel changed the aging process.

Or maybe there was something to that family joke about the Rose women getting better with age. Maybe MacNeil had known Grandma Sara when she was really young and time travel hadn't been involved. It was a mind-blowing notion.

Allie hugged her another time, taking Royce's hand. He nodded at her, and then they slipped outside into the dusk.

Tabby turned, her heart racing. Macleod remained at the fireplace, arms folded across his chest, and MacNeil was still seated at the table. He stood and walked over to her. "He tasks even my patience, finally."

She tensed. "He does have every right to hunt evil."

"He went to destroy Criosaidh to change the future."

Tabby tensed. There were no secrets. "He'll leave Criosaidh alone. I'll make sure of it."

MacNeil was skeptical. "Put a leash on him, then." He paused, his green eyes suddenly concerned. "They're so enraged they took his powers from him when he needed them most—and they'll do so again. I am worried about him."

Tabby inhaled. She had the certainty that MacNeil rarely worried about anything. "Maybe they don't know… It was only one time!"

MacNeil laughed mirthlessly. "He's been defying the gods fer a century. He's misused his powers time an' again. He swore to take his vows—but he then goes to change history. He walks a very fine line, Lady Tabitha. An' whatever he intends next, he's blocked me from his thoughts. I'd guard him well now—and send him swiftly to Iona, so he can take his vows afore the gods change their mind about him."

"Okay," Tabby whispered. That was two threats, not one, she was certain. The gods were going to take his powers from him another time, and maybe, just maybe, refuse to make him a Master of Time.

MacNeil glanced at Nick and Jan. They were staring at him, too. "The Brotherhood is secret fer many great reasons. I dinna care much fer intruders."

"Nick fights evil with all of his heart and his entire soul. He's not here to spy. He's hunting Kristin."

"Aye, but he has too many questions. We live by the Code, Tabitha. It is clear. We dinna speak openly to Outsiders." MacNeil gave the duo another cool look and vanished.

Nick said, "Shit."

TABBY STARED INTO THE bedchamber she shared with Macleod. The moment MacNeil left, he had gotten up from the table and stalked upstairs. Tabby had followed him. "Are you all right?"

He paused, about to unlock the chest at the foot of the bed, and smiled at her. "Ye worry like a wife."

His eyes were filled with affection and Tabby's heart hammered. "I love you."

He knelt and unlocked the chest, then took out the amulet in its cloth wrapping and stood somberly, holding it tightly. "Ye almost died because of me."

Tabby shook her head. "We don't know why Criosaidh's ghost is hunting me, Macleod."

"She hunts ye because of my war, my vengeance. Dinna ye feel their hatred and fury today? 'Tis worse now than before. 'Twill become worse with every passin' day." Anguish strained his face. "Ye almost died!"

"And you almost died today, too!" Tabby cried. "We're in this together."

"I brought ye back here," Macleod exclaimed.

Tabby breathed hard, aware that she must convince him this was not his fault. "The ghost found me in New York," she reminded him.

"Aye, because ye fought with it at An Tùir-Tara!"

"And that is written, Macleod."

He shook his head grimly. "When ye can leap, ye can find anyone at any time, Tabitha. Each moment in our lives will always be happenin'. Ye call it *parallel dimensions,* but the cycle has to have a beginnin'."

"What are you getting at?" she cried worriedly.

"MacNeil said ye have never been at Blayde till now. I started this when I brought ye here."

"I'm glad you brought me here!"

He appeared ravaged. "I only wanted to keep ye safe. I failed ye, Tabitha."

Tabby cried out and rushed to him, suddenly seeing him as a boy on the beach, bloody, sandy and weeping. She embraced him. "Let me help you!"

He jerked. "What did ye say?"

"Let me help you," she implored. "I love you, Macleod. You have never failed me and you never will! You did not fail your father, your mother, your family. You did your best to defend them—you were only a boy. And you defended me. I am alive because of you!"

"I would die fer ye...I will die fer ye, Tabitha."

Was he telling her that he loved her? Or was he telling her something else?

"The boy failed them...I willna fail ye."

"He didn't fail."

"I hate that boy!" Macleod raged, twisting away from her.

Tabby started to cry for him. "I love him," she said.

He whirled. "Ye love me!"

"I love that lost little boy and I always have and I always will. He is a hero—my hero—just as you are!" She went to him and took his face in her hands. "Macleod, I know you would die to save me, if you had to, but dying won't bring them back. And I won't let you die—no one is dying here!" Tabby realized his eyes were moist.

A long moment passed as he breathed hard, trembling. "Criosaidh's ghost must be stopped."

Tabby tensed. It was almost as if she could read his mind, she thought, because she knew he was also thinking about failing to destroy Criosaidh that day. He wanted her destroyed still. "We can't change what is meant to be. She's not meant to die now. She will be at An Tùir-Tara…with me."

His face hardened.

Tabby cried out, "Haven't you learned your lesson? They took your powers from you when you needed them most!"

"I canna stand by an' wait fer evil to destroy ye."

"Stop!" She touched his mouth. "I can accept Fate. You have to, too. Macleod, even if it takes me a hundred years, I am going to convince you that the massacre is not your fault—and that this is not your fault, either."

His eyes softened fractionally and his mouth shifted just as much. "We are at an impasse, Tabitha."

In that moment, she loved him so much that it hurt. "We really don't know what happens at An Tùir-Tara. It's a long time from now. Let's just take this one day at a time. We've been through hell. We need a respite. And…I need you, Macleod."

He unwrapped the cloth and the gold pendant glowed brightly in his palm. "Ye'll take this now. Ye'll wear it an' it will keep ye safe."

Tabby stared at the bright gold palm, feeling its powerful

magic more strongly than ever before. More tears came, filling her vision. Of course she would accept it now—but at what cost? "Whatever you are planning, please don't do it."

He walked behind her and lifted her hair, settling the necklace around her throat, the pendant warm on her skin in the neckline of her dress. He dropped her hair and clasped her shoulders from behind and spoke against her ear. "It suits ye, Tabitha."

Tabby felt how hot and hard he was, and how desperate. He wanted her, but his urgency meant something terrible. She turned to face him and found herself in the circle of his arms. "Tell me what you intend, damn it!"

He pulled her close and murmured, "To make love to ye."

"That isn't what I meant," she cried, afraid. "You're giving me the pendant as if this is goodbye."

"If ye keep the pendant," he said hoarsely, "I will always be able to find ye."

He abruptly lowered his face, claiming her mouth frantically with his. Tabby was so afraid for him, but as their mouths fused, it felt as if it had been so long. She seized his shoulders, kissing him back desperately, so hard their teeth grated and she tasted his blood.

He bent her backward, over the bed, lifting up her gown. Tabby raised her leg high, hooking her calf over his waist, the movement familiar and natural now. He grunted, the sound harsh and sexual, triumphant. Tabby couldn't stand the anticipation. He knew. As her back hit the mattress he smiled and plunged into her. Their union was so intense, so powerful and so right that Tabby cried out, instantly overwhelmed with the power of their love. And so much pleasure began.

He gasped her name and somehow Tabby opened her eyes, reeling in the blinding rapture. Their gazes met. She clasped his face. "I love you."

His eyes blazed. And he gasped and she felt his seed, hot and burning, as he joined her. He murmured her name, and then he held her, hard, as they soared wildly through the stars together.

But it didn't last. They were barely over the precipice when he stilled, only his mouth moving as he kissed her cheek and ear. It was never over so quickly. It took her one heartbeat to become sane and know this was some kind of ending—a goodbye. "Why are you giving me the pendant now? Why do you think that, with it, you won't lose me? Damn it!" She hit his shoulders repeatedly.

He stroked her hair, once, and got up from the bed. "I must do what I must do, Tabitha. I plan to come back to ye. If I dinna, summon MacNeil to take ye home."

"No!" She rose to her feet.

"I'm going to An Tùir-Tara to finish this once an' fer all."

ALTHOUGH HE HAD only just been given the power to leap, he was confident that he had mastered it—as long as the gods did not interfere with him now. The landing dazed him but he was prepared for that. As he opened his eyes, the light was blinding. He was in Melvaig's large central courtyard but the sky above was on fire.

And even though stone could not burn, chunks of the gray stone slabs were falling from the sky, and the rocks were ablaze, sizzling as they slammed down, only to burn holes into the bailey ground. Men, women and children were running for the castle's front gates, screaming in terror and trying to escape the inferno. Macleod pushed himself to his feet, searching Melvaig with his senses for Tabitha. He felt her above him, where there was so much hatred and evil. She was in the central tower.

Tabitha screamed, the sound bloodcurdling.

Criosaidh roared in answering rage, the sound triumphant.

And the tower swayed in the fiery night and more blazing stone blocks sheared from it, crashing to the earth below.

He was afraid he was too late. Macleod ran for the tower and pounded up the narrow stairs. As he reached the uppermost landing, the heat from the fire inside the tower chamber intensified, but that was not why he faltered. A fire wall blazed, dividing the tower chamber in half. Tabitha was on one side, Criosaidh on the other. A man stood on the threshold, blocking him from entering the room.

Macleod breathed hard, shocked as the man shouted Tabitha's name. He wanted to rush forward and help Tabitha, but he didn't dare, for he recognized the man.

He had just encountered himself.

And suddenly he did not think he could breathe.

Suddenly his knees felt weak, as did his entire body.

Was this what happened to a person if he encountered himself in another time? Was this why it was forbidden?

He reached out to steady himself as his older self screamed Tabitha's name, as Criosaidh taunted them. And Tabitha was trapped against the far wall by the fire, the flames dangerously close to her velvet skirts.

He was terrified for her and he knew without attempting to help her that he was suddenly powerless. No one had seen him and he had the sudden certainty that they could not see him, even though he was there. As he held the wall with one hand, he was determined to find his power, and he tried to blast Criosaidh. But he had been right, he had no power; in fact, he couldn't even stand up. It became harder and harder to breathe, but not because of the smoke. And he could barely decipher their words as they fought.

But just before he collapsed, Tabitha looked right at him.

He didn't know if she saw him or sensed him, but he thought he heard her whisper, "No."

And as he finally crumbled to the floor, he saw the fire wall shifting from Tabitha to Criosaidh, and he felt his older self using his mind to help her with her magic. But Criosaidh was casting her spell and Tabitha was starting to helplessly cry, tears slipping down her face. He was terrified of what this signified.

But he felt the terror in the other man, too, shockingly— sickeningly. And as his fear grew, so did Macleod's, and their feelings of horror became one. He felt himself slipping away, as if dying, the entire grotesque tragedy becoming more and more distant, yet he was in Macleod's mind now, in his heart and his soul. He felt his every thought, all of his fear, and the power of his love.

Was he dying? Was he dead? Was he now disembodied, and a part of his future self?

"Fire be hungry, fire be quick, get the Macleod bitch," Criosaidh said harshly.

Even as she spoke, he knew, and he roared "No!" while blasting the black witch again. This time, taken unawares, she gasped in pain and was driven back into the untouched wall, but it didn't matter.

Tabitha went still, as the flames circled her.

He seized Criosaidh. "Stop the fire or die!"

She sneered at him and vanished.

Tabitha screamed.

In horror, he turned and saw her lavender velvet gown on fire. And then his wife was engulfed in the flames, only a portion of her pale, frightened face visible to him.

I love you...

He knew these were her last, dying words.

But she did not finish speaking. Instead, the fire erupted, reaching the tower roof, consuming her completely.

"Tabitha!" he screamed.

Then the fire was gone, and there was only the charred ruin of the tower room.

He could not breathe. He could not move. In shock, he stared.

And across the room, upon the floor, he saw the gold necklace she had worn for two-and-a-half centuries, the amulet he had given her. The talisman was an open palm, a pale moonstone glittering in its center.

It had survived the fire, untouched and unscarred; his wife, who had powerful magic, had not.

"Tabitha," he moaned. And it struck him then, in the most shattering moment of his life, that she was gone.

"No!" He leaped into time, vanishing.

On the floor, Macleod lay still, sensation returning to his body, his limbs. The smoke was so thick now he choked, and his mind returned to life. The sensation of becoming separate from his future self hurt, as if he was physically being ripped in two. Slowly, he sat up.

And then he began to tremble.

He had leaped through time to finish Criosaidh and save Tabitha. Instead, he had watched her die.

TABBY RAN INTO THE HALL. "Good," she cried, the moment she saw Nick and Jan. "You haven't left!"

"Where's the hubby?" Nick asked quietly, now clad in fatigues and a vest. A pair of packs was on the table.

"He's gone to 1550 to get rid of Criosaidh, once and for all!"

Nick's eyes widened slightly. "He went to An Tùir-Tara?"

Tabby seized his sleeve. "What do you know about the fire?"

"Your sister seems to think you might wind up there eventually."

Tabby went still. Leave it to Sam to be hot on the trail of the exact same lead that she was chasing. Nick probably knew exactly what happened during the fire. "Nick, I don't know how you time-travel, but Macleod is defying the universe with his actions and I have to stop him before he winds up in the kind of trouble he can't get out of. I need to get to An Tùir-Tara."

Nick smiled at her. "What do I look like, a yellow cab with a supersonic engine?"

"Please," Tabby said.

Jan came forward. Tabby had only met her once or twice, and didn't know her at all, but she said to Tabby, "Do you know how dangerous it is to run around in history, out of your time? You shouldn't even think about it. People go back and are never heard from again. And there are worse things than getting lost in time—like dying in another time! You're lucky you're here and okay. Apparently, this is your Fate. I wouldn't press my luck if I were you."

"You're not me," Tabby said sharply. "And I know this— Macleod isn't supposed to be there. He's supposed to be fighting the war on evil here in 1298. Nothing good can come of his leap. Nick?"

"Don't look at me," he said. "Jan and I are going back to Melvaig, on the off chance that Kristin is still there. If she's not, our time has run out and we're going back to the Big Apple. Now, if you want a lift in that direction, I'll help you out."

Tabby was so upset she didn't respond. Nick hefted a pack and handed it to Jan, who said, "Thank God these damned missions are limited to twenty-four-hour runs. I am ready for a hot bath and some really good wine."

Tabby was enraged that they would not lift a finger to help her out.

"I have a feeling he'll be back," Nick said, by way of consolation.

When they were gone, she walked over to the table and sank down there. No good was going to come of Macleod trying to interfere with history and she was terrified for him. What if he encountered his sixteenth-century self? Would he implode? That would change history, all right! And she was stuck at Blayde in 1298. That was unacceptable.

She would have to try to use magic to get to him, she thought. Maybe she'd be lucky, because her magic seemed to be getting stronger by the day.

A noise from the staircase made Tabby turn.

"You don't need to use magic," Kristin said. "I'll take you to An Tùir-Tara."

Very slowly, Tabby stood up. "And what do you get out of it?"

She smiled. "Your death."

CHAPTER NINETEEN

Melvaig, Scotland
June 19, 1550

HE REMINDED HIMSELF that he would go home to the thirteenth century, where Tabitha was alive. But instead of doing that, he sank down on the stairs, shocked. *Tabitha would die at An Tùir-Tara.*

He could not move and he could barely think. He was consumed with grief. But all he had to do was return to Blayde in the thirteenth century and she would be there, waiting for him. A sense of confusion began. He could not live without her. Nothing had ever been as clear. He loved this woman. But he hadn't had the power to prevent her death—not now, and not as an older, even more powerful man.

He breathed hard and realized he was crying.

Watching Tabitha die was something he would never forget.

Even if they spent two-and-a-half centuries together, he could not watch her die again. An Tùir-Tara had to change! But how could he possibly accomplish that?

He began to tremble, rage joining the grief and the guilt. Was her death written? If so, he would never forgive the gods!

A shadow fell across the dark stairwell. Macleod took another breath and somehow looked down the stairs. MacNeil stood there. His fury knew no bounds now. But the walls didn't shake, the stairwell did not move and no stones fell from the ceiling.

He hadn't felt the Abbot's power, either.

Beginning to realize what had happened to him, Macleod slowly stood. "I willna allow her to die here."

MacNeil's face was as hard as stone, but the light in his eyes was pitying. "Ye dinna learn."

"Ye cold, heartless bastard! Tabitha is kind an' good. She deserves immortality. I will find a way to save her!"

MacNeil's face never changed, but his gaze flickered. "Ye'll never trust in Fate. Ye'll never trust the gods."

He wanted to murder MacNeil with his bare hands. He wanted to curse the gods loudly enough so that they knew he was through with them, so that his curses came true. "Never," he snarled.

MacNeil stared, pity still in his eyes. "Yer temper doesna serve ye well, lad."

"What do ye want o' me now?"

"Ye should know by now that yer temper only causes ye more grief."

"What do ye want?" he shouted. "Tell me or be gone an' get out of my way!"

"We want nothin' from ye."

An inkling began, but he dismissed it. MacNeil had hounded him for most of a century, demanding he give up his vengeance and take his vows. The gods would never really disown him. Of course, he could never take those vows. How could he? Fate would claim Tabitha, taking her from him. Her Destiny was written by the Ancients. He would never serve them now and that was his revenge against them.

But Tabitha was waiting for him in 1298—and his decision to take his vows had pleased her more than anything else he could ever do.

He could not think clearly, he realized. He was too upset, too sick, too shocked. But maybe he could bargain for her life. "Tell them to change An Tùir-Tara. Let Tabitha live. Let her die a natural death. An' then I will serve them."

MacNeil made a dismissive sound. "Ye're done, Guy. The gods dinna want ye to serve them. Yer own grandfather has disowned ye."

He did not care—did he? Tabitha would care. Somehow, he would explain it to her. But to do that, he had to get back to Blayde in 1298, and once there, he would find a way to change Fate. He faced the fact that he was empty inside now. "Where are my powers? Did they take them, or is this the reason no Master should go back or forward in time and see himself?"

"When ye encounter yerself in another time, one of ye will lose power." MacNeil stared. "But ye'll never lose the power to leap, otherwise, how will ye get back to the time where ye belong?"

Macleod tensed. "I dinna have the power to leap. 'Tis gone."

MacNeil's face twisted in anguish. "I am sorry, lad. When I told ye they've disowned ye, I meant it. They've taken yer powers. Ye're mortal now."

If he was mortal, he would not be able to leap back to 1298. He began to breathe hard. "I have to get back to Blayde. I have to get back to Tabitha."

"Did ye think to defy us fer ninety-seven years and walk away unscathed?" MacNeil turned away.

"Send me back," Macleod shouted, rushing down the stairs. And he tripped, falling. *He was a mortal now.*

MacNeil ignored him, walking outside into Melvaig's central courtyard, which was still in embers.

Macleod picked himself up and ran after him. "We're friends."

MacNeil looked at him sadly. "I canna help ye, Guy. 'Tis forbidden."

It began to sink in. He had no power. He was trapped in the sixteenth century with no way to return to Blayde and his time—with no way to return to Tabitha and no way to ever help her survive the Melvaig fires. "I have to get back!"

"I am sorry," MacNeil said softly. "I had such hope fer ye."

"MacNeil! Send me back!" he begged.

"Welcome to hell." Grimly, MacNeil blasted him with his power.

And Macleod was flung backward in time—by a mere hour.

TABBY MOANED. But the world stopped spinning and she realized she clutched a rough stone floor. Breathing hard, she looked up and realized she was in a circular tower room. She tensed with dread, recalling everything. *Kristin had hurled her through time.*

"Yes, Tabitha, you are in Melvaig's tower." Kristin laughed softly.

Tabby became aware of the amulet, pulsing and warm against her cleavage. She touched it, finding comfort, and got warily to her feet. Kristin stood there, appearing terribly amused. Her heart sank. "Is it June nineteenth, 1550?"

Kristin's smile widened. "Actually, my darling, it is June first, 1550." She walked past her and paused in the doorway. "Don't bother trying to escape. The guards have been ordered to stop you by beheading you if need be. Although I much prefer being allowed to torture you to death myself. And I won't be long. I want to tell my mother that you're here."

Tabby ran to the doorway as Kristin walked out onto the landing, where two soldiers stood. "Let me guess. Your mother is Criosaidh?"

"How clever you are!" Kristin laughed softly.

As a guard started to close the door in her face, Tabby put her body between it and the wall. "Wait! Why are you doing this? Why do you want me to die? What have I done to you... to her?"

Kristin's smile vanished. "In eighteen more days, my mother dies here in the fires because of you."

Had Allie been right?

"I win?"

Kristin's face filled with fury. "No, you don't win. I won't let you win!"

Tabby decided that now was not the time to try to decipher what would happen—and the fact was that she had seen herself die in the fire.

"I was five years old the day you and my mother had your last battle here," Kristin snarled. "She died in my brother's arms, horrifically burned, while I begged her to live. I am not a powerful witch, Tabitha, not like my mother. Unfortunately, my father was just your average mortal. I have waited *hundreds* of years to find the power to gain my revenge on you. But I have that power now."

Suddenly Tabby thought she felt her sister, across time. "How did you find that power, Kristin?"

Kristin laughed. "I have my source! He is all-powerful and answers only to Satan!"

Tabby sensed the enormity of that evil and it sickened her.

"He gave me the ability to leap. He gave me the longevity I needed. I decided to hunt you while you were weak and innocent, naive and unsuspecting, in the twenty-first century, before you became as powerful as you'll be in the sixteenth century."

Tabby wished she did not believe her, but she did. A terrible source of evil was out there, and Kristin was hunting her to avenge her mother. Now, she understood the ghost's burning hatred and malevolence.

This had to end soon.

Tabby trembled. "You've brought me here to murder me. You can't change history, Kristin, not if it is written correctly. History can only be changed if it went awry, if it has veered from Destiny."

Kristin started to laugh. "Oh, dear Tabitha, we live to change history."

"What are you talking about?" Tabby cried.

"Days before the very first time the Japanese attacked the United States at Pearl Harbor, their plans were discovered and the bulk of the Japanese air force was destroyed before ever reaching your airspace. Only two of your ships sank and only a few dozen sailors died."

Tabby gaped.

"But we worked long and hard to change history—and we succeeded! The Japanese victory is Satan's work. Don't you know that right now, on September 11, 2001, hundreds of demons are trying to make certain the Pentagon is destroyed along with the Twin Towers? Sooner or later we will rewrite the history of that day! You are so naive. Right now, we are making sure that the allies drown off Normandy—that D-day fails, that Hitler survives to rule Europe, that every Jew dies, that no Gypsies survive! We do not have rules. We live to change Fate! Anarchy is our bible."

Tabby backed into the chamber. "Of course. Stupid me." She wet her lips, and silently began casting a spell on Kristin to bend her mind to Tabby's will. She had never tried to exercise mind control over anyone before, but her life was at stake. History was at stake—even if it was only the history of Melvaig and Blayde, of her and Macleod. Their future was at stake.

And she wanted that future with him. She wanted it as much as she had ever wanted anything. She would fight for it now.

She stared at Kristin impassively while silently chanting a mind spell. The amulet warmed impossibly against her skin but didn't burn her.

Kristin looked puzzled. "Why are we talking about history?"

There is one will here and it is mine. Kristin's will, bend to mine.

"Tell me more," Tabby said softly. She was wondering if the amulet's magic was helping her powers. She was acutely aware of the talisman.

Kristin looked at her, clearly bewildered. Tabby thought she was about to step into the chamber, and she prepared to assault her. But before she did so, a big, dark-haired man filled the doorway. He smiled slowly at her.

Tabby's pulse skipped and raced. She instantly recognized a much older Coinneach. He had turned into a handsome Highlander. He had to be well over two hundred years old, but he looked about forty. "Coinneach," she breathed. Surely he would save the day!

"Hello, Tabitha," he said softly. "Are you trying to enchant my sister?"

Tabby froze. She'd forgotten that they were siblings. He was Criosaidh's son—and obviously not exactly mortal.

Kristin started and her expression changed and hardened. "I almost fell under her spell."

"I can see that." He continued to smile, but it did not reach his eyes.

He hadn't been evil when he was a boy, and he didn't feel evil now. She would bet he did not have any demonic DNA. But his eyes were ice-cold and the look in them reminded her of Macleod at his most ruthless. She was afraid that he was burning with the need for Highland revenge. "Coinneach!" She needed him as an ally. Surely he would help her—he owed her. "I have to find Macleod. I helped you once, surely you remember? Please, help me now."

His cold smile vanished. "Ye brought me bread an' water. Ye cared. But that was long ago, Tabitha. I have been fighting Macleod for two hundred years."

She realized he wasn't going to help her.

"That's right, Lady Tabitha. An eye for an eye. He murdered my father and I will bring your head to him now."

She backed up. "You would never murder me."

His eyes blazed. "Think as ye wish, as if it comforts ye!" He turned to Kristin. "If ye torture her, make sure ye silence her. I dinna wish to be annoyed with her screams."

"Hmm, torture. How did you know I intend to enjoy myself fully?" Kristin laughed.

Coinneach looked at her with distaste and hurried down the stairs. Before he was even gone, Tabby put a protective spell around herself. He wasn't into sadism, but she couldn't count on him, either.

Where was Macleod? Wasn't he ten or fifteen miles to the north at Blayde, centuries older and, maybe, centuries wiser?

"Is it getting stuffy in here, or is it my imagination?" Kristin murmured.

"I can breathe well enough."

"Really? *Noose, tighten.*" Kristin smirked. "I murdered my roomie this way."

Tabby tensed, briefly sickened by the snide remark, which she was certain was the truth. But she did not feel any pressure around her throat, which meant her protective spell was rock solid—for now.

"And I almost got your sister. Did you know that? I'll bet my spell felt like a butcher knife going through her stomach."

This was the second time that Kristin had mentioned hurting Sam. "I am not vindictive, but you will pay for hurting Sam."

Kristin sneered. "Oh, I let the bitch live."

Tabby was so angry she had to close her eyes for an instant. Anger would only interfere with her magic, and she needed her power now. She needed it as never before. It had to work.

Because as much as she did not want to fight Kristin—especially if Kristin really had the source of evil she claimed—there might never be as opportune a time. Once Criosaidh arrived, it would be two against one. And Kristin had hurt Sam.

She wished Macleod would sense her distress and help her out. She didn't care if it was her Macleod from 1298, or the older man who was currently a few miles away.

But she couldn't count on him, or anyone.

She could do this. Tabby looked coldly at Kristin. *"Fire await my very command. Fire be my weapon and my plan,"* she murmured. And heat seemed to tickle her fingertips, the way it might spark from the tip of a matchstick. She glanced down at her chest. The moonstone on the gold palm was as brilliant as a laser-cut diamond now.

Kristin's eyes widened. *"Noose, obey me. Noose, tighten!"* she cried.

There was no effect. Relieved, Tabby ordered, *"Fire arise."*

Fire blazed between them.

Kristin cried out.

"Fire arise!" Tabby cried louder.

And the fire became an inferno, cutting Kristin off from the doorway. Where Tabby stood, there was not a single spark, and the air was pleasantly cool.

Kristin began to choke. Then her skirts caught on fire and she screamed, beating at them with her hands. She screamed again, the guards rushing into the room, but before they could reach her, her skirts blazed.

Tabby knew she couldn't go through with this kind of violence and cruelty. She wasn't a Slayer. Her magic was meant to be used to help others, not hurt or destroy them. *"Fire obey me, fire go out."*

The fire died.

Kristin staggered back, her skirts falling apart, looking at

Tabby, her eyes glazed with pain, fear and hatred. Then she rushed from the room.

The two soldiers backed out, slamming the door.

As it closed, she felt Criosaidh's evil welling up from the lower floors.

Tabby's spine hit the wall. She grasped the pendant, and repeated her protection spell. The chamber shifted. The air glimmered. And Criosaidh began to materialize.

"YOU HAVE CERTAINLY improved your ability to leap. You do know, don't you, that by now MacGregor has put out a Code Red, since we've overstayed our historic welcome by an entire seventy-one minutes and five seconds."

As they paused in the central courtyard of a much more lavish and modern Melvaig Castle, Nick seized Jan's arm. "How could I not follow Tabby here?"

Jan went still. They both watched Kristin run into the courtyard, coughing, her skirts badly singed and burned. She fell to her hands and knees, gasping for air. "I wish you weren't right ninety percent of the time."

"Actually, I'm right ninety-nine-point-nine percent of the time." Nick grinned. But the words weren't even out of his mouth when fire exploded in the sky above them.

"Must be June nineteenth," Nick muttered, but he was striding toward Kristin.

"Tabitha's up there. What should I do?" Jan cried.

Kristin froze on all fours, and her gaze locked with Nick's. Slowly, with malice, she smiled. "It's not June nineteenth, Forrester. We will change your history today."

"Like hell you will." He smiled coldly back, comprehending her. He would never let the demon witch change history. A huge gust of shockingly cold air hit him, but he refused to budge or be pushed back. "Are you kidding me?"

"Noose, find him," she hissed.

He instantly blasted her, thinking about Elizabeth Adler, but as he did, he felt the rope around his neck. He knew it was her magic, and he didn't try to seize the cord, as nothing would be there. He breathed harder, choking, but he blasted her. She cried out, his energy hurling her into the tower wall.

"Noose, tighten!"

Fuck, he thought, blasting her again, but he was on his knees. Against his own will, he grabbed at the virtual cord.

"Nick!" Jan screamed. Drawing her Beretta, she began firing point-blank and repeatedly into Lafarge.

But the bullets bounced off her, deflecting everywhere.

However, the cord loosened and he stood, energy blazing. Kristin screamed, collapsing onto her back, as chunks of burning stone began falling from the tower above them.

Nick reached her, flipped her, straddled her. "Don't you fuckin' die," he said, yanking her wrists as hard as he could behind her back. He heard her bones break. "Payback for my little Sammie," he said.

Jan stood over him. "We need info, Nick," she warned. "Besides, I want the honor of dispatching her."

Nick leaned his entire body on top of her, the position dominant and sexual. She hissed in fury and he said against her ear, "Who's giving you orders, bitch? Why did you go to the Carlisle Hotel? A big, motherfucking demon there?"

She turned her face to his and spit.

They both felt the falling boulder at the same time. Nick looked up. For one moment, he thought it a small meteor. He jumped up, seizing Jan, and they dived away as it crashed to the ground, Nick making sure to land on top of Jan to protect her with his body.

And he knew.

He turned his head. The stone had buried Kristin. No one,

not even a witch with an ounce or two of demonic blood, could survive that.

He cursed.

Blayde, Scotland
June 1, 1550

ALARM CAUSED him to awaken.

Guy Macleod sat bolt upright in his bed.

Tabitha.

In that instant he knew that she was in danger. But she was in Edinburgh with her sister, Sam, a warrior whom he trusted. And he was confused, for he thought he felt her there, in a quiet and happy moment.

Instead, his senses veered south and he felt her determination, her anger—and her fear. He also felt doubt.

His confusion escalated. Something was terribly wrong! Tabitha had great magic and she never doubted her powers. And then he felt Criosaidh.

He instantly understood that she was at Melvaig. It was oddly familiar—as if he had already been in this moment.

But of course he had. Every moment in time existed infinitely in parallel dimensions—he was old enough and wise enough to understand that now. A part of him would always recognize the most fateful events of their lives.

As he rose from the bed, his gaze veered to a south-facing chamber window. The night sky was still and blue-black, glittering with a billion stars. His senses sharpened. For one moment, he thought the night sky there on fire. But that was impossible.

Or was it?

Guy Macleod leaped. He landed a scant instant later in Melvaig's central courtyard. *And the sky above was on fire....*

Incredulous, he saw huge balls of fire falling into the bailey, where men, women and children were running for the castle's front gates, screaming in terror and trying to escape the inferno. But the sky wasn't on fire—the tower above him was on fire— and it was an inferno.

Even though stone could not burn, chunks of the gray slabs were falling from the tower, the rock ablaze, sizzling as it slammed down, only to burn holes into the bailey ground.

Above him, Tabitha screamed, the sound bloodcurdling.

Criosaidh roared in answering rage.

They were at war.

He had never known so much fear. Worse, it was déjà vu— somehow, he had already been through this, but his memory escaped him. The only thing he was certain of was that she needed him as never before. For he somehow knew that only one witch would survive this night.

"Tabitha!" he roared, and he bounded to the tower door, leaping to the uppermost floor. As he reached the landing, the heat from the fire inside the tower chamber blasted him, burning his face, chest and hands. He saw the fire scorching a solid wall across half of the tower room, and his wife, trapped against the far wall by it, the flames dangerously close to her velvet skirts.

His horror briefly paralyzed him.

Criosaidh stood on the fire wall's other side, where the rest of the chamber was untouched by the flames. She turned arrogantly to him. "You are too late, Macleod. Tonight she dies…and your life as you know it is over." She laughed.

The heat had caused him to crouch. He straightened, shocked. In that moment, as Tabitha's gaze met his, he knew he was looking not at his wife but at the woman he had fallen in love with two-and-a-half centuries ago. Tabitha had crossed time!

The woman in so much jeopardy was achingly innocent and

so terribly young. She'd come from their past, from their first days together. She was inexperienced, no match for Criosaidh now.

"Macleod!" she cried desperately.

He choked. She hadn't called him by his clan name in centuries.

And she knew he was from her future, because her eyes were wide and shocked.

He hardened. If she died in that fire, the life they had spent together, the life they had built across two-and-a-half centuries, the children and grandchildren they had begotten and raised, would all be destroyed.

And it was what Criosaidh wanted.

Yet in the back of his mind, he had an acute awareness of having tried to save her this way once—and of having failed.

Too much was at stake. Worse, he needed to remember, but the gods always made certain to erase life-altering memories. He had resolved his differences with them over time, but sometimes their ways still angered him.

He blasted Criosaidh with his power, at once furious and determined, but she had wrapped herself in a protective spell and his power fell harmlessly away from her. Now, as it hit the floor and was diverted to the walls behind her, as rock and stone cracked apart, it remained so damned familiar.

He looked at Tabitha, refusing to panic. He'd forgotten how young she'd once been, but she was as beautiful and brave as ever. He was aware that she was using her powers, even before the fire wall shifted and moved back toward Criosaidh. He tried to join his mind with hers as he always did when they battled evil, and he felt her surprise as his power touched and enabled hers. Their eyes met again. It was her first time—it felt like the first time for him, too.

Can ye hear me? Let me aid ye now.

I can hear you… I will not die today, Macleod. I won't!

And he fell in love with her all over again. He felt a hundred and eleven years old, the age he'd been when he'd first seen her in the flesh in New York.

"Fire be hungry, fire be quick. Get the Macleod bitch," Criosaidh said, breaking the moment of union.

Even as she spoke, he knew and he roared "No!" while blasting the black witch again. This time, taken unaware, she gasped in pain and was driven back into the untouched wall, but it didn't matter.

Tabitha went still as the flames circled her dangerously.

He ran to Criosaidh and seized her with his bare hands. "Stop the fire or die!"

She sneered at him and vanished.

Tabitha screamed.

In horror, he turned and saw her blue velvet gown on fire. And then she was engulfed in the flames.

Tabitha's frightened amber gaze met his and it was all he could see of her now. But he heard her.

I love you…

He knew these were her last, dying words.

She could not die, not when she was only twenty-nine! It would change their lives, their history, and it would destroy their greatest creation—their children and grandchildren!

And he could not, would not, live without her!

He had lost her this way, before…

"No!" he roared.

The fire erupted, reaching the tower roof, consuming her completely.

"Tabitha!" he screamed.

Then the fire was gone, and there was only the charred ruin of the tower room.

And across the room, upon the floor, he saw the gold

necklace she had worn for two-and-a-half centuries, the amulet he had given her.

It had survived the fire, untouched and unscarred; his wife, who had powerful magic, had not.

It struck him then, in the most shattering moment of his life—she was gone.

"No!" He leaped into time to find her.

CHAPTER TWENTY

An Tùir-Tara
June 1, 1550

SHE WAS ABOUT TO BE *burned alive*.

Tabby was terrified. She did not want to die, not now, not yet! Her life flashed before her eyes—and it was her life with Macleod. She hadn't even seen him take his vows! But she knew he would, because the man who'd just been with her in the central tower had been strong and old and wise…a Master of Time.

She could not die that day.

She became impossibly still, crouching. She forced the fear aside. And as she did, she started to realize that the fire blazed *around* her, but it wasn't *touching* her. She was incredulous. Several feet separated her from the flames. And there wasn't even any heat inside the small protective space where she crouched.

Tabby slowly straightened, amazed. Her spell was so strong now it was protecting her from the fire, or someone else was. She thought she felt her grandmother, hovering watchfully close by.

But Criosaidh was still out there.

Tabby knew she had to finish this.

Only one of them was going to make it out alive.

She put every thought and feeling aside now except for her sheer determination to win. *"Come to me, witch, come to me now. Enter my fire, witch. Come to me now."*

The fire roared, as high as tall fir trees, but Tabby wasn't afraid. She was entirely focused on her enemy. The fire was her ally, her friend and her weapon. Suddenly she felt the evil and hatred approaching.

She felt herself smile and she murmured, "It's so cold, isn't it, Criosaidh? You need to warm yourself in my fire."

And through the wall of flames, she saw a wind kick up, slamming all the shutters closed in the tower room.

Tabby tensed, shocked. The shutters kept slamming, cracking the stone walls, as the energy gusted through the wall of fire, blasting her face and bare chest with frigid air. There was no mistaking Criosaidh's ghost.

And the circle of fire seemed to hesitate. But fire did not like the cold.

"Not so smart, ghost," Tabby murmured. *"Fire arise!"*

It blazed.

The shutters flew from the windows, breaking apart and shattering, wood flying everywhere, the evil viciously furious now.

"Come to me, witch, come to me now. Bring me your living form," Tabby cried. She had to lure Criosaidh close now and get rid of that demonic spirit!

Through the flames, she saw the dark-haired woman on the landing. Her eyes were glittering with hatred—and shining oddly with the transfixed stare of the enchanted.

"Come to me, witch, escape the cold. Come to me, witch, warm in my fire," Tabby chanted softly.

Criosaidh started to walk toward the flames.

The wind whirled violently, turning into a spiraling cyclone, and the ceiling exploded from the roof.

Tabby cringed, covering her head with her arms, ordering the fire to protect her. And as the timbers rained down around her, Criosaidh walked into her fire.

Kneeling, Tabby looked up.

The moment she did, Criosaidh was engulfed in the blaze. As her clothes and hair went on fire, she screamed in pain and terror, her gaze meeting Tabby's.

Bitch...

Tabby came out of her trance. "Roast in hell," she screamed back.

Criosaidh staggered away, the flames burning her arms and legs, her clothes, her body. Her screams were bloodcurdling.

She fell, and there was only the blazing fire.

For another moment, Tabby stared at the inferno outside the circle of fire where she stood, almost disbelieving. She had won. Criosaidh was dead, burned alive at An Tùir-Tara, and her ghost seemed to have been vanquished, too.

But it was June 1, 1550, not June 19.

As she had that thought, her entire body gave out. Tabby collapsed.

She cried out, barely able to brace herself as she fell to the hard stone floor. Suddenly she was aware of her exhaustion. She simply could not move. She was drained, depleted, sickened and shaking uncontrollably. She couldn't think clearly. She wasn't even certain she had any magic left. She only knew that it was over—and she hated what she'd had to do.

The stone floor was cool against her cheek. Her eyes drifted closed. She was so seriously drained, she wondered if she might die from using the power that she had.

She had to go home.

It was truly over now.

Macleod.

She wanted him desperately. She would find relief in his

arms. But how was she going to get back to Blayde in the thirteenth century? Tabby clawed the stone, trying to get up, but
her body refused to heed her now.

She fell back onto her belly, her face. She needed to rest,
but only for a moment. And the fire roared around her.

Could she even get out of the circle of fire?

Tabby somehow looked at the circle of fire, shoving to her
hands and knees, too weak to even sit up. If only she could lie
there for a few moments, trying to find some of her strength.
But the urge to go home to Macleod was consuming. It was
urgent. He needed her—she somehow knew it. She was
confused, because the man who'd been in the tower with her
had been so powerful, and he only needed her love. Her head
hurt. Macleod needed her. *He was lost, suffering....*

She would have to dispel the fire. Tabby forced herself to sit
up, panting from the exertion. Instinctively she touched her chest
and she jerked. Utter dismay claimed her. The amulet was gone!

She didn't know what to do. The necklace meant everything
to her. It had belonged to Elasaid and Macleod had given it to
her so she wouldn't ever get lost. She was certain it had helped
her in her battle with Criosaidh. She breathed hard, tears
forming, suddenly dizzy and terribly confused. Of course the
talisman was gone—it had been lost at An Tùir-Tara and it
would wind up on exhibit at the Met. Except today was June
1, 1550, not June 19. What could that mean?

Tabby shook off her confusion. She was never going to figure
it out or, at least, not now. She had miraculously triumphed over
both Criosaidh and her spirit. Now she had to get out of the fire
and go home to Macleod, because he was in trouble. She had no
idea what would happen to history and maybe she shouldn't care.

She slowly stood and instantly reeled, almost falling over.
Instead she caught herself and the fire seemed to back away
from her.

Tabby closed her eyes again, fighting for strength and focus. *"Fire go from me,"* she said hoarsely.

The fire simply danced about her, but the flames were waist-high now.

"Fire go from me," she cried, trying to put power into her words. The effort was simply too much and she collapsed as she spoke, but the fires vanished.

She was so dizzy and sick that she clung to the floor. For a long moment she could not move or think. She could only lie there, too exhausted to do anything else. The battle had come close to destroying her. She fought the need to pass out, to retch. She needed help, she needed Macleod.

Determined, Tabby started to crawl from the room, across the landing to the stairs. She did not know how she would make it out of Melvaig's tower if she couldn't even walk. She looked down the stairwell and despair welled. The journey down it might as well have been a thousand miles.

Where are you, Macleod? What has happened to you?

She had almost expected an answer. There was none.

She half crawled and half slid down the stairs. On the landing below she paused, panting and out of breath. Maybe she would close her eyes and rest....

Tabitha?

About to pass out, her eyes flew open. She was certain she'd just heard Macleod close by. But she was alone on the dark landing. She crawled to the doorway and used a door to claw herself to her feet. Then she simply stood there, clinging to it.

"Tabitha!"

Tabby jerked at the sound of Macleod's voice—and it was real. She turned and saw him striding toward her, several strapping young Highlanders with him. Their eyes met; his gaze blazed. Tabby exulted. But even as she did, she saw his blisters and burns.

He was the same man who had just tried to fight Criosaidh

with her. It was Macleod, but he was the Master who lived in the sixteenth century—the Master who had tried to reach across time to her at the Met.

He was the man she loved, just older. She loved him desperately and she needed him just then terribly. And he needed her—she saw it on his face and felt it coming from him in huge, hard waves.

But before she could cry out, she felt the world tilt and begin to spin. He ran forward and caught her as she fell.

And looking into his eyes, she inhaled. *He was even more powerful now. But he was blessed. He walked in their light....*

"Ye'll be fine now," he said, kneeling with her in his arms, his eyes fierce and searching. "I'll always find ye an' I'll never lose ye, even without the pendant."

His burns had been treated, she saw, and they were already healing. There was a scar on his jaw that she'd never seen before. He looked as if he was in his late thirties—not as if he was twenty-five. But mostly, his eyes had changed. They were the eyes of someone centuries old, someone who had seen and fought everything, someone terribly wise and empowered by the gods. "You took your vows," she whispered, clasping his jaw.

His smile came and went. Moisture shone in his eyes. "Ah, Tabitha, I took those vows centuries ago."

"Are you all right?" She stroked his hard jaw. It was the same.

"A few burns canna hurt me, Tabitha, not as long as ye live."

She touched her throat, which was bare.

"Ye lost it in the fire," he said softly.

"I'm in the sixteenth century—you're from the sixteenth century," she whispered. "But I belong at Blayde in 1298."

"Aye." His mouth shifted. "I ken...ye're so sweet an' so young!"

Tabby reached for his shoulders and he held her tightly, against his broad, powerful chest. His embrace was the same—

powerful, consuming, impossibly safe and right. "After the fire, you found me at the Met."

He hesitated. "I thought ye died fer one terrible moment, after ye went up in the flames, and I leaped into time to find ye. I thought to find ye when we started this, so long ago, at the school where ye were teachin' the children."

"So there is a beginning?"

"Sometimes we're not allowed to remember everythin', Tabitha. I ken we both fought this way together in the fire here before. But I canna really recall it well. 'Tis shadowy, in my mind. I ken I feared I lost ye, that ye died. But ye dinna die."

"I didn't die—I won. Elasaid's amulet is powerful."

"Aye, ye triumphed. Ye wouldna have done so if it wasn't what the gods chose fer us."

Their gazes locked. Tabby hesitated. He had come to New York because of her spell, but their beginning had been that afternoon when she'd seen him at the Met—because of this battle at An Tùir-Tara.

"Tabitha, I came to ye at the exhibit, but ye came to me when I was a lost boy."

He'd told her that before. "What does that mean?" she whispered, stroking his face.

"Yer soul was seekin' mine. Yer soul will always seek mine. My soul will always seek yers…no matter what day it is, what month, what year." He smiled at her, a single tear falling.

Tabby hugged him, burrowing as close as she could get. His love for her was so powerful she was cocooned in it. And his smile was, impossibly, even sexier than when he was young. She looked up. "You've gotten so much better with age."

His gaze turned to dark purple fire. "Dinna tempt me."

But her body was filled with a reckless urgency now. "I need you." She needed to celebrate their life and their love. She wanted nothing more. She slid her hand into his hair, which he now wore very short, and somehow caught several strands. It crossed her mind that this wasn't really right, although she did not analyze why, and she pulled his face down. His eyes blazed; he covered her mouth with his. His kiss was hot and hard, but the deep hunger was tightly controlled as he'd never been able to control it before.

Tabby kissed him as wildly as she could, as if she hadn't seen him in centuries, until he gasped and gave over to her. She loved him as never before and she didn't care if he was young or old. She would always love him this way.

Suddenly he tore his mouth from hers.

"I love you and I want you, Macleod."

He breathed hard, his eyes dark and hot. "God, I want ye, too. I fergot how it was in the beginning fer us, with ye so hot an' bothered an' tryin' to make up fer years o' abstinence."

Her eyes widened.

His smile vanished. "I am verra tempted, but three o' the boys are standin' behind us…an' ye're in Edinburgh with Sam an' Brianna—in 2011."

She cried out, amazed, and then she threw her arms around him and held on, hard. "I don't want to let go," she whispered. "I'm afraid to let go!"

He held her back tightly, and it was a long moment before he spoke. "We've built a good life, Tabitha. I want ye as much as I always do—so badly I canna stand it. But I willna jeopardize what we have. Ye need to go back to Blayde an' wait fer me."

Tabby suddenly went still. She'd been swept up in the moment, but Macleod was out there somewhere, looking for her. "I have to go back, immediately! Do you know what's happening to us in the thirteenth century?"

He shook his head. "I canna recall. 'Tis fer the best."

The gods had thought of everything, she thought. And she sat up and turned to look at her sons.

Her sons. Tall, dark and powerful, three handsome High-landers stared at her, their eyes wide.

Wow, Tabby thought, and she smiled.

The Highlands
The summer of 1550

HE SLEPT IN CAVES or dirt trenches by day; at night he traveled on foot, trying to elude the deamhanain who tracked him. Grief and guilt were his constant companions—and the boy was his companion, too.

One hundred and nineteen days had passed since he had last seen Tabitha die in the fires of Melvaig—four times. One hundred and nineteen days had passed since he had finally crouched on the floor of that stairwell, vomiting helplessly, racked with grief, with MacNeil coldly standing over him, having meted out his punishment as the gods wished for him to do. One hundred and nineteen days ago he had begun his journey across the Highlands, resolved to do what he had to do to return to Tabitha in the thirteenth century, where she waited for him. The gods meant to trap him in the sixteenth century, to keep him from Tabitha, his final punishment for a lifetime of defiance. Let them try. Nothing would stop him from returning to Tabitha. He would not live without her and he would never accept her future death, even if the gods were telling him he must accept their will.

He had decided to make the long journey to Carrick, where he would do whatever he had to in order to convince Ruari Dubh to send him back to her.

He had spent three days fashioning a raft with a single sail, his tears making it hard to see, and then he had left the coast of Melvaig. He was a mortal man now and acutely aware of it. He was out of his time. He had no wealth—he could not purchase anything he needed, and especially not a horse or a ship. He had no clan, and therefore no soldiers to trek with him, to fight for him. He did not have any allies—he could not request lodging and food. He did not know which rivalries now prevailed or who warred with whom. He did not dare pose as his sixteenth-century self. He had to proceed with the utmost caution, avoiding everyone, whether mortal, demonic or possessed.

Except evil could sense him, as if he still had white power, but he could not sense evil in return. Not a day went by that a deamhan or its henchman did not attempt an ambush upon him. Evil hunted him now with relish, perhaps because he was weak and it knew. But in the first ninety-two days he had destroyed fifty-eight deamhanain with his sword and dagger, along with twenty-one of the possessed. A dozen humans, interested in robbery and murder, had also been dispatched. Since then he had lost count. Every time he vanquished evil, he thought of Tabitha, aware that she would be pleased. Each time he came to face-to-face with evil, the desire to cause mayhem and murder, to rape and maim, to take pleasure in pain, shocked him and hardened him and made any outcome except triumph impossible.

And because the inner sea that lay between Melvaig and Lochalsh on Skye's western side was controlled by the Mac-Dougalls of Skye in the thirteenth century, as was the nearby sound of Sleat, he had jettisoned the raft after five days of sailing. Their ships would be swifter than his and he could not take a chance on being spotted or, worse, captured. It would take him longer to reach Morvern on foot, but he could easily hide in the forest at the first sign of anyone's approach. And there was good hunting—he was always hungry now.

When he paused to rest, floating during the calm at sea, or when he was trudging along a mountain trail almost mindlessly, he became aware of the boy, who refused to let him be.

*See! This is what it is like! This is the pain and the guilt that
ye denied me!*

At first he was furious to be haunted by his childhood—the
damned boy becoming more and more real with every passing
day. His image was so vivid, like a reflection on the glass sea,
but his pain was even more tangible. He didn't want to know.
He was suffering too much himself.

He'd seen Tabitha die, and he wept when he recalled it. The
boy wept for the murders of his family.

*Now ye ken what ye denied me...now ye feel the grief, the
guilt, the pain!*

The boy was raging and crying in grief and despair. He had
lost those he loved and he had failed them, too, and his sobs
were soul-shattering. Macleod had failed Tabitha at An Tùir-
Tara, and his pain was as unbearable...but then, they were one
and the same.

They were one and the same.

Slowly, the grief lessened.

And he would watch the boy warily as they climbed
mountain after mountain, or as they sat at night beneath a
waxing moon, across the fire from each other. He cried less
now. Macleod did not cry, but he finally understood the boy
completely—he understood his grief and guilt—for they had
become too intimate for him not to know him now.

And he was sorry. He was so sorry he hadn't let him cry and
rage and indulge in his sorrow and anguish, his despair and fear.
But there hadn't been a choice. He'd had to become a hard, un-
feeling man overnight.

The grief seemed to slip away and so did the guilt. The boy
no longer wept at all.

Too late, he knew that he'd only been a boy. He had been
helpless to prevent the massacre. It had been insane to ever
think he could have done otherwise. The boy was not to blame.

He had tried to fight the enemy, but one small boy could only do so much. And that boy had accepted his duty, even though he'd wanted to wallow in grief. That boy had turned immediately to war and revenge—as he'd had to. That boy was brave. He could finally admire him.

But it was over now.

He was sorry he'd murdered Alasdair in the name of revenge, and captured and tortured Coinneach. He regretted the entire century he'd spent on revenge—it had gone on for too long! The gods were right. But it ended now. Revenge had become meaningless. What mattered was his life with Tabitha, keeping her safe—and keeping others safe, as well.

Facing evil as a mortal man made that so terribly obvious.

Someone had to defend the women like Tabitha, the children like that boy, and all that was good and innocent in this world.

And the boy was hopeful. His heart had changed, becoming buoyant and light.

Macleod was anxious to get home.

The boy began to elude him. He started noticing him less and less as he got closer to his destination. Macleod would look around at the forest as he crossed a game trail, only to realize that he was now alone. As he made a bed of grass and leaves to sleep in a foxhole by day, he would wait for the boy to appear, but he did not. And then one day, when he was but a week or so from Morvern, he realized he hadn't seen the boy in days and that he wasn't coming back. But it didn't matter now, because Tabitha was waiting and he had so much to tell her…and he couldn't wait.

He began another ascent at midnight. Only one more mountain lay between him and Carrick. Wolves were tracking him, hoping to make him their next meal. When one came too close he used the sling he had made, shooting a stone between its eyes. His shots were usually fatal and this one was no different.

The forest sighed.

He was wary and alert. He knew a deamhan would soon attack, not because he sensed it, but because there hadn't been any ambush yet that night. He did not dread the encounter—he looked forward to it. Facing evil now felt like his due, his cause, his right.

The attack came during a bloodred dawn.

A deamhan on a warhorse charged him from the forest, powers blazing. Macleod had heard the horse an hour earlier, even though its hooves were wrapped in skins, and he was prepared for the assault. He moved behind a huge tree, which cracked apart, then dove behind a boulder. He let the deamhan blast him again, repeatedly, waiting for him to tire as it destroyed his small stone defense. Another mortal might have died, but he thought of Tabitha and of the gods, determined to survive. And when there was a lull in the assault, he stood, sending his dagger into the horse's heart. The beast collapsed and the deamhan vaulted from it. Macleod was already racing for the giant, and as its power blazed he cleaved his head from its shoulders.

The red-black power scattered harmlessly, like burning embers. Breathing hard, Macleod dusted himself off. He stood over the decapitated deamhan and watched it begin to disintegrate.

"A Thabitha."

He breathed again. Thinking of her—slaying evil in her name—replenished him like a sip of fresh water. He only had another hour left before daylight. He started to walk toward the mountain pass.

CHAPTER TWENTY-ONE

"HEY, NICK." Kit Mars smiled at him, her eyes wide with interest. "I see you guys made it back in one piece."

Nick looked up at her, still in his camouflage. He and Jan had just gotten back and he was mad as all hell that Kristin Lafarge was dead. He knew with every fiber of his being that she could have led him to some big bad demon honcho, because she was small-fry, interested only in petty revenge. Jan had gone home. It had been an interesting jaunt, even if they'd failed in their mission. And nothing bad had happened to any of the good guys. "Stop drooling. You'll get your turn when you're ready." He knew what she wanted.

Kit smiled at him, wishing he'd let her go back in time soon. "Sam went back and she wasn't even on board here for a week."

"Sam is an experienced soldier."

"I was a cop," Kit pointed out.

"Sam is a Slayer. She's been on the streets doing the dirty since she was a kid."

Kit sighed. "I thought you might like to see this. It just came in. Courtesy of the Russian."

Nick took the file, pleased, and opened the folder and saw a pile of glossies. The top shot was the exterior of the Carlisle, one of Manhattan's most exclusive hotels, second home to the city's top politicos as well as visiting heads of state and other foreign dignitaries. The Saudis especially liked it. It was a nice hotel. He flipped to the next photo. "I asked Rose to get on this."

"It gets better," Kit said.

Nick stared at the interior of the ten-thousand-dollar-a-night presidential suite, noting the time and date stamp on the upper right corner. It said October 20, 2008, 10:02:38 p.m. It had been taken just a few months ago, not the other night, when Lafarge had booked it.

The room was empty and he flipped to what seemed to be the exact same shot—except the time stamp on top showed it was two minutes later.

He leaned closer. He stared at the shadows in the barely lit room, but he was not mistaken. One of the shadows glowed, its demonic aura unmistakable. A demon had obviously just entered the living area of that suite.

Suddenly Jan walked into his office, her hair wet, wearing jeans and a sweater. She plopped a pizza carton down on his desk, along with a really cold bottle of Michelob Ultra. She glared at him and said to Kit, "I'm not coming in tomorrow. And don't even think it. It's not worth it." She stalked out.

He smiled at her backside. He was clearly forgiven. "Thank you," he called.

She didn't answer.

Then he looked at Kit before turning the top photo over and inhaled. Kristin Lafarge was now standing beside the demonic shadow, but she was clearly visible—and completely naked.

He was not surprised. Demons needed to feast on sex and power nightly, even a demon posing as a part of the city's establishment or a foreign dignitary. And a witch lover with some demonic blood was a pretty good pairing—except that the demon couldn't get his jollies by finishing the evening off with murder. Not if he wanted to use Lafarge, as he obviously did.

He flipped through the glossies, and saw Kristin in action in bed with the demonic shadow.

"She had a demon lover," Kit said unnecessarily. "Someone who could afford one of the city's most expensive hotel rooms."

"I knew it." He stood. "I bet she met with lover boy just before she went back in the past. Do you have those photos?"

Kit shook her head. "No."

"Who paid for the room?"

Kit hesitated. "There's a problem with the hotel records. We're working on it."

He was incredulous. "Who was registered there on October twentieth?"

Kit grimaced. "John Smith."

His frustration knew no bounds. "Find out where she was and who she met on December ninth, damn it." He'd known Lafarge could lead him to a major player, and now she was dead. "I want the demon who's cruising our town, posing as one of the good guys," he said. "Where is Rose?"

"She's on her way back from a personal trip," Kit said.

He stiffened. Kit was trying to block him from her thoughts. "She went to Scotland? For what?" he asked dangerously.

"She wouldn't tell me." Kit looked nervous.

"Get her in on this," he said. "And, Mars? Tell Sam to stay away from her bad boy. I happen to know that Maclean isn't one of us."

Kit paled.

Blayde, Scotland
The summer of 1298

TABBY LANDED IN THE bedchamber she shared with Macleod. She took a long moment to recover from the leap, sitting in the center of the room on the floor. She was thrilled to be back. But as the room stopped spinning, as all the pain vanished, her senses returned and she knew instantly that he wasn't present. *He wasn't at Blayde.*

Her heart sank with dismay. Dread began. She reminded herself that even though he had gone to An Tùir-Tara, or had intended to go there, it was over now and he had survived, just as she had.

But where was he?

She couldn't feel him anywhere. Tabby got to her feet, glancing outside. The sky was brilliantly blue and it was pleasantly warm. It was surely summertime. She had arrived with Macleod in the past on June 10, and his attempt to destroy Criosaidh at Melvaig had been five days later. She was worried now about which day she'd arrived back at their home.

Then she recalled her sense that he was lost and that he needed her.

For one instant, she thought she saw him in a night-blackened forest, holding a sword in one hand. And evil surrounded him....

She inhaled, terribly frightened now. Tabby hurried downstairs, but only a housemaid was in the hall. She ran outside. It took her a moment to espy Rob on the ramparts. She called out to him, waving. He saw her and hurried down to the bailey. Tabby raced across the yard to him.

"My lady!" he cried, clearly relieved to see her. "Is Macleod with ye?"

Her heart lurched with more fear. "No, he's not. Rob, how long has it been since he returned Coinneach to Melvaig?"

"'Tis been two days." Rob's blue eyes blazed and his face was grim. "I have heard Coinneach is arousing his allies an' plans war on us now, an' his mother is usin' her magic to help him."

Tabby went still. *Criosaidh was still alive.* Of course she was—she wouldn't die until June 1, 1550, if Tabby had changed history. Now it seemed as if they would be rivals for the next two-and-a-half centuries. She shivered. She was a Rose. If she had to fight that witch for two-hundred-and-fifty more years, she would do so and she'd win.

"The MacDougalls are always plottin' against us," Rob added quickly, as if to reassure her. He then said, low, "He told me he would leap into the future to save ye in another time. I dinna realize he finally had his powers. I begged him not to go. What has happened to him? Why hasn't he come back to us?"

"I don't know what has happened. But I know he's coming back—I am sure of it."

Rob looked at her with worry but Tabby couldn't reassure him. She kept seeing Macleod in that forest, and evil was stalking him. Where was he?

She reminded herself that he survived. She knew it because she'd just been in his arms.

It's all right, she told him silently. *I'm here and I'm waiting for you.*

She couldn't imagine defending Blayde for the next two-hundred-and-fifty years without him. Tabby felt sick. She held her stomach, thinking about how Fate—and history—could be changed. Maybe the gods were angry with her for what she'd just done at An Tùir-Tara. Now, she began to really worry. She'd just been with him on June 1, 1550, but he'd gone to Melvaig on June 19, 1550. If he was meddling at An Tùir-Tara and being punished for it *after* she'd been with him in the sixteenth century, their entire life could be destroyed.

A terrible headache began. She refused to think about being at Blayde for the rest of her life without him. Being able to leap into the past at any point in time meant that if someone made one slip, history could be undone and rewritten. But the Book of Roses stated emphatically that history would only change if it had been miswritten.

"He'll return." Rob was adamant, but his expression remained worried.

The day passed endlessly. Tabby found herself on the ramparts, waiting for him to return, as if he was traveling by horseback. At dusk she gave that up, because he wasn't a mortal and he would return by leaping time. She paced the hall, unable to eat, until Peigi insisted.

She fell asleep in his great chair before the fire, his wolf-hounds at her feet.

And she dreamed about him. In her dreams, he was somewhere in the night, always walking, his face grim and set, his feet bloody and blistered. In her dreams, there were demons and wolves, and his sword dripped their blood. Sometimes she saw him wandering through the forests as the fourteen-year-old boy. When she awoke, he hadn't returned, and she was even sicker with fear for him.

Something terrible had happened to him, she thought uneasily.

The sense she'd had before, that he was lost, escalated.

The hounds whined.

Tabby couldn't even pet them. "C'mon," she said hoarsely, feeling as if she hadn't slept at all that night. She crossed the hall, the hounds racing her to the front doors, tails wagging. They began to bark in excitement.

Tabby opened the doors, the bright morning sunlight almost blinding her. Macleod was crossing the bailey.

He had come home. Tabby cried out in joy, flooded with relief. Then he stepped out of the shadows cast by the walls and her happiness vanished. She was stunned by his appearance.

His clothing had been reduced to rags and it hung from his body in tatters, revealing the fact that he had become terribly thin and far too emaciated for his large frame. He no longer looked like a knight or a bodybuilder—he looked like a marathon runner, and a sick one at that! He was long and lean now, all muscle and bone. Disbelieving, she realized his face was hollow and gaunt, too.

She started to cry and ran into his arms. He wrapped his arms around her in return, as if afraid to ever let her go again. Tabby clung desperately, so overjoyed that he was alive, and apparently unhurt—and that he was home. But what had happened to him?

In his hard, equally desperate embrace, she felt and understood the depth of his love for her.

"What happened?" she cried, looking up.

And the moment their gazes met, she realized what was wrong. *He had no power.*

She should have sensed his vast white power, because the hot waves always cloaked and cocooned her. It was gone.

But he smiled at her, his eyes shining with moisture and love. "Tabitha," he murmured. "I'm afraid ye're a dream."

Tabby hesitated, frantic to comprehend what had happened, and in that single moment, she felt something else, too. Macleod's power had always been tinged with a dark weight. Now, his presence was buoyant and light—like the look in his eyes.

The burden of guilt and grief was gone.

"I'm not a dream. Thank God you're home!" She looked into his eyes and saw so much light—she saw joy and love. "You've healed," she managed, shocked.

His mouth curved and even his smile was different. "I've forgiven myself, Tabitha," he said simply.

She clasped his face. "I'm so happy for you."

"An' learned I canna live without ye—but I have lived without ye fer many months now," he said hoarsely. "So let me kiss ye, woman."

He pulled her close and kissed her. Tabby gave in, clinging, crying with sheer joy. He was home and nothing else mattered.

When he tightened his grasp on her, his body telling her he

was about to heave her over his shoulder and carry her upstairs, Tabby finally pushed away, wiping her damp face. "What happened?" She reached for his face and held it in her hands again. He was still beautiful. He was her hero, more so now than ever, no matter what they had done to him.

"The gods dinna want me now, Tabitha. I went too far—I defied them one time too many. I've been banished from the brethren. There'll be no vows." He was grim. "But I will fight fer mankind anyway."

She realized he had been banished from the Brotherhood by the gods for what he'd done at An Tùir-Tara, and with that punishment, he had been stripped of all his powers, every single one. He was a mortal now, unlike the Master she'd met in the sixteenth century. He was frustrated but resigned. "I don't care that you're mortal. I love you just the way you are. But it is wrong, Macleod, wrong that you are denied your Destiny."

"Can ye read my mind now?" he asked.

It was such a terrible irony. Tabby slipped into his mind and she saw that he had walked across the Highlands, fighting evil with his sword and his bare hands, in order to get back to her. She realized the extent of his ordeal—how he'd been hunted by evil daily, how he'd had to hide in order to survive. His companion had been his memories of the time spent with her and his tragic childhood. And he had worked through his repressed grief and guilt.

She stroked his jaw. "I can read your mind now." She started—he believed she would die at An Tùir-Tara!

MacNeil had made him watch her go up in flames four times! And she had thought the stocks a cruel punishment! She started to cry. "I thought MacNeil was your friend!"

He cradled her in his arms. "Dinna cry fer me. I am home now, with ye, Tabitha, where I will always be. An' I am *happy*."

"I hate what they did to you," she cried, her face wet with

tears. "And I don't die in the fire, Macleod! I *hide* in the fire! It's Criosaidh who dies there."

He gasped, and it was the first time she had ever seen him shocked. Then he tilted up her chin and his eyes blazed. "MacNeil was furious with me because I dinna trust in Fate. Now I ken why. O' course the gods would let ye live. Ye're everythin' fine an' good in this world, Tabitha. An' what of her deamhan ghost? Has it come back?"

She tried to stop crying and trembled, breathing hard. "I vanquished Criosaidh on June first, not June nineteenth, in 1550. And I destroyed the ghost when I destroyed Criosaidh. It imploded, Macleod."

He was thoughtful. "But what if her deamhan ghost was born another time?"

Tabby nodded. "I think it likely her ghost is a part of history. One was destroyed, the other created, on June first. And if Criosaidh's ghost was just born, I believe it will still go to early December 2008, seeking revenge on me there, before you take me into the past."

"So she'll hunt you in New York an' then follow ye to Blayde, till ye go to 1550 to destroy both the ghost an' the witch, a few days later." He smiled, satisfied.

"I think the ghost is trapped in that triangle of time," Tabby whispered, chilled. "She is created in June of 1550, she goes to December 2008 and follows me to June of 1298. Then I go to An Tùir-Tara and the cycle starts all over again. The dates might change a little, but it's all really the same—it's the history the Ancients wrote."

"Good." He was fierce. "Let the puny ghost suffer eternally in that triangle of time! I am proud of ye, Tabitha."

She was surprised. "Really?"

His smile revealed one small dimple. "Ye dinna ken how much I admire ye—even with yer independent nature?"

Tabby bit her lip, but she was thrilled. "It's mutual, Macleod. I admire you, too, more than you can possibly know!"

"But I'm medieval…barbarian…a savage," he murmured, pulling her back into his arms.

She laughed. "You are so medieval, and you know what? I think I like it."

He was pressing with some urgency against her now, and he said softly, his eyes gleaming, "Ye *think* ye like it?"

Desire reared up and hollowed her. "It's been too long," Tabby whispered.

His hands slid low. "I may be mortal now," he said softly, "but ye'll never notice."

She inhaled. "I have no doubt."

"Let me prove it," he said. His mouth tightened, and he turned her around.

"Prove it," Tabby ordered as her backside hit the edge of the trestle table.

His mouth curved. "Shrew," he whispered.

Tabby felt her own mouth turn upward, while her body exploded with feverish excitement. "Barbarian," she managed to say.

He reached for her leg and hooked it around his hip. He slid her gown up her calf, her knee, her thigh…her hip. "I'd cross a thousand Highlands fer ye, Tabitha," he said. "A thousand more times."

And she realized he would fight his way back to her time and again if he had to. "I love you, Guy."

He started—she'd never called him by his name before. His gaze unwavering and fierce on her face, he slid his massive length into her, and a moment later they were joined. Tabby held on to him, crying. Nothing could ever feel as right as being in his arms, except for becoming one.

"I'm home now," he said. "'Tis our home, Tabitha."

She somehow nodded. She would never leave him. She'd figure out how to be a modern woman in medieval times, with a medieval Highlander as her soul mate. He made love to her on the table, and although mortal now, Tabby broke into more ecstasy than ever before, maybe because she loved him more than ever and finally understood him. When they were both breathing hard and almost sated, the light coming inside from the open doors was the soft faded hues of an approaching dusk.

He kissed her neck and moved off her, helping her up as she rearranged her clothes. Then he held out his arm and Tabby went to stand against his side. "Will ye stay with me?"

He couldn't read her mind anymore. "Of course I will. But I need to see my sister—and I need to get the Book of Roses, too."

"Ruari can help us." He suddenly tensed. Tabby was confused, as well. She sensed so much white power, rapidly growing, and it was familiar—but that was impossible!

"Guy?"

"Tabitha," he whispered, his blue eyes wide. "I can hear yer every thought." He stopped. He flexed his hand. He gave her a look and pointed at the bench. Silver blazed; the bench exploded into tiny shards and pieces.

Tabby cried out. "You have your power back!"

Macleod stared in disbelief. Then he breathed hard and said, "I can leap if I wish to—I can feel it!"

Tabby seized his hand. "They're giving you back your power!"

But Macleod jerked toward the hearth—as did Tabby. MacNeil materialized in a cloud of shimmering golden air, his majesty unmistakable.

Tabby thought about what he'd done to Macleod and she was so angry she inhaled, clenching her fists.

Fully present, he smiled a little at her, as if expecting her wrath and dreading it. "I dinna have any choice. The gods were done with him."

"There is always a choice!" she cried. "You tortured him!"

Macleod took her hand, silencing her. Tabby blinked, realizing she'd been the one to lose her temper, not him. She realized he wasn't angry. "Let's hear what he has come to say."

MacNeil smiled, approaching, and to Tabby's amazement, he pulled Macleod into a bearlike embrace. "I'm proud of ye, lad," he then said, releasing him. "The gods decided yer punishment. 'Twas harsh, I agree, but they gave ye one last chance to redeem yerself. Ye have triumphed over every deamhan sent to stop ye. Ye forgave the gods, even though ye thought Tabitha dead. An' ye learned the truth about yer life—that yer reason to live is to defend God's creatures, all o' them, as long as they are Innocent."

Macleod was flushed, probably from MacNeil's warm hug. Tabby was amazed. "You forgave the gods?"

He nodded grimly. "An' I am sorry, verra much so, that it has taken me so long to learn the truth."

MacNeil clasped his shoulder, and Tabby saw that he was overjoyed and close to tears. "I saw Lady Tabitha in yer Destiny, Guy. The gods decided long ago she would be yer better half, an' that she would guide ye to the truth. I will admit I became afraid she would fail. Ye can be the most stubborn of men! But I can see now that I shouldna have ever feared fer ye." He turned to Tabby. "Thank ye, Lady Tabitha, fer all ye have done."

Tabby nodded, tearing up. "You're welcome. He's sort of hard to resist."

MacNeil grinned. "They like to make a man mad with desire, when it helps their cause."

Tabby realized it was all Fate, and that was fine with her.

"Ye'll come to Iona tomorrow." MacNeil smiled and vanished.

Tabby rushed over to Macleod. "You are redeemed," she whispered unsteadily, taking his hands. "You are forgiven. Tomorrow you take your vows!"

He inhaled, clearly shaken. "Tabitha," he whispered. "Those vows mean everythin' to me now."

THE BEACHES WERE the color of pearls. The morning sunlight was bright and warm, the sky azure, without a single cloud, and the sea was the color of lapis. Not a bird chirped, not a leaf stirred—the morning was absolutely silent. Macleod stood before Iona's holiest shrine, making his vows upon the ancient Book of Wisdom, which MacNeil held. The Abbot was cloaked in red and gold robes, while Macleod wore a leine so richly dyed that it was gold. The neckline and hem were lavishly embroidered, and his red-and-black brat was pinned across his right shoulder with his father's lion brooch. The huge, gilded and bejeweled ceremonial sword he held dated back to the first days of the Brotherhood—two centuries before Christ was born. As he spoke, his voice resonated powerfully in the otherwise silent morning.

Tabby was overcome.

They were not alone. Fifty or so Masters were present, most of them bare-legged Highlanders in leines and brats. But a few of them were Lowlanders, Englishmen and Norsemen. Tabby was the only woman there.

The monastery, which was a sanctuary for the Brotherhood, reeked of warrior power and testosterone—it was highly charged and solidly male.

But there was more. Behind the brethren, she could almost see the Ancients in their robes and gowns, shimmering in the morning light, fiercely pleased now. Clearly they would celebrate later, too. Their splendor and majesty was inspiring, and she had never felt so small, so insignificant and so humble.

Macleod went down on one knee.

She knew he felt it all, too.

Because this was his Destiny—serving the gods, keeping Faith and protecting the Innocent. And he was her Destiny. Tabby thrilled.

MacNeil laid both his hands on his shoulders, speaking softly now.

Tabby's heart turned over, bursting with pride. If only Sam were present.

Then she felt a caress upon her shoulder.

She turned and Grandma Sara smiled at her.

For one impossible moment, Tabby saw her grandmother standing there, but not as a wrinkled old woman. She saw a young, beautiful woman, in ancient robes. Then the morning sunlight washed over Sara, and she was gone.

Tabby trembled, even more undone. She had not a doubt her grandmother had just come to join her in the most important moment of her new life. And if her suspicions were correct, Grandma was no stranger to the world of the Masters—just the opposite was true.

Tabby pinched herself. She was incredibly proud of Macleod, deliriously happy as never before, and wildly in love. Macleod was her Destiny and she was his. She had been meant to go back in time to set him free from his past, so he could take his vows. And while Criosaidh was her arch enemy, and they would war for a few centuries more until she was vanquished, so what? Her powers were growing and so were Macleod's. She already knew the kind of Master he would become, and she was confident about her own powers, too. There would be other forces of evil to battle and fight—it was the law of the universe.

They were about to embark on a lifetime that would encompass centuries. They would fight evil, protect Innocence, make love, argue a bit—and make babies. Eventually she would have at least three strapping sons, not to mention a few magically talented daughters—or so she hoped. And while she missed Sam, she would see her again. Of that, she had no doubt.

She felt her smile widen. Macleod hadn't asked her to marry him yet, but she knew he would—she'd heard him thinking about it that dawn.

She laughed silently to herself. She could read his mind now and she loved it! He was still terribly macho and he'd probably be medieval until the Renaissance, but she could manage him, oh, yes. After all, she was a Rose.

The ceremony was over. Macleod had risen and MacNeil was shaking his hand, when suddenly the brethren erupted into a single, shockingly powerful roar. Tabby looked at Macleod as their cry of acceptance and triumph echoed over and over again and he looked directly at her.

She inhaled. He had already changed. His power, his confidence and dependability were increasing in leaps and bounds. The man she'd met in the sixteenth century was starting to emerge before her very eyes. And she had to admit it was such a turn-on....

It took him a while to reach her. Every Master reached out to grab his hand or clasp his shoulder and pummel his back. Tabby didn't move, breathlessly happy now and already thinking of a few ways to celebrate. She couldn't help it. He'd awoken her as no other man ever had, or ever could. She hadn't lost the best parts of the old Tabby, but the new Tabby was sexually voracious and not going anywhere, ever.

He finally slipped free of his brothers and reached her. "Have ye ogled enough Masters today?" But he was amused as he pulled her close.

"I'm trying to find Sam her match." That was actually the truth and she knew he was teasing her, anyway.

He wasn't jealous—how could he be? Last night she'd given him far more than her body—she'd given him her heart and her soul. He undoubtedly knew it, as he still lurked without compunction. "Yer warrior sister would drive a man to madness."

"There's someone for everyone. I am so proud of you," Tabby said.

His eyes darkened as he held her. "I dinna ken why I was so angry, so guilty, why I refused to serve the gods and the good men, women an' children o' the world fer so long."

"I am glad the past has been laid to rest," she whispered.

"Aye, me, too, because now we have the present to live in an' the future to plan." He pulled her against him and murmured, "An' how will we celebrate tonight?"

She wet her lips. "I think I can come up with an idea or two."

His grin was quick, wicked and it revealed that slight dimple. "Have I taught ye *too* well?"

"Tonight you can find out…when I teach you a thing or two." Tabby grinned and gave him her hand.

He grinned back at her. "So ye'll teach me?"

"If you can handle it."

He laughed. The sound was warm and deep. And they walked back to the other Masters, hand in hand. The celebration beginning was one that would last a lifetime—or two.

EPILOGUE

New York City
A few days later

"WHY THE URGE to suddenly go back to the exhibit on An Tùir-Tara?" Sam asked, feeling a bit cross and restless. But she was jet-lagged from the two-day trip to Scotland, and Nick had laid into her when she'd gone to work that morning.

No more personal anything, he'd ordered. Who the hell did he think he was?

And he damn well hadn't been reading her mind, because then he'd know that there hadn't been anything personal going on with Ian Maclean. And there never would be.

"Because I came across a reference to An Tùir-Tara when I was going over my file before closing it," Kit said, hurrying up the stairs. They were at the Met, and because it was so close to closing, it wasn't very crowded. "It was bothersome. A usually good historian got some dates wrong."

Sam didn't care. Nick had told her that Tabby was fine and at Blayde in 1298—and apparently, head over heels in love with her medieval Highlander. Hadn't Sam predicted that? But he didn't think she could have survived An Tùir-Tara. He'd been there, he'd said, and it had been an inferno. The good news was that he was certain Criosaidh hadn't made it out alive, either.

Sam refused to believe that Tabby would go back in time to

the thirteenth century, find a nearly immortal soul mate with superpowers, and then die while battling evil a few centuries later. She still disliked Macleod for taking Tabby away from her, but she knew he'd move mountains—and Fate—to keep Tabby alive until she died from really old age. By now, Tabby probably knew that the Rose women kept a lot of secrets.

Sam still missed her, enough that it hurt.

Kit's rapid steps finally slowed. Her gaze was soft, sad. "Hey. I know what it's like to lose your best friend ever."

Sam tensed. "Tabby's where she's meant to be." Then she felt like a total heel. "Hey, I'm sorry." Kit never talked about her dead twin sister, but everyone knew about Kelly.

"You have nothing to be sorry for. You and Tabby were as close as sisters can be. I get it. It hurts that she's gone, even if it's her Destiny. And it will take a long, long time to adjust."

Sam felt like pointing out that Kit had never adjusted to her loss, and her sister had been murdered when they were eighteen—almost ten years earlier.

"Oh, and I forgot," Kit said. "Nick thinks Maclean is bad news."

"Wow," Sam mocked, trying not to spit in anger as she thought of Ian, "for once we are in absolute agreement on something!"

"I guess he pissed you off," Kit muttered, and she hurried ahead of Sam to the big glass case displaying the Wisdom of the Celts exhibit. "Sam!"

Sam hurried over, and instantly, she understood why Kit was shocked. Because winking at them from the inside of the case was the gold palm amulet, with its bright moonstone center.

"What does that mean?" Kit gasped. "Macleod stole it a few days ago!"

Sam elbowed past her, not meaning to be rude. Even the facts had changed. "Listen to this," she said hoarsely. "On June first,

1550, a terrible fire destroyed the central tower of Melvaig Castle. While most historians cannot agree on the cause of the fire, the most common hypothesis is that the fire was a result of the kind of treachery so often seen in the ongoing clan war between the MacDougalls of Skye and the Macleods of Loch Gairloch. But that bloody feud ended with the demise of the Lady of Melvaig, a victim of the fires. To this day, locals claim that An Tùir-Tara was the last battle in a great war of two Highland witches." Sam reeled in shock as she spoke.

"That's the date I found in my files, and I thought I'd missed it the first go-round!" Kit exclaimed. "Sam, the facts—the date of An Tùir-Tara, even the text—have changed! And the amulet is back!"

"You didn't miss it and it wasn't a mistake," Sam whispered, staring at the pendant. It glowed magically now. "History has changed."

Kit was silent, but only for a moment. "Okay, so what on earth does it mean?"

Sam began to smile. "It means Tabby was meant to lose the pendant at An Tùir-Tara, and apparently, she did."

"Sam?"

"It means she got a bit impatient to do battle, don't you think?" Sam turned to Kit and uncharacteristically put her hand on her shoulder. "It means Tabby won." Then she sighed, groaning inwardly. "And it means she's living happily ever after with Macleod."

The two women exchanged glances, smiled, and Kit said, "Pizza?"

"Why not?" But as they left, Sam looked back at the glowing pendant and silently cheered for her sister and her soul mate.

The moonstone kept winking.

* * * * *

Dear Reader,

I hope you have enjoyed the first two books of THE ROSE TRILOGY. I love writing about these superpowered, macho medieval heroes—men who are men, make no apologies about it and the ladies beware! However, something new has happened. I'm really enjoying writing about some of the strongest heroines I've ever created. Working with these modern Rose women and taking them on their personal journeys has been a blast. I hope you enjoyed Tabby's courageous struggle with evil—and her equally courageous journey to find true love with Macleod.

By now you all know Sam Rose's story is next—and that she will go head to head with Ian Maclean!

Sam is truly a modern woman and is probably the strongest heroine I've done yet. She is powerful, sexy, independent and a Slayer. Romance is not in her vocabulary—a true soldier lives alone, fights alone and dies alone. Sam might miss Tabby now, but she'd never admit it, not even to herself. Her life is the war on evil, period. Except for one itty-bitty grudge she is holding—against Ian Maclean.

You see, Sam believes in payback. She will never forgive Ian for walking out on her and leaving her naked in *Dark Victory*. She can't wait to meet him again and bring him down. But what she doesn't expect is for them to meet and be on opposite sides of the war. Because Maclean has come to town, and he has something everybody wants: the good guys, the bad guys and, of course, Sam….

Ian Maclean ranks right up there with the handful of best heroes I've ever done. Society assumes he is what he appears to be—a wealthy and powerful jet-setting playboy. But Maclean spent sixty-six years as a child in demonic captivity, and he has far more than scars—he has dark secrets. He is tortured. He rarely sleeps—he can't handle his dreams—and he suffers daily from terrible flashbacks. And, as rich as he is, he lives a life of isolation, without family, without friends. He struggles with the truth about himself. But he is oh-so-sexy, anyway. And he knows it.…

He comes to New York to steal a page from the Duisean, which has wound up in an art collector's hands. However, he hasn't forgotten Sam. He knows she will be hunting the page, too. And Ian can't wait to play this game with her, certain of its outcome. Because women never say no to him for very long. Of course, he's never met a woman like Sam before!

Dark Lover is an amazing story—but a word of caution: it is *dark*. What Ian has gone through is horrific, and it's a miracle he's survived. *Dark Lover* is a story of an incredibly wounded man seeing that thread of light at the end of a dark tunnel and slowly being helped toward it. It is a story of good and evil, courage and fear, true love and dark desires. It is a story of two strong, proud, furiously independent people daring to look past the obvious and reach out to one another. And mostly, it is once again a story of the healing power of love.

Happy reading!

Brenda Joyce

Turn the page to read an excerpt from
DARK LOVER, the final book in
THE ROSE TRILOGY.
Every Rose Woman Has Her Destiny.

IT WAS LATE ENOUGH that no one was on the street. Ian went to the front door of the turn-of-the-century building and keyed in the door code, Sam close behind him, still handcuffed to him. He'd left the lights on in the entry foyer, which had double ceilings. As he closed the door he glanced at her bleeding arm, then at the torn dress. She seemed indifferent to the gash on her ribs.

Sam was eyeing his furnishings, which were mostly antiques from previous centuries. She put her messenger bag on an Irish library table from the seventeenth century. Even the chandelier above them was from fifteenth-century France. Above the front door were a pair of genuine sixteenth-century swords. "Interesting choice of decor for a modern playboy," Sam said. Her gaze was sharp. "Though, come to think of it, your mansion on Loch Awe is as Old World."

"I like old things," he said. "Ye're bleedin' all over my twenty-five-thousand-dollar rug."

"Sorry. I'll get you a new one in the twenty-second century, when I'm rich and famous."

He tugged on the cuff and she came forward, tripping in the broken sandals. He caught her by her hips, which were hard and muscular beneath his hands. Already in overdrive, his sexual tension soared further. Sex would push the last of his memories away. Why wait? "Do ye want to tend the wound?" he asked softly.

"Not if it means letting you out of my sight." She seized his wrists but didn't step back. "What, no butler to wait on us?"

"Gerard is sleeping at this hour." He pulled her closer, and her eyes calmly met his as she came into contact with his huge arousal. "Afraid to be alone with me?"

She took a breath. "I'm never afraid. Hey, I have a great idea. Call Gerard and have him arrange some evening entertainment for you—before you explode."

He grinned. "Will ye watch?"

"I'm not leaving," she said flippantly.

He thought about performing for her again. But that wasn't what his body was screaming for. He tightened his grasp on her, their gazes locked, wedging her against a hall table.

"Don't think it," she murmured.

"I canna think of anything else. Especially with yer body shackled to mine an' quiverin' so hotly."

"You can't ever think of anything else, whether we're shackled together or not."

He decided not to answer and slid his hand down her hip instead.

She went still. "Make a pass—at your own risk."

He smiled. It was hard to restrain himself. He wanted to put his hand between her thighs or turn her around and bend her over the table. She knew. She wouldn't object very much. Her words were sharp and caustic, but her tone was thick. Those violet-blue eyes were smoldering.

"Ye weren't afraid tonight." He touched the bloody, crusting tatters of the jersey dress, her left breast brushing his hand, and felt her flinch.

"I'm a Slayer, Maclean." She was wry.

"Are ye ever afraid?"

She stared into his eyes. "Not for myself."

Admiration swept through him. Her breast was heavy on the

back of his hand. He pressed upward and felt her inhale. The gasp had nothing to do with pain from the gash on her ribs. "How much does it hurt?" he whispered.

"What are you, a high-testosterone version of Florence Nightingale?"

He took her bodice in his hands and snapped it down below her breasts.

She stiffened, tightening her hold on his wrists.

His mouth went dry. Very slowly he looked up into her eyes. "Turn around, Sam."

She looked down at what was between them. "As good as that looks and feels, no, thanks."

He reluctantly looked past her breasts at the open, bleeding knife wound. She wasn't immortal. She should take care of the cut. He looked up. "I can pleasure ye more than ye've ever been pleasured."

"I'd rather pleasure myself."

"Ouch," he said, but he grinned. He was going to enjoy the hunt, more than he had in a long time, if ever. His hands were positively itching, and he finally let go of her bodice. He knew he'd pay, but he cupped her bare breasts anyway.

Her spike heel bored into his instep. He released her, cursing.

"Hands off," she warned. She jerked the dress up.

"Mayhap ye should have thought twice about handcuffin' us together."

"If you didn't have the power to leap, I'd handcuff you to the wall," she snapped. "No, to the bed—but alone. I'll bet that would torture you."

He tensed, but hid it, forcing a smile. "Ye ken we'll have to sleep together? Bathe together? Use the bathroom together?"

"I can handle it, Maclean. So let's go. It's almost one-thirty. I need to clean up and then I'm putting you to bed."

He stared at her. "I'm no gentleman."

"No kidding. But you're not a rapist, either."

The images flashed of the little boy, hiding under the bed. *He hid in the closet, beneath coats and jackets, barely able to breathe, as they searched for him. The fear was cloying. He'd been imprisoned only weeks ago—it was all new and terrifying. Still, he knew what they wanted, what they would do. Tears streamed. He prayed for his father.*

Then the door was torn off its hinges, and the monk stood there, red eyes glowing. Ian stopped breathing, paralyzed. And the monk laughed, reaching down for him....

From *New York Times* bestselling author

Gena Showalter

Enter a mythical world
of dragons, demons and nymphs...
Enter a world of dark seduction
and powerful magic...
Enter Atlantis...

Catch these thrilling tales in a bookstore near you!

THE NYMPH KING • Available now!

HEART OF THE DRAGON • Available January 2009

JEWEL OF ATLANTIS • Available February 2009

THE VAMPIRE'S BRIDE • Available March 2009

"Lots of danger and sexy passion give lucky readers a
spicy taste of adventure and romance."
—*Romantic Times BOOKreviews*
on *Heart of the Dragon*

We *are* romance™

www.HQNBooks.com   PHGSAT2009

REQUEST YOUR
FREE BOOKS!

2 FREE NOVELS
FROM THE ROMANCE/SUSPENSE
COLLECTION PLUS 2 FREE GIFTS!

YES! Please send me 2 FREE novels from the Romance/Suspense Collection and my 2 FREE gifts (gifts are worth about $10). After receiving them, if I don't wish to receive any more books, I can return the shipping statement marked "cancel." If I don't cancel, I will receive 4 brand-new novels every month and be billed just $5.49 per book in the U.S. or $5.99 per book in Canada, plus 25¢ shipping and handling per book plus applicable taxes, if any*. That's a savings of at least 20% off the cover price! I understand that accepting the 2 free books and gifts places me under no obligation to buy anything. I can always return a shipment and cancel at any time. Even if I never buy another book from the Reader Service, the two free books and gifts are mine to keep forever.

185 MDN EF5Y 385 MDN EF6C

Name _____ (PLEASE PRINT) _____

Address _____ Apt. # _____

City _____ State/Prov. _____ Zip/Postal Code _____

Signature (if under 18, a parent or guardian must sign)

Mail to **The Reader Service:**
IN U.S.A.: P.O. Box 1867, Buffalo, NY 14240-1867
IN CANADA: P.O. Box 609, Fort Erie, Ontario L2A 5X3

Not valid to current subscribers to the Romance Collection,
the Suspense Collection or the Romance/Suspense Collection.

Want to try two free books from another line?
Call 1-800-873-8635 or visit www.morefreebooks.com.

* Terms and prices subject to change without notice. N.Y. residents add applicable sales tax. Canadian residents will be charged applicable provincial taxes and GST. Offer not valid in Quebec. This offer is limited to one order per household. All orders subject to approval. Credit or debit balances in a customer's account(s) may be offset by any other outstanding balance owed by or to the customer. Please allow 4 to 6 weeks for delivery. Offer available while quantities last.

Your Privacy: Harlequin is committed to protecting your privacy. Our Privacy Policy is available online at www.eHarlequin.com or upon request from the Reader Service. From time to time we make our lists of customers available to reputable third parties who may have a product or service of interest to you. If you would prefer we not share your name and address, please check here. ☐

BOB08R

BRENDA JOYCE

77334	DARK EMBRACE	___ $7.99 U.S.	___ $7.99 CAN.
77219	DARK RIVAL	___ $7.99 U.S.	___ $9.50 CAN.
77233	DARK SEDUCTION	___ $7.99 U.S.	___ $9.50 CAN.

(limited quantities available)

TOTAL AMOUNT	$ _____
POSTAGE & HANDLING	$ _____
($1.00 FOR 1 BOOK, 50¢ for each additional)	
APPLICABLE TAXES*	$ _____
TOTAL PAYABLE	$ _____

(check or money order—please do not send cash)

To order, complete this form and send it, along with a check or money order for the total above, payable to HQN Books, to: **In the U.S.:** 3010 Walden Avenue, P.O. Box 9077, Buffalo, NY 14269-9077; **In Canada:** P.O. Box 636, Fort Erie, Ontario, L2A 5X3.

Name: _____
Address: _____ City: _____
State/Prov.: _____ Zip/Postal Code: _____
Account Number (if applicable): _____

075 CSAS

*New York residents remit applicable sales taxes.
*Canadian residents remit applicable GST and provincial taxes.

HQN™

We *are* romance™